Dickens, Religion and Society

Dickens, Religion and Society

Robert Butterworth

palgrave
macmillan

First published 2016 by
PALGRAVE MACMILLAN

Palgrave Macmillan in the UK is an imprint of Macmillan Publishers Limited, registered in England, company number 785998, of Houndmills, Basingstoke, Hampshire RG21 6XS.

Palgrave Macmillan in the US is a division of St Martin's Press LLC, 175 Fifth Avenue, New York, NY 10010.

Palgrave Macmillan is the global academic imprint of the above companies and has companies and representatives throughout the world.

Palgrave® and Macmillan® are registered trademarks in the United States, the United Kingdom, Europe and other countries.

ISBN 978–1–137–55870–1

This book is printed on paper suitable for recycling and made from fully managed and sustained forest sources. Logging, pulping and manufacturing processes are expected to conform to the environmental regulations of the country of origin.

A catalogue record for this book is available from the British Library.

Library of Congress Cataloging-in-Publication Data
Butterworth, Robert.
Dickens, religion, and society / Robert Butterworth, independent scholar UK.
pages cm
Summary: "Dickens's social criticism is one of the most famous and important aspects of his works. This book explores the centrality of his religious attitudes to his attacks on the social ills of his day. After discussing how deeply engaged Dickens was with his religion, the author links him to a group of political and religious campaigners who were pioneering the application of Christian moral precepts to social issues. The perspective this gave him on society is examined in detailed studies of several novels. Looking at his works from this angle sheds important new light on a number of cruxes and controversies in Dickens's oeuvre, including the portrayal of Fagin as a villainous Jew, the hostile depiction of trade unions in Hard Times, the apparent weakness of Dickens's remedy of a 'change of heart' to society's ills, and the presence of sentimentality in his novels"— Provided by publisher.
ISBN 978–1–137–55870–1 (hardback)
1. Dickens, Charles, 1812–1870—Religion. 2. Dickens, Charles, 1812–1870—Social and political views. 3. Religion in literature. 4. Social problems in literature. 5. Social ethics in literature. 6. Dickens, Charles, 1812–1870—Criticism and interpretation. 7. Literature and society—England—History—19th century.
I. Title.
PR4592.R4B88 2015
823'.8—dc23 2015019854

Typeset by MPS Limited, Chennai, India.

To the memory of my grandmother
Annie Elizabeth Butterworth,
the most admirable, most unselfish person
I have ever met. Her values and outlook
are part of the deep background to this book.

Contents

Acknowledgements

Earlier versions of Chapters 3 and 6 were published as 'The Significance of Fagin's Jewishness', *The Dickensian*, 105 (2009) and 'Dickens the Novelist: The Preston Strike and *Hard Times*', *The Dickensian* 88 (1992) respectively. Parts of Chapter 2 appeared in 'Thomas Hood, Early Victorian Christian Social Criticism and the Hoodian Hero', *Victorian Literature and Culture* 39 (2011). Copyright Cambridge University Press. Reprinted with permission.

1
Dickens's Engagement with Religion

In April 1869, in the middle of a series of public readings, ill-health forced Dickens to abandon the remainder of the tour. Some weeks later, in one of his final *Uncommercial Traveller* pieces, 'A Fly-leaf in a Life',[1] Dickens reported indignantly some of the reactions to this development:

> I had experiences of spiritual conceit, for which, as giving me a new warning against that curse of mankind, I shall always feel grateful to the supposition that I was too far gone to protest against playing sick lion to any stray donkey with an itching hoof. All sorts of people seemed to become vicariously religious at my expense. I received the most uncompromising warning that I was a Heathen: on the conclusive authority of a field preacher, who, like most of his ignorant and vain and daring class, could not construct a tolerable sentence in his native tongue or pen a fair letter. This inspired individual called me to order roundly, and knew in the freest and easiest way where I was going to, and what would become of me if I failed to fashion myself on his bright example, and was on terms of blasphemous confidence with the Heavenly Host. He was in the secrets of my heart, and in the lowest soundings of my soul – he! – and could read the depths of my nature better than his ABC, and could turn me inside out, like his own clammy glove. But what is far more extraordinary than this – for such dirty water as this could alone be drawn from such a shallow and muddy source – I found from the information of a beneficed clergyman, of whom I never heard and whom I never saw, that I had not, as I rather supposed I had, lived a life of some reading, contemplation and inquiry: that I had not studied, as I rather supposed I had, to inculcate some Christian lessons in books; that I had never tried, as I rather supposed I had, to turn a child or two tenderly towards the knowledge and love of our Saviour; that I had never had, as I rather supposed I had had, departed friends, or stood beside open graves; but that I had lived a life of 'uninterrupted prosperity,' and that I needed this 'check, overmuch,' and that the way to turn it to account was to read

> these sermons and these poems, enclosed, and written and issued by my correspondent! (pp. 389–90)

These correspondents were not alone in their opinion. Three days after Dickens's death, for instance, a country preacher described him as a writer 'who never ceased to sneer at and vilify religion'.[2]

My position in this book is that these critics could not have been more wrong, and that Dickens's religion is absolutely central to his work. I am writing in the tradition of commentators ranging from the contemporary critic of *Little Dorrit* who described the author as a 'deeply religious writer'[3] to modern commentators such as Angus Wilson and his contention that Dickens 'thought of himself as centrally a Christian ... in profound ways the Christian religion make sense of his work';[4] I think Dickens's interest in religion goes to the very core of his work and shall be arguing that it underpins and determines the social criticism that is one of the most famous and important aspects of his work. Approaches to criticism that have developed over recent decades have brought to prominence such concepts as the intentional fallacy, distinguishing between what writers set out to achieve in their works and what they actually do achieve. Before such approaches can be applied successfully to Dickens, however, it is necessary to bring fully into focus what Dickens intends to do in his works; and this is my aim here. Writing about Dickens as a reformer, Hugh Cunningham observes that

> There were others with a claim to the title of reformer who had much clearer diagnoses for and solutions to British ills than did Dickens. Dickens stood on shifting and uncomfortable ground amongst such reformers, his responses to situations often seeming to attract the label of 'conservative' as much as 'radical'.[5]

My contention is that Dickens's position is not at all shifting, and that he does have a clear diagnosis of what is wrong with society and an established view as to how to set things right: namely, that Christianity is the solution to all society's problems, and a failure to follow its precepts is the cause of all that is wrong. Evidence that such was Dickens's own view of his work is provided in a rare statement of his position written in response to criticism from Rev. David Macrae of his portrayal of Christians in his writings:

> With a deep sense of my great responsibility always upon me when I exercise my art, one of my most constant and most earnest endeavours has been to exhibit in all my good people some faint reflections of the teachings of our great Master, and unostentatiously to lead the reader up to those teachings as the great source of all moral goodness. All my strongest illustrations are derived from the New Testament: all my social abuses are shown as departures from its spirit; all my good people are humble,

> charitable, faithful and forgiving. Over and over again, I claim them in express words as disciples of the Founder of our religion; but I must admit that to a man (or woman) they all arise and wash their faces, and do not appear unto men to fast. Furthermore, I devised a new kind of book for Christmas years ago ... absolutely impossible, I think, to be separated from the exemplification of the Christian virtues and the inculcation of the Christian precepts. In every one of those books there is an express text preached on, and the text is always taken from the lips of Christ.[6]

Not only does the author explicitly place Christianity at the centre of his work here; he also makes it clear that his diagnosis of the ills of society is made from a religious perspective and with a religious solution: the 'social abuses' are 'departures' from the 'spirit' of the New Testament. I shall return to this letter later, when I shall be arguing that, in the aspects of this statement relevant to our study, we can take Dickens at his word.

At Dickens's funeral, Dean Stanley declared him to have had 'a simple but sufficient faith'.[7] A simple faith, can, of course, be of more than one type: it might be naïve, superficial and relatively uninformed; or it might be a faith that is considerably more sophisticated and well-informed but in which all that is not essential is stripped away. Critics have disagreed about which of these was nearer the truth, and how cognisant about and engaged with religion Dickens was. To Sir Arthur Quiller-Couch, Dickens 'simply disregarded' it.[8] In *Dickens and Education*, Philip Collins argues that 'his theology was not rigorous ... he might ... be described as a "New Testament", a "Four Gospels", even a "Sermon on the Mount" Christian ... it is probably useless to try to define some consistent position or development in his religious beliefs'.[9] As far as Dickens was concerned, 'for adults as well as children, theological niceties seemed ... of secondary importance, a distraction from the clear moral doctrine and spirit of Christ's ministry'[10] and 'his was an ethical Christianity, hardly touched by the sacramental or supernatural'.[11] It would be wrong to look for deeply considered positions on religion in Dickens:

> In his religion, as in the rest of his life and work, Dickens was lacking in intellectual rigour. He naively skirted the difficulties he found in the Bible, by the simple device of writing off the Old Testament, and he seems to have been almost unaware of those disputes about Christian Evidences which made 'honest doubt' so familiar to his generation.[12]

More recent commentators have found greater sophistication in Dickens's religious outlook In her book *Literature and Religion in Mid-Victorian England,* as Carolyn Oulton explores the impact of evangelicalism on Dickens and Wilkie Collins, her emphasis from the start is on the 'complexity' of their response.[13] Of the final passage by Philip Collins quoted above she remarks that it is 'unfair to Dickens, who held strong views on the question of Biblical criticism',[14] and her discussion presents Dickens as having thought-out, developed positions on a range of religious issues, including such theological matters as Original Sin and Providence. Gary Colledge examines Dickens's theology as revealed in *The Life of Our Lord* in detail, and warns against being misled by what Dickens chose to concentrate on in his religious writings: if he seems unconcerned about 'Purity of doctrine, perfecting formulations of theology, and a preoccupation with ecclesiastical polity', it is because these are relatively unimportant to him: 'What mattered to Dickens was the practice of Christianity, and that meant imitating Jesus and following his teaching'.[15] He may not have been a 'serious theologian', but he was a man who 'thought carefully about his faith'.[16]

My aim here is to underline that Dickens did indeed have a sophisticated understanding of and engagement with his religion. We may examine, to begin with, a passage from one of the letters Dickens sent to the *Daily News* on the subject of capital punishment, which he regards as contrary to Christianity. There can be no doubt about the matter he claims:

> The case is far too plain. The Reverend Henry Christmas, in a recent pamphlet on this subject, shows clearly that in five important versions of the Old Testament (to say nothing of versions of less note) the words 'by man,' in the often-quoted text, 'Whoso sheddeth man's blood, by man shall his blood be shed,' do not appear at all. We know that the law of Moses was delivered to certain wandering tribes, in a peculiar and perfectly different social condition from that which prevails among us at this time. We know that the Christian Dispensation did distinctly repeal and annul certain portions of that law. We know that the doctrine of retributive justice or vengeance, was plainly disavowed by the Saviour. We know that on the only occasion of an offender, liable by the law to death, being brought before him it was *not* death. We know that He said, 'Thou shalt not kill'. And if we are still to inflict capital punishment because of the Mosaic law (under which it was not the consequence of a legal proceeding, but an act of vengeance from the next of kin, which would surely be discouraged by our later laws if it were revived among the Jews just now), it would be equally reasonable to establish the lawfulness of a plurality of wives on the same authority.[17]

The case here is closely argued, in quite a scholarly way. Dickens shows himself to be well-informed about the latest theological thinking. Even if he has derived his points from the pamphlet he mentions, he nevertheless shows a grasp of the arguments. This is not a passage written by somebody with only a superficial engagement with religion.

Dickens is often, though not uncontroversially, associated with the Broad Church party in the Victorian Church of England, reflected, for instance, in his reaction to A.P. Stanley's *Life and Correspondence of Thomas Arnold*: as he wrote to Forster, 'I respect and reverence his memory beyond all expression ...

Every sentence that you quote from it is the text-book of my faith'.[18] This again may have caused some misapprehension: by no means was adherence to Broad Church principles a default position rather than an adopted one, neither were members of the Broad Church party people casual and therefore vague about their religion. That as religiously literate a man as F.D. Maurice subscribed to Broad Church principles reflects that it was not a refuge for the relatively unthinking, only generally and loosely committed Christian B.G. Worrall identifies five characteristics of members of the Broad Church: 'toleration of breadth of opinion within Christianity'; the influence of German theology 'generally thought to be rationalistic and hostile to traditional faith'; a 'willingness to adopt a critical attitude to Scripture' in the light of modern science and Biblical criticism: 'the appeal to morality' for 'authoritative guidance', with its 'moral ideal' as 'the heart of Christianity'; and 'a remarkable optimism and belief in progress', in which education would free people 'from superstition and fear of authority' and facilitate their being guided by 'the moral law within'.[19] In examining Dickens's religious position, we shall see how the ideas important to him among these principles weave together in his religious outlook, and that he engages in a sophisticated rather than superficial way with Christianity.

I want to suggest that there are five aspects to Dickens's engagement with religion. He is alert to and well-informed about developments in religion in his time; in taking a practical approach, against a theological background, to Christianity, he is primarily concerned with its moral teaching; he is impatient with theological, denominational or other disputes when they are a distraction from, or irrelevant to, the promotion of Christian moral values; he takes an interest in such debates only when he sees them as furthering the promotion of Christian morality; and he sees that morality as having a social, and not merely personal, dimension.

It would be possible to see these aspects of his engagement reflected by ranging widely over his writings. However, below I explore how the five aspects of Dickens's engagement with religion are exemplified in his reactions to developments within the Church of England, of which he was a member for most of his life.[20]

The pattern of Dickens's reaction to such developments is set by his response to administrative and pastoral changes. In these regards, the Church of England at the beginning of the Victorian age was emerging from a long period of torpor. The Church's governing assemblies, the Convocations of Canterbury and York, which were eventually to convene again in 1852 and 1861 respectively, had not met since 1717; and, for instance, despite ongoing urbanisation, the diocesan and parochial structures had not been reformed for over five hundred years. The Victorian period was to see large-scale change, both internally organised and in the shape of Acts of Parliament. There was large-scale reform of the diocesan and parochial system, there was considerable church extension, and, from 1843, it no longer took an Act of Parliament to create a new parish. The issues of pluralism, absenteeism and non-residence were tackled. The need for more clergy was recognised, and changes made to raise the educational level of clergy and improve their training. There was a revival of the pastoral ideal, affecting both bishops and parish priests.

Dickens's reaction to these is characteristic of his reaction to other developments in the Victorian Church. His awareness of these changes generally is reflected in the occasional allusions he makes to them. In *The Mystery of Edwin Drood*, for example, the Dean goes to 'the snug old red-brick house where he is at present "in residence"' (p. 13),[21] a reference, as David Paroissien notes[22] to the requirement for deans to be resident at their cathedrals for eight months each year, laid down in the 1841 Ecclesiastical Commissioner's Act.

Dickens, however, gives more attention to the associated matter of pastoral reform, in the shape of the professionalisation (or re-professionalisation) of the clergy. Victorian clergy felt, as Brian Heeney remarks, that 'they lived in an era of clerical renaissance, when the profession of which they were members had been given a new life':[23]

> Mid-Victorian churchmen, high, low and broad, looked back to the late eighteenth century and to the early years of their own century as a time when the parishes were manned by lax and inefficient clergy. In 1845, John Sandford, author of *Parochialia*, could write that 'an age of energy and inquiry has succeeded a long night of secularity and torpor'. He listed the characteristics of the eighteenth century church: 'effete theology; a lax and licentious tone of morals; an ignorant and secular priesthood; an untaught and neglected population, empty churches; desecrated Sabbaths'.[24]

Similarly, in 1863, a high churchman declared that 'the typical eighteenth century parson gambled and rode and drank and swore. Sins ... less mentionable often polluted the clerical life'.[25] In the Victorian era, there was a new emphasis on what Heeney sums up as 'the uniquely spiritual quality of the ministerial call':[26] Bishop Samuel Wilberforce stressed that the clergyman must have 'some desire at least to live nearer to Christ in employment and pursuit than worldly callings render possible'.[27]

With the salvation of souls clearly identified as central to the clergyman's pastoral role, he had a number of identified duties, which he must be helped to perform as well as possible:

> Preaching, catechizing, direct religious instruction, the reading of services and the celebrating of sacraments, were obviously all important professional activities of English parish priests. Mid-Victorian writers of pastoral theology devoted a good deal of space to their improvement and to the private study, reading and personal prayer which supported such public religious activities. Equally important was private pastoral activity with

> individual parishioners, activities which included visiting in sickness and in health, personal interviews, counselling, and even confession.[28]

The clergyman was on duty at all times, as an anonymous pamphleteer of 1863 emphasised: 'Ordained priests ... are priests always and at all seasons', and there must be 'no dropping our customary prefix of "Reverend" in order that we may indulge in amusements inconsistent with that title'.[29]

In addition, the clergyman's character had to be of the right type, as Ashton Oxendon observed in *The Pastoral Office*: 'what manner of man ought he to be – how unworldly, how heavenly-minded, how separate from sin'.[30] The setting up of theological colleges was considered helpful in preventing young men being corrupted by university life.[31] Heeney identifies qualities expected of the Victorian clergyman as including 'Patience and joy, punctuality and hospitality, "gravity" or seriousness, and courage', but above all, two qualities which 'appeared on virtually every list' and 'were always emphasized'.[32] The first of these was sympathy, defined by Heeney as 'deep personal understanding, a man's capacity to put himself in the place of the parishioner with whom he was dealing',[33] involving an ignoring of any social differences. It involved heavy demands, not only, Heeney remarks, 'that the clergyman be constantly open to the calls of his parishioners, but that he become personally involved in each case'.[34] Sympathy would be important in bridging the social and educational gap between priest and parishioners; ordinands were warned to expect a culture shock 'when they moved from university towns to the backwaters of rural curacies'.[35] The second supreme pastoral quality expected of the Victorian clergyman was self-discipline, 'the capacity to order one's time, to develop and stick to a plan of work', as Heeney puts it.[36] Idleness was to be deplored.

Furthermore, the clergyman's wife was expected to play a prominent role in his work. *Hints to a Clergyman's Wife*, published in the 1830s, emphasised that she would need similar qualities of earnestness and serious commitment: 'habits of perseverance, punctuality, application, and industry, and the still more important habits of self-control, self-denial, and self-examination'.[37] Her duties, particularly involving the women and girls of the parish, are suggested as including cottage readings, private instruction of the parish's young women, superintendence of the girls at Sunday school, but also 'let it be her delight to supply comfort to the aged ... her delight will be to be found in the poorest cottage, at the bedside of the sick and dying, and employed in the humblest offices of Christian benevolence and love'.[38]

Again it is emphasised that the clergyman and his wife are more or less never off duty:

> With this desire predominant in her heart, the Clergyman's wife will call but a very small portion of her time her own, but, with her husband, will be ever ready to listen to the calls of ignorance and distress[39]

and she too will need self-discipline:

> In order ... to carry her rules into execution, some arrangement of her time will be necessary. Every moment of the day must have its appropriate employment; every hour must bring with it its own portion of allotted duty.[40]

The phenomenon of the professionalisation of the clergy is one that stirs Dickens's interest. His early writings present scathing depictions of unreformed clergy. In *Sunday Under Three Heads*, from 1836, he describes a service being conducted by a clergyman only too evidently of low calibre, and corrupted at university: he is 'a young man of noble family and elegant demeanour, notorious at Cambridge for his knowledge of horse-flesh and dancers, and celebrated at Eton for his hopeless stupidity'. Despite supposedly doing a job of work, his skin retains the pallor aristocrats prided themselves on as a sign that they did not work, and he is revealed also as worldly and vain as 'he applies his white hand, studded with brilliants, to his perfumed hair' (p. 479);[41] there is no sign in him of attempting to be unworldly or of trying to bridge the social gap with his parishioners. When the writer moves on to discuss Sunday 'As It Might Be Made', he takes as a model a clergyman he has met in a country parish, who is a great deal more pastorally committed, 'intimately acquainted with the circumstances of all his parishioners' (p. 496), and thus showing the requisite sympathy, and instrumental in helping them find healthy recreational activities. In *Oliver Twist*, the clergyman at a mere pauper's funeral, untroubled by any feeling of a need to be either punctual or serious, does his job so thoughtlessly and carelessly that he arrives over an hour late (apparently a habit, because the clerk is able to predict that this will happen) and then only 'read as much of the burial service as could be compressed into four minutes' (p. 44);[42] by the time of *Our Mutual Friend*, Dickens is noting that some clergy take their role so seriously, have such scruples and tender consciences that they 'found themselves exceedingly uncomfortable in their minds, because they were required to bury the dead too hopefully' (p. 327),[43] a reference, as Adrian Poole notes, to the way some clergymen by the 1860s 'were unhappy about uttering the assurance of eternal life over the graves of those who obviously did not deserve it, drunken adulterers and so on. The critical words were "in sure and certain hope of the Resurrection to eternal life"'.[44] Consequently, as Michael Cotsell notes, 'some argued that the words of the service should be changed, others that church discipline should not require the service to be read over everybody'.[45] The reference immediately after to clergy being 'required to do one or two other things (say out of nine-and-thirty) calculated to trouble their consciences' (p. 327) is, of course, a reference to the Thirty Nine Articles of the Church of England, which clergymen needed to subscribe to, but which, as Cotsell remarks, 'Many Victorian clergymen had difficulty subscribing to'.[46]

Beyond this, though, he gives detailed portrayals of the new model of clergy. It is precisely this vision of the life of a clergyman that Dickens presents in his depiction of Rev. Frank Milvey and his wife in *Our Mutual Friend*. Milvey's is a life of commitment despite being 'wretchedly paid' (p. 107) and having to do teaching and translating to make ends meet. His life, far removed from that of eighteenth century clergy with time to spend on botany and other scholarly pursuits, is one of self-discipline, in which he has 'repressed much in himself that naturally belonged to his old studies and old fellow-students, and taken up among the poor and their children with the hard crumbs of life' (p. 109). He is the model of a man open to the calls on his time of his parishioners, for Milvey's time is everybody else's; he is, as Dickens sardonically observes, 'generally expected to have more time to spare than the idlest person in the parish' (p. 107). Despite his 'very modest income' (p. 107), it is part and parcel of his life, taken for granted, that he will be charitable, as if he had 'more money than the richest' of his parishioners (p. 107) *Hints to a Clergyman's Wife* warned that the spouse of a clergyman would need

> to regulate her inclinations, to set bounds to her desires, to govern her temper, to subdue her natural propensities, to watch against a trifling spirit and a wandering mind, and to consider herself as a responsible creature[47]

and this Mrs Milvey has taken on board, for she,

> something worn by anxiety ... had repressed many pretty tastes and bright fancies, and substituted in their stead, schools, soup, flannel, coals, and all the week-day cares and Sunday coughs of a large population, young and old. (p. 109)

Milvey and his wife work as a team. He remarks that she is 'indispensable' (p. 107) to him, and their discussion about which orphan Mrs Boffin might adopt shows that they both have an intimate knowledge of their parishioners. They are a 'kind, conscientious couple' (p. 110). Dickens even indicates that he feels Milvey is burdened in a 'needless' way; but he is conscious that Milvey himself does not baulk at his life and would have been unsympathetic to 'any decent layman who would have adjusted such burdens as his' (p. 107).

The professionalisation of the clergy is also the context for the account of the work of Rev. Stephen Roose Hughes in the early *Uncommercial Traveller* piece 'The Shipwreck'.[48] Much of the emphasis of the piece is on the work of the clergyman in the wake of a shipwreck involving great loss of life that took place just off Llanallgo where his parish was. Hughes exemplifies sympathy: throughout, Dickens stresses the dedication, sensitive care and compassion displayed by the clergyman, as well as the hospitality expected of a man in his profession. Before visiting him, Dickens has already heard of him

> as having buried many scores of the shipwrecked people; of his having opened his house and heart to their agonised friends; of his having used a most sweet and patient diligence for weeks and weeks, in the performance of the forlornest offices that Man can render to his kind; of his having most tenderly and thoroughly devoted himself to the dead, and to those who were sorrowing for the dead. (p. 31)

The details the writer gathers during his visit reinforce this: when recovered dead bodies were brought into the church, Hughes 'worked alone for hours, solemnly surrounded by eyes that could not see him, and by lips that could not speak to him, patiently cutting off ... anything that might lead to subsequent identification' (pp. 32–3). Later we learn that 'my clergyman alone had written one thousand and seventy-five letters to relatives and friends of the lost people' (p. 34); that having made careful arrangements for the burial of unidentified bodies, he had logged the bodies as meticulously as possible, so that if subsequently identified, they could be exhumed and reburied after a second funeral, and that, 'in all such cases, he had performed the funeral service a second time, and the ladies of his house had attended' (p. 34); that the strain of these tasks had affected him in such a way that he was 'unable for a time to eat or drink more than a little coffee now and then, and a piece of bread' (p. 35). Dickens reprints a number of letters from the relatives of those involved in the shipwreck and others as further testimony, in various ways, to the standing Hughes had achieved, including one from a husband asking for the pastoral support of 'a consoling letter to prevent my mind from going astray' (p. 36) and one from the Chief Rabbi commending him for 'your acts of humanity and true philanthropy' (p. 38). In line with the Victorian model for the clergyman that had developed, his wife and family are also actively involved:

> The ladies of the clergyman's family, his wife and two sisters-in-law, came in among the bodies often. It grew to be the business of their lives to do so. Any new arrival of a bereaved woman would stimulate their pity to compare the description brought, with the dead realities. (p. 33)

All in all, with the 'cheerful earnestness' (p. 34) of a dedicated man, Hughes is presented not simply as a good person, but specifically as a 'good Christian minister' (p. 34).

As John Drew points out, 'opinion was mixed as to the propriety of Dickens's praise of the priest: the *Saturday Review* considered it "questionable taste" to have "thus placarded ... the virtues of a Welsh clergyman ...

for this helping the sufferers"',[49] and it might be said that this is a sign that such commitment in a clergyman was by no means by this time so unusual as to be beyond what might be expected of a clergyman and thus worthy of comment, but expected as the norm in such a man. Dickens makes clear his motives: the clergyman embodies the 'practical Christianity' that Dickens is interested in:

> I read more of the New Testament in the fresh frank face going up the village beside me, in five minutes, than I have read in anathematising discourses (albeit put to press with enormous flourishing of trumpets), in all my life. I heard more of the Sacred Book in the cordial voice that had nothing to say about its owner, than in all the would-be celestial pairs of bellows that have ever blown conceit at me. (p. 32)[50]

He is equally explicit about why it is this development in the Church that he sees as more important to draw attention to than mere administrative reforms:

> Convocations, Conferences, Diocesan Epistles, and the like, will do a great deal for Religion, I dare say, and Heaven send they may! but I doubt if they will ever do their Master's service half so well, in all the time they last, as the Heavens have seen it done in this bleak spot upon the rugged coast of Wales. (p. 40)

The emphasis here on pastoral commitment and on the clergy setting an example of Christian moral behaviour reflect Dickens's over-riding concern to encourage the propagation of Christian ethics in daily life; for all that he is aware of mere administrative developments, them, this is much more important than they are.

Dickens's approach is similar with respect to other kinds of developments within the Church. Doctrinally and theologically, Evangelicalism was already a powerful force within the Church of England, and was to continue to be so. It had gained ground when the first bishop to be an Evangelical was appointed in 1815, followed by two more in the 1820s,[51] and this process was to reach a climax during the premiership of Palmerston (1855–65), who relied on the advice of his step-son, Shaftesbury, when appointing bishops, leading to a number of Evangelical preferments.[52] However, from the 1830s onward, the Oxford Movement, among whose leaders were Edward Bouverie Pusey and John Henry Newman, was also to be very influential. As Gerald Parsons writes, members of the Oxford Movement

> sought to deny the essentially Protestant nature, character and identity of the Church of England and asserted instead its Catholic roots, traditions and identity. They stressed the authority of the church, of the

> priesthood, of the sacramental system, and of the early Christian Fathers. They sought to downgrade, and even to denigrate, the Reforms. And they sought to give a consistently Catholic interpretation of the Thirty-Nine Articles and the Book of Common Prayer.[53]

It stimulated theological debates in the 1830s, 1840s and 1850s concerning tradition and Scripture, the authority of the ministry and the nature of the sacraments. In addition, as historical criticism of the Bible became established, and as developments in geology, astronomy and biology began to bring into question the early chapters of Genesis, further challenges for theological debate emerged. In the period 1850–70, matters such as the divine inspiration of the Bible, the notions of divine judgement and eternal punishment, miracles, revelation and the literal fulfilment of prophecy all came up for discussion. Certain figures and publications became the centre of controversy. Rev. George Gorham was one such figure. In 1847, the Bishop of Exeter refused to appoint Gorham to a living because of Gorham's Calvinist views on baptism, the Bishop judging them to be inconsistent with the doctrines of the Church of England. The Bishop's decision was upheld by the ecclesiastical Court of Arches, but eventually, in 1850, the Judicial Committee of the Privy Council's decision went in Gorham's favour. The judgement itself then stirred up further controversy, members of the Oxford Movement disapproving of its downplaying of the sacraments, and that the matter had been settled by a secular court. Similarly controversial were the views of the Tractarian A.G. Denison concerning the real presence in the Eucharist; again, court cases followed. In 1861, John William Colenso, the Bishop of Natal, questioned the atonement and everlasting punishment on moral grounds, and in 1863 published a book questioning the authorship of the Pentateuch. He was tried for heresy. In 1860, the volume *Essays and Reviews* caused enormous controversy given that its various chapters

> called for a thoroughly historical and critical approach to the Bible, for recognition of the moral and spiritual worth of religious traditions outside the Bible, and for acceptance of the findings of science concerning both the age of the earth and its geological history, and the possibility (or impossibility) of miracles. It also argued that the moral demands of the Christian life had a priority over dogma and doctrinal formulae.[54]

Dickens is impatient with doctrinal and theological debates as a distraction from the important aspects of Christianity and because of their negative effect on the thriving of religion:

> Dearly beloved brethren, do you know that between Gorham controversies, and Pusey controversies and Newman controversies, and twenty other edifying controversies, a certain large class of minds in the

> community is gradually being driven out of all religion! Would it be well, do you think, to come out of the controversies for a little while, and simply be Apostolic thus low down![55]

Elsewhere, he is even more emphatic about the debates stimulated by the Oxford Movement being a distraction from the moral teachings of Christianity:

> In the minds of the persons employed in the University of Oxford, such comprehensive words as justice, mercy, charity, kindness, brotherly love, forbearance, gentleness, and Good Works, awaken no ideas whatever; while the evidence shows that the most preposterous notions are attached to the mere terms Priest and Faith.[56]

Just after the Colenso controversy and *Essays and Reviews* had dominated discussion at the Church Council of October 1864, Dickens declared that he was 'sick of' the Church:

> The spectacle presented by the indecent squabbles of priests of most denominations, and the exemplary unfairness and rancour with which they conduct their differences, utterly repel me.

Partly this was because it went against the whole spirit of Protestantism with its emphasis upon individual conscience and belief, as opposed to the priest-imposed beliefs of the Roman Catholic church:

> the idea of the Protestant Establishment, in the face of its own history, seeking to trample out discussion and private judgment, is an enormity.

It also meant, though, that in getting wrapped up in theological disputes, people were distracted from Christ (and His teachings):

> Here, mere Popery – there, mere methodism – as many forms of consignment to eternal damnation, as there are articles, and all in one forever quarrelling body – the Master of the New Testament put out of sight, and the rage and fury almost always turning on the letter of obscure parts of the old Testament which itself has been the subject of accommodation, adaptation, varying interpretation without end – these things cannot last.[57]

Dickens seems utterly untroubled by the developments in science of his time. Though *Vestiges of the Natural History of Creation* had caused a stir in religious circles, Dickens, in reviewing another scientific book, takes a positive view of what he calls 'that remarkable and well-abused book', crediting it with 'rendering the general subject popular' and with having 'created a reading public – not exclusively scientific or philosophical – to whom such offerings can be hopefully addressed'.[58] As Michael Slater points out, a review of Darwin's *Origin of Species* was printed in *All the Year Round* in July 1860;[59] and Dickens himself owned a copy of the book.[60] Dickens was confident that, 'nothing is discovered without God's attention and assistance', and sees science as serving God's purposes in a process of progressive revelation: 'I suppose every new knowledge of His works that is conceded to man to be distinctly a revelation by which men are to guide themselves'. He is undisturbed by scientific accounts of things that seem different from what is suggested in the Old Testament; these were accounts that served their purpose when man was in his infancy. He refers, for instance, to the Biblical account of rainbows as instituted by God as a promise never to inflict another Flood on the earth:

> inasmuch as ever since there was a sun and there was vapour, there *must have* been a rainbow under certain conditions, so surely it would be better now to recognise that indisputable fact. Similarly, Joshua might command the sun to stand still, under the impression that it moved round the earth; but he could not possibly have inverted the relations of the earth and the sun, whatever his impressions were.

His attitude is not blindly cavalier: he recognises that scientific developments may trouble 'the more thoughtful and logical of human minds' but is confident that there is no need to 'lose' them if the right approach is taken.[61]

Dickens saw himself as fighting a great deal of the time against attitudes derived from the Old Testament. Sabbatarians, for instance, were basing their position on an Old Testament which Dickens saw as superseded:

> the declared authority of the Christian dispensation over the letter of the Jewish law, particularly in this especial instance, cannot be petitioned, resolved, read, or committee'd away.

The matter ought not even to be controversial:

> One Christian sentence is all-sufficient with us, on the theological part of this subject, 'The Sabbath was made for man, and not man for the Sabbath'.[62]

Undue attention to the Old Testament more generally results in 'miserable error', he wrote to Frank Stone:

> Half the misery and hypocrisy of the Christian world arises (as I take it) from a stubborn determination to refuse the New Testament as a sufficient

> guide in itself, and to force the Old Testament into alliance with it – whereof comes all manner of camel-swallowing and of gnat-straining.[63]

In the novels, over-attachment to the Old Testament rather than the New leads to the version of Christianity Dickens so critically portrays in Mrs Clennam and other characters; and despite his impatience with theological disputes, he hence does engage with theological debate when he sees it as serving the purpose of helping promote the New Testament and Christ's teachings.

Thus, he owned a copy of *Essays and Reviews*,[64] and approved of what he saw as the argument there put forward for regarding the Old Testament as superseded, at least in parts, and thus no longer relevant:

> The position of the writers of '*Essays and Reviews*' is, that certain parts of the Old Testament have done their intended function in the education of the world *as it was*; but that mankind, like the individual man, is designed by the Almighty to have an infancy and a maturity.[65]

Liturgically and ceremonially, public worship in the Church of England at the start of the 1830s was 'a comparatively dull, plain and unceremonious event'.[66] With Matins and Evensong the main Sunday services, and Holy Communion only celebrated once a quarter, services were dominated by the sermon, and responses and psalms spoken rather than sung. Often the only participation of the congregation in the service consisted of singing such hymns as were used. During the Victorian period, public worship was revitalised. Among other changes, Holy Communion commonly came to be celebrated every week, and hymns became central to services, accompanied by robed choirs and organs, part of a thrust to give a greater participatory role to congregations. As Ian Bradley observes, 'hymn singing was a novel experience for most Victorian church-goers';[67] while Methodist, Baptist and Congregationalist services had been featuring hymns since the middle of the eighteenth century, 'the practice was not officially sanctioned in the Church of England until the 1820s and gradually became the norm in Anglican churches in the following two decades'.[68] Only in 'the first decade of Victoria's reign' did hymns become 'fully accepted in the Church of England' and 'even then there were bishops and others who remained opposed to their use'.[69] In the 1830s and 1840s, church music reformers such as John Antes La Trobe and John Hullah 'proposed the introduction of properly-trained choirs, pipe organs and simpler and more dignified hymn tunes'.[70] Even by 1843, Hullah was complaining that in the majority of Anglican churches 'congregations generally do not sing at all ... it is not genteel to sing in church'.[71] Between 1830 and 1870, there was a choral revival in the Church of England;[72] and while by 1800 most London Anglican churches had organs,[73] at the time of Victoria's accession, most churches and chapels in Britain did not, a situation that was to be more or less totally remedied over the period of her reign.[74] The choral service became 'the most fundamental Anglican liturgical development of the Victorian period'.[75] While these developments found wide acceptance, Tractarians wanted to introduce further changes which proved more controversial. Topics such as the eastward position of the priest at Eucharist, the wearing of full Eucharistic vestments, the use of lighted candles, of incense, of unleavened wafer bread and similar matters were debated and such practices followed in some churches.

Such developments are reflected in *Sketches by Boz*, in which the account of 'Our Parish' includes the description of an old lady who 'subscribed twenty pounds towards the erection of an organ in our parish church' (p. 14)[76] and a half-pay naval officer who 'finds fault with the sermon every Sunday, says that the organist ought to be ashamed of himself, offers to back himself for any amount to sing the psalms better than all the children put together, male and female' (p. 15). In *Sunday Under Three Heads*, organs and choirs are apparently as yet the showy prerogative of wealthy churches and their less-than-enthusiastically engaged congregations: 'The organ peals forth, the hired singers commence a short hymn, and the congregation condescendingly rise, stare about them, and converse in whispers ... The organ is again heard; those who have been asleep wake up, and those who have kept awake, smile and seem greatly relieved' (pp. 479–80). By the time of his *Uncommercial Traveller* piece 'City of London Churches', Dickens is giving an ironic account of the modern choral service in a church with a sparse congregation: 'Organ plays. Organ-loft is in a small gallery across the church; gallery congregation, two girls. I wonder what will happen when we are required to sing'. He comments on 'the brisk clerk's manner of encouraging us to try a note or two at psalm time' and 'the gallery-congregation's manner of enjoying a shrill duet, without a notion of time or tune'.[77] Meanwhile, when in 1846 he wrote 'The Hymn of the Wiltshire Labourers', the form was appropriately of the moment for a highly topical theme.

Dickens is again impatient that liturgical and ceremonial matters should be at the centre of people's religious focus:

> A vast number of witnesses being interrogated as to what they understood by the words Religion and Salvation, answered Lighted Candles. Some said water; some, bread; others, little boys; others mixed up the water, lighted candles, bread, and little boys all up together, and called the compound, Faith. Others again, being asked if they deemed it to be a matter of great interest in Heaven, and of high moment in the vast scale of creation, whether a poor human priest should put on, at a certain time, a white robe or a black one; or should turn his face to the East or to the West; or should bend his knees of clay; or stand, a worm on end upon

> the earth, said, 'Yes, they did'; and being further questioned, whether a man could hold such mummeries in contempt, and pass to everlasting rest, said boldly 'No'.[78]

As Michael Slater points out, in a letter from the same period (1843), the author similarly writes

> I find I am getting horribly bitter about Puseyism ... Good God to talk in these times of most untimely ignorance among the people, about what Priests shall wear, and whither they shall turn when they say their prayers.[79]

In the national and constitutional sphere, the position of the Church of England was being somewhat eroded during the Victorian era. Disestablishment was a topic under consideration from 1832 onwards, and indeed, in Ireland took place in 1869. Compulsory church rates were abolished. In 1854 and 1856, the need to subscribe to the Thirty Nine Articles as a requirement for taking a degree at Oxford or Cambridge was abolished. The oath taken by new Members of Parliament was relaxed for Jews. Civil registration of births was introduced, and hence there was no need to register births in the parish register; equally, marriages could be solemnised elsewhere than in the parish church. There was a reduction of the religious element in divorce law, and the blasphemy laws were interpreted more liberally. The Liberation Society campaigned in opposition to the domination of the Established Church, through its British and Foreign Schools Society and National Society, in education.

Of these matters, Dickens felt strongly about the issue of education in schools. In 1843, Ashley's Factories Regulation Bill had failed to get through Parliament because it proved impossible to gain the agreement of the Nonconformist interest to its clauses about education, which would leave the Established Church in control of the schools. Dickens's position was clear: he offered to Macvey Napier, editor of the *Edinburgh Review*, to write an article which would 'come out strongly against any system of Education, based exclusively on the principles of the Established Church'. His article would show 'why such a thing as the Church Catechism is wholly inapplicable to the state of ignorance that now prevails; and why no system but one, so general in great religious principles as to include all creeds, can meet the wants and understandings of the Dangerous Classes of Society'. Once again, he is impatient of what he sees as irrelevancies such as denominational differences getting in the way of doing Christian moral duty: 'Mysteries and Squabbles for Forms, *must* give way', he insists, in a situation so urgent, with 'people in a state so miserable and so neglected, that their very nature rebels against the simplest religion ... to convey to them the faintest outlines of any system of distinction between Right and Wrong, is in itself a Giant's task'.[80]

In an 1850 article, 'A December Vision' he gives a damning portrait of the hindrance of denominational squabbling to the cause of education. He writes of 'a low dull howl of ignorance' and of how

> The Minister of State, whose heart was pierced by even the little he could hear of these terrible voices ... went among the Priests and Teachers of all denominations, and faintly said:
>
> 'Hearken to this dreadful cry! What shall we do to stay it?'
> One body of the respondents answered, 'Teach this!'
> Another said, 'Teach that!'
> Another said, 'Teach neither this nor that, but t'other!'
> Another quarrelled with all the three; twenty others quarrelled with all the four, and quarrelled no less bitterly among themselves.[81]

He also concerned himself with religious matters affecting university education. As K.J. Fielding notes,[82] Dickens's speech of 12 April 1864 in praise of University College Hospital was delivered just as an (eventually unsuccessful) Bill to abolish religious tests for students taking degrees at Oxford was passing through Parliament. He remarks how the Hospital has helped bring attention to University College – 'I cannot separate it in my own mind from the establishment of the London University and the granting of degrees there'. He then continues with a pointed reference to the secular 'Godless colleges' of Belfast, Cork and Galway, established in 1845:[83]

> I will go further, and say that I think it no great stress of imagination to pursue the wholesome influences of this place even away into the Queen's Colleges of Ireland, and at home again into the rubbed eyes and quickened steps of those famous old universities that we all admire. (p. 329)[84]

He then goes on to talk about how,

> Among the students of University College, there have been Parsees, and other native youths from the far East, who have been enabled to obtain medical education there owing to the absence of religious tests, and who have carried home to their countrymen the blessings derivable from their skill and knowledge. (p. 330)

Religious tests are thus an obstacle to the doing of good in the world.

If Dickens's reactions to developments in the Victorian Church of England widely reflect the five aspects of his engagement with religion that I identified above, the concern with education here strikingly shows how inseparable social issues are to him from religious concerns. To Dickens, religion is never a mere matter of personal piety. He is always interested in the broader context of religion and religious developments within his society. His attack on the Sabbatarian movement in his *Sunday Under Three Heads* springs out of a concern not for himself, but for ordinary working people, as the Dedication to the Bishop of London announces. Bishop Blomfield is singled out as 'among the first, some years ago, to expatiate on the vicious addiction of the lower classes of society, to Sunday excursions'. Blomfield, in his elevated position has 'countless opportunities' for doing good, 'increasing the comforts and pleasures of the humbler classes of society ... by merely sanctioning with the influence of your example, their harmless pastimes and innocent recreations'. The Bishop's support for Sabbatarianism instead makes the life of these people worse, denying them desperately needed harmless pleasure:

> That your Lordship would ever have contemplated Sunday recreations with so much horror, if you had been acquainted with the wants and necessities of the people who indulged in them, I cannot imagine possible. That a Prelate of your elevated rank has the faintest conception of the extent of those wants, and the nature of those necessities, I do not believe. (p. 476)

The lives of ordinary people, he goes on to argue in the main text, are unlike those of 'The pampered aristocrat, whose life is one continued round of licentious pleasures and sensual gratification' (p. 477); for 'those whose lives are spent in sedentary or laborious occupations' (p. 478), Sunday is 'their only holiday' (p. 477) and they are 'accustomed to look forward to it through their whole existence, as their only day of rest from toil, and innocent enjoyment' (p. 478). Sabbatarianism is thus portrayed as cruel to the least privileged members of society.

Well over twenty years later, Dickens's social concerns involving religion persist. An *Uncommercial Traveller* piece, 'Two Views of a Cheap Theatre',[85] reflects Dickens's concern for the spiritual welfare and religious commitment of ordinary people. The day before the 1851 Census, a Religious Census was taken. In the official analysis that followed, Horace Mann considered that 'The most important fact' to emerge from it was 'the alarming number of the non-attendants' at church. Well over five million people had not attended church on the day of the Census, leading him to conclude that 'a sadly formidable portion of the English people are habitual neglecters of the public ordinances of religion'. Furthermore, this phenomenon seemed to be class-based, for the absentees were mainly 'the *labouring* myriads of our country'. It is a problem that occurs 'More especially in cities and large towns'.[86] In 1860, in a number of places, including London and Liverpool, as an experiment, services began to be held in theatres. The purpose of the clergymen involved in this 'bold step in the right direction', the *Liverpool Courier* explained, was the 'great work of evangelising the masses';[87] and the reports of such services tended to concentrate on how successfully this aim was achieved. Thus, of a service at Hengler's Circus in Liverpool it was reported that 'the greater portion of the audience appeared to belong to that class for which the services are intended' and the presence of 'many rough, and in some instances, *ragged* people' was noted; while at the same city's Adelphi theatre there were 'not fewer than 1,400 persons present, including many of the very class meant to be reached by the service in this place, who listened with the deepest attention'.[88] Similarly, it was reported of a service at the Victoria theatre in Lambeth that 'the pit and boxes of the theatre were well filled by the poor of the district'.[89] It is with precisely the same focus and concern that Dickens attends his theatre service. The piece describes the Uncommercial Traveller's visit to the same theatre on a Saturday evening, and then to the religious service there on a Sunday evening. While concerned that 'the lowest part of the audience of the previous night, *was not there*' (p. 61), and critical of various aspects of the service, he is gratified that 'there must have been full four thousand people present ... Every part of the house was well filled' (p. 58), that the congregation listened to a discourse 'with the most exemplary attention and uninterrupted silence and decorum' (p. 59), that the preacher gave 'reiterated assurance to the people that the commonest among them could work out their own salvation if they would, by simply, lovingly and dutifully following Our Saviour' (p. 60) and that 'whenever he struck that chord, or whenever he described anything which Christ himself had done, the array of faces before him was very much more earnest, and very much more expressive of emotion, than at any other time' (pp. 60–1).

Dickens's conception of the social dimension to Christianity, however, goes far beyond developments such as Sabbatarianism and theatre churches. To Dickens, religion cannot remain a matter of private devotions. Even subscribing to sound Christian attitudes of the brotherhood of man, and love for one's neighbour does not prevent Mr Snoady, in 'Lively Turtle' (*Household Words* 26 October 1850) from being presented satirically, because those attitudes are not translated into practical social action:

> All mankind are my brothers, and I don't think it Christian – if you come to that – to tell my brother that he is ignorant, or degraded, or dirty, or anything of that kind. I think it's abusive, and low. You meet me with the observation that I am required to love my brother. I reply 'I do.' I am sure I am always willing to say to my brother, 'My good fellow, I love you very much; go along with you; keep to your own road; leave me to mine; whatever is, is right; whatever isn't, is wrong; don't make a disturbance!' It seems to me, that this is at once the whole duty of man, and the only temper to go to dinner in.[90]

Evidently from this, not to detect a social imperative in Christian values is to have a distorted understanding of them. The Church of England is to be condemned for its lack of social involvement. Ragged Schools were initially set up, Dickens tells us, by 'a few unaccredited messengers of Christianity, whom no Bishop had ever heard of'.[91] Elsewhere, we are scornfully told of the tardiness of social concern within the Church: writing in 1848, the author declares that it was only 'in the year of grace eighteen hundred and forty-eight that a Bishop of London first came out respecting something wrong in poor men's social accommodations'.[92] At times, the social imperative in Christianity is insisted on in emphatic terms, as in 'To Working Men' (*Household Words* 7 October 1854), when the writer asserts that unless people

> set themselves in earnest to improve the towns in which they live, and to amend the dwellings of the poor, they are guilty, before GOD, of wholesale murder.[93]

Is Christianity adequate, however, in Dickens's opinion, to address successfully the problems of his age? A number of critics have concluded that he does not think it is up to the job. In her book *Dickens and the Broken Scripture*, Janet Larson challenges critics' assumption that 'whatever else might be fractured in his world, the Bible according to Boz is an unbroken book'.[94] Larson contends that Dickens had a 'deepening sense that his culture had outgrown the Bible's scheme, perhaps any scheme – a historical fact that exposed even the biblical ideals the prophetic Dickens invoked as impossible fictions of belief';[95] and that 'all around him far reaching cultural dislocations were shaping a world that seemed no longer to fit the Bible's concordant design of history'.[96] Later she claims that, 'On occasion in the novels Dickens even shifts from implicit to direct statement about the inadequacies of Scripture to modern life'.[97] As 'a writer so much attuned to his time', Dickens could only be expected to 'revise, not merely receive, his Bible at a time of needful revision and even radical rewriting'.[98] Vincent Newey, in his *The Scriptures of Charles Dickens*, agrees in seeing the Bible as no more than a general starting point for Dickens. Newey argues that in the Victorian age literature served as 'the provider of a new canon, a substitute bible, a secular scripture informed by and disseminating ... "an alternative set of liberal-humanist values"'[99] and sees Dickens's works very much in this context. Dickens has not abandoned Christianity, but is acting on a sense of its inadequacy. Thus, *A Christmas Carol* is

> manifestly about 'constructing ideals'... though Dickens embraces New Testament morality and even retains an element of the 'supernatural' in the visitation of the Spirits, he is actively committed to 'natural happiness' as the grounds of well-being. Duty to God and concern for the

> state of the immortal soul have been succeeded by an insistent interest in healthy feelings and fruitful relationships with the outer world.[100]

This is later summed up: 'the *Carol* replaces one ideology (old-style religion) with another (humanism)'.[101] If the text describes Scrooge as a 'sinner', 'the concept of sin ... is transferred from a religious to a social plane'.[102] Dickens's other works are seen in a similar way. As regards *Oliver Twist*, for instance, 'within the value-system of the book religion itself is entirely subservient to the valorisation of familial community'.[103] In *Great Expectations*, Christianity is one of a number of 'hollow creeds'.[104] Dickens 'to a large extent runs with the "Religion of Humanity"' in which 'the orthodox credo of "God is love" is displaced with the humanist principle of "Love is god"'.[105]

Some critics, indeed, argue that Dickens lost, or did not have, even a residual faith. Barry Qualls asserts that 'Carlyle never doubts the existence of the unknowable God' but that 'Dickens does'.[106] He talks of 'Dickens's progressive disenchantment with the idea of "supernatural"... reality'.[107] By the time of *Our Mutual Friend*, 'all effort to suggest a God above "the prison of this lower world" has been abandoned'[108] and 'Death is not envisioned ... as the passage from a dunghill world to glory; it is simply an escape from life in a "hopeless city"'.[109] The constant Christian allusions are merely perfunctory, and Dickens's true feelings revealed in his style. Larson comments on the merely 'conventional religious language' and 'Allusions that call upon the reader to do no creative work, merely to respond to an abstract stimulus':

> The Bible and the Prayer Book become repositories of clichés from which to draw to evoke automatic reactions for certain kinds of novelistic occasions, such as the child's deathbed or the exaltation of the heroine's virtues.[110]

For Qualls, in *Dombey and Son*,

> The luxuriant prose which surrounds the death of little Paul and calls attention to divine love and the 'older fashion' of immortality undoubtedly comforted his readers in a religious way. But the excesses of the prose and the very conventionality of the rhetoric indicate, I think, Dickens' fear that he does not know what he can believe.[111]

Quall finds in a sentence apparently alluding to Heaven that 'the wan belief of the Dickens of *Little Dorrit* is signalled by the dragging phrases'.[112]

The notion that, at least by the end of his life, Dickens had little or no religious faith simply won't hold water. As we have seen, matters that helped precipitate the more general Crisis of Faith, such as developments in science, do not bother him; he regards them as largely irrelevant. Writing shortly after the author's death, John Forster confidently asserted Dickens's 'unswerving faith in Christianity',[113] and returning to the subject towards the end of his biography, Forster quotes a letter of September 1868 written to his youngest son who was setting off to Australia. Dickens emphasises the need to follow the Christian moral code:

> Never take a mean advantage of anyone in any transaction, and never be hard upon people who are in your power. Try to do to others as you would have them do to you, and do not be discouraged if they fail sometimes. It is much better for you that they should fail in obeying the greatest rule laid down by Our Saviour than that you should. I put a New Testament among your books for the very same reasons, and with the very same hopes, that made me write an easy account of it when you were a little child. Because it is the best book that ever was, or will be, known in the world; and because it teaches you the best lessons by which any human creature, who tries to be truthful and faithful to duty, can possibly be guided.[114]

Dickens thus sees his own religious attitudes as the same as when he wrote *The Life of Our Lord* over twenty years before. Although the morality of Christianity is central to Dickens, that is not all that religion involves, for though

> You will remember that you have never at home been harassed about religious observances, or mere formalities. I have always been anxious not to weary my children with such things, before they are old enough to form opinions respecting them.

he urges his son

> Never abandon the wholesome practice of saying your own private prayers, night and morning. I have never abandoned it myself, and I know the comfort of it.[115]

Forster assures the reader that 'every word there is written from his heart'[116]

Furthermore, in his will,[117] made in 1869, only just over a year before his death, he wrote

> I commit my soul to the mercy of God through our Lord and Saviour Jesus Christ, and I exhort my dear children humbly to try to guide themselves by the teaching of the New Testament in its broad spirit, and to put no faith in any man's narrow construction of its letter here or there.[118]

There is no convention about placing such religious sentiments in a will; if he had lost his faith, he could simply not have included this passage.

Furthermore, the emphasis of the passage upon the spirit rather than the letter of Christian teaching is once again consistent with attitudes Dickens showed throughout his life rather than indicating changes in his thinking about religion.[119]

Nor will it do to argue that what Dickens believes in is a Religion of Humanity. I have been emphasising the importance to Dickens of the moral teachings of Christ; but this does not mean that the metaphysical aspects of Christianity are unimportant to him. We have just seen his concern about the religious belief and observances of ordinary people reflected in his keen observation of the church service at the theatre. In addition, when he visits a Ragged School, he observes the pupils' 'benighted ignorance in reference to the Deity' as well as to 'any social duty'. Though he isn't uncritical of the school, he notes with satisfaction that

> it had inculcated some association with the name of the Almighty, which was not an oath, and had taught them to look forward in a hymn (they sang it) to another life, which would correct the miseries and woes of this.[120]

It is equally reflected in his novels. In *Bleak House,* Mrs Pardiggle's efforts are condemned because she puts the brickmakers off going to church rather than inspiring them to go; and what is religiously shocking about Jo's death is not that he is dying in ignorance of a moral code but in ignorance of God. In *Hard Times,* Dickens is concerned that for all the churches in Coketown, no-one seems to attend them. As we shall be seeing, Dickens is concerned with the spiritual welfare of the members of his society as well as their physical welfare.

Though these critics think Dickens finds Christianity unequal to the challenges of his age, I shall be arguing that, on the contrary, he finds Christianity the complete answer to the problems of his age. More than once, Dickens refers to the 'sufficiency' or 'all-sufficiency' of religion as he sees it. We have already come across the letter to Frank Stone in which he complains about some people's 'determination to refuse the New Testament as a sufficient guide in itself and to force the Old Testament into alliance with it'.[121] Equally, in a letter to Rev. R.H. Davies of 24 December 1856 Dickens asserts that,,

> there cannot be many men, I believe, who have a more humble veneration for the New Testament or a more profound conviction of its all-sufficiency than I have.[122]

In the former of these instances, 'sufficient' seems to mean 'enough, without reference to the Old Testament'; and this may or may not be what he means by referring to the 'all-sufficiency' of the New Testament in the letter to Davies. Even if the meaning is the same in both cases, it is notable that its application is not limited: he does not specify areas in which it is all-sufficient, but seems to be using the word in the normal sense in which we would use it, as meaning 'meeting all situations, covering all eventualities'. Certainly when he uses the term (or its cognates) in other contexts, such as when describing the 'demented disciples who push arithmetic and political economy beyond all bounds of sense (not to speak of such a weakness as humanity) and hold them to be all-sufficient for every case',[123] he seems to use the word in precisely this sense. It is not unreasonable, then, to take Dickens as having confidence that Christianity has the answers not only to problems of belief and personal conduct, but to wider and broader problems. I shall be arguing later that Dickens finds no need to attach himself to a political creed, because Christianity provides him with a creed that leaves no need for a political analysis of society and political solutions. More comprehensively, his religion provides him with an approach to making sense of society and of solving its problems. Far from being inadequate to dealing with the problems of Victorian society, he thinks Christianity is the only answer to them. In the next chapter, we shall attempt to explore the precise nature of his religious social criticism and to put it in the context of contemporary religious social attitudes.

2
Dickens and Early Victorian Christian Social Attitudes

> The late and present distress of the manufacturing population of Great Britain must be deemed, in the case of multitudes, in a very considerable degree, attributable to themselves ... in prosperous times of trade, the habits of the operatives are very commonly deserving of the severest reprehension. They are marked by idleness, selfishness, extravagance, and brutish intemperance.
>
> Rev. Thomas Gisborne[1]

Though perhaps slightly surprising to the modern reader, the social views of Rev. Gisborne expressed here would by no means have struck his contemporaries in the 1820s as unusual, even for a clergyman. Prevailing religious social attitudes in the early part of the nineteenth century and continuing into Victoria's reign have been summed up by Gerald Parsons:

> Poverty was morally tolerable because it was the inevitable product of immutable economic laws which were themselves the product of a divinely ordained and ordered world ... whilst charity might alleviate poverty, it would be impious, as well as fruitless, to contemplate reform ... the practice of charity ... was to be directed towards the deserving poor, whose poverty was identifiably not the result of their own improvidence, intemperance or indolence. Much poverty, it was confidently claimed, was in fact the result of precisely such personal failing, and hence a recompense for sin[2]

Of the four ideas Parsons expounds here, all can be seen reflected in the Church of England, of which Dickens was a member for most of his life, in the writings of John Bird Sumner (1780–1862). Sumner was thoroughly part of the mainstream of his church in his day: in 1848 he became Archbishop of Canterbury, after twenty years as Bishop of Chester. The first Bishop of Manchester was not enthroned until the same year that Sumner left his position, and so, significantly for the views he held, the Diocese of Chester at the time of his incumbency covered the whole of industrial Lancashire, including Manchester, Salford, Preston, Blackburn and the other major centres of manufacturing and mining.

In 1844, having seen the problems of industrial society at first hand, he remained committed to the view that though 'We see wealth and poverty in close contact and violent contrasts; both in extremes' yet 'It would be unreasonable to complain of this ... the inevitable course of things ... Legislation cannot reach the case ... but like every other providential arrangement, the evils belonging to it have a corresponding remedy'[3] – by which he meant what he called in 1841 'the economical dole of public charity'.[4] Attempts to interfere more radically in the system would upset the order of society – 'machinery ... cannot be safely meddled with. When we attempt to regulate one wheel, we set other wheels in motion of which we had not known the power, and the result is confusion'.[5] No permanent change can be made by man in the general pattern of society: 'He cannot reverse the original decree, that man shall eat bread in the sweat of his brow'.[6]

His longstanding view was that the poverty of the lower orders gives them an opportunity to be moral through the practice of patience and learning to be content with the little they have. The poor are so because 'their ancestors have been either less prudent or less fortunate'; they need 'the constant exercise of patient contentment' and should aim at 'preserving a cheerful equanimity under those hardships which no discontent can remove or alleviate'.[7] The distinction between the deserving and undeserving poor introduced here with the separation of the 'less prudent' from the 'less fortunate' and the implication of moral failing in the former is developed further. Sumner distinguishes between 'poverty' and 'indigence'. Poverty is 'the natural lot of many in a well constituted society'. Indigence is not the natural lot of anyone, 'but is commonly the state into which intemperance and want of prudent foresight push poverty: the punishment which the moral government of God inflicts in this world upon thoughtlessness and guilty extravagance'.[8]

It is perhaps not surprising, then, that Sumner and his fellow Bishop Blomfield of London were members of the Poor Law Commission whose work paved way for the 1834 Poor Law Amendment Act.[9] The reception of the Act in religious circles is a reflection of how commonly held the attitudes behind it were. As Owen Chadwick points out, the Act was widely welcomed in religious spheres both within the Church of England, and beyond, warmly received by such publications as the Evangelical *Christian Observer* and the Unitarian *Monthly Repository*.[10] The prominent Scottish Presbyterian clergyman Thomas Chalmers was a keen advocate of the Act; earlier, as a Malthusian, and in line with the views of Ricardo and others, he had been in favour of abolishing the Poor Law altogether,[11] to strengthen for the poor what Malthus called 'incentives to sobriety and industry and consequently happiness'[12] and to encourage them to look to what Ricardo referred to as 'their own exertions' and to make them develop 'prudence and forethought'.[13] The 'remedy against the extension of pauperism', Chalmers stated, was to 'reform the improvident habits of the people'. Less than a tenth of English pauperism, he considered, arose from 'unavoidable misfortune'.[14] Many contemporary clergy concurred with the view that under the old Poor Law immorality was promoted in that it encouraged idleness and bastardy (since it granted child allowance).[15] G. Kitson-Clark remarks on 'the commitment of a large number of the clergy to the administration of the Poor Law' once the reforms had been put into place.[16]

These types of views seem a long way from those we would associate with Dickens, and so, in trying to account for his attitudes, we might look for any alternative religious views on social issues at the time. The Unitarians might suggest themselves here: Dickens was a Unitarian for four years in the early 1840s, and they were well known for holding progressive views. Indeed, the author himself perceived them in this light. During his visit to America not long before becoming a Unitarian, he had been greatly impressed, as he wrote in *American Notes*, by the Unitarian minister William Ellery Channing and 'the bold philanthropy with which he has ever opposed himself to that most hideous blot and foul disgrace – Slavery' (p. 34).[17] He observed similarly during a visit to St. Louis that:

> The Unitarian church is represented, in this remote place, as in most other parts of America, by a gentleman of great worth and excellence. The poor have good reason to remember and bless it; for it befriends them, and aids the cause of rational education, without any sectarian or selfish views. It is liberal in all its actions, of kind construction, and of wide benevolence. (p. 194)

At the time he joined them, he described them as people 'who would do something for human improvement if they could, and who practise Charity and Toleration'.[18]

Writings by Unitarians, however, reveal that they held similar views to the ones already outlined; if anything, they tend to be even more hardline about such matters. Harriet Martineau's *Illustrations of Political Economy* (1834), for instance, was written specifically to preach acceptance of the new economic system and its accompanying outlook. Thus, one of the stories, 'A Manchester Strike', is a tale of a strike for higher wages, which strike brings about much suffering before the workers are ultimately defeated. At a late stage, the striking workers are addressed by Mr Wentworth at a public meeting:

> 'All you can do now, is to live as you best may upon such wages as the masters can give. You must watch every opportunity of making some little provision against the fluctuations of trade, contributing your money rather for your mutual relief in hard times than for the support of strikers ... you

> must discourage in them [i.e. your children] the imprudent early marriages to which are mainly owing the distresses which afflict yourselves and those which will for some time, I fear, oppress your children. You ask me what you must do. These things are all that I can suggest.'
>
> 'But these things, sir, will not guard our children any more than ourselves from the fluctuations in trade you speak of.'
>
> 'But they will prevent those fluctuations from being so injurious as they now are.' (pp. 102–3)[19]

We are then told that the workers present 'were pleased to be reasoned with by one whom they esteemed, and to obtain, by these means, a better insight into their affairs than was given them by leaders who were all of one party' (pp. 104–5). The hardline position is evident here: the economic system will operate inexorably, wages will unavoidably be determined by the laws of supply and demand, and there will be fluctuations in trade just as a fact of life. In the light of this the workers can best act prudently, avoiding marrying early and bringing children that they cannot support into the world. They should not be improvident, spending all their money in the good times; rather, they should save to get them through the tough times that will inevitably come.

Similar attitudes are evident in non-fiction of the period. In an early edition of the Unitarian weekly *The Inquirer*, for instance, a writer discusses the bill Lord Ashley had introduced into Parliament to ban women, girls, boys under thirteen years of age and parish apprentices from working in mines. The writer professes support for the bill, but it soon becomes evident that this is on very specific terms. Interference from the law must only take place within well-defined limits: 'useful legislation confines itself to the suppression of fraud, violence and tyranny'. In such circumstances, 'The prevention of oppression and brutality is not to be put off for a day from any reference to laws of political economy, which only express the natural circumstances affecting the price of labour'. Humanitarianism must not, however, lead to other legal attempts to interfere in the economy: we must 'remember that we cannot by any law place all our countrymen in the situation in which we should wish to see them, and that ignorant and injudicious attempts at relief only aggravate their sufferings'. Attempts to 'oppose the laws laid down by the political economists by appeals to humanity and religion' reveal only ignorance of political economy, which 'does not pretend to lay down laws, but to give us the knowledge of natural laws equally existing whether we are acquainted with them or not'. Forbidding the labour of women and children will affect the income of families, and it would be a 'delusion' to try to force men's wages up by law to compensate, for 'The variation of the rate of wages is as much under the influence of natural laws as the changes in the tides. You cannot controul them'. The employment of children is 'far from being necessarily and in itself an evil', and observation of working children shows 'in abundant instances, that they are cheerful and happy under the labour required from them'.[20] A few weeks later, a writer in the same publication considering Chartism assesses the motives of those involved in the campaign. Apparently, some simply 'want better wages, and they fancy if they demand them they must have them. These people have no idea why they receive wages at all, or what circumstances affect their amount; they feel their own wants and seek the most obvious remedy, but success is impossible and clamor vain'. The writer fears that if the Charter is granted, 'they might even do more harm by ignorance than has hitherto been done by selfishness. All good must come from an acquaintance with the natural laws affecting our social condition'.[21]

If these attitudes do not seem progressive, they have to be seen against a background in which reactions to the new industrialised society included one which wished to reject that society and return to a former way of life. The most famous manifestation of this was the Young England movement of the 1840s, but it was a view held also by others. Among a group of people to whom we are shortly to turn, for instance, the Member of Parliament (M.P.) Michael Sadler longed for a time when 'every cottager had a cow and every cottager's wife had a spinning wheel';[22] the campaigner Richard Oastler considered that 'domestic manufacture ... would be the greatest blessing that could be introduced into Old England',[23] and in his speeches constantly gave his hearers what Cecil Driver calls 'the simple story of a happier England that once had been, when the recognised ties of mutual obligation bound men together into a commonwealth – a tacit contract sealed by the old Poor Law of 43 Elizabeth, which the capitalists for their own evil purposes were now seeking to abrogate'.[24]

In this context, Unitarians were indeed being progressive in wholeheartedly embracing recently developed ideas and accepting the reality of the new society. As Raymond V. Holt argues, 'their very faith in science' caused them to believe 'that the generalizations of contemporary economists were as much statements of natural laws as generalizations made by chemists and geologists from their observations'.[25] Ricardo himself was a Unitarian,[26] and subscription to Malthus's theory of population and to wage-fund theory 'convinced them that it was not possible to cure distress by raising wages'.[27] From this it becomes logical that while supporting progressive causes of the time such as the Anti-Corn Law Movement and the Co-operative Movement,[28] they opposed trades unions as 'futile conspiracies to defeat the laws of nature' and strikes as 'inevitably hopeless'.[29]

Holt asserts that Unitarians 'were to some degree torn asunder by the divergence between their humanitarian and their economic and social theories',[30] and a notable feature of Unitarian writings at this period is that compassion is a factor in their thinking about the poor. Compassion must, however, be reined in by not losing sight of the laws of political economy. Thus William Rathbone Greg, a member of a manufacturing family well known for being enlightened, nevertheless argues that benevolence must not interfere with the operation of the laws of the market and thus of the universe: an employer must not

> gratify himself with the luxury of paying higher wages than his neighbours, either out of vanity or from benevolence ... The plain truth is, that neither the most boundless benevolence, nor the most consummate ability can fight against the clear moral and material laws of the universe. If the field of employment is too limited for the numbers who crowd into it, no power and no goodness can prevent wages from falling.[31]

Compassion is much in evidence in Elizabeth Gaskell's *Mary Barton* in her tracing of the sufferings of the working classes of Manchester during the Hungry Forties. She is unstinting in her depiction of people reduced to the most rudimentary of existences:

> Parents sitting in their clothes by the fireside during the whole night for seven weeks together, in order that their only bed and bedding might be reserved for the use of their large family ... others sleeping upon the cold hearthstone for weeks in succession, without adequate means of providing themselves with food or fuel (and this in the depth of winter) ... others being compelled to fast for days together, uncheered by any hope of better fortune, living, moreover, or rather starving, in a crowded garret, or damp cellar, and gradually sinking under the pressure of want and despair into a premature grave.[32] (p. 85)

Gaskell nevertheless acquiesces with the need simply to accept the ideas of political economy. In the discussion of issues between employer John Carson and working class Job Legh at the end of the novel, Carson's assertion that

> We cannot regulate the demand for labour. No man or set of men can do it. It depends on events which God alone can control. When there is no market for our goods, we suffer just as much as you do

goes unchallenged by Legh, who, though claiming he is 'not given to Political Economy', says he is aware of that (p. 384); and indeed, the divine source of economic laws lies at the heart of the whole novel. The author's description of the story of John Barton (after whom the novel was originally to be named) is 'the tragedy of a poor man's life' (p. 372), and the term is being used here in its Greek or Shakespearean sense. In his activities as a Chartist and trade unionist, Barton is rebelling against the order God has established in the universe; as always in tragedy, God's will prevails, and rebellion against it is futile and leads to the destruction of the tragic hero. As is conventional, Barton is a good man with a fatal flaw linked to his admirable qualities: he is

> a good, steady workman, and, as such, pretty certain of steady employment. But he spent all he got with the confidence (you may also call it improvidence) of one who was willing, and believed himself able, to supply all his wants by his own exertions (p. 24)

Gaskell has already classed Barton as one of those who are resentful during hard times at how the sufferings of the employers seem so much less than those of their employees, but remarks on how 'with child-like improvidence, good times will often dissipate his grumbling' (p. 24). His moral flaw can be traced back to his upbringing, an inheritance from his parents, for the 'scanty living' he suffered during childhood was partly the result of 'improvident habits' (p. 7). The word is applied to no-one else in the novel, though the trait can also be seen in the other character who suffers a downfall, Esther, whose improvidence compounds her predicament. Having run away with her lover, when he departs for Ireland she makes poor use of the fifty pounds he gives her:

> I might have done better with the money; I see now. But I did not know the value of it then. Formerly I had earned it easily enough at the factory, and as I had no more sensible wants, I spent it on dress and on eating. While I lived with him, I had it for the asking; and fifty pounds would, I thought, go a long way. (p. 162)

This moral flaw, and most centrally with John Barton, is at the root of the decline and downfall of these characters.

Otherwise, though, the sufferings of the characters in their poverty are not their own fault and not a punishment for sin. For these deserving poor, the writer has Job Legh suggest that it would not be at all impious – indeed quite the reverse – to mitigate the effects of the God-imposed dispensation by charity from the more fortunate:

> surely it's also a part of His plan that so much of the burden of suffering as can be should be lightened by those whom it is his pleasure to make happy, and content in their own circumstances ... when God gives a blessing to be enjoyed, He gives it with a duty to be done; and the duty of the happy is to help the suffering to bear their woe. (p. 385)

The masters, Job says, will have to answer to God ' whether you've done, and are doing all in your power to lighten the evils that seem always to hang on the trades by which you make your fortunes' (p. 386).

In Greg's review of Mary Barton for the Edinburgh Review,[33] he takes issue with the novel in a number of ways, but seizes on the idea of Barton's improvidence, to underline a familiar moral lesson, noting that

> he never, when in receipt of the highest wages ... lays by a farthing for a time of sickness at home or stagnation of trade. Meanwhile, whenever these periods come, he is found cursing his masters instead of his own improvidence; spending his time and money on trades' unions, when both his child and himself are unsupplied with the barest necessaries of life; and wasting, (as so many operatives do), in subscriptions for such objects, funds which, duly husbanded, would have saved his only son (whose loss, we are told, has warped his temper) from an early grave ... if ever there was a clear case in which a man had himself to thank for most of his sorrows and misfortunes John Barton was that case. On the contrary, he is painted as utterly unconscious, even to the last, of his own improvidence and of its sinister influence on his condition. (p. 413)

Greg goes on to argue that for workers to save is 'easy' but 'rare' with 'much' of their money 'wasted at the ale-house ... squandered in subscriptions to trades' unions and strikes' and devoted to 'gambling' (p. 417). If, as in the novel, the workers perceive their employers as coping better during times of a slump, it is because the latter 'in the days of prosperity, had laid by a portion of their earnings and ... the operatives had not'; hence, 'they could subsist out of their previous savings, while the improvident operatives had no savings to fall back upon' (p. 415). The notion of the deserving and undeserving poor is plainly in his mind as, cautious about the idea that the rich should help the poor in their distress, he argues that the poor themselves are the best ones to help the poor, being in a better position to be confident that they are not bestowing charity on the undeserving:

> Immense difficulty is experienced by the rich, when they attempt to discriminate between cases of imposture and cases of real destitution, – between cases which it would be a duty and delight, and cases which it would often be a sin and mischief to relieve. (p. 411)

If the novel depicts the suffering of the working classes, Greg asserts, the writer should have 'drawn attention also to those intellectual and moral deficiencies by which this distress is so often caused or aggravated' (p. 434).

An alternative religious view was famously to emerge with Christian Socialism in 1848. However, in the 1830s and earlier 1840s, there was already a body of Christians with a decidedly more critical view of social issues. Writing from a religious point of view, Fanny Trollope in her 1840 novel *Michael Armstrong* has her heroine investigating whether the poor actually are characterised by 'intemperance and extravagance' and are 'poor because they are extravagant' (p. 168),[34] and discovering a quite different reality. At the beginning of the 1830s the campaigner Richard Oastler cried out in the face of the factory system, which, among other things employed child labour yet was supposedly 'Practised by men called Christians': 'What are the ministers of religion doing? Would that they would raise their voices and resolutely interfere for these lambs'.[35] When in 1841, Lord Ashley, the future Lord Shaftesbury, visited the industrial North of England, he was shocked at the indifference of local clergy to the suffering he saw, and attacked them for being 'cowed by capital and power'.[36] As J.C. Gill records, clergy such as Revs. Richard Oglesby, Wyndham Maddock, J.C. Frank, J.C. Boddington and many others were active in the movement for factory reform from the 1830s onwards.[37] Nicholas Edsall further observes that numerous Christians viewed the New Poor Law of 1834 as 'a violation of the Constitution and of the Laws of God'[38] and G.D.H. Cole relates that the Malthusian doctrines behind it were seen as 'contrary both to Holy Scripture and decent human feeling'.[39] The Cambridgeshire parson, F.H. Maberly, led an early campaign against the New Poor Law,[40] and an 'extraordinary number'[41] of both Church of England and Nonconformist clergy subsequently joined the anti-Poor Law movement. Most prominent among the clergy outspoken in their criticism of society during the early Victorian period were the Revs. Joseph Rayner Stephens and George Stringer Bull.

They were joined by a number of politicians and political activists, including Michael Sadler M.P., Lord Ashley, Oastler and John Wood. At the same time, a similar alternative religious critique of society was being reflected in the works of writers such as Thomas Hood, Elizabeth Barrett Browning, Fanny Trollope and Charlotte Elizabeth Tonna.[42]

Of the figures in these three groups, many, though not all, were involved in the Factory (or Ten Hours) Movement of the 1830s and 1840s.[43] The Movement had its origin in a conversation between Wood, a Yorkshire worsted spinner, and Oastler, in which the former had expressed his unhappiness at the conditions under which he was having to force the children he employed to work as he tried to remain competitive. He and two other master spinners had tried to institute a ten hour working day but had met with opposition to the move from other masters and had had to drop their plans.[44] The account he gave of working life in the factories prompted Oastler to write a letter to the *Leeds Mercury* exposing such conditions in the factories[45] and from this the Movement was born. George Stringer Bull joined the campaign in 1831,[46] and Michael Sadler, a longstanding friend of Oastler's, took up the cause in Parliament. When Sadler lost his seat, Lord Ashley took up the Parliamentary campaign to get legislation passed to control what went on in factories.

Stephens, already a committed factory reformer,[47] met Oastler in 1835, and pledged himself to the latter's cause in August 1836.[48] Some of the writers also had links to this group. Before writing *Michael Armstrong*, Fanny

Trollope obtained letters of introduction from Ashley to the Movement's leaders, and met Wood, Bull and Oastler.[49] Bull appears lightly disguised in *Michael Armstrong* as Rev. Bell, and the factory run by Wood and his business partner is named and singled out for praise. For a period during the 1830s, Charlotte Elizabeth Tonna edited the *Christian Lady's Magazine*, which was published by Robert Seeley, close friend and eventual biographer of Sadler. Seeley also published a number of Tonna's books,[50] and the two of them were among the leaders of the Christian Influence Society.[51] In Tonna's 1842 novel *Helen Fleetwood*, Ashley is singled out as the man who is going to remedy the evils the novel explores.

Centrally, what all these figures did was to measure their society against Christian values. As Rev. Joseph Rayner Stephens declared, his aim, for instance, was 'to apply the rule of God's commandments to various institutions of the social system' in order 'to bring the operations of the manufactures, commerce and legislation of this professedly Christian land to the standards of God's Holy Word'.[52] Thus, in response to the Report of the Children's Employment Commission concerning the Employment of Women and Children in Mines and Collieries, Ashley, in a speech in Parliament on 7 June 1842, denounced aspects of female employment as

> evils of so hideous a nature, that they will not admit of delay – they must be instantly removed – evils that are both disgusting and intolerable – disgusting they would be in a heathen country, and perfectly intolerable they are in one that professes to call itself Christian.[53]

In measuring their society both against the general thrust of Christianity and its individual precepts, they found it seriously wanting. The ills of society had a single ultimate source: as Oastler remarked, 'The real cause of our general distress may be found in our entire abandonment of the great principles of the Divine Legislator'.[54]

The group's two main targets for criticism were the unrestrained operation of the economic system and the new Poor Law, though Stephens for one saw these as twin aspects of a vision of society to which the Christian critics were fundamentally opposed, claiming that 'the connection between this cursed Poor Law Bill and the factory system is intimate and inseparable',[55] and Oastler expressed the opinion that the New Poor Law was 'only *one* branch of the Factory System, *intended* to drive the agricultural poor into the Factories'.[56] A number of these figures were concerned about the workings of the economic system, taking, as mentioned above, prominent roles in the Ten Hours Movement, which campaigned to reduce the working day from as much as sixteen hours a day to ten (and in the early days of which Michael Sadler appealed to 'the words of Scripture itself' to argue that 'the termination of labour should correspond to that of the day'),[57] and against the use of child labour in factories and mines. Considering his own employment of child labour, John Wood told Oastler, referring to the Bible, 'I have been reading this Book and in every page I read my own condemnation'[58] In Tonna's *Helen Fleetwood*, Richard Green speaks for the author in labelling child labour of up to ten hours a day 'a disgrace to a Christian country' (p. 239).[59] More generally, in an 1844 speech, Richard Oastler, for instance, pointed out the lack of accord between the values of 'a Christian country' and the 'immense heaps of wealth that have by the cruel factory system, been acquired, in utter disregard both of the physical and spiritual interests of the nation'.[60]

Oastler equally condemned the New Poor Law as 'that unchristian and unconstitutional statute'[61]; in an 1839 speech given in London, Stephens 'besought the people no longer to remain subservient to so unlawful, so unchristian an enactment' and declared with regard to the Poor Law Commissioners that 'The acts of these men had for their object turning religion into infidelity'.[62] Among his specific grounds for objecting to the Act were that it ' treats the poor worse than the felon ... makes marriage a mockery,[63] and offers brutal violence to the holiest feelings of our nature, degrading the creature and dishonouring the Creator'.[64] In *Helen Fleetwood*, as the board of guardians at a workhouse conscientiously carries out official policy, and attempts to work out 'upon how scanty a quota of necessary sustenance might life be supported, so as to avert from its object the climax of actual starvation' (p. 19), Tonna remarks:

> the calculators were necessarily in imminent peril of sacrificing on the shrine of supposed public duty, not only all finer feelings of humanity, all brotherly observances that man owes to man, but also the obedience due from every professing follower of Christ to the explicit, unmistakeable command of his divine Master, 'Do ye unto all men even as ye would they should do unto you.' (p. 20)

Prominent in the outlook of this group of religious social critics was the notion of the brotherhood of man. Ashley, for instance, in his speech to Parliament of 4 August 1840 advocating a Royal Commission to investigate children's employment asserted that

> I have been bold enough to undertake this task, because I must regard the objects of it as being created, as ourselves, by the same Maker, redeemed by the same Saviour, and destined to the same immortality[65]

In Trollope's novel, it takes only a change of clothing for the eponymous hero of *Michael Armstrong* to be symbolically transformed, as another character remarks, from 'a beggar-child' into 'the genteelest looking little fellow' (p. 106). Equally, the novel's heroine, Mary Brotherton, the privileged daughter of a manufacturer, always believes that 'she was formed of the same sort of materials as the wretches who toiled for him' (p. 126), and faced with the 'utter destitution' of the workers, shows a Good Samaritan-like sense of brotherhood in resolving that she will not 'pass along on the other side' (p. 219). Hood's 1843 poem 'The Song of the Shirt', inspired by the desperate plight of seamstresses existing on wages so low, as a result of the unrestrained operation of market, that it was hard to subsist,[66] measures this state of affairs against Christian values:

> It's Oh! to be a slave
> Along with the barbarous Turk
> Where woman has never a soul to save
> If this is Christian work. (lines 13–16)[67]

Hood has his seamstress appealing to the idea of universal brotherhood and sisterhood in the hope of alleviation of her plight, addressing her employers as

> Oh, Men, with Sisters dear!
> Oh, Men, with Mothers and Wives! (lines 25–6)

Being one's brother's keeper involved three over-riding shared concerns, about the immediate hardship and suffering of the less fortunate in their daily lives; anxiety that their humanity should not be diminished or fail to be developed; and a watchfulness about the state of their immortal souls. Concerns about the physical sufferings of child labourers, for instance, are expressed by an 1840 correspondent to *The Times* who signed himself 'The Children's Friend'. Deploring that 'such barbarities are practised in a civilised and Christian country', the writer describes the effects of such labour:

> The physical consequences of these cruel impositions upon infant strength are consumption, scrofula, stunted growth, and rheumatism of a character sometimes so severe as to entirely incapacitate the sufferer from labour.[68]

In her poem, 'The Cry of the Children' (1843), Elizabeth Barrett Browning focuses on the same group of labourers and stresses the physical debilitation that arises from sheer hard work. Their physical state, with their 'pale and shrunken faces' (line 25)[69] is unhealthy. They suffer from utter exhaustion, 'weary' (line 65) and with 'heavy eyelids drooping' (line 71). The pace of their work is relentless: the machines turn 'all day' (line 77), unremitting and monotonous,

> 'Till our hearts turn, – our heads, with pulses burning' (line 79)

Their whole being is taken over by the machinery. The seamstress in Hood's 'The Song of the Shirt' is physically debilitated, with 'fingers weary and worn' (line 1) and 'eyelids heavy and red' (line 2) as she exists in an environment of ' poverty, hunger, and dirt'(line 6).

Anxiety about the dehumanisation of people lies behind Stephens's concern above that the workhouses were 'degrading the creature', and Hood picks this issue up in his poem 'The Pauper's Christmas Carol'. Reflecting the famous custom of giving workhouse inmates a treat on Christmas Day, the poem springs out of Hood's perception that for the rest of year, inmates of workhouses, not allowed any personal expression, became stultified and reduced to what Sidney and Beatrice Webb called 'a state of blankmindedness'.[70] Thus, the emotionally-alive human being is resuscitated and his full humanity restored only on one day of year:

> Frozen cares begin to melt
> Hopes revive and spirits flow-
> Feeling as I have not felt
> Since a dozen months ago. (lines 46–9)

Laissez-faire capitalism was seen as having the same effect. Ashley worries in his 1842 Reply to the Lancashire Short Time Committee that

> Over a large surface of the industrial community man has been regarded as an *animal,* and that, an animal not of the highest order; his loftiest faculties when not prostrate, are perverted, and his lowest, exclusively devoted to the manufacture of wealth[71]

That they often perceived the position of the poor as very similar to that of slaves, with the implication not merely of financial exploitation but that those involved were being deprived of full human status, is reflected, for example, in the letter by Richard Oastler's letter concerning factory children, published in the *Leeds Mercury* which initiated the whole Factory Movement: 'the system of infantile Slavery in Bradford is what I have described it to be – "*More horrid than Colonial Slavery*"'[72] or Ashley's description of child employment as 'a system of slavery under the sanction of law'.[73]

The correspondent to *The Times* was also worried about the child labourers' spiritual welfare:

> The moral effects are obvious: for the system precludes all possibility of education, except by attendance at Sunday schools, which can impart but little instruction to children so exhausted by the watching and toil of the week as to be incapable of giving wakeful attention to the teacher. The gambling and other vicious habits of the men are naturally imitated by many of the children ... a tendency to drinking is generated...[74]

George Stringer Bull was similarly concerned:

> What knowledge having a religious or moral tendency can the factory child acquire? Suppose children have learned in infant schools or national schools to read the New Testament tolerably well before they become Factory Children, which is commonly the case at 8 or 9 years of age, what chance have they of improving or even maintaining what they have learned? At 5 a.m. (or even at 4 a.m.) they leave their beds; they return at 7, 8 or 9 p.m. The factory system annihilates, as nearly as possible, the offices of parents or religious instructors to all intents and purposes.[75]

One of Oastler's arguments in favour of the Ten Hours Bill was equally that

> It has been found utterly impossible to inculcate moral and religious principles into the minds of human beings who are engaged in factory labour, or any other labour, for a longer period.[76]

The 1842 and 1843 Reports of the Royal Commission of Inquiry into Children's Employment, set up as a result of the campaigning of Ashley, among much else heightened awareness of working children's ignorance of religion, as reflected in the remarks of eleven year old Henry Jowett: 'I do not know who God is – Jesus Christ is heaven'.[77] Christian social critics worried that in addition to mere ignorance, the experiences of the poor would make them sceptical of religion. The children in 'The Cry of the Children' are presented as in a state of sheer lack of knowledge concerning religion, and barely know how to pray, but in as far as they do pray, find God unresponsive:

> 'If He heard us, He would surely
> (For they call Him good and mild)
> Answer, smiling down the steep world very purely,
> "Come and rest with me, my child."'
>
> 'But, no!' say the children, weeping faster,
> He is speechless as a stone;
> And they tell us, of His image is the master
> Who commands us to work on.
> ...grief has made us unbelieving –
> We look up for God, but tears have made us blind. (lines 121–8, 131–2)

The narrator then sums up the situation:

> God's possible is taught by His world's loving –
> And the children doubt of each. (lines 135–6)

It is to this last group of Christian social critics,[78] of course, that Dickens belongs. From the time that Christian Socialism emerged, a new perspective on social issues began to form and have fruits within religious circles; however, in drawing many of my examples below from the early part of his career, my intention is to show that Dickens's social attitudes were formed long before the influence of Christian Socialism might be felt. Just as the figures discussed above do,[79] he constantly measures society and its institutions against Christian values. In the face of the scandal that erupted in 1849 when cholera broke out killing a hundred and eighty pauper children who were farmed out to the private Drouet's baby farm Dickens, in an article in *The Examiner*, called it 'a disgrace to a Christian community' and 'a stain upon a civilised land'.[80] In *Oliver Twist*, their failure to match Christian standards are a damning judgement on Mr Bumble and the workhouse:

> 'By the bye,' said Mr. Bumble, 'You don't know anyone who wants a boy do you – a porochial 'prentice, who is at present a dead weight – a millstone, as I may say – round the porochial throat? Liberal terms, Mr. Sowerberry – liberal terms;' and as Mr. Bumble spoke, he raised his cane to the bill above him, and gave three distinct raps upon the words 'five pounds,' which were printed thereon in Roman capitals of gigantic size.
>
> 'Gadso!' said the undertaker, taking Mr. Bumble by the gilt-edged lappel of his official coat; 'that's just the very thing I wanted to speak to you about. You know – dear me, what a very elegant button this is, Mr. Bumble; I never noticed it before.'
>
> 'Yes, I think it is rather pretty,' said the beadle, glancing proudly downwards at the large brass buttons which embellished his coat. 'The die is the same as the parochial seal, – the Good Samaritan healing the sick and bruised man. The board presented it to me on New-year's morning, Mr Sowerberry. I put it on, I remember, for the first time, to attend the inquest on that reduced tradesman, who died in a doorway at midnight.'
>
> 'I recollect,' said the undertaker. 'The jury brought in "Died from exposure to the cold, and want of the common necessaries of life", didn't they?'
>
> Mr. Bumble nodded.
>
> 'And they made it a special verdict, I think,' said the undertaker, 'by adding some words to the effect, that if the relieving officer had –'
>
> 'Tush – foolery!' interposed the beadle. 'If the board attended to all the nonsense that ignorant jurymen talk, they'd have enough to do.'
>
> 'Very true,' said the undertaker; 'they would indeed.'(p. 29)[81]

Not only does Mr. Bumble signally fail to follow in the Good Samaritan's footsteps, but the reference to Oliver as a 'millstone' is, as several editors of the novel have pointed out,[82] meant to remind us of Matthew 18: 6 – 'But whoso shall offend one of these little ones which believe in me, it were better for him that a millstone were hanged about his neck, and that he were drowned in the depth of the sea'. We might also think in this context of such moments in Dickens's later novels as when, in *Hard Times*, Mr Gradgrind's view of life is revealed as damningly at odds with Christianity when we see him deciding that 'the Good Samaritan was a Bad Economist' (p. 207).[83]

In the early part of his career, the same issues concerned Dickens as provoked the concern of the others that we have been talking about. The operation of the New Poor Law is obviously a major focus of *Oliver Twist*, and Dickens was also concerned about the operations of laissez-faire capitalism. When, in July 1842, Ashley was attempting to get his Mines and Collieries Bill through Parliament and the Bill was having trouble getting through House of Lords, Dickens sent a strategically timed letter to the *Morning Chronicle*:

> for very many years, a state of things has existed in these places, in the heart and core of a Christian country, which, if it had been discovered by marines or missionaries in the Sandwich Islands, would have made the fortune of two quarto volumes, filled the whole bench of bishops with emotion, and nerved to new and mighty projects the Society for the Propagation of the Gospel in Foreign Parts

He draws on a Biblical reference (to Joshua 9:21) to help make his point that the Bill had 'for its sole object the improvement of the condition and character of one great class of hewers of wood and drawers of water'.[84]

Dickens's belief in the brotherhood of man is an ever-present element in his work, as is reflected in the two references we have already seen to the parable of the Good Samaritan, with its message that all men are brothers. Equally, in *The Chimes*, Will Fern makes a speech about how social conditions are setting the classes against each other, and betraying the notion of brotherhood so that Biblical statements such as that made by the Moabite Ruth in solidarity with her Israelite mother in law (Ruth 1:16) will be reversed: 'thy people are Not my people; Nor thy God my God' (p. 133).[85] The book ends with the wish, 'So may each year be happier than the last, and not the meanest of our brethren or sisterhood debarred their rightful share, in what our Great Creator formed them to enjoy' (p. 154).

Dickens's concern for the immediate hardship and suffering of members of the brotherhood of man is straightforwardly reflected in the famous incident of Oliver Twist asking for more. The point of the episode, of course, is not that the workhouse is being badly run, but that it is being run exactly in accordance with the philosophy behind New Poor Law. The Utilitarian principle of 'the greatest happiness of greatest number' demanded that workhouse conditions be severe, to discourage people from resorting there, and so keep costs to the taxpayer down; this famous scene makes plain that the consequences are that children are going hungry. The idea of brotherhood is betrayed as people look after the money in their own pockets and adopt an attitude of 'devil-take-the-hindmost' towards everyone else.

Dickens is also concerned about the diminishment of people's humanity. In *The Old Curiosity Shop*, as Nell and her grandfather approach the industrialised areas of the Midlands, people seem less than human:

> Men, women, children, wan in their looks and ragged in attire, tended the engines, fed their tributary fires, begged upon the road, or scowled half-naked from the doorless house. Then came more of the wrathful monsters, whose like they almost seemed to be in their wildness and their untamed air. (p. 340)[86]

The narrator goes on to describe 'night, when the noise of every strange machine was aggravated by the darkness; when the people near them looked wilder and more savage' (p. 341). In a speech in 1844, Dickens expressed support for Polytechnic Institutions as counteracting the dehumanising effect of the industrial system:

> For surely it cannot be allowed that those who labour day by day, surrounded by machinery, shall be permitted to degenerate into machines themselves; but, on the contrary, they should be able to assert their common origin in that Creator from whose wondrous hands they came, and unto whom, responsible and thinking men, they will return.[87]

In Dickens's Christmas book for 1848, *The Haunted Man*, Mrs Swidger brings home a homeless boy, and the hero Redlaw later sees him:

> something rushed past him into the room like a wild-cat, and crouched down in a corner ... A baby savage, a young monster, a child who had never been a child, a creature who might live to take the outward form of man, but who, within, would live and perish a mere beast.
>
> Used, already, to be worried and hunted like a beast, the boy crouched down as he was looked at, and looked back again, and interposed his arm to ward off the expected blow.
>
> 'I'll bite,' he said, 'if you hit me!' (pp. 336–7)[88]

Dickens picks up the idea that industrial workers can be compared to slaves: in *Pickwick Papers*, we are told that the inhabitants of Muggleton

> mingling a zealous advocacy of Christian principles with a devoted attachment to commercial rights ... have presented at divers times, no

> fewer than one thousand four hundred and twenty petitions, against the continuance of negro slavery abroad, and an equal number against any interference with the factory system at home (p. 98)[89]

Similarly, in the 'Full Report of the Second Meeting of the Mudfog Association for the Advancement of Everything', published in September 1838, Mr. Tickle displays 'his newly invented spectacles, which enabled the wearer to discern ... objects at a great distance, and rendered him wholly blind to those immediately before him'; these, he claims, are 'based strictly upon the principle of the human eye'. When the latter idea is challenged, Mr Tickle backs his assertion up with evidence including that 'a large number of most excellent persons and great statesmen could see, with the naked eye, most marvellous horrors on West India plantations, while they could discern nothing whatever in the interior of Manchester cotton mills' (p. 546).[90]

Dickens's concern for the state of the immortal souls of the poor is evident in his 1846 poem 'The Hymn of the Wiltshire Labourers'. The poem, inspired by the urgent pleas for bread made at a meeting of the wives of agricultural labourers in Wiltshire, is an attack on the sufferings of the poor arising out of the Corn Laws. Talking about their 'lords and gentry' (p. 16), the labourers' wives plead:

> Oh God! teach them to feel how we,
> When our poor infants droop,
> Are weakened in our trust in Thee,
> And how our spirits stoop; (lines 17–20)[91]

Most famously, it is a concern later reflected in the desperate attempt by Allan Woodcourt to teach the Lord's Prayer to the dying Jo in *Bleak House*.

All in all, Dickens's works challenge fundamentally the four aspects of mainstream Christian social attitudes Parsons identifies. He does not consider that poverty is morally tolerable and that economic laws are part of a divinely ordained order. On the contrary, he believes that in a society arranged in accordance with God's commandments and Christian values, poverty would not be tolerated. Second, he plainly dissents from the idea that attempts at reform would be both futile and impious; implicit throughout his works is the notion that society can be changed fundamentally through the application of Christian values. The other two ideas – that charity is only for the deserving poor, and that most people are poor because of their own improvidence, intemperance or indolence – are addressed directly in *The Chimes*. The latter idea is clearly reflected in the protagonist, Trotty Veck, pondering the notion that 'we are born bad' (p. 87), Mr Filer, when talking about the poor, speaking of 'their improvidence; their wickedness' (p. 98), and Sir Joseph Bowley describing the poor as 'this improvident and impracticable race' (p. 109). What the story shows, however, is that it is not sin that makes people poor, but poverty that makes people sin. Hence Richard's state of being 'wasted by intemperance and vice' (p. 134) is the product of his suffering as a poor man, not its cause; he started as a fine, upstanding young man. Dickens puts his views plainly in his article about the Preston Strike, 'On Strike'.[92] On the train to Preston, he engages in conversation with Mr Snapper, who refers to 'the improvident and unreasoning habits of the common people'. Dickens, however, is not willing to entertain the idea that qualities long regarded as inherent in the working class, and the supposed explanation, as we have seen, for their poverty, are any such thing:

> I doubt the existence at this present time of many faults that are merely class faults. In the main, I am disposed to think that whatever faults you may find to exist, in your own neighbourhood for instance, among the hands, you will find tolerably equal in amount among the masters also, and even among the classes above the masters. They will be modified by circumstances, and they will be the less excusable among the better-educated, but they will be pretty fairly distributed. I have a strong expectation that we shall live to see the conventional adjectives now apparently inseparable from the phrase working people and lower orders, gradually fall into complete disuse for this reason. (p. 199)

Through sentiments expressed by Mr Plornish of Bleeding Heart Yard in *Little Dorrit*, he comments on how ready the more fortunate members of society, many of them in no position to criticise, are to leap on any evidence that will confirm their prejudices and absolve them of any requirement to show any responsibility towards the poor or give them help:

> Then you see, some people as was better off said, and a good many such people lived pretty close up to the mark themselves if not beyond it so he'd heerd, that they was 'improvident' (that was the favourite word) down the Yard. For instance, if they see a man with his wife and children going to Hampton Court in a Wan, perhaps once in a year, they says, 'Hallo! I thought you was poor, my improvident friend!' Why, Lord, how hard it was upon a man! What was a man to do? He couldn't go mollancholly mad, and even if he did, you wouldn't be the better for it. (p. 157)[93]

Dickens is, then, a figure in the vanguard of a new set of religious attitudes to social problems, being one of the first to insist that Christian moral teaching had a social dimension as well as applying to the individual and individual conduct. As Driver argues, the 'militant declaration' in Richard Oastler's writings that 'the public relationships of mankind, no less than the private, have to be judged by the ethical standards given by the Christian revelation'[94] is one of the reflections that he was 'one of the first men in the nineteenth century to affirm the relevance of Christianity for an industrial society'.[95] In *Michael Armstrong* Trollope has Rev. Bell put forward the idea that purely personal charity is inadequate to deal with the evil aspects of the new society in which people now live and that action on a social and political scale is demanded. Commenting on 'the total inefficiency of individual benevolence to heal the misery', Bell declares that the 'oppression' is 'too overwhelming' to be tackled by 'any agency less powerful than that of the law' (p. 298).

The notion that Christian moral principles had a social dimension was sufficiently novel for Trollope to have the characters in her 1843 critique of the Poor Law, *Jessie Phillips*, discuss it at some length. Mr. Lewis, the lawyer, has objected to people unlearned in the law passing judgement on it, and the clergyman Mr. Mortimer takes up the issue:

> 'I plead guilty to this accusation ... the fact is, that though we have very decidedly the fear of the law before our eyes, we have the fear of the Gospel also. The law, if I understand it rightly, Mr. Lewis, seems to assume as a principle that the poor, who, we are told, we have always with us, have no natural RIGHT to assistance from the rich. Now this, I take it, is the point upon which a vast number of us who have never studied jurisprudence hitch. Not, I believe, that there are many who would undertake to dispute this terrible dictum by any arguments suggested by a process of abstract reasoning, but a good many of us think that the doctrine of the Gospel is at variance with it'.
>
> 'Of course, sir, now that you have got upon your own ground, I cannot presume to follow you,' said Mr. Lewis ... 'That's all we ask on our side, Mr. Rimmington. Let those learned in the Gospel stick to the Gospel; and those learned in the law stick to the law'.
>
> 'I should be sorry to think that they must of necessity be divided,' said Mr. Rimmington.
>
> 'Not a bit of it – not a bit of it,' cried Captain Maxwell ... 'I am neither lawyer nor priest, but I know just enough of both callings to be certain that they were meant to dove-tail into one another, as neat as my nail. We shall never do any good, Lewis, to the poor or the rich either, if we set off with that notion. It is more likely, I think, to lead us right a-head towards the truth if we say that first and foremost what we have got to remember is, that the Gospel tells us we *are* to take care of the poor; and next, that it is but wise and fitting and like good prudent citizens, that we should set about making laws to put us into the best way of doing it'. (pp. 182–3)[96]

The innovative nature of this approach is further reflected in contemporary reactions to the real-life clergy involved in the campaign for reform.

At a meeting in December 1831, Bull told the audience that, 'As I entered this room, I heard a person say, "What have the parsons to do with it?"', to which Bull's answer was:

> Sir, they have a good deal to do with it; and I conceive that a most fearful responsibility rests upon these Ministers of the Gospel to oppose all the influence they possess against any system which tends to prevent the moral improvement and religious advance of the people. I have not been invited to take part in the proceedings of the day, but I did not need an invitation.[97]

Stephens was increasingly inclined explicitly to claim ground as within the parameters of Christian concern. Having been dubbed a 'raving, ranting parson' who ought to 'stick to his Bible', Stephens proclaimed

> I have been told by these men to stick to the Bible and leave the spindle to them.[98] I mean to stick to the Bible; and if anyone wants to know why I am a factory reform agitator, I tell them it is because I know that the system is repugnant to the word of the living God, and that as long as we have his blessed book in our hands and in our hearts, we must live to see the downfall of that tyranny which is now grinding you to the dust.[99]

Later, Stephens was to go even further, responding to the cry that there should be no politics in the pulpit by saying

> unless a priest of the living God be a politician in the pulpit, he has no business there at all ... Law and religion can never be separated. If you attempt to disassociate them or to disunite them, it is like attempting to disassociate and disunite the soul from the body of man, and expect after you have done so, to find a living being before you ... Read this book from the beginning to the end, and tell me whether in the whole of its code of laws, you find one law out of them all that does not apply to this world and to this world only. These are the laws of God ... 'Thy will be done on earth, as it is in heaven'.[100]

Like these figures, Dickens insists that Christian moral teaching has a social dimension as well as applying to the individual and to individual conduct. His novels represent an exploration of the implications and ramifications of these attitudes.

3
Oliver Twist and Fagin's Jewishness

Dickens's presentation of Fagin as a villainous Jew remains a major source of controversy about *Oliver Twist.* In David Vital's 1999 book *A People Apart: The Jews in Europe 1789–1939*, for instance, he links Dickens and his portrayal of 'the Jew Fagin as a monster of criminality' to Cobbett, whose view Vital quotes as being that 'Jew has always been synonymous with sharper, cheat, rogue. This has been the case with no other race of mankind', and who denounced Jews as the murderers of Christ, blasphemers of his Gospel, and parasites.[1]

The question of Dickens's attitude to Jews and whether it was enlightened or prejudiced is complicated, as is evident from the studies of the subject. Harry Stone, for instance, considers Dickens to have been anti-semitic at the time he wrote *Oliver Twist*,[2] and Deborah Heller similarly writes of 'Dickens's shifting attitudes towards Jews'.[3] Dickens himself, however, seems not to have been aware of anti-Jewish feeling inside himself. In 1854, he declared with some bewilderment that 'I know of no reason the Jews can have for regarding me as "inimical" to them'.[4] That he was not a dyed-in-the-wool anti-semite was something, furthermore, he himself set out to prove in his depiction of Mr Riah in *Our Mutual Friend* and of which he assured Eliza Davis privately in a letter of 10 July 1863: sending her a donation towards a convalescent home for the Jewish poor he asserted that,

> I have no feeling toward the Jewish people but a friendly one. I always speak well of them, whether in public, or private, and bear my testimony (as I ought to do) to their perfect good faith in such transactions as I have ever had with them. And in my *Child's History of England*, I lost no opportunity of setting forth their cruel persecution in old times.[5]

His attitudes may have changed over the years imperceptibly to himself of course. However, the evidence for anti-semitism that Stone, for instance, adduces from outside the novel consists largely of what might be seen as casual and unconsidered statements rather than ones expressing a vicious and hurtful attitude towards Jews. In deliberated work, such as is involved in the invention of major characters, he could hardly be unconscious of it if he was being anti-Jewish.

One might argue that, in any case, more central than Dickens's personal attitudes are those of his readers, and thus of society at large. When Dickens wrote *Oliver Twist* he was trying to consolidate his newly established position as a highly popular author. He would be ill-advised to write something grossly out of tune with the attitudes of his readers; at the same time, if sufficiently attuned to his audience's outlook, he could play on it in pursuing his literary aims.

Examination of the historical context reveals that if Dickens set out to be anti-semitic, he was neither swept along by nor pandering to a groundswell of anti-Jewish feeling. Two sets of attitudes seem to have been current in the 1830s, a new tolerance co-existing with lingering, more prejudiced perceptions inherited from the past. As regards official discrimination at least, the 1830s saw significant progress in the acceptance of Jews into society. David Englander traces the story of British Jews in the nineteenth century as one of assimilation into society; and significantly, great steps forward in that process were already being made in the 1830s. The position of British Jews in the early nineteenth century was already considerably better than that of their European co-religionists. They did not have to wear distinctive clothing, were not forced live in ghettos, could settle wherever they liked, were not barred by law from any business or manufacturing activities or from dealing in any commodity, and could hire non-Jewish labour.[6] Jews were granted British citizenship and even those born abroad found it easy to become naturalised.[7]

However, the emancipation of Roman Catholics in 1829 paved the way for advances made by British Jews in the 1830s. As late as 1818 the courts maintained Lord Coke's doctrine that in law Jews were perpetual enemies 'for between them, as with the devils, whose subjects they are, and the Christian there can be no peace'.[8] By 1833, however, a ruling by Lord Brougham declared that Jews were:

> born to all the rights, immunities and privileges of His Majesty's other subjects, excepting so far as positive enactments of law deprive them of those rights, immunities and privileges.[9]

Throughout the 1830s and beyond, Jews were increasingly being accepted into mainstream British society and attempts being made to alter the law when necessary to allow this process to continue. Sir Robert Grant repeatedly, albeit unsuccessfully, introduced a bill to remove the disabilities suffered by British Jews in 1830, then again in 1833, 1834 and 1836.[10] In Edinburgh in 1834, similarly, the Lord Provost spoke at a meeting held to call for 'a removal of the disabilities under which the Jews of His Majesty's dominions now labour, and to place them in the same situation with all others of His Majesty's subjects'.[11] In 1831, provision by the Common Council of the City of London for those taking up the freedom to take the requisite oath in a form agreeable to their religious convictions allowed Jews to become freemen, to carry on trade in the City and to become members of Livery Companies. David Salomons promptly applied to join the Coopers' Company; in 1835 he was elected sheriff and Parliament passed the Sheriffs' Declaration Act so that he did not have to make his statutory declaration 'on the true faith of a Christian'.[12] In 1837, Moses Montefiore became the sheriff of London and subsequently became the first Jewish knight in over a century. The first Jewish hereditary baronet was appointed in 1841.

The first Jewish barrister was called to the Bar in 1833 and the earliest known Jewish juryman served in 1835.[13] Changes in the law in 1835 and 1836 respectively enfranchised Jews and gave statutory recognition to the Board of Deputies as an authority competent to certify Jewish places of worship. The incorporation of the non-sectarian University of London in 1837 made it possible for Jews to take degrees, as they could not at Oxford and Cambridge.

Some of these developments, as has been indicated, faced opposition, and it was to take decades more for the process of emancipation to be completed, but the evidence shows that despite some lingering of older attitudes, there was a powerful impulse towards an end to discrimination. A letter sent to *The Times* in 1835 reflects how Jewish people felt their position to be altered. The correspondent is bold enough to complain at the way the newspaper always points out the Jewishness of any miscreants whose crimes are reported in the paper: in a newly more secure position, the correspondent feels able to object to this practice, and the newspaper feels impelled to answer that this is not done 'in reproach to his ... nation'.[14]

At the same time, as regards prejudice (as opposed to discrimination), attitudes were ambivalent. The decline of discrimination does not necessarily mean the decline of prejudice. As Vital points out, for instance, though the Chartists supported Jewish emancipation in principle, this did not stop Chartist writers lumping Jews in with 'other parasitical and oppressive enemies of the working class' and he cites an 1833 article from the Poor Man's Guardian describing Britain as 'a country of Jews and usurers, and parsons and plunderers, and hangmen, and lawyers, and shopcrats, and vampires, and soldiers and "statesmen" and bloodhounds'.[15] However, attitudes to Jews had become more sympathetic from the end of the eighteenth century onwards. Richard Cumberland's play *The Jew* featured a Jew as its hero and Maria Edgeworth's 1816 novel *Harrington* featured a gentleman Jew. Attempts by Evangelicals to convert Jews led to the development of a new attitude, as Roth comments: 'they were approached in a spirit ... almost of veneration, as the ancient people of God ... it was freely admitted that Christendom owed a profound debt of shame in respect of the past centuries of persecution and maltreatment'.[16] A review in *The Times* in 1830 of a history of the Jews notes changing attitudes: commenting that until recently, Jews were 'endured because mankind had become habituated to their presence, rather than tolerated on any liberal principles', the reviewer now perceives 'the rapid spread of the spirit of toleration, forbearance, and Christian charity'.[17] Reporting in 1851, Henry Mayhew implicitly contrasts his present day with the eighteenth century when 'popular feeling ran very high against the Jews'. To Mayhew as an early Victorian it seems that 'the wholesale prejudice against them was absurd'.[18] In an 1833 speech in Parliament, indeed, cited in Anne Aresty Naman's *The Jew in the Victorian Novel,* Thomas Macaulay had dissected Jewish stereotypes and anti-semitic prejudices:

> We drive them to mean occupations, and then reproach them for not embracing honourable professions. We long forbade them to possess land; and we complain that they chiefly occupy themselves in trade. We shut them out from all the paths of ambition; and then we despise them for taking refuge in avarice. During many ages we have, in all our dealings with them, abused our immense superiority of force; and then we are disgusted because they have recourse to that cunning which is the natural and universal defence of the weak against the violence of the strong.[19]

In this climate it is perhaps not so surprising that Grant's 1830 Bill was supported by a Londoners' petition of 14000 signatures and another, from Liverpool, was signed by twenty thousand inhabitants including the Mayor and the Corporation; there were also further petitions from other places that had Jewish communities.[20] Prejudice had by no means ended. Mayhew acknowledges that, 'among some the dominant feeling against the Jews on account of their faith still flourishes' and relates an anecdote hinging on the persistence of a prejudice that Jews, having spat at Christ, were no longer able to spit.[21] On the whole, however, prejudice seems to have begun to decline, to have become less entrenched, particularly in the more enlightened echelons of society, and at the very least to have become more ambiguous. The columns of *Punch* in the 1840s exemplify the ambivalence of the age. Sometimes, for instance, articles seem to fall back satirically on prejudices about Jews while others attack such prejudices and show great sympathy for Jews. Thus, an 1845 article, 'The Ruins of the Fleet', refers to the closure of debtors' prisons, which a Jew contemplates, debt collecting and the running of spunging houses having been common Jewish occupations:

> Two tears – big and bright as his diamond shirt studs, stood in his precious eyes, for Jews' eyes are proverbially costly. With laudable thrift he safely dropt them in his pocket-handkerchief.[22]

An 1848 article, 'Old Israel to Young Israel', has a Jew reflecting on the putative achievement of equality, with Baron Rothschild apparently about to be admitted to the House of Commons:

> For I don't know how many hundred years we've had nothing to do with the 'sweat of the brow'; we've left all that to the Gentiles. But since they're going to make us equal, as they call it, they won't stand no shirking.[23]

On the other hand, a speech made by Mr Justice Corney in the Common Council, suggesting that Jews had an 'intuitive fondness' for money prompted an 1847 article, 'Young Israel in Parliament', satirising such prejudices:

> Yes; we believe it to be a lamentable fact, that the young Jew, having amassed his first five hundred pounds, has an 'intuitive fondness' towards making the five ten, the ten twenty, the twenty forty – and so on; a disgusting habit, of which Christian tradesmen know nothing[24]

Furthermore, the treatment of Russian Jews by Tsar Nicholas I, who had recently visited London, where he was enthusiastically received, prompted a scathing attack in an 1844 article, 'Nicholas and the Jews':

> he should have waited some time longer, when the wrongs and sorrows of another one-hundred-and-fifty-thousand of his fellow creatures would, if possible, have made him more lustrous in the eyes of his worshippers.[25]

The ambivalence of these attitudes is something Dickens is able to play on in *Oliver Twist*. At a time when prejudices persist but are not so entrenched as to close minds, he is able to exploit these prejudices without necessarily sharing them.

His awareness of popular prejudices and stereotypes about Jews is undoubted. Stone discusses how Fagin is given traditional features of the literary Jew, such as red hair and a shuffling gait.[26] Heller discusses how Dickens draws on negative stereotypes of the Jew, making Fagin financially unscrupulous, 'dishonest, thieving, treacherous, avaricious, ultimately cowardly'.[27] She goes on to comment on:

> Dickens's readiness to exploit the whole compendium of terrifying associations that have clustered around the stereotype of the Jew in the popular imagination from the Middle Ages onward: the Jew as devil (or his close associate), as subhuman monster, as poisoner, as kidnapper, mutilator, murderer of innocent Christian children, on whom, perhaps, he cannibalistically feeds in observance of alien rituals ... Dickens seems to have been appealing to an anti-Semitism already present in his readers, which

> he was simply willing to exploit in creating his first major representation of evil in its confrontation with childhood innocence ... in his portrayal of Fagin's villainy, Dickens, as a young writer, chose to rely on ready-made, deeply rooted associations to a supposedly specifically Jewish brand of villainy.[28]

More recently, Efraim Sicher has written of the influence of Romanticism on the creation of Fagin as, 'a malicious omnipresence who reflects Romantic hostility toward urban capitalism'.[29] Nevertheless, he too is very aware of the influence of 'mythical material rooted in English and Western culture that resounded with theological meaning and cultural meaning',[30] so that Fagin is also 'a spendthrift Shylock who exerts a merciless hold on his victims'.[31] However, if Heller talks of Dickens exploiting stereotypes, it remains open in what way he exploits them. I want to argue that it is in a subtler and more sophisticated way than has commonly been assumed.

It is possible that Fagin is a Jew simply because his real-life original, Ikey Solomons, was a Jew. In his letter to Mrs Davis of 10 July 1863 the author explained that 'Fagin ... is a Jew because it was unfortunately true of the time to which that story refers, that that class of criminal almost invariably was a Jew'.[32] Even if this is so, however, Dickens is careful to present him as an unrepresentative Jew. Towards the end of the novel he is shown as uninterested in the consolations of his religion:

> Venerable men of his own persuasion had come to pray beside him, but he had driven them away with curses. They renewed their charitable efforts, and he beat them off. (p. 445)[33]

Strikingly, the process of portraying him as unrepresentative of Jews begins with our first encounters with him. The sausages he is cooking when we first meet him in Chapter 8 may or may not be pork, but there is no ambiguity when, soon after, we see him breakfasting on ham (Chapter 10) and eating a saveloy (Chapter 13), thus breaking even the most basic of his religion's food laws. It might be thought that Dickens is here reflecting a laxness common among Jews living on the sorts of desperate social level that Fagin inhabits. Evidence indicates, however, that this was not the case. Mayhew's testimony reveals that, generally, Jews were meticulous in following the precepts and traditions of their religion. He does report that Jewish old-clothes dealers 'seldom go to a synagogue' and 'are not particular about eating "tryfer" – that is, meat that has been killed by a Christian';[34] and on another occasion a Jewish boy tells him that, 'other Jew boys' have eaten ham sandwiches. The speaker himself, however, declares 'Pork! Ah! No, I never touched it; I'd as soon eat a cat; so would my father ... I don't know why it shouldn't be eaten, only that it's wrong to eat it.'[35] Similarly, an adult street-seller tells Mayhew, 'No, I never touch any meat but "Coshar"'.[36]

Indeed, Mayhew notes fastidious adherence to observances among Jewish old-clothes dealers:

> he will never use the same knife to cut his meat that he previously used to spread his butter, and he will not even put his meat on a plate that has had butter in it. The objection to mix butter with meat is carried so far, that, after partaking of the one, Jews will not eat of the other for the space of two hours.[37]

To see what function this apostate Jew Fagin might serve in *Oliver Twist*, we need to consider Dickens's aims and intentions in the novel as a whole.

Though a picaresque novel, *Oliver Twist* by no means adheres to the tradition of taking for its hero a rascal living on his wits on the edge of criminality and in constant danger of being hanged – not, at least, as a result of any action springing out of his own moral choices. Oliver is a very different kind of picaro, and the contrast between him and, for instance, the hero of one of Dickens's favourite novels, *Tom Jones*, is instructive. In Fielding's novel, we both follow the hero's moral progress and are given a panorama of contemporary society. Tom is a good-hearted young man but the moral flaws in his character need to be ironed out before he becomes 'all-worthy' and thus deserves the place in his society which the revelation of the truth about his background yields; for his society, as depicted in the novel, though it has its share of rogues and rascals, is a good one, benign and moral, with the likes of the virtuous Squire Allworthy presiding over it. In *Oliver Twist* the situation is reversed: Oliver's surname is ironic, for he is a good little boy and it is society, not Oliver himself, that needs straightening out; society is hellish, cruel and callous. Oliver is the first of a long line of orphans in Dickens's works, and is used by the author as the others will be: helpless and vulnerable, with no family to protect them, the treatment they receive at the hands of individuals and society is a touchstone of the moral character of those individuals and of society. Cates Baldridge, in his study 'The Instability of Inheritance in *Oliver Twist*'[38] is only one of many critics who have been exercised as to how Oliver can possibly be so virtuous given the environment in which he has been raised, and, as they point out, to the extent that Dickens attempts to explain this, he merely creates further awkward problems for himself. Essentially, though, Oliver's goodness is simply a *donnee*; within the scheme of the novel, he does not have to grow morally in order to earn a place in his society; rather, society is on trial for the way it treats a blameless, vulnerable young boy, and it is this that is the focus of the novel. Significantly, Oliver is never to be safe until he finds his family, one's only refuge, in the perspective of the novel, from a harsh and hostile outside world.

This, then, is Dickens's vision: he sees around him an utterly malign society. This orphan at the mercy of the parish suffers the rigours of a workhouse where he and others are treated callously and underfed, subjected to the indifference and harshness of Bumble and all the others who are supposedly tending him, and ultimately flees straight into the hands of unscrupulous and evil criminals who are determined to corrupt him as they have so many others.

The chapters featuring Fagin thus fulfil straightforwardly one of Dickens's aims in the novel. Their second function, though, is in line with one of Dickens's main principles of organisation in *Oliver Twist*: the use of comparison and contrast, between characters, between scenes, ultimately between different worlds within the novel. Within this scheme of organisation, the worlds of the parish, with Mr Bumble at its centre, and the criminal underworld, with Fagin at its centre, are compared and contrasted; but this is done in a more ambiguous light than might be expected.

Certainly Fagin is depicted as a villain. It is he who attempts to corrupt Oliver as he has corrupted Nancy and so many others. He can be violent, as he is in Chapter 16, beating Oliver with a club. Murder is never very far away from his mind: fear of Oliver betraying him makes him consider that he may 'stop his windpipe' (p. 104). When Monks suggests murdering Nancy, Fagin's response is that 'that sort of thing is not in our way, or one of these days I might be glad to have it done' (p. 214). In Chapter 44 he plans to persuade Nancy to kill Sykes; and in Chapter 47 he is the one who sets Sykes on Nancy and thus indirectly is the cause of her death.

Nevertheless, while Fagin is clearly a villain, the question is whether respectable society is any more virtuous. For when Fagin's world is placed alongside Bumble's, it can be seen to have virtues that the world of the parish signally lacks; and the two worlds stand in uneasy contrast.

Indications that Oliver is not necessarily going to an in all ways worse world as he enters the criminal underworld are there right from his first encounter with it. The last scene depicted in detail before Oliver arrives in London is his conversation with Dick – weak, sickly, cowed Dick, brought up by the parish. The next character Dickens portrays Oliver with is also a boy – but this time it is the lively, pert, self-confident 'roystering and swaggering' (p. 60) Artful Dodger, in the care not of the parish but of Fagin. In direct contrast to the timid and hesitant Dick, the Dodger is purposeful, taking control of Oliver and establishing himself as his patron: 'you want grub, and you shall have it' (p. 61). This is what happens: they have a loaf, some ham and beer between them. It is the first time in the novel that Oliver has had food substantial enough to call grub; up to this point he has lived, while under Mr Bumble's general care, largely on gruel, bits of bread and scraps of meat intended for the dog.

This is a pointer for things to come, as is seen when Oliver is taken to meet Fagin for the first time, and is fed sausages – not rich food, certainly, but substantial, homely fare. This is not the only type of new experience Oliver has in this first meeting with Fagin. Fagin greets Oliver by making a low bow and shaking his hand; this is, to be sure, mock-politeness, that of the spider inviting the fly into his parlour, but it is the first time in the novel that anyone has treated Oliver with courtesy. The courtesy continues when, again for the first time in the novel, concern is shown for Oliver's comfort: 'draw a tub near the fire for Oliver' (p. 66). When he is put on one of the sacks that serve as beds, he is 'gently lifted' (p. 66) – an act displaying a tenderness he has encountered nowhere before in the book.

All this continues in the next chapter. Oliver is again well fed, on coffee, hot rolls and ham. There is here the first scene of laughter and fun in the novel, Charley Bates, as so often later, particularly enjoying himself. Fagin becomes the first person in the novel to show any tact towards Oliver, quickly changing the subject when the boy blushes with embarrassment at Charley's remark about his being 'so jolly green' (p. 70). He is also the first person ever to praise Oliver ('You're a clever boy, my dear' (p. 72)) and to pat him on the head; and though others have offered Oliver violence, Fagin is the first to try to soothe him afterwards, pretending he picked up the knife 'in mere sport' (p. 69).

Much of Fagin's behaviour here is duplicitous, cunning and ultimately motivated by self-interest, but there is in him also a simple humanity, plain on a later occasion when the Dodger wants to speak to Oliver who is asleep

> so pale with anxiety, and sadness, and the closeness of his prison, that he looked like death ...
>
> 'Not now,' said the Jew, turning softly away. 'Tomorrow. Tomorrow.' (p. 162)

And so the worlds of the parish and of Fagin are set in contrast to each other, if anything, to the favour of Fagin's world. Sometimes specific scenes are set in contrast or comparison, as when Mr Bumble's denunciation of Oliver's 'treachery, ingratitude and malice' towards the end of Chapter 17 (p. 142) is immediately followed by Fagin's intimidating lecture to Oliver about 'the crying sin of ingratitude' and the pointed story about another boy's 'treacherous behaviour' (p. 144). Overall, though, it is the two worlds *in toto* that are contrasted. As we have already been seeing, food provides a characteristic touchstone. When Oliver lives in the care of the parish, he has to eat gruel, bread and butter, water, oatmeal, some rolls, some scraps of meat and part of the worst end of a neck of mutton. Because he is so underfed he is small enough to be in danger at one point of suffering the horrors of being employed by a chimney sweeper to climb up chimneys; when he asks for more, he is shut up in a room by himself. People around are dying of hunger: the woman whose funeral he attends starved to death. Those who live on are frail and weak, like Dick. Only the masters are well fed: they dine on steaks and gin. Both Mr Bumble and the masters of the workhouse are fat.

No sooner does Oliver enter the criminal underworld on meeting the Artful Dodger (Chapter 8) than he is eating 'a long and hearty meal' (p. 61); and from then on he feeds on ham, loaves, beer, sausages, gin, coffee, hot rolls and more ham. In Fagin's world, people live on saveloy, bread, beer, boiled beef, wine, rabbit pie, 'green', sugar, 'two half-quartern brans; pound of best fresh; piece of double Glo'ster' (p. 321). The masters are not the only ones who are well fed; Fagin, on the contrary, is 'shrivelled' (p. 64) and it is the others who, like Bet and Nancy, are 'stout and hearty' (p. 71). With all this meat to eat, it is no wonder that they develop, as Mr Bumble prognosticates, 'soul and spirit' (p. 53). The inhabitants of Fagin's world are lively, self-confident, mischievous, as the Artful Dodger and Charley Bates for two exemplify.

This is the appalling thing: when Oliver enters the world of an apostate and outlaw Jew he receives better treatment, as a human being, than in the respectable world. Moreover, the parish prides itself on being Christian and this is pointed up by Dickens. Oliver is urged by the board of the workhouse to pray every night 'for the people who feed you, and take care of you, like a Christian' (p. 12). Every evening at the workhouse there is 'prayer-time', and following the occasion on which Oliver asks for more food, the boys pray not only 'to be made good, virtuous, contented, and obedient', but also 'to be guarded from the sins and vices of Oliver Twist' (p. 18). The beadle has a button on his coat depicting the Good Samaritan and the same scene is used on the parochial seal. In reality, respectable Christian society lives up to none of the standards of its religion. For all his evil, an apostate Jew and common criminal does a better job. As Dickens himself wrote, confronted with Eliza Davis's accusation in a letter of 22 June 1863 that the creation of Fagin encouraged 'a vile prejudice against the reviled Hebrew',[39] 'all the rest of the wicked dramatis personae are Christians'.[40]

This, then, is a resonance to, and a significance of, Fagin's Jewishness that relates to Dickens's aims and the novel's themes. Even as he gives Fagin traditional features of the literary Jew, and exploits stereotypes, Dickens establishes Fagin's Jewish identity as such not so that he can indulge in meretricious anti-semitism but as a device in measuring his society against Christian values. Far from pandering to his readers' prejudices, Dickens plays on them to jolt his respectable Christian readers out of their complacency.[41]

4

Christian Social Vision in the Novels of the 1850s: *Bleak House, Hard Times* and *Little Dorrit*

As the 1850s arrived, there came no abatement of the need for social campaigning. By 1850, the political and religious campaigners who had been pursuing their goals since the 1830s had achieved some, but only partial, success. In 1842, Ashley had at least succeeded in getting a bill through Parliament prohibiting all employment of females and of boys under ten years of age in mines, making it illegal for anyone under fifteen to be in charge of shaft lifts, setting up a system of inspection, and outlawing the truck system of payment in kind both within and outside the mining industry.[1] The attempts made by him and others to introduce legislation affecting factories were less successful. The Ten Hours Movement briefly thought it had achieved its goals with the passing of the 1847 Factory Act.[2] However, some employers quickly started getting round the Act using a relay system, which meant that employees might have to be at their mill for up to fifteen hours a day[3]; when this practice was challenged in the courts in 1850, the jury found in favour of the masters,[4] and, in the words of J.T. Ward, 'The Ten Hours Act was thus virtually demolished'.[5] There were also moves to repeal the Act, leading to the foundation of a Society for the Protection of the Ten Hours Act,[6] and also to a rift in the Factory Movement. After the masters promised to abandon relays in exchange for an eleven hour working day,[7] Ashley, fearing an Eleven Hours Bill, supported the idea of a ten and a half hour working day,[8] prompting Oastler to say that he had 'betrayed the poor' and Stephens to describe him as having acted with 'the most unparalleled baseness'.[9] In due course, the Ten Hours Act was repealed,[10] and though there were some advances, such as the establishment of Saturday as a half-holiday, in the 1850 Act that replaced it,[11] the ten hour working day was not to be established once and for all until Disraeli's administration of 1874.[12] After 1850, the Factory Movement had what Ward describes as a 'spasmodic' existence;[13] its last agitation was in 1855.[14]

The campaign against the New Poor Law equally had little success despite such incidents as the revelations about conditions at the Andover workhouse, fully detailed in a Select Committee report published in 1846, including, among much else that was scandalous, a diet that was so inadequate that inmates who were employed in crushing bones were eating the gristle and marrow from the bones it was their job to crush.[15] Dickens himself recognised that little progress had been made. In *Oliver Twist* his two main grounds of attack had been the lack of Christian love in the callous Benthamite principles on which the workhouses were run, and the callous laziness and incompetence of those – Mrs Mann, Mr Bumble, the Board of Guardians – involved in operating the system. Nearly thirty years later, returning to the matter in the portrayal of Betty Higden in *Our Mutual Friend*, written in the mid-1860s, he remained concerned about the very same issues. In the Postscript to the novel, he is still attacking the way the New Poor Law is administered: 'I believe there has been in England, since the days of the STUARTS, no law so often infamously administered, no law so often openly violated, no law habitually so ill-supervised'. Equally, its immorality continues to disgust him: 'In the majority of the shameful cases of disease and death from destitution, that shock the Public and disgrace the country, the illegality is quite equal to the inhumanity – and known language could say no more of their lawlessness'.[16] The 'illegality' and the 'inhumanity' both remain. In 1909, the Majority Report of a Royal Commission on the Poor Law and the Unemployed found that workhouses were still 'often ill-administered'.[17] Though there had been some changes in them over the years, workhouses were not to be abolished until the Local Government Act of 1929, which came into force in 1930,[18] and it was only the National Assistance Act of 1948 that, Norman Longmate relates, 'destroyed the last vestiges of the Poor Law'.[19]

By the 1850s, the context within which Dickens was making his criticisms of society had changed in two ways. One was that new social issues, such as the need for sanitary reform, had risen to prominence. The other was that the climate of opinion within which Dickens and other campaigners worked was also developing: albeit very gradually, social attitudes among Christians had begun to change. The emergence of Christian Socialism in 1848 was a significant moment. Trevor May's summing up of its 'guiding ideal' as 'the application of Christian principles to all social relationships'[20] reveals some affinity with the earlier political campaigners, clergy and writers we have been discussing, and though some of their ideas differed from those held by this group, the Christian Socialists too rejected a *laissez-faire* economic system and the mainstream Christian social views of the early Victorian period:

> in their rejection of the necessity of naked economic competition and the essentially individual nature of humanity, and in their advocacy of social and economic co-operation and the essentially communal nature of human life, they struck directly at the traditions of political economy. Similarly, in advocating co-operation between classes for their mutual advancement in the realization of the Kingdom of God as a present

> reality, they presented a radical alternative to the predominant Christian social teaching that social harmony was to be maintained simply by a patient endurance of present inequality on the part of the poor, the alleviation of the worst of the suffering by a benevolent and Christian duty on the part of the better off, and a mutual recognition that in any case the present life was a preparation for eternity rather than an end in itself.[21]

Christian Socialism in this early manifestation lasted only a few years, but elsewhere, the ground was shifting and attitudes developing, if only very slowly. Norris Pope points out that in 1850, the 'normally conservative *Christian Observer*' proclaimed the importance of attending to the physical sufferings of the poor as well as their spiritual state: 'We serve a Master whose eye was as intently fixed on the bodily as on the spiritual diseases of mankind'.[22] The Slum Ritualists, Tractarian clergy working in slum parishes, became known for their attention to the material as well as spiritual needs of their parishioners: thus, for example, at St. Saviour's in Leeds, 'a community of celibate priests established soup kitchens, provided other material relief for the poor of the city, and earned the gratitude of the poor for their ministry to the sick and dying during the cholera epidemic of 1849'.[23] Though the idea of the 'Civic Gospel', which thrived in Birmingham in particular, prospered in the 1870s and 1880s, its roots lay back in the 1850s and 1860s, in the preachings of George Dawson, whose message 'socially and politically centred on a vision of civic brotherhood and of the city as a community in which a common municipal purpose transcended the interests of individual classes and groups'.[24] After his arrival in Birmingham in 1853, one of the future leaders of the Civic Gospel movement, the clergyman R.W. Dale, listened to Dawson's preaching before beginning to form his own ideas about the Civic Gospel in the following decade.[25] Equally, from 1858 onwards, the Free Church in Scotland began looking into working class housing conditions and calling for reform;[26] by the second half of the 1860s, James Begg was to be proclaiming, 'our obligation to promote sanitary and social reform', which he saw as directly commanded by God, and to be asserting that 'the social reformer and the Christian minister must not only combine in seeking to alleviate and remove the destruction of many generations, but they must be combined in the same individuals'.[27] We shall see that by the time Dickens wrote *Hard Times*, there were others sharing and expressing the very Christian social attitudes he had been promoting since the 1830s.

In this changing cultural and religious environment, Dickens continued, in the 1850s and beyond, to take the same approach of measuring his society against Christian values. When he took up the issue of sanitary reform in an 1850 speech to the Metropolitan Sanitary Association, supporting their mission to bring London within the provisions of the 1848 Public Health Act, from which it had been excluded, he argued that 'it was their duty to diminish an amount of suffering and a waste of life which would be a disgrace to a heathen land' and that given the consequences of this state of affairs in deaths, illness and suffering, 'They claimed for the metropolis of a Christian country that this should be remedied'.[28] When proposing a toast to the Royal Hospital for Incurables at a dinner in 1856 marking its first anniversary, he commended, 'the great Christian humanities of a hospital designed for the permanent care and comfort of those who, by disease, accident, or deformity, were hopelessly disqualified for the duties of life'.[29] In 1863, in his *Uncommercial Traveller* piece 'The Short-Timers'[30] Dickens's narrator wrote of how:

> Within so many yards of this Covent Garden lodging of mine, as within so many yards of Westminster Abbey, Saint Paul's Cathedral, the Houses of Parliament, the Prisons, the Courts of Justice, all the Institutions that govern the land, I can find – *must* find, whether I will or no – in the open streets, shameful instances of the neglect of children, intolerable toleration of the engenderment of paupers, idlers, thieves, races of wretched and destructive cripples both in body and mind, a misery to themselves, a misery to the community, a disgrace to civilisation, and an outrage on Christianity. I know it to be a fact as easy of demonstration as any sum in any of the elementary rules of arithmetic, that if the State would begin its work and duty at the beginning, and would with the strong hand take those children out of the streets, while they are yet children, and wisely train them, it would make them a part of England's glory, not its shame – of England's strength, not its weakness – would raise good soldiers and sailors, and good citizens, and many great men, out of the seeds of its criminal population. (p. 239)

The use of the church here as a symbol of Christianity is typical of Dickens's practice throughout his works, in which churches are rarely mere topographical details. In his article 'On Duty with Inspector Field', for instance, the chiming of church clocks represents an indictment of the unholy state of things in the abandoned environments in a Christian country:

> Saint Giles's church strikes half-past ten. We stoop low, and creep down a precipitous flight of steps into a dark close cellar. There is a fire. There is a long deal table. There are benches. The cellar is full of company, chiefly very young men in various conditions of dirt and raggedness. Some are eating supper. There are no girls or women present. Welcome to Rats' Castle, gentlemen, and to this company of noted thieves! ...
>
> Saint Giles's church clock, striking eleven, hums through our hand from the dilapidated door of a dark outhouse as we open it, and are stricken back by the pestilent breath that issues from within. Rogers, to the front with the light, and let us look!

> Ten, twenty, thirty – who can count them! Men, women, children, for the most part naked, heaped upon the floor like maggots in a cheese.[31]

In his novels too, references to churches suggest the angle of Dickens's vision of his society: the earthly world is being viewed in a metaphysical context. All events are seen against a background of religious concepts and the teachings of Jesus; the brotherhood of man and other central ideas of Christianity remain at the centre of the author's concerns. We are never allowed to forget that earthly actions have a larger context. In *Bleak House*, for example, we are constantly reminded, as the actions of earthly courts are described, of a more ultimate court on the Day of Judgment. The mad Miss Flite tells Esther, Ada and Richard, 'I expect a judgment. Shortly. On the Day of Judgment. I have discovered that the sixth seal mentioned in the Revelations is the Great Seal' (p. 47).[32] Even if Miss Flite is wrong, the calamities the Bible asserts will follow on earth in the wake of the opening of the sixth seal seem to be coming about, as the novel shows. The enraged Gridley inveighs against the legal system – 'I will accuse the individual workers of that system against me, face to face, before the great eternal bar!' (p. 252). As Richard becomes corrupted and destroyed by his involvement with the Jarndyce and Jarndyce case, the narrator ponders, 'would Chancery be found rich in such Precedents too, if they could be got for citation from the Recording Angel?' (p. 631). In *Hard Times*, not only do the titles of the three Books it is divided into –'Sowing', 'Reaping', 'Garnering' – indicate that events are being seen in the light of Biblical teaching ('Whatsoever a man soweth, that shall he also reap' Galatians 6:7), but the title of the first chapter, based on a phrase used by Jesus is set in immediate tension with the values of the world of the novel in the third sentence of the chapter. In Luke 10:42, Jesus states that the 'one thing needful' is to be devoted to God's service; Mr Gradgrind's version, however is that, 'Facts alone are wanted in life' (p. 9).[33] *Little Dorrit* is replete with references to the metaphysical, reminders again that we are in a universe that has a metaphysical meaning, not just a physical one, and all mortal life is to be seen, and earthly actions assessed, in that context. The first chapter thus ends by saying that 'so deep a hush was on the sea, that it scarcely whispered of the time when it shall give up its dead' (p. 29).[34] Arthur Clennam worries about the possible responsibility of his mother for the fate of the Dorrits: 'What if the prisoner now sleeping quietly ... by the light of the great Day of Judgment should trace his fall back to her' (p. 104). The deaths of the Dorrit brothers take them 'before their Father; far beyond the twilight judgments of this world' (p. 682). The scenes of Clennam in the Marshalsea contain the famous reference to 'the prison of this lower world' (p. 796). In the immediate term, the metaphysical dimension to life can be ignored as false, worldly values are adhered to, but ultimately it is of supreme importance, and its existence lends significance to, for instance, the contrast between

Mr Merdle who, through Fanny's watery eyes, seemed to 'leap, and waltz, and gyrate, as if he were possessed by several Devils' and Physician, of whom we are told a few lines later:

> much irreconcileable moral contradiction did he pass his life among; yet his equality of compassion was no more disturbed than the Divine Master's of all healing was. He went, like the rain, among the just and the unjust, doing all the good he could. (p. 734)

The insistence of this perspective is part of Dickens's development as a novelist. The difference of approach in Dickens's presentation of social evils between his early novels and his later ones, summed up by Kathleen Tillotson as being that 'a pervasive uneasiness about contemporary society takes the place of an intermittent concern with specific social wrongs'[35] has become a critical commonplace. Tillotson furthermore suggests that 'After Carlyle the poetic, prophetic and visionary possibilities of the novel are fully awakened';[36] and Michael Goldberg sees Carlyle's central general influence on Dickens as bringing him to a sense of the deeper factors underlying particular social evils:

> from Dombey and Son forward Dickens' novels project his sense of a society thwarted by monstrous pressures for which individual villainy no longer supplied an adequate explanation and for which personal benevolence no longer provided an effective remedy ... The social vision of the novels from Dombey onward, with their sense not merely of faulty institutions but of a sick society inhabited by tyrants, who are at least in part the victims of the forces they represent, owes more to Carlyle than to any other man.[37]

I see this as Carlyle's over-riding influence on Dickens: the Christian vision Dickens already has, and the religious analysis he makes of society, moves from being something he refers to at pertinent moments and becomes the foundation of his novels. Writers such as Goldberg see the influence of Carlyle as greater, and that it is Carlyle's ideas too that pervade Dickens's novels. As we have seen, however, another set of ideas had already been formative in shaping Dickens's vision of society, and this thus did not need to be totally derivative on Carlyle; much of the time Carlyle's ideas synchronise with the specific Christian outlook Dickens had already developed, and it is here, perhaps, that Carlyle's influence is at its strongest. *Hard Times*, for instance, was dedicated to Carlyle, and Dickens told him, 'I know it contains nothing in which you do not think with me'.[38] Goldberg asserts that:

> In content *Hard Times* bears the unmistakable imprint of Carlyle's influence. It makes its attack on statistical methods even less temperately than

> Carlyle had done in 'Chartism' and it endorses his unflattering view of the 'dismal scientists'...[39]

One does not have to deny the influence of Carlyle here to see equally the influence of Christian ideas of needing at all times to regard fellow human beings as brothers and sisters, not to be dehumanised into mere figures; and significantly, at the end, Mr Gradgrind turns away from a total reliance on statistics, and begins to accommodate Christian perspectives into his world view, 'making his facts and figures subservient to Faith, Hope, and Charity' (p. 286).

Founding his novels on his Christian vision rather than merely alluding to it when relevant makes his scrutiny of society all the more searching. It is in this context that in the early novels, piecemeal solutions seem to allow happy endings. Oliver Twist finds his family and a home that provides the refuge from an evil society that he needs, and his problems are resolved, though the evils, such as those of the workhouse, remain. There is still an implicit belief that if workhouses and Yorkshire schools can be got rid of, society is redeemable and will be sound. By the time of his mature novels, causes such as child labour, long working hours and the workhouses may still need attention, but to enact reforms would only be a stop-gap on the way to more fundamental change. A Christian society is more pervasively absent than the author apparently at first perceived. Society cannot be brought back into line by a few Acts of Parliament; wholesale cultural reform is demanded, with the building of a society based on Christian values rather than Utilitarian or mercenary values.

Part of the trouble lies in the acceptance by society of those alternative values, and this is reflected in how villainy itself receives a new emphasis in the novels. A number of the early villains are in a rather traditional mould. Figures such as Fagin, Quilp and Jonas Chuzzlewit are on the edges of their society or outside it. Eventually they come to a nasty end and society is no longer in danger from them. This type of villain is still to be found in the later works – Orlick in *Great Expectations* is an example – but increasingly the villains are of a different nature. If Fagin and the others are outsiders, lurkers in corners in their society, villains are increasingly 'insiders'. From the early novels, there are 'respectable' villains such as Mr Bumble, Mr Squeers and Mr Pecksniff, who on the surface appear to subscribe to socially acceptable values. These people can be exposed for what they are, and their villainy thus defused – which is what happens to them. Exposing their villainy robs them of further power or influence; society is now safe from them. Ralph Nickleby commits suicide because his socially unacceptable behaviour has been revealed. Both these types of villains operated within a generally accepted set of values; they may have broken the moral code flagrantly, or done no more than paid lip-service to it, but they did not challenge that moral code; they paid implicit obeisance to it even while transgressing openly or secretly against it. Fagin and his fellow criminals knows what their end will be, and accept that is the way things are for people who flout the values of their society. They acknowledge their conduct as an outrage to society, and are far from questioning its consequences, which instead become the subject of grim humour, as when Fagin gives a message to the landlord of The Three Cripples for his other customers: 'go back to the company, my dear, and tell them to lead merry lives – *while they last.* Ha! ha! ha!' (p. 208).[40] Increasingly, though, the villains in Dickens subscribe, brazenly and shamelessly, to values that are evil according to traditional (and Christian) ethics, while all the time remaining perfectly respectable. We thus see Mr Vholes calmly and shamelessly exploiting and destroying Richard Carstone. A typical moment occurs when, after a court session, Richard 'flings himself into a chair, half sighing and half groaning; rests his aching head upon his hand and looks the portrait of Young Despair'; at the same time, Vholes, detached from the case and unconcerned about any deleterious effects it is having on his client, is 'quiet and unmoved' (p. 623). As he milks Richard of all his money, he does nothing that is illegal or not respectable. He cannot be exposed because he is doing nothing society condemns. There is just a hint that somewhere deep inside, Mr Vholes has a bad conscience about the way he behaves, for he constantly justifies himself by reference to the need to support his daughters and father; but the conscience is firmly suppressed as he does something evil that society regards as completely acceptable.

Mr Bounderby perhaps is the supreme example, asserting as he does his set of alternative and evil values even more blatantly, and with a characteristic confidence. He takes his place among the community of Coketown industrialists whose bullish attitudes Dickens reports:

> They were ruined, when they were required to send labouring children to school; they were ruined, when inspectors were appointed to look into their works; they were ruined when such inspectors considered it doubtful whether they were quite justified in chopping people up with their machinery; they were utterly undone, when it was hinted that perhaps they need not always make quite so much smoke. (p. 111)

He shamelessly parades his own values in conversation with Harthouse:

> First of all, you see our smoke. That's meat and drink to us. It's the healthiest thing in the world in all respects, and particularly for the lungs. If you are one of those who want us to consume it, I differ from you. We are not going to wear the bottoms of our boilers out any faster than we wear 'em out now, for all the humbugging sentiment in Great Britain and Ireland ... Now, you have heard a lot of talk about the work in our mills, no doubt. You have? Very good. I'll state the fact of it to you. It's the pleasantest work there is, and it's the lightest work there is, and it's the

> best paid work there is. More than that, we couldn't improve the mills themselves, unless we laid down Turkey carpets on the floors. (pp. 125–6)

Such attitudes are not ones Dickens has invented for satirical purposes. Edward Baines the younger declared of factory work that 'it was scarcely possible for any employment to be lighter'.[41] Nassau Senior considered that 'the extraordinary lightness of the labour' made long hours in cotton factories 'practicable' as well as 'desirable'.[42] In *Notes of a Tour in the Manufacturing Districts of 1842*, William Cooke Taylor claimed that 'the toil was not very great, nor was it incessant ... an operative in a cotton factory was at rest one minute out of every three'[43] and in his 1844 book *The Factory System*, the same commentator, J.T. Ward reports, 'optimistically surveyed industry, claiming that accidents were rare and the fault of the injured; allegations about industrial conditions often rested on the frauds of lifelong cripples, posing as hurt operatives'.[44]

If these values are regarded as socially acceptable, it is hard to expose their holders as the villains they are. In a society of moral chaos, evil values are evidently tolerated. To the extent that villains such as Bounderby can be exposed, their evil is not defused. Mr Bounderby is indeed exposed, in that the truth about his past emerges and undermines his philosophical justification for his callous attitude to his workers; but he can still continue to exploit them. The apparently benign Mr Casby is exposed as a cruel landlord who has hidden behind Pancks for years; but he remains a landlord, still able and entitled to be harsh to his tenants. Neither of them is forced to sell up.

Furthermore, villainy has become more than a matter of individual conduct; as many critics have commented, it has become institutionalised. In as early a novel as *Oliver Twist*, Dickens had exposed how much of the institutional villainy in the world is perfectly respectable. The workhouses were officially sanctioned and their representatives such as Mr Bumble had status in society; this did not stop the institution and its personnel being callous and cruel. The villainy is not the work of individuals; it has become anonymised, its appointees taking no individual responsibility but merely administering the system. By the time of *Bleak House*, this is being explicitly underlined. As a distracted Gridley says of the law, 'The system! I am told, on all hands, it's the system. I mustn't look to individuals'. The judge cannot be appealed to as an individual responsible because he 'knows nothing of it. He sits there to administer the system' (*Bleak House*, p. 251); Gridley anticipates, though, that some day such people will be able to make no excuse in front of God, when he accuses 'individual workers ... before the great eternal bar' (p. 252). The law, the factory system, the debtors' prison and everything that goes with it are in themselves, at least in the form in which they are seen operating in the novels, evil and the villains are those who subscribe to these institutions and are their apparatchiks. Evil is embedded in the fabric of society, from Mr Bumble the beadle to Thomas Gradgrind M.P.

The institutions Dickens attacks in these novels are evil because they damage or destroy people. The Circumlocution Office grinds people down into despair; debtors' prison causes a deep shame the likes of Mr Dorrit never recover from even when they become wealthy; the factory system causes people to live wretched, miserable lives; the law drives people to madness, suicide or fatal debilitation. The suffering is caused not by abuses of these institutions but by their functioning in precisely the way society approves of. Everyone is thus involved in the evil of this society, morally compromised by gaining a livelihood from these institutions, or at the very least by tolerating and accepting them. The wickedness is, to use the discarded title of *Little Dorrit*, 'nobody's fault', in that it is not the work of a rogue individual; rather, though the phrase is an attempt to shrug off any responsibility, it is everybody's fault. Everyone is caught up in and implicated in the guilt. It is not possible to live independently of society, and it is a salve to people's consciences to claim that the things going wrong are nobody's fault, and responsibility need not be taken. When Arthur Clennam insists that the ruin of Doyce's business he causes via speculation in Merdle's scheme is not nobody's fault but is his, and is determined to take responsibility for it, he is standing out against the trend of his society: the greed for money into which he has been tempted (albeit for the best of reasons) is perfectly respectable in his society and the idea that he should be punished for it, any more than is inescapable, is alien to the world in which he lives. The corruption of values spreads as insidiously as diseases do. People are not perturbed by things that should be intolerable in a truly civilised society.

Dickens is not willing to accept that the way the institutions of society operate, whether from vested interest or sheer inaction, is inevitable and so tolerable. That things are the way they are is not 'nobody's fault'; they can and must be changed. And they will be changed by making Christian values the basis of society. The moral code of the Good Samaritan, a sense of the brotherhood of man, Christian love, doing unto others as you would that they should do unto you: these are the routes to a good society in which cruelty, misery, suffering and injustice will be eradicated. In his social novels of the 1850s, Dickens exposes the evils of society for what they are, and simultaneously suggests the solution to them.

5
Bleak House: Law, Religion and Civilisation

In a letter to Rev. David Macrae quoted in Chapter 1, Dickens, alluding to the New Testament, stated that in his works, 'all my social abuses are shown as departures from its spirit'.[1] From a slightly different angle, he similarly commented, in a letter to the *Daily News* on the subject of capital punishment that 'if an Institution or Custom is wrong and bad' then 'IT CANNOT BE a part of the law laid down by the Divinity who walked the earth'.[2] *Bleak House* depicts a society gone seriously wrong because it has attempted to build civilisation merely on the basis of law. Christianity has been ignored as the foundation of society; and there is moral chaos rather than a shared moral code in its daily operation. It is no wonder that the 'social abuses' are as serious as they are.

I

The first two phrases of *Bleak House*, referring to its setting and to legal terms – 'London. Michaelmas term lately over' (p. 13)[3] – hint at an England blessed by the rule of law, and with it, in a state of civilisation. The law, after all, in bringing order to society, is the bedrock of civilisation. Dickens then immediately, however, contradicts this impression through imagery that suggests that we are not in civilisation but in a primeval, or at least primitive,[4] world:[5] the mud is such that it is 'as if the waters had but newly retired from the face of the earth, and it would not be wonderful to meet a Megalosaurus, forty feet long or so, waddling like an elephantine lizard up Holborn Hill' (p. 13). On the surface there is nothing objectionable about the law and its operation: Chancery proceeds 'so smoothly', is 'a polite show' that 'went calmly on from day to day, and year to year, in such good order and composure' (p. 396). It appears the very epitome of civilisation; below the surface, it is to emerge, things are very different.

The phrase 'Michaelmas term', furthermore, reminds us of a (theoretical) link between the legal world and a religious festival; but it is an ironic reference, for the law in all its aspects is unholy. Later, indeed, it is to be implied that people need help when in 'the valley of the shadow of the law' (p. 504) just as much as the narrator of the 23rd Psalm does when passing through the valley of the shadow of death: the two environments are both evil. The law is a kind of priesthood, but one that far from succouring the public causes them damage and harm: 'the laity sometimes suffer in peace and pocket' (p. 621). In the early pages of the novel, its institutions may be reminiscent of holy places, with 'stained glass windows' and a 'sanctuary' (p. 15) but the halo ('glory' (p. 14)) round the head of the Lord High Chancellor is one of fog, not holiness. This is a system of law quite disconnected from Christianity. Theoretically it promotes moral and social values, but not as it is practised in this society: as some remarks of Mrs Bagnet reflect, ' truth and justice' are quite separate from 'law and lawyers' (p. 841). The lawmakers themselves are, 'some graceless jokers' have suggested, in need of 'the prayers of the congregation' for 'six hundred and fifty-eight gentlemen in a very unhealthy state' (p. 645). The prison system reflects the distorted values of society in that it takes better care of wrongdoers than society does of the innocent: as John Jarndyce remarks of Jo, 'if this wretched creature were a convicted prisoner, his hospital would be wide open to him, and he would be taken care of as any sick boy in the kingdom' (p. 494).

Centrally, though, of course, Dickens concentrates on the operation of the courts and Chancery in particular. Through his presentation of this Dickens brings out how the legal system undermines civilised values rather than promoting them. From the start it is presented as immoral: it is a place where 'monied might' prevails over 'the right' (p. 15). It is a thriving ground for 'trickery' and other forms of evil (p. 17). It ruins people, reducing them to poverty, as instanced in the 'ruined suitor, with his slipshod heels and threadbare dress, borrowing and begging' (p. 15). It is corrosive of virtues, of 'patience, courage, hope' (p. 15). Gridley's morals have, by his own account, been eroded through his involvement with the law: he is 'quarrelsome ... irascible ... not polite' (p. 249), for having been 'dragged for five-and-twenty years over burning iron' in court; he has 'lost the habit of treading upon velvet' (p. 250). Gridley has become aggressive, he says, because 'if I took my wrongs in any other way, I should be driven mad' (p. 250). If his rage has been caused by the operation of the law, the law will operate to protect itself and contain that rage rather than altering its operations. After an 'alarming' visit from Gridley, Mr Tulkinghorn decides that, 'We are not to be put in bodily fear, and that ill-conditioned fellow shall be held to bail again' (p. 259).

Above all, it is destructive of life and sanity, and divisive of families. The first character we meet in the novel is a victim of the law, 'a little mad old woman in a squeezed bonnet' (p. 15), apparently Miss Flite, whose sanity has certainly been affected. Mr George appositely predicts of Gridley in his long legal entanglement that that 'He will be worn out soon ... You may file a strong man's heart away for a good many years, but it will tell all of a sudden at last' (p. 395). The Jarndyce and Jarndyce case drove Tom Jarndyce to suicide, and in the course of the novel we see how it destroys Richard Carstone. John Jarndyce sees it as fatally influential in the indecisiveness over his career that does Rick so much harm:

> How much of this indecision of character ... is chargeable on that incomprehensible heap of uncertainty and procrastination on which he has been thrown from his birth, I don't pretend to say; but that Chancery, among its other sins, is responsible for some of it, I can plainly see. (p. 197)

When Esther later notes in Rick 'no habits of application and concentration', she concludes that 'the uncertainties and delays of the Chancery suit had imparted to his nature something of the careless spirit of a gamester, who felt that he was part of a great gaming system' (p. 265). If the case has created these attitudes, they lead to his depending totally on it: with regard to the court case, he gradually moves from a position that, 'We know it better than to trust it' (p. 215) to coming to thinking that if 'I devote myself to it' and make it 'the object of my life' (p. 599), that it will sort out his life for him.. Aware that the case 'taints everybody', and that 'it has a little twisted me' (p. 597), he nevertheless gets so desperately caught up in it that in his later days he is 'thin and languid, slovenly in his dress, abstracted in his manner, forcing his spirits now and then, and at other intervals relapsing into a dull thoughtfulness' (p. 926) and it kills him when the case collapses. He is not alone in the effect the court case has on him: 'ten thousand' are similarly affected (p. 630).

In a novel which, as we shall see, centres around the idea that the whole of humanity is one family, the law is portrayed as splitting such family togetherness as there is and as dividing people from one another. Her introduction to Jarndyce and Jarndyce causes Ada to reflect in distress that she may be

> the enemy – as I suppose I am – of a great number of relations and others; and that they should be my enemies – as I suppose they are; and that we should all be ruining one another, without knowing how or why, and be in constant doubt and discord all our lives. (p. 78)

As he pursues the case, Richard becomes estranged from John Jarndyce, acknowledging the case to be the cause: 'all this business puts us on unnatural terms', he remarks (p. 599). He allows for the possibility that he may be 'mistaken in John Jarndyce', but will not contemplate a reassessment until the case is over: 'My head may be clearer when I am free of it' (p. 599).

That the law is not made for people like Richard Carstone is reflected in the people it does seem made for, such as the Smallweeds – otherwise insubstantial people, as their name suggests, who, as we shall see, are able to exploit the law to gratify their greed for money and power, transforming them into intimidating figures. The physical deformity of Grandpa Smallweed is an obvious symbol of the inner twisted nature of their characters.

That the law is disconnected from, and in many ways the antithesis of, civilisation is also driven home through the portrayal of the novel's legal officers, people who not only make their living out of the law but are also portrayed as being guided by it alone in the conduct of their lives. The inadequacy of the law to establish civilisation is underlined in the presentation of two of its chief representatives.

As a professional, Mr Vholes's behaviour, for instance, is impeccable. Kenge describes him as 'Diligent, persevering, steady, acute in business' (p. 622). He describes himself as 'exact and open' in business (p. 607), and as 'cool and methodical' (p. 624), He is dutiful, assiduous and diligent. His 'duty', he says is 'attending to your interests' and this he does, even during vacations when 'Other professional men go out of town' (p. 625). Apparently, he sacrifices his health to his professional duties, for while 'rest might improve' his troublesome 'digestive functions', 'I shall not rest, sir, while I am your representative' (p. 628). Indeed, he bases his claims for payment by Richard on his professionalism, on 'the zealous and active discharge ... of my professional duty' (p. 629). His professional integrity meant that he declined to offer any 'opinion or advice as to your interests, while those interests were intrusted to another member of the profession' (p. 628). He shows scruples in his behaviour to his client: he proclaims that honesty 'is my golden rule' (p. 779) and it is true that 'I never give hopes', though Richard would dearly like him to; Vholes resists because he is 'constantly considerate of my good name' (p. 625).

Any personal moral virtues, though, are not in evidence. His personal moral code is revealed parenthetically: we see him discussing how as long as a client 'laid down a principle which was not of an immoral (that is to say, unlawful) nature, it devolved upon me to carry it out' (p. 925). Vholes lives upon the principle that whatever is legal is moral. Nothing he does in the novel is illegal. However, taking what is legal also to be moral means that he is able to do some deplorable things without ever breaking the law. He behaves towards his clients without any Christian love or a sense of responsibility. The lack of any personal scruples means that he perfectly content to pursue Rick's case quite cynically, even as it is evident that it is causing Rick to go into decline. He is unruffled, 'quiet and unmoved', after another fruitless visit to court, even though Richard 'looks the portrait of Young Despair' (p. 623); to Vholes, the whole thing means simply more income. He is perfectly happy to cause family division: 'I must not shrink from a professional duty, even if it sows dissension in families' (p. 628). Brotherhood, even within families, is quite unimportant. In his behaviour towards Rick he is quite devious. Well aware of Richard's impatience to get the court case resolved quickly, he will emphasise how expeditiously he behaves, drawing attention to how there is nothing of 'the languid and routine' in his 'discharge' of his duties (p. 629) and that, with regard to the case,

> being informed by one of my clerks last night after post time that it stood, rather unexpectedly, in the paper for tomorrow, I put myself into the coach early this morning and came down to confer with him. (p. 606)

This produces the desired, calculated effect. Richard is delighted that they are not doing things 'in the old slow way, now' (p. 606). There is no breaching of Vholes's professional integrity here: everything he says is perfectly true, if very deliberately calculated. His lack of scruples in exploiting Rick, however, is presented as making him, not a civilised human being, but rather as someone dehumanised. His name suggests an animal-like nature and Dickens has Esther describe him when discussing Rick's decline as speaking 'as though there were not a human passion or emotion in his heart' (p. 923).

His lack of care for his client is seen, in this corrupt society, as an impersonality that is an admirable mark of his professionalism. The absence of other moral values perverts even his professional ones. Detachment is part of professionalism, and Vholes makes clear to Richard that there is no human relationship between them, only a professional and economic one: there will be no tie of loyalty or friendship. If the case succeeds 'you will owe me nothing' beyond money, and there will be no enduring relationship, for 'My duty prosperously ended, all between us is ended' (p. 629).

The other chief figure who brings out the inadequacy of the law to establish civilisation is Mr Tulkinghorn, a man whose life and personality are shaped by his profession and whose conduct is restrained only by the law. Tulkinghorn is the reverse of Wemmick in *Great Expectations*, because in him there is no distinction between his professional and private selves. Significantly, his rooms are both 'his house and office' (p. 159). He displays the qualities, standards and professional ethics of a man in his job as a solicitor. Professionally attentive – 'I proceed upon the troublesome principle of begging leave to possess my clients with any new proceedings in a cause' (p. 26) – he is simultaneously therein professionally circumspect, 'a cautious man ... taking no more responsibility than necessary' (p. 26).

Centrally, he is discreet, as a man trusted with private, confidential information needs to be. When we are first introduced to him, it is as 'the silent depository' of 'family confidences' and 'noble secrets' (p. 23), 'Mute, close ... like his clothes' (p. 23). He is 'a great reservoir of confidences', the sole repository of such, for he has 'no clerks'; his great professional abilities mean that 'His clients want him; he is all in all' (p. 159).

In determining his personal conduct, he is guided not by a moral code but by professional standards:

> Whether his whole soul is devoted to the great, or whether he yields them nothing beyond the services he sells, is his personal secret. He keeps it, as he keeps the secrets of his clients; he is his own client in that matter and will never betray himself. (p. 192)

Secrecy has become a way of life, his *modus operandi* in all situations: 'He never converses, when not professionally consulted' (pp. 23–4), so that in social situations he is 'speechless but quite at home, at corners of dinner-tables in great country houses and near doors of drawing-rooms' (p. 24). When he arrives at Chesney Wold on one occasion in Chapter 12, he engages only in the most banal of small talk, and in a later, non-business conversation about some elections, he has 'no political opinions; indeed, no opinions' (p. 647). At all times 'An Oyster of the old school, whom nobody can open' (p. 158), even the narrator cannot wholly penetrate his secretiveness, having to speculate on what 'perchance' (p. 433) Tulkinghorn is thinking. Furthermore, his detachment, a requirement of any professional, goes well beyond the merely professional. When Nemo is found dead, he is willing to 'testify ... if it should ever be necessary, that all was fair and right' as he sets Krook to search through Nemo's things (p. 170), but otherwise shows a detachment throughout the scene, 'aloof', 'impeturbable', his face 'inexpressive', 'unmoved' (p. 168), in contrast to the reactions of the others present, from Krook's 'horrible interest' (p. 167) to Miss Flite's 'awe' (p. 168). Woodcourt takes 'a young surgeon's professional interest in death' (p. 168) but this is 'quite apart from his remarks on the deceased as an individual': Woodcourt has earlier sympathetically commented that 'to judge from his appearance and condition, I should think it a happy release' (p. 168). There is no such duality of reaction in Tulkinghorn. When later pressed for an opinion of the man, he snootily pronounces him 'the commonest of the common' (p. 195). Professional manner reflects, or has shaped, a coldness in his personality; he is 'no more like flesh and blood, than a rusty old carbine is', George is later to comment (p. 727).

These aspects of his personality carry over into his moral character. A man who habitually wears an 'expressionless mask' (p. 192), 'close and dry ... watchful behind a blind' (p. 433) is to others morally a blank slate on which they create a moral character in accordance with their preconceptions. Traditionally, the solicitor of an aristocratic family is a devoted and loyal retainer, so faithful as to be practically a member of the family. So Sir Leicester sees even Tulkinghorn's dress as 'retainer-like' (p. 24) and Mrs Rouncewell sees him as 'part and parcel' (p. 109) of Chesney Wold. Moral qualities such as loyalty, however, are not part of Tulkinghorn's make-up. 'The peerage may have warmer worshippers and faithfuller believers than Mr. Tulkinghorn, after all, if everything were known' declares the narrator towards the middle of the novel (p. 433), and Lady Dedlock describes him as 'mechanically faithful without attachment' (p. 581). He rarely discusses things in moral terms, beyond a professional expression of support for a client's cause, as when he describes Boythorn to Sir Leicester as 'obstinate' (p. 193), or in a rare burst of bad temper (possibly calculated, to disquieten and worry) when frustrated by George's unco-operativeness, refers to Gridley, identified as one of George's 'associates' as 'A threatening, murderous, dangerous fellow' (p. 445).

For the rest of the time, though, Tulkinghorn's conduct is restrained only by the law, which allows him plenty of scope to behave deplorably badly and cruelly. His behaviour is carefully calibrated to stay within the law. When Smallweed, in dealing with George's reluctance to hand over a sample of Hawdon's handwriting, wishes he could 'tear the writing away from him', Tulkinghorn is firm and clear: 'Violence will not do for me, my friend' (p. 437). The law, however, allows him a lot of scope to lie and deceive, which he often does. He tells Snagsby on a visit made deliberately to him that he 'just happened to be passing' (p. 161) and later that he is not going into Krook's shop whereas once Snagsby is out of the way he 'enters it straight' (p. 163). Part of his secretive manner is that when Hawdon's dead body is discovered, Tulkinghorn affects not to have noticed a portmanteau of interest to him until it is brought to his attention by Snagsby, even though 'he is standing so close to it, and though there is very little else' (p. 171). He will not explain to George why he wants the sample of Hawdon's handwriting, lying by claiming professional necessity: 'confidential reasons, very harmless in themselves, for many such wants, in the profession to which I belong' (p. 436).

This, however, is the least of it. Secrecy is so central to Tulkinghorn's life that it has become his religion: he is the 'high priest of noble mysteries' (p. 661). As his devotion to secrets facilitates an ability to remain discreet, Tulkinghorn is in a position of power. When relaxing, he wallows in the confidences he possesses: 'he sits, and drinks, and mellows as it were in secrecy; pondering at that twilight hour, on all the mysteries he knows' (p. 353). And without ever breaking professionally gained confidences, he is a man who loves to exercise power, whether it be to force a document he wants out of George or to torment Lady Dedlock. His victims are very aware of this aspect of him. George describes him as a 'slow-torturing kind of man' (p. 727) and Lady Dedlock tells Esther that, 'His calling is the acquisition of secrets, and the holding possession of such power as they give him' (p 581). He is utterly ruthless and merciless, and if his victims are people of simple honest decency, like the Bagnets and George, they are so much more easily his prey. Mrs Bagnet's advice to George, on behalf of her husband, is 'to do nothing in the dark, to be a party to nothing under-handed or mysterious'; Tulkinghorn is one of those 'people who are too deep for him' (p. 443). Such straightforward, unduplicitous people have no hope against a man described at one point as having no 'compunction, remorse or pity' (p. 459), and who is perfectly willing to put people through torment, as George finds out: 'What does he care?' He causes him 'more restlessness, and more uneasiness, and more dissatisfaction with myself, than all other men put together' (p. 727). At no point, though, does he break the law when exerting his power. Far from breaking the law, he is able to use it ruthlessly as a weapon against George and the Bagnets. In alliance with his client Smallweed, he uses the threat of prosecution as leverage to get the document he wants out of George. Smallweed is owed money which neither George nor Bagnet can pay back:

> Very well! Then you just pay it between you, or you must both be sued for it, and both suffer. You have had the money and must refund it. You are not to pocket other people's pounds, shillings and pence, and escape scot free. (p. 551)

At the same time, he knows how to take recourse in the law to protect himself from intimidation he in his turn may experience. The way the law operates is destroying Gridley, but an 'alarming' visit from him to Tulkinghorn's rooms prompts no qualms about the law in the solicitor, merely a determination that, 'We are not to be put in bodily fear, and that ill-conditioned fellow shall be held to bail again' (p. 259). Equally, he uses the threat of 'keys of prisons' and 'houses of correction (where the treadmills are, for women)' (p. 667) to try to restrain and control Hortense.

In uncovering Lady Dedlock's secret, Tulkinghorn is on no self-righteous moral mission to expose vice and immorality. It may be that some of the pleasure he gets out of it is because he is a misogynist. A bachelor himself, he expresses the opinion that 'most of the people I know would do far better to leave marriage alone. It is at the bottom of three fourths of their troubles' (p. 658), an observation made in the context of the distress the revelation about his wife is going to cause Sir Leicester. We have already had it reported to us that Tulkinghorn's view is that, 'There are women enough in the world ... – too many; they are at the bottom of all that goes wrong in it' (p. 259). Later, the announcement of a visit from Mademoiselle Hortense prompts the reaction, 'These women were created to give trouble, the whole earth over. The Mistress not being enough to deal with, here's the maid now!' (p. 664). Once Lady Dedlock, through her reaction to the legal document, followed by her affected unconcern, followed by her feeling faint, has given away there is some disturbing secret she does not want revealed, Tulkinghorn is set on taking the matter further as a means of pursuing his dislike of women and confirming his prejudices about them.

Centrally, though, Tulkinghorn is arbitrarily indulging the love of secrets and power that is so mixed up with his professional personality, and is perfectly able to make her life a torment well within the law. He does nothing illegal, such as blackmailing her; the distress he puts her through is enough. From the small beginning of a curiosity to know what lay behind Lady Dedlock's reaction to the sample of Hawdon's handwriting, he pursues an evident secret at first with no idea where it will lead. It becomes a battle for power between two secretive people, used to giving away nothing in their demeanour or speech. Tulkinghorn admires the skill with which his antagonist does this: 'The power of this woman is astonishing. She has been acting a part the whole time', he thinks at one point (p. 743). After the story he tells Sir Leicester reveals that Tulkinghorn knows her secret, in Lady Dedlock's conversation with him, Tulkinghorn, aware of 'Anger, and fear, and shame. All three contending' in her, thinks admiringly, 'What power this woman has, to keep these raging passions down!' (p. 653). When things come to a crisis, 'There is nothing in her manner to express weakness or excite compassion', leaving Tulkinghorn fascinated, considering her 'a study', and he 'studies her at his leisure, not speaking for a time' (p. 746). However, her control over herself is not as total as Tulkinghorn's over himself. As he relates her story in anonymised form to Sir Leicester, he describes how the 'train of circumstances' that 'led to discovery' began 'in an imprudence on her own part one day, when she was taken by surprise; which shows how difficult it is for the firmest of us (she was very firm) to be always guarded' (p. 650). When she speaks to Tulkinghorn after this scene, her imperfect control is again evident. While 'In her carriage and all else, she looks as she looked down-stairs two hours ago', she cannot hide 'a wild disturbance ... in her eyes', which she can only suppress successfully enough to make Tulkinghorn uncertain whether it is 'fear or anger' (p. 653). She is thus a worthy opponent for him to take on in a deadly joust; but also, perhaps, to punish her for her lack of total control will vindicate Tulkinghorn's own impulses for maintaining total control, total impassivity, total secretiveness. It is as if she has committed an offence against his standards of behaviour and must be punished. Her ruin will confirm his sense of the need for total reserve.

Early on, she shows impressive command of her own reactions. After a momentary lapse on seeing the legal document, she immediately looks 'full at' Tulkinghorn 'in her careless way again' (p. 26) and pretends that her interest in it was only 'to vary this detestable monotony' (p. 27). The fragility of her self-control, though, is already apparent when she is taken faint soon after. By the time he has tracked down who wrote the document and counters with a far from casual, prodding message that he has 'something to tell her' (p. 183), she has regained command, and affects to find it 'very odd' that he took the trouble to find out the information (p. 194). She pretends to think his interest sprang out of his (otherwise never evident) considerate nature – 'It was like you to remember the circumstance' – while at the same time trying to misdirect him by claiming the matter to be of no real interest to her, one that 'I had quite forgotten' (p. 193). When he has discovered the full story, he returns to the fray, assaulting her with an anonymised version of the story told to Sir Leicester in her presence. The episode is so satisfying to his appetite for power that while maintaining his 'severely and strictly self-suppressed nature' means that he is not apparently 'triumphant', he is 'sedately satisfied'. He has 'a rather increased sense of power', and the excitement this causes him is reflected in how he for once is 'not in a business mood', despite the important place work normally occupies in his life. Eventually, however, he begins to get over his excitement, 'subsiding, if a man so cruel may have any need to subside' (p. 652). When Lady Dedlock comes to see him, he reasserts self-control, facing her with 'the same formal politeness, the same composed deference ... the same dark, cold object, at the same distance' (p. 653).

Essentially, though, from this point onwards he has won the battle and is able to revel in his power. Lady Dedlock is aware of herself as 'the woman under your foot', reduced to begging for 'mercy' (p. 654). All her strength of character is as nothing in the face of his power. They both know that, 'He has conquered her' (p. 656), though he is not quite secure in the enjoyment of his power: he gives a 'jealous glance' as she heads for the window and he fears she is going to jump to a suicide that will end his power (p. 656).

Such is his relishing of his power, combined with the coldness of his manner on top of his moral insensibility, that as Lady Dedlock now weakens, there is no relenting on his part. Her distress and desperate plans when she realises her secret has been uncovered leave him 'quite unmoved' (p. 655). Instead, he feels himself entitled to be merciless. He would have shown consideration for Lady Dedlock, he claims, 'if the case had admitted of it; but unfortunately it does not' (p. 659). He 'cannot at all consider' her in his future actions (p. 658). He takes over the running of her life. Claiming concern for Sir Leicester and how he will react to the news, until Tulkinghorn has decided what to do, he says, she must not run away but continue with her life as before; she has no choice but to acquiesce in being thus 'tied to the stake' (p. 659).

Part of the competition between them is to retain as much reserve as possible in front of each other; once Lady Dedlock is in private, though, the cruelty of Tulkinghorn's behaviour is apparent, with 'her figure twisted as if by pain' (p. 660).

When they have further dealings, his triumph and the increased power over her that he revels in are apparent. She has been so shaken that she has lost 'the belief she of old reposed in herself, as one able to reserve whatsoever she would under her mantle of pride' (p. 735). His sense of increased power is revealed in the 'indefinable freedom in his manner, which is new' when he is in conversation with Lady Dedlock (p. 744). He objects to her doing things, such as making arrangements for Rosa, which are not controlled by him: 'both the letter and the spirit of our arrangement altogether precluded any action on your part, founded upon my discovery' (p. 745). He is unresponsive, in his lack of compassion and moral scruples, to any argument that

Rosa needed to be spared the shame of association with Lady Dedlock once the secret is revealed: 'As to sparing the girl, of what importance or value is she?' (p. 745). As far as Tulkinghorn is concerned, in his unyielding exertion of his power, Lady Dedlock 'cannot be spared – why should she spare others?' (p. 746). If he controls her actions, though, he refuses to allow her any control over his actions: he will not let himself be pinned down over when he will reveal the secret to Sir Leicester. 'I would rather say no more', he says, than that it merely 'may be to-morrow' (p. 747). Able thus to torment, Tulkinghorn's enjoyment of his power is brought to an end only with his death, though even then, the suffering which is the result of his actions continues for Lady Dedlock.

The callous, ruthless cruelty of Tulkinghorn, all within the law, again dramatically demonstrates how inadequate the law is to establish civilisation and civilised values.

II

The rule of law certainly obtains in the society portrayed in *Bleak House*, but it establishes only what is legally right and wrong, not what is morally right and wrong. People are left to find their own, makeshift moral codes, with the result that this is a society in moral chaos. The moral code of Vholes and Tulkinghorn, that whatever is legal is moral, is only one of a number of different codes, moral or otherwise, by which people are living their lives in this society, the best of them inadequate, the worst deplorable. It is noticeable that some people effectively live their lives without any moral code at all.

The only constraint on Grandfather Smallweed's behaviour seems to be his own physical limitations. The law barely reins in his behaviour: as Bucket remarks, Smallweed is involved in 'conspiring to extort money' out of Sir Leicester (p. 828). His aggressive, violent nature is constantly in evidence: as we have seen, he would like physically to tear away the sample of Hawdon's handwriting from Mr George and finds it 'chafing and galling' (p. 437) not to be able to. He is furious with Hawdon for dying:

> 'He owed us immense sums, all round. I would sooner have strangled him than had no return. If I sit here thinking of him,' snarls the old man, holding up his impotent ten fingers, 'I want to strangle him now.' (p. 348)

It is only his physical decrepitude that restrains him. He would grab the document from George 'If I wasn't as weak as a Brimstone Baby' (p. 437). The narrator comments that, 'his powerless figure is suggestive of a baleful old malignant, who would be very wicked if he could' (p. 337). He does not seem to mind the effect on himself as long as he can be as aggressive as possible within his limitations: thus, he throws the spare cushion that he 'always' has by him at his wife even though 'the necessary exertion recoils on Mr Smallweed himself, whom it throws back into his porter's chair, like a broken puppet' (p. 334). Physically limited, his aggression is redirected into a ruthless, merciless love of power. Tempted in his rage at George to throw his pipe at him, and barely restrained from doing so, he dashes it to the ground instead but promises him 'I'll smash you. I'll crumble you. I'll powder you'. (p. 547).

Uninfluenced by 'ideality, reverence, wonder' (p. 332), Smallweed has no guiding moral principles, religious or otherwise, that he endeavours to live up to. Instead, he comes from a line of worshippers of money: of his father it is said 'this old pagan's God was Compound Interest' (pp. 332–3). A money-lender, he views his fellow men not as brothers but as potential victims ripe for exploitation. Even members of his family are potentially to be exploited: as Bucket remarks, 'there ain't one of the family that wouldn't sell the other for a pound or two' (p. 947). Mr George is well aware that, 'You'll sell me up at last I suppose, when I am a day in arrear' (p. 344), though, despicably, Smallweed does not have the courage of his own rapacity, pretending it is 'my friend in the city' who is the real exacting and hard-hearted taskmaster (p. 344). Morality only enters his conceptual framework when it suits his mercenary purpose: speaking to the highly moral John Jarndyce, having produced a document found at Krook's relating to the Jarndyce case, he 'left it to Mr Jarndyce's honour not to let him lose by his honesty' (pp. 946–7).

The lack of even the most basic standards of morality and decency in Smallweed is astonishing. His violence and vituperativeness towards his wife shows not only a lack of family love and loyalty but also, given that she is senile, a lack of even the most basic compassion for the vulnerable. This is all the more remarkable in that Smallweed himself, in his decrepitude, is also very vulnerable. He is an insecure man, frightened, and perhaps conscious of himself as hated, when he visits George's shooting-gallery as to whether 'anything goes off here, accidentally' (p. 426). He also has the constant anxiety of a man himself of sharp practices and few ties of loyalty: when Bucket is discussing the Jarndyce will Smallweed has found, the hard-of-hearing and 'suspicious' (p. 944) by nature Smallweed listens 'anxiously, with his hand at his ear' (p. 945), frightened Bucket is going to trick him into damaging admissions. Dependent on others to carry him about, he is constantly worried about his own safety. When Mr George asks Phil Squod to carry Smallweed back to his coach, the old man is nervous, and driven to a rare show of respectful address: 'Are you sure you can do it carefully, my worthy man?' (p. 431). He prefers, however, not to depend on moral qualities in others, such as kindness or compassion and is happiest when not relying on them. He prefers to depend instead on the sort of monetary incentives that would motivate him, being carried around by a cab-driver whose service in this respect is 'by agreement included in his fare' (p. 423). The mercenary relationship, involving no link of sympathy, no debts of obligation for kindness received, and everything strictly business, just suits Smallweed.

Mr Turveydrop is guided through life not by a moral code but by following a particular lifestyle. Turveydrop's life is lived in imitation of that of the Prince Regent, whose world Turveydrop regards as the acme of civilisation:

> We have degenerated ... A levelling age is not favourable to Deportment. It develops vulgarity ... England – alas my country! –has degenerated very much, and is degenerating every day. She has not many gentlemen left. We are few. I see nothing to succeed us, but a race of weavers. (p. 228)

There is virtue, therefore, in perpetuating the lifestyle of the Prince Regent:

> I will do my duty to society, and will show myself, as usual about town ... I have been faithful to my post, since the days of His Royal Highness the Prince Regent; and I will not desert it now. (p. 379)

The idle and superficial life of the Prince Regent hardly impressed Dickens and this is reflected in his portrayal of Turveydrop, who leaves others to 'work, be industrious, earn money' (p. 379) as he urges his son; but it is worse than this, for Turveydrop uses his Deportment to intimidate others and thus to indulge his utterly selfish way of life. His Deportment is used as leverage. Setting himself up as a model which others fall short of, their feelings of inadequacy mean that they are intimidated into being submissive to him. His wife is dead: he 'had worked her to death, or had, at the best, suffered her to work herself to death, to maintain him in those expenses which were indispensable to his position' (p. 226). He has not educated his son properly, because Prince has had to work 'morning, noon and night' to keep his father, but Caddy is keen to excuse and indulge this behaviour: 'what did it matter? She could write letters enough for both' (p. 231). His Deportment and the associated qualities are always to be deferred to. Caddy and Prince have not told him of their engagement for fear it might be 'too great a shock':

> 'For old Mr Turveydrop's deportment is very beautiful you know, Esther,' added Caddy; 'and his feelings are extremely sensitive.' (p. 374)

His outer refinement is held to reflect an inner refinement, and he must be indulged and presented with nothing discomforting. When Turveydrop ensures that even when married they will stay with him and look after him, Esther comments on how

> The power of his Deportment was such, that they really were as much overcome with thankfulness as if, instead of quartering himself upon them for the rest of his life, he were making some munificent sacrifice in their favour. (p. 379)

He had 'such a long prescriptive right to this Deportment' that the slightest declaration of not putting himself first causes Caddy and Prince 'to be melted to tears by these affectionate self-sacrifices' (p. 773).

In reality, Turveydrop is egocentric, as a lifestyle based on narcissistically devoting oneself solely to looking impressive encourages, and exploitative. Prince's engagement to Caddy is 'An arrow launched at my brain, by my own child!' (p. 376); Prince is pressurised by his reaction into promising that in their marriage they will provide his comforts 'before anything' (p. 377). In practice, he becomes the subject in their marriage of 'innumerable precautions':

> If the baby cried, it was nearly stifled lest the noise should make him uncomfortable. If the fire wanted stirring in the night, it was surreptitiously done lest his rest be broken. (p. 772)

Mr Turveydrop is only a believer in family values in so far as he can take from his family: he expects and receives respect and consideration from his son and daughter-in-law while giving very little back. He equally perverts religious concepts. If we are all our brother's keepers, he was willing, as we have seen, to let his wife work herself literally to death to keep him, without reciprocating or ever emerging from his 'absorbing selfishness' (p. 227). His attitude to his son is unwittingly revealed by his having given him a name more suited to a dog.

Significantly, Esther always sees through him. The elegant compliments that go with his Deportment are weapons he uses to manipulate people; but she is impervious to his suggestion that she 'conferred a charm and a distinction on London' (p. 227); and she finds his gallantry 'very disagreeable' (p. 229). A few others see through him, such as the old lady who declares that 'he never does anything else' than be a model of Deportment (p. 226); but largely Turveydrop gets away with being admired without showing any moral virtues. At the very end of the novel, he is 'still believed in, in the old way' (p. 987).

To the extent that his persona is genuine, Mr Skimpole is pre-moral in the way an infant is. If he is, as he constantly asserts, a child, he is childish rather than childlike, and is a very young child at that. His stance is that of someone who thinks the universe revolves around him and that everyone and everything exists for his benefit. In thinking about someone who is bold enough to go to the North Pole, he considers that 'he may go for the purpose – though he don't know it – of employing my thoughts as I lie here' (p. 295). Similarly, slaves in America may have 'an unpleasant existence' but 'they people the landscape for me, they give it a poetry for me, and perhaps that is one of the pleasanter objects of their existence' (p. 295). It gives him an uncritical view of the *status quo*. Aristocrats such as Sir Leicester:

> are public benefactors. They are good enough to maintain a number of delightful objects for the admiration and pleasure of us poor men; and

> not to reap all the admiration and pleasure that they yield, is to be ungrateful to our benefactors (p. 682)

It is a perspective that enables him to develop a sanguine theodicy: he:

> felt that he appreciated health the more, when somebody else was ill; didn't know but what it might be in the scheme of things that A should squint to make B happier in looking straight; or that C should carry a wooden leg, to make D better satisfied with his flesh and blood in a silk stocking. (p. 593)

With this view of life, he manages to see himself as a benefactor of others, not a parasite on them: getting Richard rather than John Jarndyce to pay Skimpole's debt becomes an act which will 'develop generosity in a new soil, and in a new form of flower' (p. 95).

Skimpole is also like a child in being sheltered from the harsh realities of the world; except that in his case, it is himself, rather than loving parents, doing the shielding. Early on, after declaring that 'I know nothing' of the world, he wishes that for Ada 'there should be no brambles of sordid realities' (p. 93). Much later, he is reluctant to let Esther discuss something unpleasant: 'Why should you allude to anything that is not a pleasant matter? I never do' (p. 931). When asked not to be a drain on Richard's finances, he is immediately compliant: 'When I go anywhere, I go for pleasure. I don't go anywhere for pain, because I was made for pleasure' (p. 931). Richard, as he disintegrates in his absorption in the court case is no longer a source of pleasure for Skimpole. Ada and Richard have lost their 'youthful poetry' and 'reduced to prose ... degenerate in the power of imparting pleasure to me' (p. 933). Skimpole has no interest in helping them as they suffer; he simply wants to avoid anything that is unpleasant. He is essentially an escapist from the real world with its challenges and difficulties.

Growing to moral maturity involves recognising that the rest of the world does not exist simply for one's own convenience, that others are capable of suffering and that there is a duty to alleviate the suffering of others as much as possible. Skimpole has no interest in such growth: he would rather remain the irresponsible parasite he is. He is unabashed that he is such. He does not care that his family suffers. The family home is in a symbolic 'state of dilapidation':

> Two or three of the area railings were gone; the water butt was broken; the knocker was loose; the bell handle had been pulled off a long time, to judge from the rusty state of the wire; and dirty footprints on the steps were the only signs of its being inhabited (p. 672)

Inside, the house is 'dingy enough, and not at all clean', has a 'shabby luxury' and a broken pane of glass (p. 672). There is no chance of his acting as a responsible parent: 'In this family we are all children, and I am the youngest' (p. 676). His sons have run away from home. Equally, he makes only the most superficial use of religious and moral concepts: 'our common brotherhood' becomes the basis of his appeal to a baker complaining of how the family have worn out some armchairs he lent them to stop getting in the way of Skimpole 'contemplating Nature' (p. 679).

Skimpole gets away with this type of conduct precisely because there is no shared set of moral values in this society; the likes of Turveydrop and he make each other possible by expanding the notion of what is morally permissible and tolerated in the world of the novel. Furthermore, Skimpole exemplifies that even if there is a norm in any area of life, it is people who already come close to the norm who will be made to conform with it; someone who extravagantly departs from that norm is somehow allowed to get away with it. In addition, he disarms criticism and disapproval by being open about being a parasite. He has confidence enough to show 'candour' (p. 90) in describing himself as living off Jarndyce with 'neither trouble, cost, nor responsibility' (p. 91). He wins people over by being constantly charming and witty. With a butcher dissatisfied with his only meaning to pay his bill, Skimpole is ready with his riposte when the butcher declares 'I wish I had meant the lamb as you mean the money' (p. 240):

> How could that be? It was impossible. You *had* got the lamb and I have *not* got the money. You couldn't really mean the lamb without sending it in, whereas I can, and do, really mean the money, without paying it! (p. 241)

It is the sort of argument that reflects Skimpole's intelligence, an intelligence being misused, since it does not serve society (Skimpole is a trained doctor) but merely serves his self-indulgence. Nevertheless, these qualities enable him to operate a kind of sleight of hand. His 'helpless kind of candour ... lighthearted manner in which he was amused by his innocence, the fantastic way in which he took himself under his own protection and argued about that curious person ... the delightful ease of everything he said' (p. 675) all make it seem to Esther when in his presence 'unlikely ... that he could design, conceal or influence anything' (pp. 675–6); but when not under his spell and able to look at things coolly, Esther thinks the reverse. In so far as he depends on John Jarndyce to be his benefactor and thus support this approach to life, the secret lies in Jarndyce finding the society he lives in unbearable. He looks for escapes from its horrors, which he finds partly in the Bleak House Esther creates, but also in Skimpole. He sees in Skimpole 'one perfectly undesigning and candid man, among many opposites' (p. 239). After a grim visit to see the Necketts, Esther relates, 'he was such a mirthful child by the side of the graver childhood we had seen, that he made my Guardian smile' (p. 254). He sees Skimpole's function in Rick's life in similar terms: 'Such an unworldly, uncalculating, gossamer creature, is a relief to him, and an amusement' (p. 671). Jarndyce needs to believe that Skimpole stands aside from the corruption of society, so that in the face of the fact of Skimpole having been paid to introduce Rick to Vholes, Jarndyce asserts, 'There is nothing mercenary in that, with him' (p. 671). Jarndyce wills Skimpole really to be the man he constantly presents himself as.

The shocking reality of Skimpole's nature, however, is revealed when he betrays Jo to Bucket for money. Skimpole is a man who enjoys (if only in a dabbling way) the higher fruits of civilisation in the shape of art and music; but he does nothing to help establish that civilisation.

Sir Leicester Dedlock's aristocratic code of values is given justice, despite Dickens's lack of sympathy with the aristocracy, for the virtues it has. He is 'honourable', 'truthful', 'most polite on every occasion to my Lady' and shows 'gallantry' to her (p. 22). He is 'a kind and generous man' to his cousins (p. 447), a believer in family. As his moral values are tested when his wife's past catches up with her and she flees, we are told that he 'has never had a selfish thought' in connection with her, and that as scandal looms, he speaks of her with 'compassion rather than reproach' (p. 838). As the full truth emerges, he shows loyalty and forgiveness, declaring 'I am on unaltered terms with her' (p. 895). He admirably lives up to his own values:

> His noble earnestness, his fidelity, his gallant shielding of her, his generous conquest of his own wrong and his own pride for her sake, are simply honorable, manly and true. (p. 895)

Sir Leicester has a number of flaws – he is also 'obstinate', 'intensely prejudiced' and 'perfectly unreasonable' (p. 22) – but there is real moral virtue in him. However, his old-world values are quite inadequate in the modern world. He lives sincerely by them, but he is a fossil, remarkably out of touch with the world around him. He correctly feels his position in society is under threat, which he expresses in terms of a fear of Wat Tyler. In reality, he should be frightened not of Wat, but of Watt, both James Watt and Mrs Rouncewell's grandson who is named after him, each representative of the thrusting engineers and entrepreneurs whose rising influence as the Industrial Revolution developed led eventually to a seizure of the strings of power from the old aristocratic ruling class. By the time that Dickens wrote *Bleak House* the 1832 Reform Act and the repeal of the Corn Laws had made this movement of the centres of power a reality. There has been some dispute about when exactly the novel is meant to be set.[6] To the extent that we can rely on it, Esther tells us at the end of her narrative that seven years have passed since the events she has been describing, thus placing the action of the novel after the Reform Act but possibly before the repeal of the Corn Laws. Sir Leicester is aware that developments are going on – he repeats, in shock, to Volumnia that 'the opening of floodgates and the uprooting of distinctions' is taking place, with the entry of a Rouncewell into Parliament, but he seems incapable of comprehending these events. He barely knows what Rouncewell is – 'He is called, I believe, an "Ironmaster",' he declares with 'doubt ... not ... sure but that he is called a Lead-mistress or that the right word may be some other word of some other relationship to some other metal' (p. 450) – let alone comprehending the nature of the threat Rouncewell's class represents. Later on, he has apparently even forgotten the proper term for Rouncewell's job and refers to him as 'the iron gentleman' (p. 739). While Sir Leicester is all unawares, the modern world is creeping up on him:

> Railroads shall soon traverse all this country, ... as yet, such things are non-existent in these parts, though not wholly unexpected. Preparations are afoot, measurements are made, ground is staked out. (p. 839)

In a world of bustle and turmoil, 'busy times, when so many great undertakings are in progress' (p. 451) as Rouncewell puts it, Sir Leicester's domain, one where 'there is no hurry', stands in a contrast that he is proud of and 'content enough' with (p. 451); he is simply blinkered as to what is happening around him. He is comforted to find the morally reprehensible Skimpole is 'A perfectly idle man. A mere amateur' (p. 682). It consoles him to find others like himself; it reassures him, wrongly, that his way of life is not dying.

Sir Leicester and his values belong to an outmoded, superseded world, and whatever moral worth gallantry and chivalry may have had, they are of little use to meet the ethical demands of modern society. Both he and his values are redundant; he represents a strand in English society that has reached the end of the line. It is only too symbolic that he has no offspring.

However, worse than this, he is morally blinkered, sympathising only with members of his own class and not relating to his fellow human beings more generally Though a religious man after his own fashion, his religion is one that has been remade according to his class outlook: during a church service, he throughout looks upon the congregation 'as if he were a considerable landed proprietor in Heaven', an attitude Boythorn asserts Sir Leicester has inherited from his ancestors (p. 293). Safe in these attitudes of superiority, he ignores the need for universal love which his religion preaches. Notably, his kindness is directed only to those of his family and class. With his class-bound attitudes, he makes the rest of society abstract and objectifies others as merely the enemy ('Wat'), rather than his fellow human beings, and the Christian love and brotherhood he should be showing them goes by the board. But in the modern world, there is a need for Christian conduct to have not just a personal but a social dimension.

In a society in which there is no accepted moral code, it is not just the vulnerable – the likes of Jo, the Bagnets, George, Phil Squod – who have reason to feel insecure. Krook, for instance, will not ask anyone to teach him to read, because he might end up 'taught wrong'; the only person he trusts is 'my own self' (p. 237); and, as D.A. Miller points out, Guppy is paranoid.[7] Not all the characters, of course, are living by *ad hoc* moral codes. Some, as we shall see below, live by the Christian code of ethics; but so alien is this to the society presented in *Bleak House*, that when Mr Snagsby develops, out of compassion and love for his fellow human beings, the habit of giving money to the desperately poor Jo, Mrs Snagsby suspects his motive to be that Jo is his illegitimate son.[8]

How to measure the seriousness of the inadequacy of this morally chaotic, law-based attempt at civilisation? Dickens applies his usual criterion, of looking at how it treats its most vulnerable. When he does, he sees suffering and cause for concern in the three areas he had been identifying from the start of his career.

III

In *Bleak House* there is a perfect coincidence of narrative, emotional and thematic climaxes with the scene depicting the death of Jo the crossing sweeper at the end of Chapter 47. Allan Woodcourt is tending to Jo:

> 'Jo, can you say what I say?'
> 'I'll say anythink as you say, sir, for I know it's good.'
> 'OUR FATHER.'
> 'Our Father! –yes, that's wery good, sir.' (p. 734)

The opening phrase of the Lord's Prayer causes Jo to repeat the words as an exclamation of surprise. The new concept which prompts him to declare that the words are 'wery good' is that he – who told Guster that he 'never know'd nothink about' his parents (p. 416), informed the inquest on Nemo that he had 'No father, no mother, no friends' (p. 177), has been left with the impression that he belongs nowhere and to no-one, 'hustled, jostled and moved on' and left to feel that 'I have no business, here, or there, or anywhere' (p. 257), and has no concept of home ('What's home?' (p. 177)) – discovers that he does belong somewhere and is a member of a family after all. As the phrase conveys, he has a parent, who is the Father of us all. This, of course, is no sentimental suggestion here. For if God is the Father of all of us, we are all brothers and sisters. Yet there has been a singular lack of a sense of brotherhood in the way the world has treated Jo: hence the narrator's indictment of the whole of his society, from the Queen down, in the final paragraph of the chapter.

In this society not guided by the concept of the brotherhood of man, Jo has suffered in all three of the ways that we have discussed earlier Dickens saw as the result of the absence of Christian values in his society. The boy has been through a good deal of immediate physical suffering. We see him early on working on a 'wretched evening' in the dark and drizzle (p. 259) and walking on 'bare feet' over 'hard stones' (p. 261). He is afflicted with 'homely parasites' and 'homely sores' (p. 724), and a prey to what he calls 'starwation' (p. 725), and we see him in the course of the novel suffer from and somehow survive a disease often suggested to be smallpox. Second, Dickens places heavy emphasis on how Jo's humanity has been diminished or never really fully developed. He has scarcely the amount of identity any human being has: he has no known surname, and the two bare letters of his name are 'long enough for him' (p. 177). He perceives himself as a 'creature', 'scarcely human', that he 'belong[s]' to 'the horses, dogs and cattle' and not to 'the superior beings in my shape, whose delicacy I offend' (p. 258). The narrator classes him with 'the other lower animals' (p. 258). Jo and a dog both listen to some music with an equally limited, Caliban-like reaction, 'probably with much the same amount of animal satisfaction' (p. 259). At the end of his life, ill and hounded, he looks 'anxiously about him in all directions as he eats and drinks, like a scared animal' (p. 719). He is aware of himself as 'not of the same place in creation' as other people, 'neither of the beasts nor of humanity' (p. 724). Looking for a refuge for the boy, Woodcourt notes how 'this creature in human form' is 'more difficult to dispose of than an unowned dog' (p. 719).

Third, Jo is a 'savage', 'in soul a heathen', whose 'native ignorance … sinks his immortal nature lower than the beasts that perish' (p. 724). He just about knows that it is 'wicked' to lie, but 'Can't exactly say what'll be done to him arter he's dead if he tells a lie to the gentlemen' in court, having only a hazy notion that 'it'll be something wery bad to punish him' (p. 177). Seeing people go to church merely leads him to speculate 'what does it all mean' (p. 257). The cross on the top of St Paul's Cathedral he comprehends as 'the crowning confusion of the great, confused city' rather than as a 'sacred emblem' (p. 315). It is, of course, his spiritual welfare that Woodcourt is desperately, if inadequately, trying to minister to in teaching him the Lord's Prayer as he dies.

The very name of the place Jo comes from, Tom-all-Alone's, reflects the lack of brotherhood there: everyone is 'all alone'. The lack of any sense of Christian brotherhood towards its inhabitants is reflected in the way it is allowed to exist 'unventilated' and 'undrained' (p. 358). Nobody cares about this 'ruinous place' (p. 256) and the people who live there. The result is that the inhabitants live on a subhuman level. The imagery the writer uses is of the animal world: there is 'a swarm of misery' here. The people living in the buildings are compared to the 'vermin parasites' that afflict humans: 'so, these ruined shelters have bred a crowd of foul existence that crawls in and out of gaps in walls and boards; and coils itself to sleep, in maggot numbers' (pp. 256–7). Inspector Bucket is later to remark that people are dying from fever there ' like sheep with the rot' (p. 358) and he goes to see a landlady there whose room is described as 'a dog hutch' (p. 359).

It is a place of spiritual oblivion. Mr Snagsby feels that he is going into Hell as he approaches it, descending ever more 'into the infernal gulf' (p. 358), and the people there are likened to 'a concourse of imprisoned demons' (p. 362). Its alienation from anything remotely spiritual is reflected in the way that not even Christian names ('any Christian sign' (p. 358)) are used there.

The inhabitants are not, of course, naturally an inferior order of beings – indeed Mr Snagsby is 'strangely reminded' of the baby Jesus when he sees one of the brickmakers' new-born children (p. 360) – but have been made so, through a lack of care from their Christian brothers and sisters. Like Jo, the brickmakers are subject to a lot of immediate suffering. We see them living in a 'damp offensive room' (p. 130). The water they have access to smells and is dirty and 'unwholesome' (p. 132). Five of their children have died in this unhealthy environment (p. 137) and another one dies during the visit of Esther and Ada with Mrs Pardiggle. Forced to live like this, they have become brutalised and dehumanised. The man of the house speaks roughly and with a coarse sarcasm to his middle-class visitors, asking if there are any more yet to enter 'Because I thought there weren't enough of you, perhaps?' (p. 130), and he later bluntly remarks that 'So long as you goes now ... you may do what you like' (p. 133). Lack of good manners, however, is the least of it. Jenny is beaten by her husband – she has a 'bruised eye' (p. 130) and her husband openly declares 'I giv' it her' (p. 132) – and her friend's face and arms have 'the marks of ill-usage' (p. 134). At one point, in front of Esther, the husband 'openly kicked at her foot with his heavy boot' (p. 877). The women themselves are 'coarse and shabby and beaten' and Jenny's friend has 'no kind of grace about her' – except 'the grace of sympathy' (p. 134); somehow in this brutalising environment they still preserve some humanity, if in a paradoxical way: 'the heart of each to each was softened by the hard trials of their lives' (p. 135).

For all the attentions of Mrs Pardiggle, their spiritual state gives cause for concern: the man declares 'Don't I never mean for to go to church? No, I don't never mean for to go to church'; he claims he wouldn't be welcome or 'expected' there, where people are 'too genteel for me' (p. 132).

On the one hand, society is permeated with moral codes that are unequal to the task of stopping the injustices and suffering only too evident all around, and on the other, the sense of brotherhood so desperately needed is missing. Where is Christianity in this world? It is, of course, present in a number of ways in the novel; but it is having little success in solving society's problems and establishing Christian love and brotherhood as the basis of society because its proclaimed adherents, no matter how zealous, have wrong priorities. They are distracted from an emphasis on Christian morality applied socially by other religious concerns, or by their own human flaws. In the process, Christianity is being betrayed and the wrongs of society are not cured.

Religion is in the proximity of those most in need, but it does not reach them. Jo at one point contemplates St Paul's but it does not take him under its wing; indeed, he is in ignorance of what it represents and it merely seems utterly remote from him:

> And there he sits, munching and gnawing, and looking up at the great Cross on the summit of St. Paul's Cathedral, glittering above a red and violet-tinted cloud of smoke. From the boy's face one might suppose that sacred emblem to be, in his eyes, the crowning confusion of the great, confused city; so golden, so high up, so far out of his reach (p. 315)

He slips through the fingers of organised religion because its priorities are not practical Christian love and caring to those in immediate need, but other things. One day he breakfasts on the doorstep of 'the Society for the Propagation of the Gospel in Foreign Parts' (p. 258), which does not reach out to him because its focus is on abroad. He hence goes away quite ignorant of the very Gospel it has been set up to spread: 'He admires the size of the edifice, and wonders, what it's all about' (p. 258). Those who have visited Tom-all-Alone's on missionary duty have neither enlightened Jo about Christianity nor have they shown any Christian love towards him. They have not only talked in too elevated a way for him to understand, but have been preoccupied with arcane denominational or theological disputes:

> Different times, there wos other genlmen come down Tom-all-Alone's a prayin, but they all mostly sed as t'other wuns prayed wrong, and all mostly seemed to be talking to their selves, or a passing blame on the t'others, and not a talkin to us. (p. 733)

There is a lot of frantic religious activity going on in the world of the novel, but much of it is completely irrelevant to the needs of society. John Jarndyce receives a constant stream of letters from people working on committees 'in the most impassioned manner' and collecting subscriptions 'with a vehemence quite extraordinary' (p. 123); but their efforts are devoted to irrelevant projects such as the aim to establish 'the Sisterhood of Medieval Marys' (p. 123), the need for which is evidently driven by an impulse to work out the implications of Puseyite ideas rather than to do any immediate good.

None of Dickens's concerns about the less fortunate in society are being addressed through the activities of the religiously engaged that he portrays. The Gospel is not being preached effectively, and so their spiritual welfare is not attended to. Without practical Christian love being shown to them, their immediate suffering is not being relieved and their dehumanisation not prevented or remedied. In some highly critical, merciless and quietly angry portraits, he depicts those claiming to do the work of Christ but who squander their opportunities.

A failure to address the spiritual and physical welfare of the likes of Jo lies at the heart of Dickens's criticism of Mrs Jellyby and her ilk, engrossed in the predicament of people far away when there is dire need immediately at hand. Jo is not a figure able to be romanticised and sentimentalised by being remote; his is need in all its ugly and unappealing reality, a true challenge to Christian love and commitment:

> He is not one of Mrs Pardiggle's Tockahoopo Indians; he is not one of Mrs Jellyby's lambs, being wholly unconnected with Borrioboola-Gha; he is not softened by distance and unfamiliarity; he is not a genuine foreign-grown savage; he is the ordinary home made article. Dirty, ugly, disagreeable to all the senses. (p. 724)

He resembles those Mrs Jellyby concentrates on solely in that he is 'in soul a heathen', one whose ignorance 'sinks his immortal nature lower than the beasts that perish' (p. 724). If his spiritual welfare needs attention, so does his immediate physical suffering, for he is covered in 'filth', plagued by 'parasites' and 'sores', and wearing 'rags' (p. 724). That the Mrs Jellybys of society should ignore him and prefer to find some more glamorous object for their benevolence is an outrage.

Working, ironically, from an uncivilised society while aiming to bring civilisation to Africa, Mrs Jellyby may proclaim 'the Brotherhood of Humanity' (p. 58), but she does not apply the principle to those immediately around her; purporting to be tending to the needs of her wider human family, though as we have seen, neglecting it in the very city where she lives, she fails to care for her own immediate family. A sign of how wrongly she is going about things is that she provokes her family towards breaking the 5th Commandment. When Caddy Jellyby describes her mother and Mr Quale as 'ASSES', Esther is very 'shocked', as Caddy herself realises, and reminds her of 'Your duty as a child'. Caddy remains unrepentant: 'where's Ma's duty as a parent?' (p. 65).

Mrs Pardiggle is another person whose misguided conduct causes less religious obedience and commitment. Her son Egbert is also provoked into breaking the 5th Commandment, using, as Esther again points out, language of 'great impropriety ... especially in connexion with his parent' (p. 129). She mistakes form for substance in forcing her son to give his pocket money to good causes. What she thinks is an indefatigability to be proud of in her religious mission – 'You can't tire me, good people ... I enjoy hard work, and the harder you make mine, the better I like it' (p. 132) – in fact is counterproductive, alienating from religion those with whom she is being overbearing. Driven by vanity and egotism, her mission is a form of pride and self-assertion. Her work is all about her, despite her thinking otherwise, an indulgence in the pleasure of the forceful exertion of her will, rather than being motivated by the love of God and of other people. In truth, she is contravening Christian principle in treating other people as a means (to her self-gratification) rather than an end; it is another form of exploitation in a society ever ready to prey on people in a host of ways. With her insensitive, Lady Bountiful ways, far from fighting people's antipathy to religion, she is the cause of it. She insults the brickmaker by giving him a tract that was 'fit for a babby', and her 'forcible composure' as he expresses his views is, Esther opines, 'calculated to increase his antagonism' (p. 132). The element of coercion, serving her drive for self-fulfilment, in her conduct – she pulls out 'a good book, as if it were a constable's staff and took the whole family into custody' (p. 132) – is quite inappropriate, but she seems blind to the alienating effect she is having in her attempts to convert. The things she says and reads are 'ill chosen' (p. 133) and the tracts she distributes are unreadable; Jarndyce doubts that even Robinson Crusoe, desperate for some reading matter, could have got through one. The results would have been the same even if she had done these things, as she does not, 'ever so modestly and with ever so much tact' (p. 133). Inappropriate material makes her visits pointless and her bull-headed approach only provokes the brickmaker into emphasising how irreligious he remains, boasting of drinking, hitting his wife and not going to church. She is perceived as a mere busybody, stimulating comments about 'gentlefolks minding their own business' (p. 130).

Jesus enjoined people to do good by stealth, but Mrs Pardiggle fails to follow this rule in two ways. Even before she has met her in person, Esther correctly suspects that Mrs Pardiggle will be one of those 'charitable people' who 'did a little and made a great deal of noise' (p. 124). Second, in the process, she does very little good. Her approach is cast into relief by the much more appropriate and effective loving approach of Esther and Ada, who attempt to offer Christian comfort. Having noticed, as Mrs Pardiggle did not, the distress of the brickmaker's wife with her baby, they show genuine concern and compassion on witnessing the baby's death. Ada is 'so sorry' for the child and its mother; they try to give some practical help in tending to the dead child; and 'We tried to comfort the mother and we whispered to her what Our Saviour said of children' (p. 134).

If Mrs Pardiggle was at least aware of those suffering around her, even if her efforts were misjudged, Mr Chadband comes even more directly into contact with those in need of Christian love, for he meets bottom-of-the-heap Jo. He is help, though, neither to Jo's spiritual nor physical life, all the more deplorably in that he is well aware that Jo is 'devoid' of the things he needs both material and spiritual: 'devoid of parents, devoid of relations, devoid of flocks and herds, devoid of gold, of silver and of precious stones' but also 'devoid of the light that shines in upon some of us ... the light of Terewth' (p. 411). As these lines show, though, Mr Chadband too is an egotist, in love with his own grandiloquence and oratorical skills, and given to rolling, sonorous empty phrases whose meaning may well go over the heads of his listeners. Inappropriate language again hinders any effective impact his work might have:

> Though it may be, Jo, that there is a history so interesting and affecting even to minds as near the brutes as thine, recording deeds done on this earth for common men, that if the Chadbands, removing their own persons from the light, would but show it thee in simple reverence, would but leave it unimproved, would but regard it as eloquent enough without their modest aid – it might hold thee awake, and thou might learn from it yet! (p. 415)

Though Chadband sees Jo, a 'young Heathen', as a challenge, someone 'to wrestle, and to combat, and to struggle and conquer, for his sake' (p. 414), all he achieves is to send Jo to sleep. In his empty grandiloquence and lack of love, he exemplifies St Paul's remark that 'though I speak with the tongues of men and of angels, and have not charity, I am become a sounding brass, or a tinkling cymbal' (1 Corinthians 13:1). Once again, there is a contrast exemplifying the loving approach Jo needs when the 'charitable Guster' shares her supper with him, takes an interest in him, enquiring about his parents, and sympathetically pats him on the shoulder, 'the first time in his life that any decent hand has been so laid upon him' (p. 416), and when Mr Snagsby gives him the practical help of half a crown.

These ostensibly religiously concerned people, then, fail in the most important mission of all, genuinely to tend to the physical and spiritual needs of the brothers and sisters the Father of us all created. The net result of a society in which values are wrong-headed and corrupt, moral codes inadequate and Christianity traduced is that the whole of society is a Bleak House. The whole of humanity may be one big family, but the environment in which they live is no more than a 'house'; there is none of the closeness, love and mutual support to transform it into a 'home'. As such, it is a comfortless place that is indeed 'bleak'.

In the face of this, what is to be the remedy? What can be the true basis of civilisation?

IV

St Albans is named after the first English Christian martyr, and at the nearby Bleak House we find an environment and people with the sort of dedication to Christianity that St Alban took to the ultimate degree, and who suggest a route to an alternative England to the one portrayed in the novel. The concept of human beings as a family is there applied domestically, among a group of people only distantly and tenuously related, setting a model for the wider social application of the same concept.

Crucial to this is Esther: she promotes the idea of family and domestic togetherness that we have seen is so downgraded or ignored by many of the characters in the novel. Kevin Mc Laughlin notes that Esther's 'position of housekeeper or governess of Bleak House' is a 'highly ambiguous' one in that 'she is neither wife, nor daughter, nor merely hired hand'.[9] Furthermore the people she binds into a family there are essentially strangers. Since John Jarndyce is related to Lady Dedlock, he is also related to Lady Dedlock's daughter, but when Esther moves into Bleak House she is certainly not aware of this. Jarndyce is also Ada and Richard's 'cousin, several times removed' (p. 19). Basically strangers then, under the care of 'Dame Durden', despite this, they become a family. Bleak House significantly fell into disrepair, and became 'bleak, indeed' when Tom Jarndyce became so tangled up in the court case that he neglected it and it became an analogue of his decay. As John Jarndyce remarks,

> When I brought what remained of him home here, the brains seemed to, me to have been blown out of the house too; it was so shattered and ruined. (p. 119)

If it thus symbolised the effects of a callous, corrupt society, Esther embodies the opposite set of values. Through her efforts, as barely related strangers become a family, the house stops being bleak and becomes a home. At the end of the novel the house she and Woodcourt are to live in is also named Bleak House, as a kind of omen of the transformative effect she is to have there. A pointer to the religious significance of the family to the Victorians is to be found in the views of F.D. Maurice: 'Signs or foretastes of the unity of humanity may be recognised, according to Maurice, in the divine institutions of the family and the nation'[10] The attitude of loving care for one's family sets the pattern for behaviour on the larger scale towards one's brothers and sisters in the human family created by our common Father. Bleak House becomes a kind of microcosm of the kind of harmonious, close and mutually supportive environment that society as a whole needs to become. A sense of family, and of everyone as family, lies as the basis for the remedy of society as it does for the remedy of one house. And from this house, Esther brings her values to bear in the wider world too. Wherever she goes, she shows a loving concern for others, whether it be the Jellyby family, the brickmakers or Jo. Her wish is that 'I might always be so blest and happy as to be useful to someone' (p. 385). Bleak House becomes an oasis of Christian values in a corrupt society.

Bleak House's owner, John Jarndyce, facilitates this transformation; he is a kindred spirit believing in and propagating the same Christian values. He has followed the Biblical injunction to do good by stealth. Early on in the novel, Esther discovers that he has long been 'my benefactor and sole earthly dependence through so many years' (p. 81); but he is a man who 'could never bear acknowledgments for any kindness he performed' (p. 81). Throughout his estrangement from Rick, he practises forbearance and forgiveness: he shows 'gentleness and consideration' to 'poor Rick' (p. 917). He frequently alludes to the Bible. The Christian-spirited landlady who has let the Neckett family off their rent is specifically appreciated as such by Jarndyce:

> 'It's not much to forgive 'em the rent, sir.' She said; 'who could take it from them!'
>
> 'Well, well!' said my Guardian to us two. 'It is enough that the time will come when this good woman will find that it *was* much, and that forasmuch as she did it unto the least of these – ! (p. 247)

Elsewhere, he remarks that, 'I think it must be somewhere written that the virtues of the mothers shall, occasionally, be visited on the children, as well as the sins of the fathers' (p. 273). He became concerned for Esther when he realised that she was being brought up suffering under a 'distorted religion' (p. 276); in response, he has made himself into 'a Father to her' (p. 277). He thus drew on the concept of family to counter the effects of misguided religion. He too stands in contrast to his society: Esther remarks at one point that, 'A more complete contrast than my guardian and Mr Vholes, I suppose there could not be' (p. 695).

On a social scale, there are people who serve God in the true spirit of Christianity, acting from a sense of love and brotherhood and a sense that the whole of humanity is one family. We see a dramatic demonstration of such in the actions of Allan Woodcourt. In a scene that reflects *par excellence* Dickens's Christian social values, wandering Tom-All-Alone's at night, Woodcourt ministers, in his capacity as a doctor, to the needs of those he encounters, including those given ineffective attention by the likes of Mrs Pardiggle and Mr Chadband. He exemplifies Christian love in practical action. Early on, we hear about his attitude to medicine in his 'strong interest in all that it can do'. His commitment involves a 'reward' that is not financial, for it will bring 'a very little money'. His sense of serving others will make him persevere against the intransigence of the world with all the 'considerable endurance and disappointment' involved (p. 267). His job brings him 'very little ... in money', but he practises it 'night and day, at the service of numbers of poor people' (p. 277). In a climate in which Tom-all-Alone's reflects the general callousness of society, liable to 'be reclaimed according to somebody's theory but nobody's practice' (p. 710), Woodcourt wanders round it with 'compassionate interest' (p. 711) and administers practical help. He encounters the brickmaker's wife, and puts a dressing on her bruised and wounded forehead, speaking to her in a gentle and tactful manner, 'A habit in him of speaking to the poor ... avoiding patronage or condescension, or childishness' (p. 711). Later he encounters

Jo, and takes him under his wing, promising to 'find you a better place than this to lie down and hide in' (p. 718). As the two walk along, Dickens symbolically mentions that along with the streets, the high church spires are now 'so near and clear in the morning light' (p. 719).

Woodcourt continues to show kindness to Jo, buying him breakfast though Jo is steeply declining towards death and 'even hunger has abandoned him' (p. 719). Woodcourt cares for him to the end, ultimately desperately and inadequately trying to teach him the Lord's Prayer. Woodcourt shows a great deal of Christian love throughout here; he also incidentally displays Christian forgiveness, as he is well aware that it was Jo who inadvertently infected Woodcourt's beloved, Esther, with the severe disfigurement to which that led. But at the end, at least, Jo ends up in truly Christian hands. George compassionately offers Jo free accommodation and plans to spend money on getting him a bath and new clothes. As Jo stands in the shooting gallery, he is aware that they know 'what he has caused' and that they are resisting an impulse to 'shrink' from him as a result (p. 724). George is also devoted to Esther – he says that 'I would willingly be knocked on the head at any time' to please her (p. 723) – and is worried as to whether Jo is still infected, because 'we have had enough of that' (p. 723). Esther's Christian love for the boy, though, inspires them to help him rather than shun him. As George remarks:

> 'It seemed to me probable that you might take more than a common interest in this poor creature, because Miss Summerson had taken that unfortunate interest in him. 'Tis *my* case, sir, I assure you.'
>
> 'And mine, Mr George.' (p. 726)

Love breeds love: this is how Christianity works to bring about a better world. As Jo dies, these two are joined by Mr Snagsby, to form a triumvirate of true Christian men tending to a boy society has callously brought to a premature death. Woodcourt's commitment to serving the poor abides: Jarndyce brings to his attention an upcoming vacancy to be 'a medical attendant for the poor' (p. 919), appealing as 'a way of usefulness and good service' (p. 920), done as valuable in itself and not with any ulterior motive, it 'leading to no other' level in society (p. 920). It is this job that Woodcourt, with Esther by his side as his wife, both living at the service of others, commits himself to. Esther records at the end of the book that every day, her husband 'has alleviated pain, and soothed some fellow-creature in the time of need' (p. 988), facilitated by a wife whose support of her husband is crucial to his ability to serve others ('everything I do in life I do for his sake' (p. 989)), causing both of them to be praised and respected in their community.

Esther and Woodcourt have not transformed society by the end of the novel with their Christian attitudes and service. What they have done, is make a start towards the amelioration and civilising of society; everyone else needs to follow suit.

6

'Oh my Friends and Brothers': Industrialism and Trade Unionism in *Hard Times*

Bleak House depicts a society that lives under the legacy of the past. Individual lives are shaped by the past in a number of ways. As regards the central characters, the Jarndyce versus Jarndyce case is an inherited incubus on the life of John Jarndyce; he wants nothing to do with it because of the way it destroyed his brother, in a course of events over before the novel begins. This legacy of the past comes to obsess and destroy Richard Carstone. Esther grows up in the dark shadow of the illegitimacy of her birth. Lady Dedlock is eventually destroyed when her past catches up with her. The lesser characters also live with inheritances from the past. Mr Turveydrop lives his life in the present inspired by a way of life that belongs to the past. The Bayham Badgers conduct their marriage in the shadow of Mrs Bayham Badger's two previous marriages. Krook's natural habitat is among 'old parchementses and papers' and this is where he feels comfortable: 'I have a liking for rust and must and cobwebs' (p. 70).[1]

More than this, though, the social structure and institutions of this society are inherited from the past, and operate by reference to the past. Chancery 'knows no wisdom but in precedent' (p. 630); as Nicola Bradbury notes, it was governed by 'Equity, shaped by legal precedents. Thus both the legal matters and proceedings of Chancery were inherently backward-looking'.[2] As the novel turns from Chancery to the world of the aristocracy, the narrator emphasises that 'Both the world of fashion and the court of Chancery are things of precedent and usage' (p. 20). The aristocratic world, as represented by Sir Leicester Dedlock, has its roots in the past. Sir Leicester's family is 'as old as the hills' (p. 21); his home has an inheritance from the distant past, as reflected in 'the broad, flagged pavement, called, from old time, the Ghost's Walk' (p. 21). In the estate church, 'there is a general smell and taste as of ancient Dedlocks in their graves' (p. 21). Very little is new at Chesney Wold; even the housekeeper, Mrs Rouncewell, has been there for fifty years; and her long service is described as 'only ... fifty years' (p. 106). To belong to as distant a part of the past as possible is a virtue at Chesney Wold. Even the threats to his position Sir Leicester perceives are from the past: he is haunted by the figure of Wat Tyler, from five centuries previously.

Dickens depicts this society not fondly but critically, of course. He had no nostalgia for the past, and believed in progress. His 1841 poem, 'The Fine Old English Gentleman', for instance, satirises those who feel nostalgia for

> the fine old English Tory times;
> Soon may they come again (lines 5–6)[3]

These were times when

> The good old laws were garnished well with gibbets, whips and chains,
> With fine old English penalties, and fine old English pains (lines 7–8).[4]
>
> The good old days for cutting throats that cried out in their need
> The good old times for hunting men who held their fathers' creed (lines 19–20).[5]

Significantly, his heroine is uninterested in getting bogged down in the past: despite 'shadowy speculations' about 'what knowledge Mr Jarndyce had of my earliest history', Esther decides not 'to muse over bygones, but to act with a cheerful spirit and a grateful heart' (p. 103). When Jarndyce subsequently asks her if she wants to know anything about herself along these lines she is uninterested: 'I am quite sure that if there were anything I ought to know, or had any need to know, I should not have to ask you to tell it to me' (p. 122). This inherited society is presented as one as stagnated as the name 'Dedlock' implies, and thus in the decay that references throughout the novel imply is its condition.[6]

We might expect *Hard Times* to present quite a different prospect, for in this novel, in depicting the industrial world, Dickens presents a brand new society, free from the inheritance of the past. Its being new, however, is no guarantee of its being better, and in fact Dickens presents it as no improvement on the old society it supersedes. If the world of *Bleak House* was a primitive or primeval one, that of *Hard Times* is no more civilised. The imagery, some of which is to become recurrent, of the detailed description of Coketown in Book 1 Chapter 5 is insistent:

> it was a town of unnatural red and black like the painted face of a savage. It was a town of machinery and tall chimneys, out of which interminable serpents of smoke trailed themselves for ever and ever, and never got uncoiled … the piston of the steam-engine worked monotonously up and down, like the head of an elephant in a state of melancholy madness. (p. 27)[7]

Savages, serpents, elephants: this is not civilisation; it is a jungle. The recurrent image that makes Coketown sound more attractive, that of its factories as 'Fairy palaces' is a bitterly ironic one, for it is the perception gained by 'the travellers by express-train' (p. 66), speeding through, not lingering in the town, not seeing the factories close up, and knowing little of conditions inside them.

The way this society treats its poor and vulnerable, furthermore, is reminiscent of the way they were treated in the old society depicted in *Bleak House*. The predicament of the poor has some familiar features. Once again, immediate suffering is part of their lives. Coketown is an environment of 'killing airs and gases' (p. 65), and these and poor living conditions had a deadly effect on Rachael's sister who, Stephen Blackpool relates, 'died, young and misshapen, awlung o' sickly air as had'n no need to be, and awlung o' working people's miserable homes' (p. 263). Work can easily be fatal in Coketown. Lack of safety measures means there is a danger in the factories of 'chopping people up with ... machinery' (p. 111); a coalmine like the Old Hell Shaft has, as Stephen again relates, 'cost ... hundreds and hundreds o'men's lives' and has been 'a pit that ha' been wi' the'Fire-damp crueller than battle' (p. 263). Lack of fencing round it when it is disused robs Stephen of his life when he falls down it.[8]

Furthermore, this society tends to dehumanise the ordinary people within it. When Louisa visits Stephen's home, it is the first time she has encountered a Coketown worker as an individual human being rather than as a mere unit of work; previously, she has only known of 'their existence by hundreds and by thousands ... what results in work a given number of them would produce, in a given space of time', and has perceived them as more like insects than human beings, 'crowds passing to and from their nests, like ants or beetles' (p. 155). Dickens comments on the way the workers are referred to as 'the Hands' as reflective of their being perceived as no more than creatures able to do manual work, rather than as fully fledged human beings, and whom some people would have preferred if they had been 'only hands, or, like the lower creatures of the seashore, only hands and stomachs' (p. 66). Some indeed succumb under the conditions of life which prevail in Coketown and are dehumanised as a result. Stephen's wife was once, as Stephen relates, 'a young lass – pretty enow – wi' good accounts of herseln'; but 'She went bad – soon. Not along of me' (p. 73). As Bounderby says, she 'took to drinking' and 'left off working' (p. 73). By the time we meet her in the novel, she has sunk into a subhuman state, is several times described as a 'creature' (e.g. p. 70) and as engaged in an animal-like 'stupid clawing of herself with her hand' (p. 70).

The spiritual welfare of the people of Coketown is also highlighted as a cause for concern. This is a town in which 'eighteen religious persuasions' have built chapels but where 'Who belonged to the eighteen denominations' remains a 'mystery' (p. 28). Whoever else it might be, 'the labouring people did not' (p. 28). The 'barbarous jangling of bells' does not summon them to church; instead, they are to be observed on their street corners 'where they lounged listlessly, gazing at all the church and chapel going, as at a thing with which they had no manner of concern'(p. 29). Stephen's wife again exemplifies the spiritual decline that can befall the inhabitants of Coketown: she is 'A creature ... foul to look at ... but so much fouler than that in her moral infamy' (p. 70).

If Stephen's wife was simply not strong enough to cope with the conditions of life in Coketown without effectively being destroyed as a person, she is not presented as an exceptional case. Stephen himself has not succumbed, but is portrayed as clinging on desperately and fragilely. He is forty at the time of the novel, but he 'looked older', because of his 'hard life' and people call him 'Old Stephen' (p. 66); his hair is 'iron-grey' (p. 66). Behind this is the strain of his 'hard life' (p. 66), which includes the burden of a wife destroyed by the system and the consequent lack of the comfort and sustenance of a 'home he might at that moment have been seeking with pleasure and pride' (p. 82) not available with her but that he might have had with Rachael. Weighed down by thoughts of 'the waste of the best part of his life', of the way his character is changing 'for the worse every day' and 'of the dreadful nature of his existence, bound hand and foot to a dead woman, and tormented by a demon in her shape' (p. 82), he comes to the very brink of spiritual corruption soon after when watching without intervening when his wife is about to drink poison. It is only prevented by the adventitious intervention of Rachael; as he aptly remarks, 'thou hast saved my soul alive' (p. 89).

What is the fundamental flaw in this new society that makes it replicate the shortcomings and flaws of the old society? Tackling the major crux of the novel will take us to the heart of the problem. At least since F.R. Leavis's important essay on the novel this has been Dickens's surprisingly hostile portrayal of the trade union; for as Leavis's comments, 'Dickens has no glimpse of the part to be played by Trade Unionism in bettering the conditions he deplored'.[9] In essence this is perhaps an argument from history. Unions were later to play a very important role in improving the lot of working people, and were not to be the mere instruments of demagogues for causing civil strife that seems to be Dickens's version of them. Furthermore, it is well known that while preparing to write the novel, Dickens travelled up to Preston in late January 1854[10] to see for himself the Preston Strike,[11] which had been going on for over three months. During his visit, he attended two union meetings, the regular Sunday meeting of delegates bringing the weekly contributions from other towns, and the weavers' regular Monday morning meeting,[12] afterwards witnessing the weekly payout.[13] It has often been pointed out, though, that the picture of Slackbridge and the United Aggregate Tribunal does not accurately reflect what is known about George Cowell and the activities of the Preston weavers' union;[14] even the account in the journalistic piece Dickens wrote about his visit to Preston, 'On Strike',[15] gives a very different, much more sympathetic picture than the hostile portrayal in *Hard Times*. How could Dickens apparently be so wrong about the nature and intentions of unions, especially after observing the Preston weavers' union at first hand?

The matter is more complicated than might be imagined. One of the bases on which it has been contended that Dickens deliberately falsified his own experience in creating his fictional union has been the character of George Cowell. For Cowell, a Methodist and teetotaller[16] who became pre-eminent among the union leaders in the Preston Strike, was upright, restrained and reasonable, and not at all of the same mettle as Dickens's Slackbridge. Initially Cowell had been antipathetic to the idea of striking.[17] In July 1853, strikes at two Preston mills were ended when Cowell persuaded the operatives to return to work and not long after he was associated with a view that 'extreme measures in the shape of a strike should not be resorted to'.[18] After the Masters' Association announcement on 15 September 1853 that a general lock-out would begin one month later, he urged the opening of negotiations so that a peaceful settlement could be reached.[19] His attitude during the strike itself remained conciliatory. In January 1854, he made a major concession in expressing a willingness that negotiations should proceed mill by mill, the masters holding discussions with their own employees rather than with the delegates' committee;[20] and at the very time of Dickens's visit to Preston, Cowell was declaring that the strike could be ended by a meeting of equal numbers of masters and operatives 'to discuss the question calmly with a view to an amicable settlement' or by submitting the matter to arbitration.[21] Even as antagonistic an observer as the industrialist Henry Ashworth was to acknowledge that, 'he may be pronounced a man who would do honour to a juster cause'.[22]

Cowell, however, seems to have played no prominent part at the Sunday delegates' meeting that Dickens attended, and may well not have been present;[23] certainly he was not present at the Monday meeting, for he was in London on that day attending the Society of Arts' conference on strikes.[24] Furthermore, the Sunday meeting was, as H.I. Dutton and J.E. King comment 'more than usually fractious',[25] full of what the *Preston Chronicle* called 'wordy wars'.[26] In the course of the meeting, Mortimer Grimshaw (Dickens's Gruffshaw in 'On Strike'), on whom Slackbridge seems to be based, 'poured out a volley of invective',[27] or in the words of the *Manchester Guardian* 'poured out the vials of his wrath upon the committee and the operatives' of Warrington.[28]

Grimshaw, prominent at both the Sunday and Monday meetings that Dickens attended (though his contribution to the latter meeting was probably after Dickens's departure), had something of the firebrand about him. Known as the 'Thunderer of Lancashire', Mortimer Grimshaw was a weaver who, by his own account, was blacklisted in every mill in Lancashire. He had been involved in earlier campaigning in the industrial field, both for the strengthening and full enforcement of the Factory Acts, and against the victimisation of political activists at a mill in Royton, where he had lived; and he had taken part in the 'Ten Per Cent' campaign from as early as March

1853 in Stockport.[29] At the end of the strike, Charles Hardwick recorded some impressions of Grimshaw in an article in *Eliza Cook's Journal*:

> He was well known by his white hat, which, I suppose, he wore after the fashion of Hunt and Cobbett, to indicate the depth of his 'Radical' propensities ... Mortimer Grimshaw advocates liberty to the oppressed 'factory slaves' with a dogmatical invective ... more worthy of a Russian despot than an English patriot. I do not assert that he is insincere ... He appears to me to be an enthusiast, and that the warmth of his feelings, when excited, overpowers his judgement.[30]

Henry Ashworth, as might be expected, gives a less sympathetic account:

> Of Mr Grimshaw, the less that is said the better. We have heard it alleged, that every wild and violent sentiment which was uttered during the Preston strike came from his lips. He was commonly introduced as the 'Thunderer of Lancashire'. In his speeches we find the perfection of mob oratory. 'He's a stunner,' exclaimed an old woman at the close of one of his perorations; to which an admiring operative who had heard her, replied, perhaps truthfully, – 'he's nowt else.'[31]

How Grimshaw earned his living was something of a mystery, and this gave rise to accusations that he was a 'self-interested professional agitator'.[32] He can thus be seen as a clear source for much of the character of Slackbridge; and to this extent, given the prominence of Grimshaw rather than Cowell at these meetings, Dickens's portrait might be said to be a reflection of what he saw.

Nevertheless, other strike leaders that Dickens observed were quite unlike Grimshaw. The chairman of the two meetings that Dickens attended, Kinder Smith, a man of similar ilk to Cowell, is described sympathetically as a man with 'a placid attentive face, keen eyes, a particularly composed manner, a quiet voice', who glances at other delegates 'earnestly' and 'Looks extremely sensible' ('On Strike', p. 206). His is a successfully restraining influence on wilder men: 'the persuasive right hand of the chairman falls gently on Gruffshaw's shoulder. Gruffshaw stops in full boil' (p. 207). The whole meeting, indeed, is commended for its 'quietness and order' (p. 205).

Such pieces of description also indicate that Dickens's perception of unions was not blinkered by the sort of prejudices that Humphrey House identifies as common at the time, such as that the 'leaders of such unions were bound to be demagogic frauds',[33] though such attitudes are not hard to find reflected in accounts of the Preston Strike. A letter in the *Preston Chronicle* of the weekend of Dickens's visit, for instance, refers to 'these paid demagogues' and 'the vagabond banditti styling themselves delegates, who, with the basest effrontery, are sucking to the very heart's-core the life's-blood of their deluded victims'.[34] In similar vein, Henry Ashworth writes of the workers 'ignorance', which makes them 'the more docile', for 'where they do not see clearly, they submit to be led'; and 'a mass of operatives of this character offers a fine field for the demagogue'.[35] Dickens, however, was hardly a natural ally of men like Henry Ashworth, and it is questionable whether their views would coincide very much. Indeed, as Patrick Brantlinger points out, Dickens scorns such attitudes through Stephen Blackpool's rejection of Bounderby's theory of 'mischievous strangers';[36] and the evidence of 'On Strike' is that Dickens sees the strikers and their union in a rather different light.

It is not, then, easy to explain Dickens's attitude to the unions on the basis of his visit to Preston; and perhaps an explanation is to be found rather in considering the broader background to the writing of the novel. For while 'On Strike' may be said to give an impressionistic account of the Preston Strike, it can be argued that *Hard Times* is also impressionistic – this time about the state of England – and that it is a novel to which Dickens's visit to Preston was in some ways incidental. It does not concern itself with a particular real-life union, let alone a particular strike (there is, of course, no strike in the novel); Dickens is concerned no more than in 'On Strike' with minutiae, but rather with a perception of a society that may be new, but is fundamentally flawed and diseased. Part of the context is that of the longstanding interest we have seen Dickens had in industrial matters, and conditions that had by this time spawned a number of 'Condition of England' novels. There are also, however, some specific features of the background to the novel that are particularly important to *Hard Times*.

The period of the Preston Strike was a time of considerable industrial unrest. Though none of them was epoch-making, strikes were rampant:

> In the spring of 1853 there developed throughout the country a movement for higher wages ... The Manchester brickmakers struck in January, followed in February by masons and joiners at Ashton, and by farm labourers near Salisbury. March saw strikes in several Liverpool crafts, in the Batley and Dewsbury woollen mills, and on the land in Oxfordshire. In April boys struck at a Liverpool engine works and a shipyard at Birkenhead, and strikes broke out among waggonwrights and bricklayers at South Shields, seamen at Ipswich, Liverpool shoemakers, brickmakers and joiners at Wigan, and the joiners of Sutherland and Hartlepool.[37]

Henry Ashworth recalled industrial unrest over wages running through 'the whole of 1852 and the first half of 1853', agitation which, he noted, 'was not confined to those northern districts, or indeed to any particular trade, but spread pretty equally throughout the kingdom':

> Commencing with those employed in the production of iron and coal, it passed through most of the building trades, affected the branches of

> industry which are connected with Nottingham and Leicester, and even extended to the porters and dock labourers of such towns as Liverpool, Bristol and Hull. In some places, as in Manchester and Liverpool, the police struck for an advance of wages ... Agricultural strikes were now heard of ... A rise of wages was also universal in the ship-yards of the Clyde and the Wear, the Mersey and the Thames.[38]

It is little wonder that an article that appeared in the same issue of the *London Illustrated News* as a piece on the Preston Strike adopted a tone intended to be reassuring. 'Sketches of Strikes and Riots in the Cotton Districts' sought to calm any anxieties the reader might have had about the spate of strikes by emphasising that strikes, far from being a worrying new phenomenon, pre-dated the Industrial Revolution:

> though most persons who have written of them date their commencement at the period when spinning mills arose – namely, between 1765 and 1769. Strikes were as frequent before the invention of the jenny in 1765 as since; but they affected fewer persons.[39]

It was in the context of a society in this state that Dickens came to write about the industrial world and to portray an England splitting into contentious factions willing to use their collective power to gain the ends of their members.[40]

Contemporary views of industrial relations, unions and strikes, furthermore, included certain elements somewhat uncommon in later views. 'On Strike' itself raises the issue of whether terms like 'Capital' and 'Labour' should be use in preference to 'employers' and 'employed' ('On Strike', p. 199) and the phenomenon of contemporary documents that sometimes use the one set of terms and sometimes the other indicates that this was a period of transition in the public's perception of the industrial world.[41] To use words such as 'Capital' and 'Labour' in connection with industrial relations is to see them from what may very broadly be called a political point of view and this is probably the most common view of industrial relations today. In the 1850s, however, many people's perspective on them was not fully politicised but rather, the evidence suggests, moral, and religious, possibly influenced by the political and religious campaigners we discussed in Chapter 2. It is necessary to go no further than 'On Strike' to find evidence of this. The placard transcribed by Dickens refers to

> This love of justice and hatred of wrong ... a noble feature in the character and disposition of the working man ... gives us hope that in the future, this world will become what its great architect intended, not a place of sorrow, toil, oppression and wrong, but the dwelling place and abode of peace, plenty, happiness and love, where avarice and all the evil passions engendered by the present system of fraud and injustice shall not have a place. (pp. 201–2)

The manufacturers, furthermore, are attacked for their contention that 'the *impartial* God intended that there should be a *partial* distribution of his blessings' (p. 202). Much Biblical or pseudo-Biblical phraseology and imagery – 'the fruitfulness of the soil', 'plant and reap all the grain', 'a mess of porridge' – is used, and the Biblical precept 'Those who will not work shall not eat' (p. 202) is cited. Soubriquets on a balance sheet include 'Bear ye one another's burthens' and 'We'll stand to our text, see that ye love one another' (p. 204). A hymn sung at the Monday meeting of the strikers is quoted:

> To thee, O God, thy children cry
> Thy needy creatures on Thee call
> ... no good thing hast thou denied;
> But men of wealth and men of power,
> Like locusts, all our gifts devour.

The hymn ends with an exhortation to 'ye sons of toil' to

> Demand your rights; let tyrants see
> You are resolved that you'll be free. (p. 209)

Many similar references may be cited. Around the time of Dickens's visit, a correspondent of the *Preston Pilot*, deploring 'these ruinous and devastating "strikes" which are the order of the day, and which rage like a pestilence around us', averred that 'In that blessed curse, –"By the sweat of thy brow thou shalt eat bread", we have politics in perfection'.[42] A letter to the *Preston Chronicle* refers to the strike as 'the present unfortunate, un-English, anti-Christian struggle'[43] and one to the *Preston Guardian* to 'the present unchristian warfare'.[44] In the same week's issue of the *Preston Pilot*, a correspondent bemoaned that, 'It will require many years of prosperity, unity and peace to remedy the sad evils, both temporal and spiritual' resulting from the strike. The writer, 'Clericus', went on to suggest that ministers of religion might act as mediators between the two sides. He expressed the hope that the masters 'as God has been pleased to bless many of them with great and long-continued prosperity ... will be induced, in a kind, conciliatory spirit, to make as large concessions as they possibly can'. From the workers, Clericus asked for 'A disposition to meet their employers in a friendly manner', which 'would ... contribute much to their future happiness and welfare, and, above all, it would be pleasing and acceptable to Him whose name is LOVE'.[45]

The leaders of the strike too viewed matters from a religious perspective. Geoffrey Carnall notes a speech made by George Cowell that is echoed in *Hard Times*,[46] and which appeared in print in the *Preston Guardian* on the very day Dickens arrived in Preston:

> Political economy! What is it? The doctrine of buying cheap and selling dear – a doctrine utterly irreconcilable with the divine precept, 'Do unto others as you would that they should do unto you.' The sooner we

> can rout political economy from the world, the better it will be for the working classes of this country.[47]

Mortimer Grimshaw picked up this idea, and extended it in a lecture given at Accrington soon after, in which, in addition to arguing from the text 'the labourer is worthy of his hire', he maintained political economy to be 'at variance with Christianity, true reason, equity, and justice':

> Christianity is either false or political economy is false. Buy cheap and sell dear! The great founder of Christianity said – 'Love thy neighbour as thyself. Do unto others as you would have others do to you.' The 'buy cheap and sell dear' principle says no such thing.[48]

The chairman of that same meeting, the Baptist minister, Rev. Charles Williams, made an interesting qualification when acknowledging the cogency of Grimshaw's argument:

> I have no hesitation in saying that I think buying cheap and selling dear, when carried on rigorously and without mercy, is unchristian in its character. Both parties, however act upon it, and what is wanted, in my opinion, is this, the introduction of a moral principle to modify the working of this hard maxim, and except there be the moral principle of justice, love and brotherhood, that principle will prove the ruin of Lancashire and of England. I wish there were a little less of selfishness; to fill a man's pockets seems to be the order of the day ... Political economy must ever have its place in political life ... but there are higher considerations, and when the lower considerations are found to clash with the higher, then I say you ought to make interest give way to principle and morality.[49]

The measuring of political economy against Christian values follows an approach to assessing society that we have seen Dickens had long taken, and the remarks of Williams here parallel Dickens's own views, particularly the argument that both sides act upon the same unholy precepts, with the workers following the example set by industrialists ('Both parties, however, act upon it') and the emphasis on the need for the Christian virtues of 'justice, love and brotherhood'. For against the background of the widespread use of the strike weapon in the years immediately preceding the writing of the novel, and in a society in which some people share his approach to analysing the industrial world from a moral and religious point of view, Dickens presents a religious analysis of what is wrong with this society, and what he finds at heart of the problem is along lines that are by now familiar. The new Britain he depicts in *Hard Times* is a nation splitting into factions, a society in which men do not recognise all other men as their fellows. The concept of the brotherhood of man has been lost as the powerful in this society have in effect ceased to recognise ordinary workers as fully human. Instead, conceived of not as individuals but 'generically', they are dehumanised, as we have seen, into being merely 'the Hands' and are 'a race who would have found more favour with some people, if Providence had seen fit to make them only hands, or, like the lower creatures of the seashore, only hands and stomachs' (p. 66). Once the powerful no longer acknowledge their common humanity with working people, they have little conscience about the suffering their deeds or negligence cause to their fellow human beings; it is in vain that miners, themselves, as Stephen points out, 'fathers, sons, brothers, dear to thousands an' thousands, an' keeping 'em fro' want and hunger' have

> pray'n and pray'n the lawmakers for Christ's sake not to let their work be murder to 'em, but to spare 'em for th' wives and children that they loves as well as gentlefolk loves theirs (p. 263)

Without a sense of identification with the workers and lacking a sense of their Christian obligation to them, the industrialists appear undisturbed by the deaths of such as Rachael's sister whose demise 'young and misshapen' was 'awlung o' sickly air as had'n no need to be' (p. 263). It is, of course, this trend that Stephen Blackpool is deploring when he describes what he pathetically expresses as a lack of 'drawin nigh to fok' which is accompanied by

> rating 'em as so much Power, and reg'latin' 'em as if they was figures in a soom, or machines: wi'out loves and likens, wi'out memories and inclinations, wi'out souls to weary and souls to hope – when aw goes quiet, draggin on wi' 'em as if they'd nowt o' th' kind, and when aw goes onquiet, reproachin 'em for their want o' sitch humanly feelins in their dealins wi' yo (p. 149)

Hence, also, his dying wish 'that aw the world may on'y coom together more, an' get a better unnerstanin' o' one another' (p. 264).

Against this perspective, unions, far from providing a cure for society's ills, are merely another symptom of the disease. In an article published in 1851 on 'Railway Strikes',[50] it was precisely the tendency to factionalism – to identifying only with a sector of the community, rather than with all one's fellow men – that made Dickens deplore the railmen's strike, even though he had 'friendly feelings' (p. 317)[51] towards the railmen. He there emphasised the interlocking nature of the work of all the people who had contributed to the establishment of the railway, and then bade them not to identify only with their fellow railwaymen, and thus feel it their duty to show solidarity with them, but to give regard to a much wider constituency of their fellow citizens. Each should think, Dickens wrote, of 'my duty to the public' and 'my duty to my fellow-workmen of all denominations: not only here, upon this Railway, but all over England' (p. 319). His fictional mouthpiece among the railwaymen sums up the issue:

> I leave you to judge how it serves the workman's case, at such a time, to show a small body of his order, combined, in a misuse of power, against the whole community! (p. 321)

To identify oneself with only one restricted group is to deny the brotherhood of all men; and as such, it is unChristian. The world of *Hard Times* is one in which Christianity and Christian values count for little: the Good Samaritan is 'a Bad Economist' (p. 207); right-headed people such as Sissy are scorned for thinking that the first principle of political economy, as of everything in the human sphere, is 'To do unto others as I would that they should do unto me' (p. 59); only at the very end does Mr Gradgrind come to make 'his facts and figures subservient to Faith, Hope, and Charity' (p. 286).

Unions, in Dickens's view, augment the evil in the industrial world by following, in their proceedings, the agenda set by the masters.[52] If the masters do not acknowledge the workers as fellow men, but only as 'hands', the union encourages the workers to regard the masters as enemies, 'the oppressors' that workers are to 'crumble into dust' (p. 137). It creates division even among the workers: each man becomes either a unionist or is treated as an outcast, and no longer a brother. The unchristian nature of this is reflected in the rejection of the philosophy and behaviour of the Good Samaritan; as Stephen comments,

> if I was a lyin parisht i' th' road, yo'd feel it right to pass me by, as a forenner and stranger. (p. 141)

Union leaders like Slackbridge speak the language of brotherhood and Christian principles, urging 'my friends and fellow-sufferers, and fellow-workmen, and fellow-men' (p. 136) to fight for 'the God-created glorious rights of Humanity' and 'the holy and eternal privileges of Brotherhood' (p. 137) – but they do not adhere to the values embodied in the words. As the case of Stephen and his workmates, in which 'Private feeling must yield to the common cause' (p. 142), shows, they encourage workers to regard each other not as individuals and fellow men, but as members, or not, of the faction that makes up the union. The concept of brotherhood has become profoundly distorted and narrowed.

A fundamental question Dickens raises in *Hard Times* is whether an industrial society, or, at least, one based on the principles of that he observes around him, is compatible with Christianity; and if those acting on the principles on which this society is founded are in effect being anti-Christian, this in turn raises the question of how a man should face the evil of the world in which he finds himself. At root, it is a matter of either dealing pragmatically with an evil world and making accommodations to it or of making a stand for the principles in which he believes and which he knows to be right. Even in his journalistic pieces, Dickens's position is uncompromising. He insists on an adherence to moral principle no matter what the particular circumstances. 'We dismiss from consideration, the merits of the case' is his starting point in his article about the 1851 railway dispute;[53] in 'On Strike', he is interested in depicting the character of the strike but not in arguing the rights and wrongs of the workers' or the masters' cases:

> Masters right, or men right; masters wrong, or men wrong; both right, or both wrong; there is certain ruin to both in the continuance of or frequent revival of this breach. ('On Strike', p. 210)

It is thus that Dickens can call the strike 'this mistake' (p. 200) even as he praises the operatives as motivated to persist in their strike by 'the good that is in them, and not the evil' (p. 208).

The position he adopts reflects his philosophy: refusing to take part in the factionalism of Mr Snapper – 'a man *must* either be a friend to the Masters or a friend to the Hands' (p. 198), he declares himself 'a friend to both' (p. 198). Consistently with this, he rejects as a fallacy the idea that there are real differences between people in different sections of society:

> I doubt the existence at this present time of many faults that are merely class faults. In the main, I am disposed to think that whatever faults you may find to exist, in your own neighbourhood for instance, among the hands, you will find tolerably equal in amount among the masters also, and even among the class above the masters. (p. 199)

Dickens does not pretend that for those immediately involved, it is easy to take such a stance. In the novel, Dickens does not shirk, in his presentation of Stephen Blackpool as adopting this position, the difficulties and suffering entailed in it. In a society in which the concept of brotherhood has been debased or rejected, the man who refuses to join one faction or another in the industrial world, is cast out by, and suffers at the hands of, both. The suffering is very real: on the one hand, in the wake of the workers' refusal to speak to Stephen, he finds that he 'had never known before, the strength of the want in his heart for the frequent recognition of a nod, a look, a word' (p. 143) and he finds himself 'appalled' (p. 143) by the taste of how his life is going to be henceforth; on the other hand, Bounderby's displeasure leads to dismissal, which deprives Stephen not only of his livelihood, but also, with the resulting need to leave Coketown, of the company of Rachael. Ultimately, of course, the consequence of his refusal to join the union, is, at the end of a long chain of events, his death. There is indeed a price to be paid for refusing to compromise with the evil of the world. Dickens choice of the name of the first Christian martyr for Stephen is not a loose one: Stephen loses his life ultimately because he will not abandon the Christian concept of brotherhood.[54]

In 'On Strike', Dickens eventually identifies the 'some little thing wanting in the relations between them [working people] and their employers' ('On Strike', p. 200) as a recognition by all of the humanity of those they are dealing with and a consequent modification of behaviour, with the introduction of 'a little human covering', 'a little human bloom', 'a little human warmth' to transform the 'skeleton' of political economy (p. 210). It is this, rather than what Stephen Blackpool calls 'Victory and triumph' (p. 149) by either side, that will set society on a better foundation.

Viewed from this perspective, Dickens's view of unions, if still controversial, can be seen to be more than merely naïve or ill-informed. And as an historical perspective can be used to criticise Dickens's stance over unions, it can be used as well to vindicate it, as witness all those industrial disputes in which class conflict has formed a text or unacknowledged sub-text to the actions of employers and employed. If unions have been responsible for much in the improvement in the lot of workers, it has inevitably been at the price of contributing to the fragmentation of British society, particularly along class lines.

If the union figures Dickens observed in Preston – the firebrand, the more restrained chairman – are recreated in the novel, the character of the meeting has been changed, from one dominated by 'quietness and order' in real life to one dominated by the rabble-rousing rhetoric of a professional agitator in the novel. Partly this is to be explained by Dickens's stance, for reasons already explained, of remaining neutral: the unsympathetic master, Bounderby, is balanced by the unsympathetic workers' leader, Slackbridge. But it is also perhaps to be explained by reference to the difference between journalism and fiction. In his journalism, derived directly from real life, Dickens makes some acknowledgement that unions may serve in the immediate term a valid purpose – 'The fact of their being able to combine ... may, I can easily conceive, be a protection to them' ('On Strike', p. 199) – and that the strikers may be sincere. Fiction, on the other hand is no place in which to make compromises, but to argue what the writer thinks is right. It is a place for vision and analysis. Dickens presents the same old problems recurring in the new society *Hard Times* depicts, because there has been no reform of outlook in the people who created it. It is not a society founded on brotherhood; indeed, instead, it consciously institutionalises division between people and self-interest on both sides, conceiving people not as fellow human beings but identifying them as employers or workers, and establishing masters' associations and trade unions with vying interests. The industrial society is parallel to what Dickens is going to depict in *A Tale of Two Cities*: a new society with the same old attitudes makes no improvement on its predecessor. In the process of conveying his vision of a society in the very throes of being riven into fragments, Dickens looks not to the short-term but argues rather for the fundamental reform of society on the basis of principles which will, he thinks, ensure its long-term health and happiness. For a better society, there has to be a reform of attitudes and values; it will only be created if founded on the principles of Christ's teachings.

7
Little Dorrit: Serving Mammon

The world of *Little Dorrit* is one in which the same phenomena among the most vulnerable that Dickens had portrayed in his earlier novels are again observable. At Covent Garden, Little Dorrit observes children on a level of poverty below hers enduring immediate suffering: 'miserable children in rags ... fed on offal, huddled together for warmth'. They have been dehumanised, and are 'like young rats'; they 'slunk and hid' and 'were hunted about' (p. 182).[1] Similarly, when Arthur Clennam sits in a coffee-house on Ludgate Hill, he is surrounded by homes that reflect more suffering, for they are places 'where people lived so unwholesomely, that fair water put into their crowded rooms on Saturday night, would be corrupt on Sunday morning'. There are 'miles of close wells and pits of houses, where the inhabitants gasped for air'. The River Thames nearby is 'a deadly sewer'. Once again, the humanity of the inhabitants is not recognised, as they live in what are more 'lairs' fit for wild animals than homes fit for humans (p. 44). The spiritual welfare of these people is also a cause for concern: as the bell of a local church peals prior to a service, with ten minutes to go 'it became aware that the congregation would be scanty, and slowly hammered out in low spirits, They *won't* come, they *won't* come, they *won't* come! At five minutes it abandoned hope ...' (p. 44).

In this novel, however, we are not given the detailed portrayal of the dehumanised poor that Dickens provided in his depiction of Jo and the brickmakers in *Bleak House*, for example. Their world perhaps shades into others: in *Little Dorrit*, poverty is seen to have a hierarchy, so that while the Plornishes are members of the community of poor people who live in Bleeding Heart Yard, they are one step up on the one hand from the poor of debtors' prison, where they once resided, and on the other hand the poor of the workhouse, from whom Mr Nandy temporarily escapes when he comes to visit them. For Mr Nandy, to live with his family among the poor of Bleeding Heart Yard is something to aspire to 'when Fortune should smile on his son-in-law' (p. 386). Meanwhile, Mr Dorrit at least seems to regard the workhouse as below debtors' prison, as his pitying remark about Nandy – 'Union, poor old fellow' (p. 395) – reflects. In a society in which people measure themselves by how much money they have, the hierarchy of poverty continues considerably further up the social ladder: Henry Gowan, for instance, is constantly referring to himself as poor, and his mother refers to herself as being 'as poor as ... Job' (p. 414), while Rigaud classes himself as one of 'we poor gentlemen' (p. 470), though it is, of course, all relative.

Dickens's focus in *Little Dorrit* is instead on the depiction of the corrupt values that ultimately create the sufferings of those at the bottom of society, and the effect of these values on the very people who subscribe to and propagate them. The notion that evil values harm not only the vulnerable but also the people responsible for the evil recurs in Dickens. In *Bleak House*, the people indicted over Jo's death include the members of society 'born with Heavenly compassion in your hearts' (p. 734)[2] who, by subscribing to corrupt values, have themselves been corrupted and have lost their compassion, or they would not be letting this state of things exist. The ninth chapter of Volume II of *American Notes* is entitled 'Slavery'; but Dickens focuses quite considerably not so much on the slaves as on the slave owners, and the effect of slavery on them. Though he acknowledges the existence of 'many kind masters who are tender in the exercise of their unnatural power' (p. 251)[3], his emphasis is on the corrupting effect the system has on slave owners. 'Some hearts' may be found that 'can partially resist' the 'hardening influences' of slavery (p. 251), but he sets out to show that in many cases people in slave states have become precisely hardened and brutalised. He adduces newspaper stories as evidence of whether slave owners 'are fierce or gentle; whether their social customs be brutal, sanguinary, and violent, or bear the impress of civilisation and refinement' (p. 258). The newspaper reports depict a violent society in which life is cheap and killing common, and Dickens sees the stories as 'revolting evidences of the state of society which exists in and about the slave districts of America' (p. 264). They reflect the corruption of people where slavery is allowed: he characterises the slave owner as a man who 'whenever his wrath is kindled up, will be a brutal savage' (p. 264). The consequences of the brutalising effect of slavery are dire for the helpless and vulnerable slaves. Men who 'among their equals stab and pistol ... in all the elsewhere peaceful pursuits of life, must be to their dependants, even though they were free servants, so many merciless and unrelenting tyrants' (pp. 264–5).[4]

If in *Little Dorrit* he examines the corrupt values causing the sufferings of the very poorest, and the harm those values do to the very people who subscribe to them, this is done most piquantly in the portrayal of the Dorrit family. Dickens presents them as a group of people fervently, even neurotically, subscribing to the very false and evil values of which they are victims; they unwittingly connive at their own suffering.

I

In David Lodge's novel *Deaf Sentence*, the narrator, Desmond Bates, discusses some irritants in modern-day life, commenting that:

> Somehow it is easier to focus one's anger and despair on these comparatively trivial offences to reason and decency than on the larger threats to civilisation like Islamic terrorism, Israel/Palestine, Iraq, AIDS [acquired immune deficiency syndrome], the energy crisis and global warming, which seem to be beyond anyone's ability to control. (p. 112)[5]

The attitude is reminiscent of similar ones to social problems, particularly poverty, in *Little Dorrit*. Significantly, Bates is not a religious man; from a religious point of view, his position is a nonsense. Theodicies traditionally place the sources of suffering into two categories, with no remainder. One of these is natural evil, over which man has no control[6], including such things as earthquakes, famine and flood. The other is moral evil, which embraces everything from the making of unkind remarks to murder and war; man does have control over, and is responsible for, this type of evil. Of the problems that Bates discusses, only AIDS would count as natural evil; the remainder would all count as moral evil, and thus within the scope of human beings to tackle and resolve. From a Christian point of view, the scale of these problems is irrelevant; they would all succumb to the application of Christian moral values. At a time when homelessness was a major social problem in Britain, Mother Teresa, during a visit to the country, went to meet some of those people living on the streets. When a reporter asked her who she blamed for the problem, her reply was 'You and I'. And so with the problems that Lodge's narrator identifies. Far from being things that have just happened, are beyond human control and are nobody's responsibility, Christians would argue, they are all soluble with the application of Christian ethics. They demand Christian love to overcome them.

For the first three number plans for his new novel, Dickens was calling it *Nobody's Fault*; only when he got to the fourth number plan did he change the title to *Little Dorrit*.[7] In the world of the novel, sympathetic characters far from trying to avoid blame for things, tend to refuse, rather, to take credit for things. Daniel Doyce, for instance:

> never said, I discovered this adaptation or invented that combination; but showed the whole thing as if the Divine artificer had made it, and he had happened to find it. (p. 541)

Above all, this is a tendency of Little Dorrit, as for example when her uncle tries to thank her for her care of him:

> 'You have done me a world of good. You have been so considerate of me, and so tender with me, and so delicate in trying to hide your

> attentions from me, that I – well, well, well! It's treasured up, my darling, treasured up.'
>
> 'There is nothing in it but your own fresh fancy, uncle,' said Little Dorrit, cheerfully. (p. 668)

If there is blame to be taken, they do not try to escape it. From early on, Arthur Clennam is determined to take responsibility for the predicament of the Dorrit family if it is the fault of the Clennams, and gets Pancks to investigate the matter. When the financial investments he has made turn out disastrously with the collapse of Merdle's enterprises, he makes no attempt to avoid facing his own responsibility or to dodge the consequences, even as Pancks attempts to take the blame for advising him badly:

> What do I, myself, deserve! ... I have ruined Doyce ... the man I have felt so much for, and meant to be so true and useful to; I have ruined him – brought him to shame and disgrace – ruined him, ruined him! (p. 744)

Reparation must be made for things that are his fault:

> 'My course,' said Clennam, brushing away some tears that had been silently dropping down his face, 'must be taken at once. What wretched amends I can make must be made. I must clear my unfortunate partner's reputation. I must retain nothing for myself. I must resign to our creditors the power of management I have so much abused, and I must work out as much of my fault – or crime – as is susceptible of being worked out, in the rest of my days.' (p. 745)

Adopting the position that 'I must take the consequences of what I have done' (p. 749), he ends up in the Marshalsea by his own doing, rejecting Rugg's advice about how to avoid it.

These figures, though, are on the periphery of society. Doyce's attempts to benefit society through his inventions have all been relentlessly blocked by the Circumlocution Office; the final sentence of the novel emphasises how separate Clennam and Little Dorrit are from their society as they emerge from their wedding, going 'quietly down' (p. 859) while around them 'the noisy and the eager, and the arrogant and the forward and the vain, fretted, and chafed, and made their usual uproar' (p. 860). Much more typical in this society is that bad things are considered indeed to be 'nobody's fault', and certainly not the fault of the individual.

At its most trivial and comic level, this attitude manifests itself in the way, for instance, that Affery claims that she is married to Flintwinch through no fault of her own, but merely from feebleness of character: when Clennam asks her about her marriage, Affery states, 'It was no doing o' mine ... How could I help myself?' (p. 54). In the face of arguments from Flintwinch and Mrs Clennam, both of whom wanted the marriage to take place, 'I couldn't have said a word upon it, against them two clever ones' (p. 55). A darker parallel to this is to emerge at the end of the novel, when it transpires that Arthur's father, a similarly weak, 'poor, irresolute, frightened chap', 'had no voice in the choice of his wife even, but his uncle chose her' (p. 805).

However, the matter of whether things are nobody's fault raises deeper issues concerning determinism and the shaping influence of environment. Near the beginning of the novel, Miss Wade expresses to Mr Meagles a totally deterministic view of human life and human behaviour:

> In our course through life we shall meet the people who are coming to meet *us*, from many strange places and by many strange roads ... and what it is set to us to do to them, and what it is set to them to do to us, will all be done. (p. 39)

Pancks, presenting himself as 'Pancks the gipsy' (p. 308), later pretends to tell Little Dorrit's fortune, as if the whole of her life is fixed in advance, and readable in the lines on her palm. In addition, scattered throughout the whole novel are passing references to such concepts as 'the decrees of Fate' (pp. 175; c.f. 303, 385, 707), 'destiny' (p. 300) and 'A wild destiny' (p. 457), 'Providence' (p. 391), 'the lottery of chances' (p. 446). Part of Dickens's focus in the novel is the refutation of this view of human life and behaviour.

Rigaud takes a deterministic view of his own character and the consequences for his actions. Throughout the novel, Rigaud claims that he cannot help the way he behaves, because it is simply his character, and beyond his control to do so. When Clennam criticises him for being impatient, for instance, he does not deny it, stating, 'it's my character to be impatient' (p. 569). In his final meeting with Mrs Clennam, he speaks as if there is an inevitability quite beyond choice as to how he will behave if crossed:

> I am a gentleman of the softest and sweetest disposition, but who, if trifled with, becomes enraged. Noble natures under such circumstances become enraged. I possess a noble nature. (p. 801)

Even more seriously, he seems to excuse the murder for which he is in prison at the beginning of the novel as something he could not help and should not be blamed for. He traces the factors that led to the death of his wife. Even while acknowledging pride as a fault, he speaks as if he must resign himself to its being an unalterable, uncontrollable part of his character:

> I am proud. I say nothing in defence of pride, but I am proud. It is also my character to govern. I can't submit; I must govern. (p. 25)

He takes an equally resigned attitude to other qualities relevant to the crime he committed: 'I am sensitive and brave. I do not admit it as a merit to be sensitive and brave, but it is my character' (p. 26). These qualities had an adverse effect on his marriage. As a proud man with a drive to govern, he could not stand his wife having control of her own property, or her family's attempts to spring to her aid:

> When a wife's relations interpose against a husband who is a gentleman, who is proud, and who must govern, the consequences are inimical to peace. (p. 26)

His sensitivity meant that he was angered by the stories about his cruel conduct that he alleges were spread by his wife's relations, stories springing out of his hitting his wife in his attempt to govern. Furthermore:

> When I wanted any little sum of money for my personal expenses, I could not obtain it without collision – and I too, a man whose character is to govern! (p. 26)

When matters came to a head on the night of his fatal quarrel with his wife, other apparently uncontrollable aspects of his personality exacerbated the situation: 'I grew warm, and provoked her. I admit it. Frankness is part of my character' (p. 26). On his account, nothing that happened was his fault: everything was simply the result of traits of character that are beyond his control. However, at the same time, he somewhat inconsistently denies that his apparently irresistible impulse to govern caused the outcome: it is pure 'malice' to suggest that

> my endeavouring to force from Madame Rigaud a relinquishment of her rights; and, on her persistence in a refusal to make the concession I required, struggling with her

culminated in her actual murder (p. 27). We draw our own conclusions about a man inclined to excuse his behaviour as not his fault but aware that the law would not recognise this as a defence.

When others are discussing Rigaud at the Break of Dawn it is suggested that he may have become a murderer not because of innate character, but because of the shaping influence of his environment. Influenced by 'philosophical philanthropy', one of those participating in the discussion suggests that Rigaud's wickedness has its roots in

> ... his unfortunate destiny. He may have been the child of circumstances. It is always possible that he had, and has, good in him if one did but know how to find it out. (p. 141)

The landlady has no sympathy with this point of view, dismissing philosophical philanthropy if it 'puts anybody at the mercy of such people by holding terms with them at all' (p. 142). Dickens seems to agree with her, for his narrator describes the philosophical philanthropists (Utilitarians) as morally irresponsible 'white-washers' (p. 142). Neither he nor his sympathetic characters deny that environmental influences help shape personality. When Mr Meagles and his wife were proposing to take in Tattycoram from the Foundling Hospital, their attitude was that, given her rough start in life

> ... if we should find her temper a little defective, or any of her ways a little wide of ours, we shall know what we have to take into account. We shall know what an immense deduction must be made from all the influences and experiences that have formed – no parents, no child-brother or sister, no individuality of home, no Glass Slipper, or Fairy Godmother. (p. 33)

Through all the turbulence in their relationship that follows, the Meagles remains tolerant and understanding; at the end of the novel they take Tattycoram back into their home. But while her background may have made Tattycoram headstrong, their attitude is never that this must just be tolerated. She is expected to control this aspect of her personality – 'count five-and-twenty, Tattycoram' (p. 214); her behaviour is not held to be beyond her control and thus not her fault. By the close of the book, she recognises that she has been 'bad', but that she is not hopelessly trapped in her behaviour: she holds out hopes 'that I shall get better', if only 'by very slow degrees. I'll try very hard. I won't stop at five and twenty, sir. I'll count five and twenty hundred, five and twenty thousand!' (p. 845).

Miss Wade's story, related in Book the Second Chapter 21, furthermore, demonstrates that environment does not exercise an inescapable grip over us, as she relentlessly resists the influence of hers. An orphan, she passes through a number of loving, and potentially healing, environments. She is brought up with nine other girls by a woman who is no relative, but pretends to be her grandmother:

> I must have been about twelve years old when I began to see how determinedly those girls patronised me. I was told I was an orphan. There was no other orphan among us; and I perceived (here was the first disadvantage of not being a fool), that they conciliated me in an insolent pity, and in a sense of superiority. I did not set this down as a discovery, rashly. I tried them often. I could hardly make them quarrel with me. When I succeeded with any of them, they were sure to come, after an hour or two, and begin a reconciliation. I tried them over and over again, and I never knew them wait for me to begin. They were always forgiving me, in their vanity and condescension. (pp. 693–4)

She resists another friendly environment in the same way:

> I went among young women next, and I found them no better. Fair words and fair pretences; but, I penetrated below those assertions of themselves and depreciations of me, and they were no better. (p. 695)

Human beings are portrayed in the novel as capable of controlling their drives and impulses, so that no-one's personal conduct is 'nobody's fault'. People are not at the mercy of influences on their behaviour unless they let themselves be. Arthur Clennam spends much of the novel suppressing his jealousy and dislike of Henry Gowan: thus, when Miss Wade refers to Gowan as 'your dear friend', 'The denial that he was a dear friend rose to Arthur's lips; but, he repressed it, remembering his old struggles and resolutions' (p. 689). If, in a novel about prisons, people are claiming to be imprisoned in their character or by the environment that has shaped them, their notions are given the lie by Little Dorrit. As Mr Meagles points out to Tattycoram, she was born in the prison, but the prison was not born in her:

> 'She was born here, and lived here many years. I can't breathe here. A doleful place, to be born and bred in ... If she had constantly thought of herself, and settled with herself that everybody visited this place upon her, turned it against her, and cast it at her, she would have led an irritable and probably useless existence. Yet I have heard tell, Tattycoram, that her young life has been one of active resignation, goodness, and noble service. Shall I tell you what I consider those eyes of hers that were here just now, to have always looked at, to get that expression?'
>
> 'Yes, if you please, sir.'
>
> 'Duty, Tattycoram. Begin it early, and do it well; and there is no antecedent to it, in any origin or station, that will tell against us with the Almighty, or with ourselves.' (pp. 845–6)

Instead of letting herself be overwhelmed by her environment and any stigma attached to it, Little Dorrit chooses to live by Christian moral values. Instead of allowing herself to be imprisoned by her environment, she serves 'the Almighty', 'whose service is perfect freedom', according to the Collect for Peace in the *Book of Common Prayer*'s Order for Morning Prayer.

On a social level too, this is a world in which the many problems of society are viewed as 'nobody's fault'. Catherine Waters points out that at the time Dickens was writing *Little Dorrit,* the 1855 Limited Liabilities Act had been causing much controversy.[8] As she notes, resistance to limited liability being introduced 'was largely based upon adherence to the principle of personal responsibility'[9] and the novel reflects the approach to public life the Act reflected. If the Circumlocution Office is attacked in Parliament, it is defended as 'blameless' and 'always voted immaculate' (p. 121). The Barnacle family who form the political and administrative Establishment represent governmental refusal to take responsibility for social problems. Lord Decimus Tite Barnacle

> had risen to official heights on the wings of one indignant idea, and that was, My Lords, that I am yet to be told that it behoves a Minister of this free country to set bounds to the philanthropy, to cramp the charity, to fetter the public spirit, to contract the enterprise, to damp the independent self-reliance, of its people. That was, in other words, that this great statesman was always yet to be told that it behoved the Pilot of the ship to do anything but prosper in the private loaf and fish trade ashore, the crew being able, by dint of hard pumping, to keep the ship above water without him. (p. 427)

These apparently positive principles are, of course, a mere excuse for doing nothing. Christ's miracle of the loaves and fishes was an act of public beneficence, in contrast to Lord Decimus's purely 'private' concerns in the carrying out of his office and any bounty that might accrue from it. People who in their dealings with the Circumlocution Office are trying to bring benefit to the country and to improve it find themselves stymied. Doyce has long struggled unsuccessfully with the Circumlocution Office, trying 'to turn his ingenuity to his country's service' by means of 'an invention ... of great importance to his country and his fellow creatures'. On approaching the Government with it, however, 'he becomes a public offender ... a man to be shirked, put off, brow-beaten, sneered at ... a mere outlaw, whom it is justifiable to get rid of anyhow; a man to be worn out by all possible means' (p. 134). Arthur Clennam, for all his persistence, has no more success when he takes up Doyce's cause. If Clennam thinks, however, that he is dealing merely with a badly organised, slow-moving institution in which everything is caught up in red tape, this is a miscalculation. It eventually transpires that the truth is even more shocking. When Ferdinand Barnacle visits Clennam in the Marshalsea, he blames applicants to the Circumlocution Office themselves if they are ruined through their involvement with it, or if it has other 'effects' on 'people who will not leave us alone', and it is certainly not the Circumlocution Office's fault:

> it is our misfortune to do that kind of thing now and then. We don't want to do it; but if men will be gravelled, why – we can't help it. (p. 769)

Similarly, he will talk as if it is an 'unlucky place' (as though it were merely a matter of luck, with no blame accruing to the Office) in its other 'effects upon people who will not leave us alone' (p. 769). It is not, however, inefficiency that leads to such results; that is not to look at things 'from the right point of view'. The whole purpose of the Office is the preservation of the *status quo*: 'It is there with the express intention that everything shall be left alone. That is what it means. That is what it's for' (p. 769). With this, rather than the benefit of the country and its people, its *raison d'etre*, 'nobody cares twopence-halfpenny' about Doyce's invention, and Barnacle warns Clennam off any further attempts to approach the Circumlocution Office, about which he says 'everything goes on admirably, if you leave it alone' (p. 770).

In this context, such a major social problem as poverty, with all its suffering, is perceived, as fallaciously as David Lodge's narrator perceived the social and political problems he identified, as nobody's fault, and simply there. Mr Plornish describes the predicament of the poor to Clennam. He describes women and girls working away at their jobs 'day and night and night and day' who are nevertheless 'not more than able to keep body and soul together after all – often not so much' (p. 157). There are people 'all wanting to work, and yet not able to get it' (pp. 157–8). There are old people who, despite 'working all their lives' end up in the workhouse 'much worse fed and lodged and treated altogether' than criminals in jail (p. 158). If people are 'uncommon hard up', it seems to be 'just one of those things': Mr Plornish 'couldn't say how it was; he didn't know as anybody *could* say how it was; all he know'd was, that so it was' (p. 157). In a society in which no-one is taking responsibility for the situation, it is difficult to pin down whose fault it is:

> As to who was to blame for it, Mr Plornish didn't know who was to blame for it. He could tell you who suffered, but he couldn't tell you whose fault it was. It wasn't *his* place to find out, and who'd mind what he said, if he did find out? He only know'd that it wasn't put right by them what undertook that line of business, and that it didn't come right of itself. (p. 158)

Poverty counts firmly as moral evil; the suffering it causes is remediable by man. At root, its existence arises from a lack of Christian love.

A culture, then, in which, in both in the individual sphere and on a social level, things are held to be 'nobody's fault' is widespread in *Little Dorrit*. As we have seen, in both spheres, it constitutes an abrogation of Christian duty. The acceptability of this idea ultimately leads to human beings living like rats. To see why Christian duty counts for so little, we need to look further into the values of this society.

II

If a number of things in this society are generally held to be 'nobody's fault', and hence people not held responsible, there is one noticeable exception to this. People are held responsible for offences against money. For, if no man can serve God and Mammon (Matthew 6:24), this is a society that has decided to serve and worship Mammon. If Jesus in Holman Hunt's painting was the Light of the World, the leading money-man of the age, Mr Merdle is 'the shining light of the time' (p. 538).[10] There are 'high priests' of his 'worship', 'officiators at the altar', but 'The multitude worshipped' too (p. 581). To dine with Merdle is to be admitted into 'the innermost sanctuary of the temple' (p. 585). When he dines at a hotel, he is treated as if he is a holy man like St. Peter[11]:

> As he went up the stairs, people were already posted on the lower stairs, that his shadow might fall upon them when he came down. So were the sick brought out and laid in the track of the Apostle. (p. 641)

Worship of Merdle outdoes Christianity in its intensity, as Dickens notes in recording:

> the general bowing and crouching before this wonderful mortal, the like of which prostration of spirit was not to be seen – no, by high Heaven, no! It may be worth thinking of by Fawners of all denominations – in Westminster Abbey and Saint Paul's Cathedral put together, on any Sunday in the year. (p. 645)

Worship of Merdle does not so much exist alongside Christianity as supersede it. Merdle seems to confound the teachings of Christ, for he is, 'The rich man, who had in a manner revised the New Testament, and already entered into the kingdom of Heaven' (p. 641). He reverses the lifestyle of the Apostle he is compared to 'who had *not* got into the good society, and had *not* made the money' (p. 641). Bishop, representative of the Church of England, is one of the Establishment figures who pay court to him. His wife, meanwhile, is regarded as 'a Priestess of Society' (p. 416).

It is clear that there is only one reason for the status accorded to Merdle. It is certainly not because of any traits of character, for the man is a mere cipher: 'He did not shine in company; he had not very much to say for himself', and in society 'he hardly seemed to enjoy himself much, and was mostly to be found against walls and behind doors' (p. 266). Neither do his activities have any moral worth: 'Nobody knew that the Merdle of such high renown had ever done any good to any one, alive or dead, or to any earthly thing' (p. 581). In a fallen world populated by 'the sons of Adam', he has no 'capacity' to lead and inspire morally or in any other way, able to cast not 'the feeblest farthing-candle ray of light on any path of duty or diversion, pain or pleasure, toil or rest, fact or fancy' (p. 581). (Such is his prestige that this does not stop people attributing spurious moral worth to him nevertheless: Bishop talks of Merdle's influence being 'habitually exercised in harmony with the best interests of Society' (p. 593); and his 'making so much money out of' society is generally considered 'admirable service' (p. 723).) The reality is that he is regarded as 'a wonderful man ... a great man ... a master man ... blessedly and enviably endowed' simply because he is 'a rich man' (p. 589). He is 'immensely rich' and it is 'for that reason alone' that people

> prostrated themselves before him, more degradedly and less excusably than the darkest savage creeps out of his hole in the ground to propitiate, in some log or reptile, the Deity of his benighted soul. (p. 581)

This pagan-like worship of money produces much evil. Among those who have it, it produces materialism. The dinner that Mr Merdle gives is an exhibition of opulence, conspicuous consumption and self-indulgence:

> The rarest dishes, sumptuously cooked and sumptuously served; the choicest fruits; the most exquisite wines; marvels of workmanship in old and silver, china and glass; innumerable things delicious to the senses of taste, smell, and sight, were insinuated into its composition. (p. 589)

His house is furnished with nothing less than 'unique Dresden vases' (p. 594), the more expensive because of the guarantee that they were indeed unique.[12] Mr Dorrit in his wealth indulges in unnecessary spending, so that when he wishes to speak to his daughter, it ends up involving two hired intermediaries: 'So, Tinkler the valet was instructed find Miss Amy's maid, and to request that subordinate to inform Miss Amy that Mr Dorrit wished to see her in his own room' (p. 499). Other corrupt attitudes are bred in others. As Mrs Gowan discusses what money will come her son's way when he marries into the Meagles family, she coolly looks forward to what more money he may gain when Mr and Mrs Meagles die, commenting with callousness that, however, 'they may live for ever. My dear, they are just the kind of people to do it' (p. 415). She agrees to his marrying Pet in the first place not because she, as a loving mother concerned about her only son, thinks they are suited, but merely for selfishly mercenary reasons: she 'would be freed from any little filial inroads' into her pension; and in addition, she is confident that 'Henry's debts must clearly be paid down upon the altar-railing by his father-in-law' (p. 411). Barely better is Fanny Dorrit, whose resentment at her uncle undermining the position money gives the family considers his death 'a happy release, for, if you are not presentable, you had much better die' (p. 726).

To the extent that religious bodies partake of the values of this society, they are implicated in its corruption. As the Dorrits tour Europe, we see Roman Catholic churches ostentatious in their wealth, with 'winking lamps of gold and silver ... gaudy altars ... stained glass ... massive curtains' (p. 490), while the people live in 'dirt and poverty' (p. 489) in 'squalid villages' where there is 'nothing to eat' (p. 490). The Established Church in Britain, represented by Bishop, pays court to worldly, rich men like Merdle, the epitome of society's corrupt values. Bishop is personally wealthy (at one point he 'tried ... to look as if he were rather poor' (p. 270)), and the Church seems to function as nothing more than a respectable, genteel institution: one of Mrs General's recommendations is that she is 'the daughter of a clerical dignitary in a cathedral town' (p. 471), and her references commend her as a 'prodigy' of 'piety, learning, virtue, and gentility' (p. 472), as if all four are on a par. Meanwhile, the likes of Mrs Clennam, though fervently religious, partake of the 'nobody's fault' cast of mind, tolerating the suffering all around as from God, not man.

The Dorrit family are Dickens's focus in his examination of the effect of a culture that worships money. The Marshalsea, where we meet them, is the central symbol that in this society, offences against money will certainly not be regarded as 'nobody's fault': Mr Dorrit serves a sentence of considerably more than twenty years for having got into debt when a firm in which he was a partner went bust. He apparently owed 'two or three thousand pounds' (p. 592). As the first chapter of the novel indicates, in the world of *Little Dorrit*, people are put in prison for a wide variety of offences, from the relatively venial crime of smuggling, for which Cavaletto was arrested, to the ultra-serious crime of murder, which Rigaud has committed. The Marshalsea is a different type of prison, but Dickens stresses its continuity with the prison in Marseilles, for it has within it, we are told when first introduced to it, a 'jail for smugglers' (p. 72). Though originally the smugglers had been segregated from the debtors, by the time of the story, the distinctions have broken down, so that, 'the smugglers habitually consorted with the debtors' (p. 73). There is not, then, a clear and total distinction between the establishments, and, as a prisoner in the Marshalsea, Mr Dorrit is on a continuum with murderers. Mr Dorrit is not a criminal; at worst, he is an inadequate, introduced as a man 'very amiable and very helpless' (p. 73). His younger daughter, who does not subscribe to the values of her society insists that the inmates of the Marshalsea are by no means criminals or reprehensible people:

> People are not bad because they come there. I have known numbers of good, persevering, honest people, come there through misfortune. They are almost all kind-hearted to one another. (p. 112)

She thus refuses to be 'ashamed' (p. 112) of her father. The ignominious status he is thus doomed to is a signal reflection of the values of the society in which he lives.

Those values may be false, but the reaction of the Dorrit family to Mr Dorrit's imprisonment shows that they fully subscribe to the values of their society. Of the two we meet who were adults at the time of the crisis, one is Frederick, William Dorrit's brother. Frederick internalises things, so that 'he had shown no particular sense of being ruined, at the time when that calamity fell upon him', but his reaction is manifested in how 'he left off washing himself when the shock was announced, and never took to that luxury any more' (p. 89), a course of action indicating at least a severe loss of self-respect, perhaps even a nervous breakdown. His shame is directly observable when Arthur Clennam describes the Marshalsea simply as what it is, 'The debtors' prison'; Frederick replies to him 'with the air of deeming it not quite necessary to insist upon that designation'. When asked whether he is familiar with the place, he reacts 'as if such questions hurt him' (p. 94). He is a man utterly broken by the shameful fall of the family, and now only going through the motions. He takes no interest or pleasure in his work at the theatre: he 'had never been observed to raise his eyes above his music-book, and was confidently believed to have never seen a play' (p. 255). Private life is equally empty and meaningless to him: 'in private life, where there was no part for the clarionet, he had no part at all' (p. 255). The theatre carpenters joke that, 'he was dead without being aware of it' (p. 255). He appears in the prison yard 'humbled, bowed, withered and faded' (p. 238). Even when the family become wealthy, the shame apparently lingers, for he only takes to washing again to please the rest of the family: he 'performed some ablutions as a sacrifice to the family credit' (p. 481).

The reaction of William Dorrit is, of course, portrayed in a great deal more detail. In his depiction of this character, Dickens presents a study both of a man who is pauperised and institutionalised, and of a man coping with having offended against values he accepts.

In one respect, Dickens's portrayal of Mr Dorrit is of a man thoroughly institutionalised. He goes into the Marshalsea an independent man, confident he will leave it soon, and so 'he doubted its being worth while to unpack' his portmanteau (p. 73). Soon, however, he begins to cling to the institution, finding a 'dull relief' in imprisonment, which 'kept numbers of his troubles out' (p. 79). His very weakness of character means that instead of fighting against his troubles 'he languidly slipped into this smooth descent, and never more took one step upward' (p. 79). Having embraced being institutionalised, he becomes, in the perception of Little Dorrit, fragile and incapable of fending for himself if the support of the institution were removed: as regards his getting out of prison

> I have often thought that if such a change could come, it might be anything but a service to him now. People might not think so well of him outside as they do there. He might not be so gently dealt with outside, as he is there. He might not be so fit himself for the life outside, as he is for that. (p. 113)

There is a contrast immediately afterwards with Maggie, who, for all her afflictions, 'earns her own living entirely. Entirely, sir! ... Really does!' (p. 117).

Dickens often presents people whose independence is less than complete, and who are in a position of vulnerability, as feeling the need to compensate by constructing fantasies about themselves in which they take control. In *Our Mutual Friend*, Jenny Wren's life is restricted by the disability she is apt to sum up as 'my back being so bad and my legs so queer' (p. 223).[13] Though she has to be firm with her dissolute father, she also seems to derive comfort from the fantasy of a suitor who will be kept firmly under control: as the narrator puts it, 'no intentions were stronger in her breast than the various trials and torments that were, in the fulness of time, to be inflicted upon "him"' (p. 233). Even though the suitor does not exist, and his character thus remains unknown, Jenny is determined he will be dealt with using a firm hand:

> Wherever he may happen to be just at present, or whoever he may happen to be ... *I* know his tricks and his manners, and I give him fair warning to look out. (p. 233)

Mr Dorrit lives by a similar compensatory fantasy. Grateful to the Marshalsea for shielding him from responsibilities, he is at the same time aware that his predicament represents a diminishment, a loss of independence and the dignity that goes with it. Picking up a suggestion from the turnkey, he takes on the title of Father of the Marshalsea, a soubriquet that allows him to fantasise that he occupies a commanding position, and that monetary gifts are 'tributes, from admirers' (p. 81). He becomes exacting and demanding in the role: 'All new comers were presented to him. He was punctilious in the exaction of this ceremony' (p. 81). Combined with this, though, is a deep sense of shame, which must equally be covered up and buried under fantasy. As an offender against money, Mr Dorrit has been locked up in jail. Subscribing to the values of the society around him, this eventuality causes him to feel shame; he perceives it as a humiliation that is difficult to live with. If being a jailbird makes him a social pariah, becoming the Father of the Marshalsea helps him regain status, in the perverse fantasy that enables him to cope with his predicament. As we have already seen in the case of Mr Merdle, in the world of the novel, the possession of money gives people status, and the loss of the former involves the loss of the latter; Mr Dorrit through this fantasy salvages something of what he has lost with his financial ruin. We are thus told that 'he grew to be proud of the title' (p. 80), he starts exaggerating the length of time he has been there in order to enhance his status, and adopts a superior position to the other inmates, behaving 'paternally' (p. 81) towards them. He looks down patronisingly on his brother who, unlike Mr Dorrit himself, 'had not arrived at distinction' (p. 97). He leads his family in 'pretensions' that are actually just 'miserable Mumbo Jumbo' (p. 231). Shame is compensated for by pride. He regards it as below his dignity to receive gifts from people using flippant and facetious names: he regards these as 'in bad taste' and not sufficiently respectful, leaving him 'always a little hurt' (p. 81) (though he nevertheless accepts the money tendered). Though the reality is that he is humiliatingly dependent on such gifts, he cannot bear to be reminded of this. Offered, insultingly as he sees it, a gift in halfpence, he takes control of the situation in order to preserve his pride. The stark reminder of his own dependence causes him to burst into tears; he regains control by challenging the giver – 'How dare you!' (p. 82) – and eliciting an apology, which enables him then to appear gracious in accepting the money after all. Equally, his pride will not let him accept that his family are financially supporting him rather than the other way round, so it must never be acknowledged that they work while he remains idle in prison.

The true degradation of Mr Dorrit, looked at from the point of view of those independent of society's values, such as Little Dorrit, arises paradoxically from the very fantasy that is sustaining him from his underlying sense of degradation. Deeply damaged by the shame of his imprisonment, his proper pride and self-respect, which would inhibit him from begging, are overwhelmed by his fantasy, in which, in his proud position as Father of the Marshalsea, he is perfectly entitled to remind people of the dues owed to him. He thus more or less openly begs from Arthur Clennam, pointing out that 'people who come here, desire to offer some little – Testimonial – to the Father of the place ... it is generally – ha – Money' (p. 98). Amy is not ashamed of her father being in debtors' prison, but she shrinks in profound embarrassment at his behaviour here, and presents 'a sad, sad sight' (p. 98). The agony of his shame, and the resort to fantasy in response, leads his character to degenerate, on a downward spiral:

> The more Fatherly he grew as to the Marshalsea, and the more dependant he became on the contributions of his changing family, the greater the stand he made by his forlorn gentility. (p. 88)

Even Mr Dorrit himself occasionally is forced to see how he has lost his dignity, and any entitlement to real respect, not by being put in the prison, but by the decline in his character resulting from trying to cope with being in there. After John Chivery has made romantic approaches to Amy and she has rejected them, her father, through the transparent fiction of relating a story about someone else, expresses his displeasure that she will not 'lead him on ... on her father's ... account', thus ensuring that Chivery Senior will be 'obliging and attentive' to him (p. 244). If not exactly prostituting his daughter, he at least wants to exploit her sexual attractiveness for his own advantage. After a pause, though, even he sees how low he is stooping. He sees how no longer being 'independent' (p. 245), he is 'unfortunately dependent' on men like Chivery, and this has led him to disgrace himself. He despises himself, and if Amy also despises him, 'I am hardened now, I have sunk too low to care long even for that' (p. 246).

If he has a moment of insight into the truth about himself, however, even this is not sufficient to shake him out of taking refuge in fantasy. The shame of his offence against money has too firm a grip over him. When he refers to himself at this point as 'a squalid, disgraced wretch' (p. 245), it is difficult to tell whether he is referring to his financial embarrassment or his decline, morally and otherwise, though his allusion shortly afterwards to his 'ruin and decay' (p. 246) perhaps reveals that in this moment of self-awareness, he has both in mind. Nevertheless, he is soon taking comfort from and refuge in his fantasy:

> And yet I have some respect here. I have made some stand against it. I am not quite trodden down. Go out and ask who is the chief person in the place. They'll tell you it's your father. Go out and ask who is never trifled with, and who is always treated with some delicacy. They'll say, your father... (p. 246)

One of the main points of the novel, of course, is that shame over the family's offence against money is not over but persists when the Dorrits come into wealth. Mr Dorrit is constantly anxious, neurotic that the people they now move among will discover the guilty secret in their past. He hires Mrs General to train his daughters so that nothing they do or say will reveal that they have spent their lives moving not in swish social circles but in the environs of a prison. He covers up the shame of the past by reinventing the family as one able to afford long sojourns abroad, complete with full complements of servants. His insecurity is such, however, that it only takes a momentary hesitation in his servant Tinkler in obeying an order he does not understand to provoke a rage:

> Mr Dorrit, seeing the whole Marshalsea and all its Testimonials in the pause, instantly flew at him with, 'How dare you, sir? What do you mean?' (p. 628)

He agrees to see Flora Finching, whom he does not know, simply because 'unless she were admitted she might leave some message, or might say something below, having a disgraceful reference to that former state of existence' (p. 647).

Not only is Mr Dorrit hiding the past from others, but he has constructed a new fantasy for himself in which that past never existed. Thus when John Chivery visits him, instead of being pleased to see an old friend, he regards it simply as an unwelcome reminder of reality which breaks into his fantasy. Initially objecting to it as 'an affront, an impertinence, an audacity' from a social inferior – 'How dare you do this? ... How dare you presume to come here?' (p. 660) – he eventually acknowledges that the real reason for his anger is that 'some remembrances are not happy remembrances'

(p. 662). Shame over his behaviour leads him to an unconsciously ironic gesture which is comforting by bolstering his new sense of himself: the man who once begged money from others now in return sends just such a 'Testimonial' to the inmates of the Marshalsea in the ostentatiously generous form of 'a cheque for one hundred pounds' (p. 663). Never questioning the worship of money in his society, he never questions whether being imprisoned for offences against money was just, and thus never escapes neurosis and anxiety even when he becomes wealthy.

The Dorrit children are equally ashamed of 'the sordid facts of their lives' (p. 250), and haunted by 'the death's head apparition of the family gentility' (p. 250). Fanny, as much as her father, denies the reality of their lives. Though they are as poor as he, seeing her sister out on the street with Mr Nandy enrages Fanny: 'The idea of coming along the open streets, in the broad light of day, with a Pauper!'. The effect is to 'disgrace us' (p. 390). It also punctures the fantasy version of the family Fanny likes to entertain: 'The principal pleasure of your life is to remind your family of their misfortunes' (p. 390). When the family comes into wealth, she suffers as much anxiety as her father. While all the time refusing to acknowledge that she needs any help from Mrs General, she is insecure in fearing that she may give away the family's background, and so while rejecting any suggestion from Mrs General, 'she always stored it up in her mind, and adopted it at another time' (p. 505). She is as sensitive as her father is to perceived slights. The family's arrival at a hotel to find one of their rooms temporarily occupied provokes Mr Dorrit into a rage as he feels that 'the family dignity was struck at' (p. 483); the idea that he might be different from 'other gentlemen' (p. 483) and thus to be treated differently strikes too close to home. Fanny feels equally threatened by the innkeeper's behaviour:

> Miss Fanny ... now supported her father with great bitterness; declaring, in her native tongue, that it was quite clear that there was something special in this man's impertinence; and that she considered it important that he should be, by some means, forced to give up his authority for making distinctions between that family and other wealthy families. (p. 484)

Fanny above all subscribes to society's idea that money gives status. When she is poor, she is bought off by Mrs Merdle as not good enough for her son Edmund Sparkler; when she is wealthy, she is driven by a wish for revenge to the point of wrecking her life by marrying a man she perceived from the beginning as 'almost an idiot' (p. 262). Her determination over the matter is a sign of how deeply damaged she is by the family's shame: she looks to a life in which she will 'assert myself with greater effect against that insolent woman ... I would oppose her in everything, and compete with her. I would make it the business of my life' (pp. 618–9) and in which she can be 'a thorn in her side' (p. 619). Her extreme need to do this is to be reflected later when, after mourning the death of her father for twelve hours, her top priority then becomes, as she arranges her mourning dress, 'to take every precaution that could ensure its being as becoming as Mrs Merdle's' (p. 724). The apparent triviality of triumphing over Mrs Merdle by such means as jibes about her age provokes Amy to offer a rational and common-sense response: 'My dear sister, would you condemn yourself to an unhappy life for this?' (p. 619). Fanny's reply is perhaps truer than she realises:

> It would be the life I am fitted for. Whether by disposition, or whether by circumstances, is no matter; I am better fitted for such a life than for almost any other (p. 619).

Fanny is a Child of the Marshalsea in a much deeper and more damaging way than Amy will ever be. The shame of the former family 'circumstances' have shaped and ruined her.

Her brother Edward, or Tip, is equally a Child of the Marshalsea, and he is equally ruined. The shame of his father's imprisonment for offences against money saps his moral fibre. He quite lacks earnestness, so that while attempts are made to place him in a number of careers, 'Tip tired of everything' (p. 90), and he lasts in none of them. This failure is directly ascribed to the prison and its influence over him:

> Wherever he went, this foredoomed Tip appeared to take the prison walls with him, and to set them up in such trade or calling; and to prowl about within their narrow limits in the old slip-shod, purposeless, down-at-heel way. (p. 91)

At one point, he himself is imprisoned for debt; and when Clennam arranges for the debt to be paid off by him, he consciously tries to do so without undermining 'the self-reliance and self-helpfulness of the young man, supposing him to possess any remnant of those qualities: without doubt a very wide stretch of supposition' (p. 155). When Clennam gets accidentally locked inside the Marshalsea and needs help, Tip's first instinct is to lean on other people rather than showing any resourcefulness, independence, or responsibility:

> 'We had better get hold of Amy, first of all,' said Tip, referring any difficulty to her, as a matter of course. (p. 101)

As he then goes on to show, he was perfectly capable of manifesting the requisite qualities, once Clennam has declined to trouble Amy; he was simply being lazy.

Like his father with his 'Testimonials', Tip constructs a dignifying fantasy based on a sense of entitlement and merit. Despite Clennam's earlier help, he is outraged when Clennam doesn't comply with a request for money:

> when I address what I call a properly-worded appeal, and an urgent appeal, and a delicate appeal, to an individual, for a small temporary accommodation, easily within his power – easily within his power, mind! – and when that individual writes back word to me that he begs to be excused, I consider that he doesn't treat me like a gentleman. (p. 398)

Riches bring about no reform, and only the most superficial of changes in Tip. Because the name was given to him in the Marshalsea, he declines any longer to be known as Tip; and his forms of dissolute behaviour change, from the 'horse-dealing and billiard marking' he was formerly involved with to 'diceing' (p. 504). He too has been fatally damaged by the family's past.

The Dorrit family, then, are greatly damaged and suffer a great deal, both in times of poverty and of wealth. At the root of their suffering is society's worship of Mammon, offences against which cause Mr Dorrit to be imprisoned. He and his family, though, never question the rightness of such attitudes. They too thoroughly subscribe to the values of their society, and do not question the justice of Mr Dorrit's imprisonment. This is the source of their shame, and their later constant anxiety and insecurity. They connive at the enormous harm that is done to them. The worship of Mammon is condemned by what it does to its worshippers.

One of them, of course, does not subscribe to these values. Little Dorrit serves God rather than Mammon, and is continually concerned with love for her fellow human beings. She is unconcerned with how much money Mr Nandy has; to her he is simply a 'poor old man' whom she needs 'to take care of', and cannot conceive how this might 'disgrace' her or her family (p. 390). She cares for all around her, from Maggie to her family. She tries to help Tip sort his life out by arranging, unsuccessfully, for him to emigrate. Most of all, she cares for her broken, imprisoned father. Embarrassed not at all by his being in the Marshalsea – 'If I have found it best to conceal where my home is, it is not because I am ashamed of him. GOD forbid!' (p. 112) – she is discreet because of the attitudes of society rather than her own. She does not think that 'he has anything to be ashamed of for himself'(p. 111); as we have seen she doesn't subscribe to the view that offences against money convert someone into a reprobate deserving to be in prison. As we have also seen, she can be pained at her father's humiliating behaviour as he attempts to cope with his imprisonment. His far from subtle begging from Clennam provokes her, for instance, to put her hand on her father's arm 'in mute entreaty half repressed' (p. 98). She is nevertheless always supportive, protective and forgiving towards him. She entreats Clennam not to think badly of him for having seen him in 'moments of degradation' (p. 188). When he has, disgracefully, implied that she should lead John Chivery on, because it would be advantageous to her father, she does not hesitate, as he breaks down in shame, to embrace him and call him 'Dear father, loved father, darling of my heart!' (p. 246):

> She soothed him; asked him for his forgiveness if she had been, or seemed to have been, undutiful; told him, Heaven knows truly, that she could not honor him more if he were the favorite of Fortune and the whole world acknowledged him. (p. 247)

In all this behaviour, she is inspired by the example of Christ, as her later advice to Mrs Clennam is to reflect:

> Be guided, only by the healer of the sick, the raiser of the dead, the friend of all who were afflicted and forlorn, the patient Master who shed tears of compassion for our infirmities. (p. 826)

When the family come into wealth, it means nothing to her. Indeed, it inhibits the practice of Christian compassion: having observed Amy, Mrs General tactfully points out that 'it is scarcely delicate to look at vagrants with the attention which I have seen bestowed upon them' (p. 501). It also gets in the way of her lovingly helping her father as much as she would like to. Money drives a wedge between father and daughter: 'others occupied themselves in taking care of him' and she is 'never expected' to be involved. It is the family wealth that directly causes this change. In Mr Dorrit's view, 'to occupy herself in fulfilling the functions of – ha, um, – a valet, would be incompatible' with the respect due to a woman in the social position their wealth has translated them to. Far from feeling relieved at having her life eased, she feels 'quite displaced' to be robbed of the chance to care for him (p. 488). As we have seen. Mr Dorrit sees it as befitting his wealth and position to hire a number of servants, so that a simple piece of communication between them comes to be mediated via two servants. Later, when Mr Dorrit sets off on a journey

> Little Dorrit would have been glad to bear him company ... But, though the Courier had gone on with the Bride, the Valet was next in the line; and the succession would not have come to her, as long as any one could be got for money. (p. 639)

She takes little pleasure in the life that money provides them with. Far from being dazzled by the society in which she now moves she thinks that it 'greatly resembled a superior sort of Marshalsea'. Among many other parallels she draws, she sees people as having come abroad for the same reasons people ended up in prison: 'through debt, through idleness, relationship, curiosity, and general unfitness for getting on at home' (p. 536). These people have no greater merit or moral worth than those languishing in the

Marshalsea, as is also reflected in the way that 'They had precisely the same incapacity for settling down to anything ... they rather deteriorated one another ... they wore untidy dresses, and fell into a slouching way of life' (p. 536). When she learns of the wealth that belongs to the family, she is excited solely because it will rescue her father from misery:

> Her father, her father. She spoke of nothing but him, thought of nothing but him. Kneeling down and pouring out her thankfulness with uplifted hands, her thanks were for her father. (p. 437)

What she values are family and home; and if the Marshalsea represents shame to others, not sharing their values, she sees it simply as home. Hence, if the rest of the Dorrit family are eager to make a big show of leaving the Marshalsea, for her it is traumatic: she faints 'overpowered' (p. 452) and has to be carried out, still wearing her old dress, in Clennam's arms. In a letter to Clennam from Italy, she expresses her homesickness: 'So dearly do I love the scene of my poverty and your kindness. O so dearly, O so dearly!' (p. 580). She longs for the old family life they used to have:

> If Little Dorrit found herself left a little lonely and a little low that night, nothing would have done so much against her feeling of depression as the being able to sit at work by her father as in the old time, and help him to his supper and his rest. But that was not to be thought of now... (p. 637)

To Little Dorrit, money is of interest only as a means of helping others, as what she says to the imprisoned Clennam reflects:

> I have no use for money, I have no wish for it. It would be of no value at all to me, but for your sake. I could not be rich, and you here. I must always be much worse than poor, with you distressed. Will you let me lend you all I have? Will you let me give it to you? Will you let me show you that I have never forgotten, that I never can forget, your protection of me when this was my home? Dear Mr Clennam, make me of all the world the happiest, by saying Yes! (p. 792)

Being 'poor' would not be reprehensible in Little Dorrit's eyes; what would be 'much worse' would be to show a lack of Christian love to someone 'distressed'.

The novel's hero, Arthur Clennam, generally shares Little Dorrit's outlook. Though he is happy for Mr Dorrit coming into his wealth, for instance, for him, money is nothing alongside moral worth, and so he describes Amy as 'the treasure you have been blest with here – the best of all the riches you can have elsewhere – the treasure at your side'. (p. 440). Whereas Amy remains steadfast in her attachment to the service of God rather than Mammon, though, Clennam is tempted away from his commitment. Frustrated by his struggles with the Circumlocution Office on Doyce's behalf ('A hard case it has been, and a hard case it is, on Doyce' (p. 610)), he falls prey to an 'epidemic', a 'moral infection' (p. 597) that has already infected Pancks and which the latter now passes on to him. A belief in Merdle and all he stands for causes Pancks to urge Clennam to put his money in Merdle's hands, for thoroughly moral reasons:

> Be as rich as you honestly can. It's your duty. Not for your sake, but for the sake of others. Take time by the forelock. Poor Mr Doyce (who really *is* growing old) depends on you. Your relative depends upon you ... Why should you leave all the gains to the gluttons, knaves and impostors? (pp. 611–2)

Believing that the moral can make some sort of accommodation with Mammon, though, only leads Clennam into disaster and to his ending up in the Marshalsea 'a broken, bankrupt, sick dishonoured, prisoner' (p. 790).

Throughout the novel, Dickens demonstrates the harmful effects on humanity of their society serving Mammon, on all levels, and a variety of scales, instead of God. The sufferings of the poor, neglected because their poverty makes them negligible in the eyes of a society in which Christian love and compassion hold no sway, are everywhere in evidence, be it the very poorest living like young rats, the misery of life in the Marshalsea, or Mrs Plornish who, though a young woman, has been 'so dragged at by poverty and the children together, that their united forces had already dragged her face into wrinkles' (p. 152). (There is a contrast a few pages later in the appearance of the Plornishes landlord, the well-heeled Mr Casby, who 'had changed very little in his progress through life ... There was the same smooth face and forehead, the same calm blue eye, the same placid air' (p. 160).) Those more fortunate, though, hardly fare better. Their very indifference to the plight of the poor is in itself a sign of their corruption, and, as the Dorrit family demonstrate when they come into wealth, these people are not truly happy themselves. Serving Mammon is no route to the happiness of either individuals or society. By the end of the novel, Clennam has learned the truth of this the hard way. It is serving God that is the route to happiness.

Thus, it is that at the end of the novel, Little Dorrit and Clennam emerge from their wedding to a life of Christian service of others, or 'usefulness' – including giving 'care' to Fanny's 'neglected' children and their own, and being 'a tender nurse and friend to Tip' – and thus achieving 'happiness' (p. 859). Society in turn will only improve when it abandons both the concept that its problems are nobody's fault and the serving of Mammon with which it is still obsessed, reflected in the frantic pursuit of worldly ends in the 'roaring streets' (p. 859) and the way 'the noisy and the eager, and the arrogant and the forward and the vain, fretted, and chafed, and made their usual uproar' (p. 860).

8
Dickens and Politics: Temporary and Permanent Revolution

When Dickens addressed a meeting of the Administrative Reform Association on 27 June 1855, he said it was 'the first political meeting I have ever attended'[1] and, as Michael Slater points out, this was the only political organisation he ever joined.[2] It is quite difficult, though, for the social campaigner to remain separate from politics. Some of the social evils that Dickens exposed were remedied without any involvement of the law or politicians. In his 'Preface to the First Cheap Edition' of *Nicholas Nickleby*, written barely ten years after the novel was published, Dickens was able to report that, 'There were, then, a good many cheap Yorkshire schools in existence. There are very few now'.[3] Mark Ford notes that newspaper advertisements for such schools, having been common in the 1830s, had virtually disappeared by the time Dickens wrote his 'Preface', and that it seems Dickens's mere act of exposing them had been enough to put an end to them. Ford quotes a diary entry of the American writer Francis Parkman during a visit to Yorkshire in May 1843, relating that he had visited the original of Dotheboys Hall, which 'is deserted utterly – Nicholas Nickleby ruined not this establishment alone, but many other schools with which the vicinity abounds though some of the latter were no way objectionable'; and in an 1852 lecture, Thackeray quoted the letter of a Yorkshire schoolmaster to a newspaper complaining that 'Mr Dickens's ill-advised publication has passed like a whirlwind over the schools of the North'.[4]

Many of the social abuses that Dickens was concerned about, though, were enshrined in law, and to remedy them would require a change in the law. The reform of the workhouse system Dickens exposed in *Oliver Twist*, to take an obvious example, would demand changes to, or the abolition of, the Poor Law Amendment Act of 1834. Similarly, to relieve the suffering of the poor from the high price of bread, caused by the price of corn being kept artificially high, it was necessary to abolish the Corn Laws; and so, in this instance, Dickens's social concerns led him to be involved very directly in politics. Throughout the early 1840s, if not in his novels, then in other parts of his output, Dickens directly campaigns to get the law changed, urging the repeal of the Corn Laws in order to bring the price of bread down and thus relieve the sufferings of the poor. In an article, 'The Agricultural Interest', published in the *Morning Chronicle* in 1844, Dickens ironically pretends to be on the farmers' side, taking the view that 'the country in general is in a conspiracy against this sacred but unhappy agricultural interest',[5] before more damningly declaring that, 'the agricultural interest ... never thinks of the suffering world, or sees it, or cares to extend its knowledge of it; or, so long as it remains a world, cares anything about it'.[6] At the same period, he repeatedly attacked the Corn Laws in poems. In 'The Fine Old English Gentleman', his narrator, whose attitudes Dickens is satirising, speaks of the good old days:

> Those were the days for taxes, and for war's infernal din;
> For scarcity of bread that fine old dowagers might win (lines 31–2)

and talks of how

> The bright old day now dawns again; the cry runs through the land,
> In England there shall be dear bread – in Ireland, sword and brand (lines 3–4).[7]

In another poem of 1841, 'The Quack Doctor's Proclamation', of the central character it is said:

> He's a corn doctor also, of wonderful skill-
> No cutting, no rooting-up, purging or pill;
> You're merely to take, 'stead of walking or riding
> The sweet schoolboy exercise – innocent sliding (lines 35–8).[8]

In 'The British Lion', some verses from *The Daily News* in 1846, the lion is depicted as feeble though

> He was carried about in a carawan,
> And was slav'd in country parts,
> And they said, 'Walk up! Be in time! He can
> Eat Corn-Law Leagues like tarts!' (lines 13–16).[9]

As the campaign to abolish the Corn Laws came to a climax, Dickens wrote once more upon the matter in 'The Hymn of the Wiltshire Labourers', this time speaking as one of 'us who starve and die' (p. 8),[10] and praying that, in regard to the powerful, God will

> remind them! In the bread
> They break upon the knee,
> These sacred words may yet be read,
> 'In memory of Me!'

O God! Remind them of His sweet
Compassion for the poor,
And how He gave them Bread to eat
And went from door to door! (lines 33–40).[11]

The political stance from which Dickens criticises the laws of the land and the social abuses of his time is, however, difficult to pin down. At the period he was writing these poems,, in a letter to Forster of 13 August 1841 he jokily remarks on his becoming political in a tone of amused surprise, and as if it is the last thing in the world he expected of himself:

> By Jove, how Radical I am getting! I wax stronger and stronger in the true principles every day. I don't know whether it's the sea, or no, but so it is.[12]

His direct statements about politics tend to be more in criticism of the way things operated than support for a political position. In a speech, he thus famously announced his 'political creed', which he said, 'has no reference to any party or persons', as being that, 'My faith in the people governing, is, on the whole, infinitesimal; my faith in The People governed, is, on the whole illimitable'.[13] The 1832 Reform Act seemed to him to have little improved things: 'many years after a Reform Bill, the House of Commons is, in the gross, so little changed';[14] and this view of Parliament is reflected in the novels in, for instance, *Hard Times*, in which M.P.s are characterised as the 'national dustmen' (p. 207).[15] If he disapproves of the *status quo*, however, it is equally hard to find him expressing positive support for new political movements. He is clear about the Chartists: 'we have not the least sympathy with physical-force chartism', he declares, and physical-force Chartists, 'have done too much damage to the cause of rational liberty and freedom all over the world to be regarded in any other light than as enemies of the common weal, and the worst foes of the common people'.[16] O'Connor, the leader of physical force Chartism is categorised as, 'once a popular Misleader'.[17] The Young England movement, on the other hand, is equally dismissed as an 'hallucination'.[18]

Where, then, does Dickens stand politically? Commentators on this matter have tended to take one of three approaches. The first of these has been to align Dickens with an identifiable political stance. Thus, Macaulay famously described *Hard Times* as, 'One excessively touching, heart-breaking passage, and the rest sullen socialism'.[19] T.A. Jackson sees Dickens as a Radical, whose Radicalism, 'stiffened, hardened and deepened into something that with a little outside aid might easily have emerged as positive Socialism or Communism'.[20] Jackson sees *Hard Times*, for instance, as expressing 'hardness and bitterness', which 'arose in Dickens from his acute intuition that something more was at issue than any mere betrayal of the forward movement. Another revolution is needed – as drastic and far-reaching as the great French Revolution – and Dickens's harshness arises basically from his intense disappointment and baffled rage at finding no such revolution anywhere in sight'.[21]

Equally, *A Tale of Two Cities*:

> demonstrates unmistakably – and one might add, aggressively – Dickens' sympathy with the people in revolt, with their revolt itself, and with, too, within limits, even their infuriated infliction of vengeance upon their oppressors.[22]

Vincent Newey, on the other hand, sees Dickens as taking a conservative political stance:

> his reactions to the shortcomings of, say, support for the poor seem to be rooted, if anywhere more precise than a basic Christian ethos, in a Tory paternalism such as that expressed in Fielding's novels. His socio-political stance is undoubtedly conservative in its underlying commitment to hierarchy. This too connects him with the eighteenth century, with Cowper, Goldsmith, and Soame Jenyn's widely-circulated Free Enquiry into the Nature and Origin of Evil, which averred that God in his wisdom so designed the universe that 'there is such connexion between all ranks and orders by subordinate degrees, that they mutually support each other's existence, and every one in its place is absolutely necessary towards sustaining the whole.[23]

Thus, *A Christmas Carol* 'upholds a system of social relations that is fundamentally conservative'[24] and 'The society that is framed for recommendation in *A Christmas Carol* persistently aligns solidity with hierarchy'.[25] While 'Dickens does not go so far as to argue as Oliver Goldsmith does, through his spokesman Dr Primrose, that the poor on earth are fortunate and the rich ill-fated since the former will experience the joys of Heaven more intensely ... there is a somewhat similar placatory manoeuvre at work'[26] in the presentation of the Cratchits. The work 'conceives society very much on the old model of *discordia concors*, a fixed synchrony of separate but interdependent elements'.[27] Newey does acknowledge, though, that the picture may be more complicated than this: he recognises that there is, 'a case ... for seeing Dickens as a certain type of committed radical';[28] and in commenting on one of the John Leech illustrations, he remarks on, 'The mix of "liberal" and "conservative" strains that we have noted so often'[29] in it.

A second approach has been to see Dickens as putting forward no remedy for the ills of his society. Humphrey House comments that while Dickens 'accepted none of the current curative nostrums' for the problems of his society 'without criticism', equally, 'nor did he substitute any alternative plan of his own'.[30] George Orwell comments on the 'utter lack of any constructive suggestion' and that, while he may criticise aspects of his society, this does not lead him to 'clearly suggesting what he would put in their places'.[31] He shows, Orwell argues, 'no consciousness that the *structure* of society can be changed'.[32] This view has led to the widespread opinion that Dickens has no more positive a solution to offer than the rather weak-sounding remedy of a 'change of heart': as Orwell puts it, with no 'definite remedy', Dickens recommends a 'change of spirit rather than change of structure'.[33]

A third group of critics have gone further and seen Dickens as thinking that in fact there is no solution to the problems of his society. The ending of *Little Dorrit*, has often been seen as symptomatic of a growing pessimism in the writer in this respect. Thus, F.R. Leavis, for instance, remarks that Arthur Clennam and Little Dorrit 'have no hope of making any impact on their world of "the arrogant and the forward and the vain" who will continue to make "their usual uproar" '.[34] From a slightly different angle, Nicholas Coles argues that *Hard Times* is 'as much a novel against social reform as it is a novel of social reform',[35] in which 'Dickens persistently satirizes what he knew from other contexts to be worthy or enlightened efforts at reform and improvement',[36] including such measures as the gathering of statistical data as the basis for social action. In *Hard Times*, Dickens 'generates a critical vision of society which not only cannot be addressed within available ways of talking about and doing "reform", but in fact explicitly mocks and refuses them'.[37] Coles argues that, 'Throughout the Fifties', Dickens 'despaired of the power of either prosperity or reform to affect the "frightful extent of wrong", which he sensed in the social order and dramatized in his fiction', and so in *Hard Times* 'presents a vision of society on the basis of which socially redeeming action, including his own reforming practice, is effectually impossible'.[38]

Of these three perspectives, I shall first address the second, with its view that Dickens has nothing more positive to advocate than a mere change of heart. It is helpful here to put Dickens's views in the context of those of other Christians of the time. The emergence at this period of various political solutions, often variants of Socialism, to contemporary social ills prompted some Victorian religious writers to articulate the flaw they saw in political remedies, declaring them a false trail in seeking resolution of the problems of society because transforming the structures of society would do nothing to erase the corruption of people within it, and that corruption would serve to undermine whatever changes had been introduced. There was a need to begin by changing individuals; change in society would then follow. In *The Religion of Jesus Christ Defended From the Assaults of Owenism*, for instance, the Unitarian minister John Relly Beard discussed how Christ's aim was 'a new moral creation, with a view to the universal prevalence of the highest happiness of man',[39] and his object 'the improvement of mankind'.[40] Beard pointedly details Christ's approach:

> Now it must be carefully noted that Jesus began his work with individuals. He knew that thus only could he lay a basis for a solid and durable reform. To begin with masses and 'communities' may present a more

> imposing exterior, but must, in the main, end in disappointment. The social whole is made up of its several parts, in such a way that the character of the whole is but an aggregate of the character of the parts; and until you have reformed individuals, you cannot reform societies ... You may effectually deal with masses, when you use men as mere machines for labour or for war, but if you would bring about a 'New Moral World,' you must, as Jesus did, begin with individuals.[41]

Jesus acknowledged, Beard argues, 'the power of circumstances';[42] but the political notion of seeking 'the good of man' by means of 'the external force of "improved circumstances"' will 'signally fail', by falling into the trap of 'disowning or undervaluing the native and independent power of the human breast'. Though 'Some good may result', nevertheless, 'All effectual moral reform must be begun, carried on, and completed in the hearts of individuals'.[43]

The inefficacy of politics without spiritual regeneration is an issue explored in Elizabeth Barrett Browning's *Aurora Leigh*, in which one of the themes concerns whether poetry or politics is more effective in changing the world. Aurora's cousin Romney, looking for 'some great cure' (Book II, line 282)[44] to the ills of the world, turns to politics, and socialism specifically. (Lady Waldemar, pursuing him romantically, steeps herself in socialist texts:

> 'I read half Fourier through,
> Proudhon, Considerant, and Louis Blanc,
> With various others of his socialists' (Book III, lines 583–5))

Aurora warns him early on, though, that unless people are first spiritually reformed, his efforts are doomed:

> I hold you will not compass your poor ends
> Of barley-feeding and material ease,
> Without a poet's individualism
> To work your universal. It takes a soul,
> To move a body: it takes a high-souled man,
> To move the masses ... even to a cleaner stye:
> It takes the ideal, to blow a hair's-breadth off
> The dust of the actual. – Ah, your Fouriers failed,
> Because not poets enough to understand
> That life develops from within. (Book II, lines 475–84)

Aurora's aunt prefigures what will happen in talking of Romney's

> dreams of doing good
> To good-for-nothing people. (Book II, lines 644–5)

Romney plunges ahead, and, in the tradition of Fourier, sets up a phalanstery. However, the scheme does not work and ends disastrously, precisely because the people involved had not been previously spiritually regenerated: they were 'men and women of disordered lives' (Book VIII, line 889) and they cursed Romney for 'forcing crooked creatures to live straight' (Book VIII, line 894). Romney is compelled to acknowledge that he was relying on 'unreal remedies' (Book VIII, line 804), a 'quack nostrum' (Book VIII, line 687). As Aurora says, external changes are ineffective:

> 'Tis impossible
> To get at men excepting through their souls. (Book VIII, lines 537–8)

Events have borne out her thoughts about whether,

> A larger metaphysics might not help
> Our physics, a completer poetry
> Adjust our daily life and vulgar wants,
> More fully than the special outside plans,
> Phalansteries, material institutes ... (Book VI, lines 205–9)

And Romney ultimately concludes that men,

> 'not to work in vain, must comprehend
> Humanity and, so, work humanly,
> And raise men's bodies still by raising souls,
> As God did, first ...
> Fewer programmes, we who have no prescience.
> Fewer systems; we who are held and do not hold.
> Less mapping out of masses, to be saved,
> By nations or by sexes. Fourier's void,
> And Comte is dwarfed, – and Cabet puerile.
> Subsist no law of life outside of life,
> No perfect manners, without Christian souls'.
> (Book IX, lines 851–4, 865–71)

The position of these writers, I would argue, is precisely that of Dickens. If Beard talks of a 'new moral creation', Dickens will contemplate 'a new era ... in which the Lord's Prayer will be a fulfilled prophecy upon this earth'.[45] He would agree that 'Christian souls' are a prerequisite of the success of any social change and that 'until you have reformed individuals, you cannot reform societies'. As we shall see, in *A Tale of Two Cities* he presents a revolution that ends up producing no better a society than before, but rather one that is strikingly similar, because the characters of the French citizens, far from being reformed, are as corrupt and evil as the old system made them.

The only way to effect permanent rather than temporary revolution is by precisely the change of heart in each individual that many of Dickens's critics consider to be a weak remedy; but unless people are spiritually reformed and committed to Christian values, a better society will never come about. Merely to change the personnel in power, as happens in the French Revolution, ultimately changes nothing. The change of heart, far from being a weak, milk-and-water solution, is the key to reforming society.[46]

Dickens is neither in search of, nor in need of, a political ideology with which to supplement his religious views. His religion is his politics. Christianity provides the answer to everything. Nor was this a particularly unusual stance for him to take. The notion of the inseparability of politics from religion was reflected for instance in the assertion by the Christian Socialists that 'Politics for the People cannot be separated from Religion' and Richard Oastler's declaration that he 'gathered his politics from the Holy Scriptures ... and so, without any ceremony declined to separate his politics from his Religion'.[47] Thus, it is a mistaken endeavour to try to identify allegiance to a particular political philosophy in his work. What may seem a political attitude in Dickens should rather be seen as a religious one. When relating the story of Betty Higden in *Our Mutual Friend*, for instance, he breaks off to comment on how 'we have got things to the pass that with an enormous treasure at disposal to relieve the poor, the best of the poor detest our mercies, hide their heads from us, and shame us by starving in the midst of us'. This, he says, is 'a pass impossible of prosperity, impossible of continuance' (p. 496).[48] 'My lords and gentlemen and honorable boards' have 'piled up a mountain of pretentious favour' (p. 495) and must now 'off with your honorable coats for the removal of it, and fall to the work with the power of all the queen's horses and all the queen's men, or it will come rushing down and bury us alive' (pp. 495–6). In the long term, the consequences of such perverted moral attitudes will be dire: 'We must mend it, lords and gentlemen and honorable boards, or in its own evil hour it will mar every one of us' (p. 496). One might see these statements as either those of a Conservative, anxious to preserve the *status quo*, or those of a Radical or Socialist, threatening the powers that be with revenge. These are not so much political statements, though, as theological ones: disregard of God's instructions about loving our neighbour will breed the evil these instructions were designed to prevent. Lack of a sense in the powerful of their brotherhood with the poor will lead eventually to a vengeful breakdown altogether of brotherhood. Blatant disregard of how God intends the world to work merely stores up trouble. Society at the moment is not being run on the basis of the Gospel, but 'the Gospel according to Podsnappery' (p. 496); and the things Dickens has said would not form 'the text of a sermon, in the Returns of the Board of Trade' (p. 496). He is uttering, though, universal truths that are part and parcel of the way God made the world: 'they have been the truth since the foundations of the world were laid, and they will be the truth until the foundations of the universe are shaken by the Builder' (p. 496). Dickens speaks properly in a prophetic role, as one who can predict the future because he sees clearly, as prophets traditionally do, in the Bible and elsewhere. A society that does not live by the moral code taught in the New Testament can breed only suffering and resentment, not happiness and contentment, and everything will ultimately go wrong.

Equally, Dickens's religious perspective means that he does not think there is no solution to the state of his society. His criticisms of the attempts at reform that Coles discusses are based on his perception that they are operating outside a context of Christian love. At the end of Hard Times, statistics have not totally been abandoned by Mr Gradgrind, but he now makes his 'facts and figures subservient to Faith, Hope, and Charity' (p. 286).[49] Beyond this, however, we need to examine the importance to Dickens of the concept of usefulness.[50] 'Useful', with its implications of service and doing good is one of the highest terms of praise in Dickens's lexicon. In his speeches for instance, he regularly uses it to commend the bodies he is addressing. The 'objects' of the Charitable Society for the Deaf and Dumb are 'of the most useful and praiseworthy character'.[51] The Manchester Athenaeum, an organisation concerned with 'the moral and social elevation, the harmless relaxation, the peace, happiness, and improvement, of the community at large' is characterised by its 'usefulness';[52] Dickens disclaims that there is any 'merit' in his attending the soiree, stating that he would take it as 'the very highest mark of your favour and distinguished regard' if they would allow him 'to be useful in like manner' again on another occasion.[53] Similarly, he hopes that each passing year will find the Glasgow Athenaeum 'richer in its means of usefulness'.[54] In discussing the 'usefulness' of the chairman (John Forster) at the second anniversary dinner of the Newsvendors' Benevolent Institution, Dickens remarks that 'no man could possibly descend from his station to be useful', for

> However exalted his station he must ascend from it to be useful to mankind; and this was one of the greatest principles and greatest truths of the greatest history with which mankind was acquainted.[55]

Dickens thus explicitly links the idea of usefulness to Christian service; and it is moreover, a term he uses in relation to the work of Christ himself. In *The Life of Our Lord* he presents Jesus, in the wilderness just before his ministry begins, 'praying that He might be of use to men and women'; the next paragraph then relates how 'When he came out of the Wilderness, he began to cure sick people'.[56] At the end of *Bleak House*, Esther, who throughout has wanted 'to be useful to some one' (p. 385), goes with her husband, Allan Woodcourt, as he takes up a job as a doctor to the poor, 'a way of usefulness and good service' (p. 920). Part of the comfort for Sydney Carton in his putative vision of the future is that his sacrifice of his life will not only save the lives of others, but that those lives, unblighted, will be 'useful' (p. 389),[57] and thus good will come out of his losing his life. These characters, then, are dedicated to a life of Christian service and love; and in doing so, they are helping to bring about the Kingdom of Heaven on Earth, which will be achieved, as we have seen, one person at a time rather than by a sudden upheaval of society. If the challenge seems tougher in *Little Dorrit*, as Amy and her new husband set out on a life of 'usefulness and happiness' (p. 859),[58] all the more reason to face it with patience and perseverance. Sanguine, steady dedication rather than despair is the Christian reaction to adverse circumstances.

Dickens, then, believes that Christianity should be at the heart of political life. It is the continuing lack of Christian principles guiding governments that leads him to conclude that the 1832 Reform Act made little difference. In Parliament there is still a lack of brotherly concern for the welfare of the population as a whole: 'bills which cramp and worry the people, and restrict their scant enjoyments, are so easily smuggled through that place, and ... measures for their real service are so very difficult to pass'. There is little interest there in 'the health, the taxation, the education, of a whole people'.[59] The lack of connection between Parliament and Christian values is made explicit in an ironic passage in *Hard Times*, describing Mr Gradgrind, as an M.P., as

> one of the respected members for ounce weights and measures, one of the representatives of the multiplication table, one of the deaf honourable gentlemen, dumb honourable gentlemen, blind honourable gentlemen, lame honourable gentlemen, dead honourable gentlemen, to every other consideration. Else wherefore live we in a Christian land, eighteen hundred and odd years after our Master? (pp. 92–3)

What he believes in, though, is a civic political system which acts on Christian principles, rather than a theocracy. Part of his opposition to Roman Catholicism is that it is a theocracy, with all power resting with the Pope and his ministers right down to the local priest. In *A Child's History of England*, the Pope's attempts to assert his power are portrayed damningly. He arrogantly 'pretended that no one could rightfully wear the crown of England without his gracious permission' (p. 413).[60] Mary Queen of Scots and her husband the king of France 'styled themselves King and Queen of England, and the Pope was disposed to help them by doing all the mischief he could' (p. 414). There is 'a great conspiracy of the Pope and some of the Catholic sovereigns to depose Elizabeth, place Mary on the throne, and restore the unreformed religion' (pp. 421–2). The Pope is 'so hot in the matter' that he excommunicates Elizabeth and 'all her subjects who should continue to obey her' (p. 422). This naked attempt to exercise political power by the Pope personally stands condemned as do the deeds of his instruments. In *Pictures from Italy*, visiting the Palace of the Popes and the 'ruins of the dreadful rooms in which the Inquisition used to sit' (p. 21),[61] Dickens brings out fully the horrors involved in the Church's exercise of power. The dungeons 'in which the prisoners of the Inquisition were confined for forty-eight hours after their capture, without food or drink, that their constancy might be shaken, even before they were confronted with their gloomy judges' (p. 22) are the least of it. We are introduced to 'The Chamber of Torture' with its special funnel-shaped roof 'to stifle the victim's cries'; the 'wheel of heavy blows ... An endless routine of heavy hammers. Mash, mash, mash! upon the sufferer's limbs' (pp. 22–3); the 'stone trough' for 'the water torture' (p. 23); 'the furnace' where 'they made the irons red-hot' (p. 23). In reaction to 'Les oubliettes de l'Inquisition', Dickens's 'blood ran cold', but he feels a 'thrill' on seeing their ruined state and 'the sun shining in'. As he ironically comments, 'I felt exalted with the proud delight of living in these degenerate times, to see it ... The light in the doleful vaults was typical of the light that has streamed in, on all persecution in God's name' (p. 24). A *Child's History of England* relates a rule of fear in England with 'an Act of Six Articles, commonly called at the time "the whip with six strings;" which punished offences against the Pope's opinion, without mercy, and enforced the very worst parts of the monkish religion' (p. 387).

Even where physical punishment is not involved, Dickens sees an all powerful Roman Catholic church as having oppressed through a suppression which enabled it to retain all power. In, again, *A Child's History of England* he writes of a new prominence gained during the Reformation for 'the New Testament which the priests did not allow to be read, and which contained truths that they suppressed' (p. 375); he comments on the Evangelists and Saint Paul 'who had been for some time shut up in a strange language so that people could not get at them' (p. 413); and refers to Coverdale translating the Bible into English 'which the unreformed religion never permitted to be done' (p. 385). Thus the Reformation 'made England free' (p. 435), for it 'set the people free from their slavery to the priests' (p. 315). As Carolyn Oulton points out, in a letter of 1863, referring to the Roman Catholic church, Dickens warns there are 'politicians wanting despotism, and idiots wanting a sensation, who would do it if they could'.[62]

While there can be no denying, of course, that *Barnaby Rudge* and *A Tale of Two Cities* are historical novels, they are so only in a particular fashion. On the one hand, John Bowen points out that *Barnaby Rudge* follows the model of the historical novels of Scott and Victorian historical novelists in a number of ways, including that it traces 'the progress of a number of characters, from a range of classes, and shows how their interlinked fates develop through the course of a great historical action'.[63] As against this, though, Andrew Sanders observes that in *A Tale of Two Cities*:

> Dickens's concern with the details of an historical period does not extend far beyond the obvious; there is little concern with descriptions of costume,

> diet, speech, or manners, a concern which so obsessed Bulwer and Reade and which was to haunt George Eliot in Romola. Apart from the opening chapters with their comments on the state of the roads and the authorial barbs directed against the law or the unthinking prejudices of the past, there is not much sign of an interest in everyday historical detail.[64]

Dickens's lack of interest in what Sanders calls in the same passage 'ephemeral details' reflects that essentially these two works are, more than historical novels, political novels, and political novels written by someone whose religion is his politics. They present studies of two political events from the past seen from a Christian perspective and subjected to a Christian critique.

9
Barnaby Rudge and the Struggle for Brotherhood

Dickens's other historical novel, *A Tale of Two Cities*, is concerned with a revolution, but *Barnaby Rudge* is concerned with an anti-revolution. Gordon and his mob of rioters are opposing a change rather than trying to precipitate one. The riots, in trying to preserve an old *status quo*, are an attempt to hold back progress towards a more enlightened society with a stronger element of brotherly love. Dickens presents a sharply critical view both of the rioters and of the society from which they emerge. Gordon and his followers are supposedly adherents of Christianity; the writer brings out that they, like their society, lack what he sees as the essentials of Christianity. Centrally, in their attitude to Roman Catholics, the rioters lack any sense of the brotherhood of man and of 'Universal Love' (p. 239).[1] Indeed, their professed Christianity does not go deep at all, the result of which is the terrifying events and situations which arise during the riots. The events of the novel, and the historical occurrences that are at their centre, are used to expose the urgent need for each of the individuals who make up society to adopt Christianity and its ethic of brotherly love.

It may seem surprising that Dickens should give such a sympathetic portrayal of Roman Catholics and their predicament, when he is normally so hostile to Roman Catholicism. I hope to show here that there is no such contradiction. There are two main aspects of Roman Catholicism to which he is opposed. Partly his objection to Roman Catholicism is that many of its practices are, to him, alien, misconceived and pointless. His observations about pilgrims on the Scala Santa on Good Friday during his sojourn in Rome, described in *Pictures from Italy*, are typically reflective of his more general reactions. The Santa Scala, he tells us,

> is composed of eight-and-twenty steps, said to have belonged to Pontius Pilate's house, and to be the identical stairs on which our Saviour trod, in coming down from the judgment-seat. Pilgrims ascend it, only on their knees. (p. 156)[2]

The sight, however, of 'a hundred people, slowly shuffling up these stairs, on their knees, at a time' strikes him merely as 'ridiculous' and 'unpleasant' – 'ridiculous in the absurd incidents inseparable from it; and unpleasant in its senseless and unmeaning degradation' (p. 157). It has no meaning as far as he is concerned because it is an outward show, a reflection of a 'dangerous reliance on outward observances, in themselves mere empty forms' that are a substitute, he seems to think, for true inner devotion. The pilgrims may think that they are showing their love for God through making this climb, and thus obeying the first of the two commandments of Christ; but Dickens writes of it as if it has little value, and that the pilgrims are wrong in their sense of virtue when they 'came down, very sprightly and fresh, as having done a real good substantial deed which it would take a good deal of sin to counterbalance' (p. 157). It is a 'senseless' ritual to go through in that it achieves nothing practical at all, and perhaps leaves pilgrims deceived, by substituting an outward act for the need for inner dedication to God, as to their own state of virtue. To Dickens, it is possible and more useful to obey both of Christ's commandments at once by giving practical help to one's neighbour; thus, in an 1856 speech urging his hearers to help the Royal Hospital for Incurables, he urged their aid 'for the love of God; for the love of man – which was one'.[3]

More centrally he is, as we saw in Chapter 8, opposed to what he sees as the Roman Catholic church's tyrannical and oppressive wielding of its power and theocratic tendencies:[4] in 'A Crisis in the Affairs of Mr John Bull, As Related by Mrs Bull to the Children',[5] written in response to the so-called 'Papal Aggression', Mrs Bull relates that the Bulls of Rome laid claim 'to have some influence in our family' (p. 302); they are an 'insolent, audacious, oppressive, intolerable race' (p. 302), and being rid of them is 'liberty' (p. 303). He also sees the Roman Catholic church as the enemy of progress. According to Mrs Bull, referring to the Bulls of Rome, 'wherever they go, they perpetuate misery oppression, darkness, and ignorance' (p. 303). Miss Eringobragh, a symbol of the Ireland where Roman Catholicism is dominant, 'presented a most lamentable spectacle of dirt, disease, rags, superstition and degradation' (p. 303). Overall, Mrs Bull concludes, 'our knowledge, liberty, progress, social welfare and happiness, are wholly irreconcileable and inconsistent with them' (p. 303).

This is, however, far from the end of the matter, for Dickens is, at the same time, a thorough believer in religious tolerance. In *Pictures from Italy*, he condemns 'all persecution in God's name' (p. 24) and an examination of *A Child's History of England* reveals him to be consistently in favour of religious toleration. He relates an episode in which Oliver Cromwell appears as a hero in championing religious tolerance:

> Oliver found that the VAUDOIS, or Protestant people of the valley of Lucerne, were insolently treated by the Catholic powers, and were even

> put to death for their religion in an audacious and bloody manner. Instantly, he informed those powers that this was a thing which Protestant England would not allow; and he speedily carried this point, through the might of his great name, and established their right to worship God in peace after their own harmless manner. (p. 490)[6]

Since Dickens is himself a Protestant, one might expect him to be in favour of Protestants being tolerated. His sympathies are not narrow, though. He presents in a highly critical light clergy of the Church of England who behaved in a 'disgraceful' (p. 497) way

> because they hoped to get the nonconformists, or dissenters, thoroughly put down in this reign, and to have but one prayer-book and one service for all kinds of people, no matter what their private opinions were. This was pretty well, I think, for a Protestant Church, which had displaced the Romish Church, because people had a right to their own opinions in religious matters. (pp. 497–8)

Furthermore, Dickens defends the right to be tolerated of groups with which he has little sympathy, such as the Puritans. He reports how Parliament urged James I 'to have some little consideration for the poor Puritan clergy who were persecuted for preaching in their own way' (p. 445), and comments on how in disputes with Puritans

> It was comfortably settled that there was to be only one form of religion, and that all men were to think exactly alike. But although this was arranged two and a half centuries ago, and although the arrangement was supported by much fining and imprisonment, I do not find that it is quite successful even yet. (p. 438)

In similar vein, he deplores a lack of tolerance to Roman Catholics while not at all subscribing to their version of religion. In talking of the reign of Edward VI, he remarks on it as one of the 'pleasanter' features of that period that 'not a single Roman Catholic was burnt in this reign for holding that religion' (p. 396). He writes approvingly of Elizabeth I in her religious tolerance:

> Some of the Queen's advisers were for seizing the principal English Catholics, and putting them to death: but the Queen ... rejected the advice, and only confined a few of those who were the most suspected, in the fens of Lincolnshire. The great body of Catholics deserved this confidence; for they behaved most loyally, nobly, and bravely. (p. 431)

He is critical of how, after the Gunpowder Plot, intolerance of this religious minority intensified: 'the Catholics, in general, who had recoiled with horror from the idea of the infernal contrivance, were unjustly put under more severe laws than before' (p. 444). He deplores the victimisation of Catholics: when writing of the Great Fire of London, he observes that 'An inscription on the Monument long attributed it to the Catholics; but it is removed now, and was always a malicious and stupid untruth' (p. 503). His position is thus analogous to that of people in the multi-faith Britain of the twenty-first century who are perfectly tolerant of the various religions to be found among minorities, without wanting to live under their rules or laws.

Furthermore, there is a distinction to be made between Roman Catholicism and people who are Roman Catholics. They are our brothers and sisters, no matter how misguided, from Dickens's perspective, their opinions and practices and no matter how harmful the institution to which they belong. To the Christian, even people who do serious wrong are not excluded from love: as the saying goes, hate the sin, but love the sinner. How much more, then, are people sincerely trying to serve God, albeit as part of an institution Dickens disapproves of, entitled to Christian love. Hence the damning portrayal of their persecution in the novel.

Barnaby Rudge is probably one of the least popular and least regarded of Dickens's novels, yet when Dickens reaches the Gordon Riots and their aftermath themselves, the narrative is a superb, prolonged *tour de force*, fast-moving and exciting. It may be that it is the early part of the novel that is off-putting. In thematic terms, the father–son relationships focussed on by Steven Marcus[7] introduce the theme of authority and rebellion. In narrative terms, though the murder mystery involving Barnaby's father is set up, and the story of the opposition of the Chester and Haredale families to the romance of Edward and Emma is developed, with its religious element introducing the denominational division that will later come to the centre of the narrative, much of the rest of the narrative does not superficially seem thrusting and purposeful. Barnaby Rudge may be the hero of the novel but he is not particularly prominent at this point, neither is Gabriel Varden, even though the novel was originally to be called *Gabriel Vardon The Locksmith of London*. The point of their being in the novel, and of the details we are told of them – for instance, for the moment, nothing is made of Gabriel's profession as a locksmith despite its being highlighted in the original title – may seem unclear; and the same could be said for a number of the other characters.

In fact, the early chapters of *Barnaby Rudge* are intended to be a prelude to the main action – though perhaps, at thirty-two chapters and some two hundred and seventy pages, a long prelude. What are established here are aspects of the characters and identities of the various figures that will come to be fateful at the moment of crisis. Barnaby's being a simpleton will lead eventually to his taking a prominent part in the riots, all unaware of what he is doing, and thus almost cost him his life. Haredale's identity as a Roman Catholic will cause him to be physically attacked, and his house burnt down when anti-Catholicism explodes. Gabriel's profession as a locksmith will bring him to a highly dangerous moment of testing when the mob tries to force him to use his skills to open up Newgate prison. Dolly's beauty puts her in peril during the Riots, when she is kidnapped in accordance with the amorous intentions of Tappertit and Hugh. Hugh's brutal nature will later get the chance to be fully expressed and indulged as the rule of law breaks down during the riots, and he will forfeit his life as a result.

Beyond this, though, Barnaby and Gabriel will emerge, each in his own way, as heroes of the novel. Dickens uses Barnaby as he uses Oliver Twist and Little Nell, as a measure of the quality of the society around him, of its compassion or callousness towards a vulnerable figure. Barnaby is a simpleton with an impenetrable innocence. His lack of moral, social and political awareness means that he is not responsible for his actions. As he becomes implicated in riot and disorder, he imagines he is building a golden future for himself and his mother. Society though, comes to the very point of hanging him. It is a society without compassion, one that shows no understanding and no mercy: the harsh treatment of Mary Jones, hung for merely contemplating stealing some cloth reflects this and it is reinforced by the death sentence passed on an uncomprehending idiot boy. It is an indictment of the rioters that they exploited Barnaby's simple nature; but the punishment meted out to him is an indictment of the supposedly civilised and orderly society that once again prevails by the end of the novel. Even Hugh – brutal, savage Hugh – is more civilised than that: aware that Barnaby's life will be lost 'through me', he has been expecting some intervention from the authorities over Barnaby, and that 'this one life would be spared'. That it apparently is not going to be spared leaves Hugh without any hope for 'any mercy in this hardened, cruel, unrelenting place' (p. 646). A society with law but no mercy is little different from the society with no law and no mercy we glimpsed earlier in the novel.

If Barnaby is the hero in this way very characteristic of the early Dickens, Gabriel Varden is heroic in more straightforward ways, exemplifying the values Dickens espouses. Though Gabriel is quite an old man, he is depicted as not weighed down by the past, setting him aside, as we shall see, from many around him who are fervently attached to it. He is introduced as one of those whom time 'lays his hand lightly upon' (p. 25); even though 'past the prime of life', he is 'hale, hearty, and in a green old age' (p. 25), one of those with 'hearts and spirits young and in full vigour' (p. 25). As he remarks about himself, he has 'a pretty stout arm considering my years' (p. 76). Even at the end of the novel, like the rest of his family, living in 'cheerfulness and content', which, we are told, are 'famous preservers of youthful looks', it is 'a *very* long time' before Gabriel and the other members of his family 'looked five years older' (p. 685).

Gabriel's is a religious household, but the religion in it takes two distinct forms. One is that espoused by Mrs Varden, supported by Miggs. This is a very ostentatious version of Christianity, of which the 'mighty show of humility and forgiveness' (p. 162) that she manifests during a quarrel with Gabriel, and for which she is lavished with praise by Miggs ('I never see such a blessed one as she is for the forgiveness of her spirit' (p. 165)) is typical. Her speech, recorded directly or indirectly, is replete with religious references and terminology:

> to take a draught of small ale in the morning was to observe a pernicious, irreligious, and Pagan custom, the relish whereof should be left to swine, and Satan, or at least to Popish persons, and should be shunned by the righteous as a work of sin and evil. (p. 160)

Mrs Varden knows all the theory of Christianity, or thinks she does, and practises it thoroughly, or thinks she does. In fact, she is deceived on both counts. Her Christianity goes a lot less deep than she imagines, and her strict puritanical aspirations are constantly being undermined by her genuine impulses. Though she is ready to denounce places where alcohol is served, on her arrival there her heart 'warmed towards the Maypole bar ... directly' (p. 168). Shortly afterwards, she passes swiftly from holding forth on the religious topic of 'the nothingness of good works' to focussing on 'the somethingness of ham and toast' – 'with great cheerfulness' (p. 183). Having enjoyed the worldly delights of the Maypole, with religion of 'the retrospective order', she can later denounce 'the sinfulness of such junkettings' (p. 191). She preaches on the need for the Christian virtues of 'great fortitude and forbearance' in marriage, the display of which Miggs is ready to exalt in Mrs Varden, praising her as 'the mildest, amiablest, forgiving-spirited, longest-sufferingest female as ever she could have believed' and which Mrs Varden herself believes she has shown 'supported by a strong principle of duty' (p. 188). The reader, however, knows different; it is Gabriel who shows all the forbearance with his awkward, moody wife.

This is not hypocrisy, merely self-delusion, mainly comical. She convinces herself of her own virtue by constantly proclaiming it. This is eventually, though, to be exposed as other than harmless. When John Chester utters completely empty religious sentiments –

> 'Let us be sincere and Protestant, strictly moral, strictly just (though always with a leaning towards mercy), strictly honest, and strictly true...'

Mrs Varden takes him completely at face value: 'now, to be sure, Mrs Varden thought, here is a perfect character ... a meek, righteous, thorough-going Christian' (p. 227). To Mrs Varden, in his case as in her own, to profess such values is to have them. But of course, she is deceived, the only distinction being that she sincerely believes in what she says whereas his statements are mere acts of calculation. The shortcomings of her version of religion are exposed further in this scene in another way. Lacking humility in her Christianity, and actually victim to 'her share of vanity, obstinacy and love of power' (p. 233), she is very susceptible to the flattery he offers. By the time he leaves, she has agreed to help him, in a 'secret treaty of alliance ... with her insinuating visitor' (p. 233), to frustrate the plans of Edward Chester and Emma Haredale; having already decided that he is 'a saint' (p. 232), she 'really did believe that in so doing she furthered the ends of truth, justice and morality' (p. 233). Even Dolly, though young, is not so gullible, and detects that Chester 'was making game of us' (p. 233). Regarding herself as a model of moral correctness, Mrs Varden is duped by Chester's flattery, which seems to confirm it, into doing bad.

Equally, her very partial awareness of the true meaning of Christianity causes her firmly to link herself to denominationalism. She is strongly Protestant, constantly consulting the Protestant Manual and supporting the Protestant Association with her collecting box. She seems totally oblivious to the idea that such fierce attachment may be at odds with Christian principles of brotherhood.

If Mrs Varden's Christian name, Martha, indicates that she is, like her Biblical namesake, at least a genuine follower of Jesus, Gabriel's name marks him out as an angel. His version of Christianity is the reverse of hers in almost every respect. His religion is understated. Only occasionally does he make religious allusions, as when he describes a version of events heard by Dolly as 'true as the Gospel' (p. 43), or talks light-heartedly of Miggs as 'all the plagues of Egypt in one' (p. 163). He does not, thus, constantly parade himself as a Christian, and this is very much in keeping with the type of Christianity that Dickens recommends to his own children in *The Life of Our Lord*:

> It is Christianity to be gentle, merciful, and forgiving, and to keep these qualities quiet in our hearts, and never make a boast of them, or of our prayers or of our love of God, but always to shew that we love Him by humbly trying to do right in everything. (pp. 67–8)[8]

The need for humility as a Christian has also been emphasised earlier in that work when he tells his children, the original readers, 'we are never to be proud, or think ourselves very good, before God, but are always to be humble' (p. 33) or when he concludes from the parable of the widow's mite, 'Let us never forget what the poor widow did, when we think we are charitable' (p. 38). Humbly living by Christian moral values is precisely what Gabriel does, whether those values be the 'Charity, Forbearance, Universal Love and Mercy' identified in *Barnaby Rudge* as values not adhered to by the worldly (p. 239), or the remaining ones taught in the Bible. Early on, he displays 'compassion and humanity' (p. 53) in his concern for Mrs Rudge. In relation to his wife, he is tolerant and forgiving; 'all of us have our faults. I'll not be hard upon hers' (p. 69). Believing in such patience, tolerance and forbearance himself, he urges them on others: if blessed are the peacemakers, that is a role Gabriel attempts to take on in his dealings with John and Joe Willet:

> The honest locksmith alone addressed a few words of coherent and sensible advice to both parties, urging John Willet to remember that Joe was nearly arrived at man's estate, and should not be ruled with too tight a hand, and exhorting Joe himself to bear with his father's caprices, and rather endeavour to turn them aside by temperate remonstrance than by ill-timed rebellion. (p. 31)

Later, he is to counsel Joe that, 'We must be patient, Joe, and bear with old folks' foibles' (p. 117). He subscribes to the principle of universal love: we are told that he 'felt kindly towards everybody' (p. 337), and he declares that 'I don't hate anybody' (p. 345).

Gabriel tolerates his wife's adherence to the Protestant Association, but he never subscribes to such denominationalism himself; he never, for instance, puts any money in the collecting box. His attitude changes, though, when the consequences of such an attitude become clear: such factionalism leads to a sharpening of attitudes towards those outside the faction and casts them as something approaching an enemy, who are then prone to victimisation or violent attack. This contravenes all principles of Christian love towards one's neighbour (and towards one's enemy). Denominationalism becomes an instrument of hate. Gabriel's moment of insight into all this comes when Tappertit offers the Vardens a piece of paper with a message from Gordon which will act as 'a protection' (p. 425). If some are to be protected, on the grounds of their Protestantism, Gabriel realises, other fellow human beings will not, and will be subject to the malice of the mob. He reads the document 'with an altered face' (p. 425), and is then prompt in his condemnation. As he significantly remarks, 'What threat does it imply? What devil is abroad?' (p. 425) From now on, Gabriel's vision crystallises, and he identifies what is going on in the riots as evil.

Gabriel has already been put in a morally awkward and compromising position by Sim's account of his activities. Tappertit has just spoken openly of his involvement in violence. At Westminster, he 'kicked a county member ... he tapped a lord ... blood flowed from his nose, and ... he tapped a lord' (p. 423), and shows them a bishop's tooth he has knocked out. Gabriel is aware of the responsibility of the Protestant Association, 'your great association', as he describes it to his wife, as potentially being 'the cart that draws men to the gallows' (p. 423). In the moral dilemma of whether to protect Sim or not – 'I am not sure that I do right in screening him from the punishment he deserves' (p. 424) – Gabriel nevertheless decides to be loyal to his apprentice, on the assumption that the latter, on calm reflection, will be sorry for what he has done and will recognise the evil of it.. He urges

Sim to 'sleep for a couple of hours that you may wake penitent ... Be sorry for what you have done, and we will try to save you' (p. 424), and he comes up with a plan for spiriting Sim out of London. It quickly becomes clear, though, that Tappertit is not at all repentant, and stands by what he has done. Violence is apparently all right under the right circumstances, causing him to say to Gabriel, 'do you suppose, sir, that I am base enough to accept your servile proposition?' (p. 424).

These two incidents bring affairs into focus for Gabriel. Shortly after, he smashes the collecting box that is the symbol of Protestant denominationalism in his house. He also rejects utterly the idea of making use of the protective note from Gordon that the family have been given. To do so would be to show a lack of brotherly solidarity with those who are not Protestants, and he would unflinchingly rather face whatever violent and destructive consequences there may be than do that: 'Use it! Let them come and do their worst' (p. 428). The factionalism which has been so important to his wife he now condemns as one of the 'good things perverted to evil purposes' and as 'very wrong' (p. 428). Having achieved such clarity of vision, Gabriel knows exactly where he stands, and is staunch. As Stephen Blackpool will do, in a parallel situation which arises for the same reasons, in the central episode of the locksmith's story, Gabriel finds himself strongly at odds with, and being bullied by, the very people an outside observer might see as his own people, doggedly resisting pressure from them – in Gabriel's case, to further their aims by picking the Newgate lock. As with Stephen, the point is that Gabriel refuses to identify with one sectional group and thus to deny the brotherhood of all men, and so refuses to help further a factional cause: 'I tell you, beforehand, I'll do nothing for you' (p. 525). He is fully aware of the danger of his position: in refusing to engage in discussions with them, 'Gabriel was in imminent peril, and he knew it; but he preserved a steady silence; and would have done so, if they had been debating whether they should roast him at a slow fire' (p. 526) He is defiant: he talks of how 'My heart is green enough to scorn and despise every man among you' and calls them a 'band of robbers' (p. 526); he will, he says, 'not ask mercy at such hands as yours' (p. 525). At the jail itself, his attitude remains, 'that I will not do it, come what may of the refusal' (p. 530), and by refusing to join the rioters' side he becomes subject to violence as they turn on him.

It would be wrong to say that there is no secular element in Gabriel's defiance. Gabriel has appeared earlier as a supporter of civil order and the rule of law. His profession entails making locks that shut up criminals and evil-doers. (Locks also, of course, keep people safe, protecting them in their own homes as well as locking up the criminals who might attack them, and thus 'do good' in the world. Locksmithing may thus be seen as a moral profession.) He is a member, furthermore, of the civic militia. His religious views, however, inform even his membership of this body. He has plainly considered whether his religious beliefs can be squared with it, for when

Mrs Varden criticises his membership of the volunteers as unchristian, he is clear in his defence of it:

> 'what on earth do you call it unchristian for? Which would be most unchristian, Martha – to sit quietly down and let our houses be sacked by a foreign army, or to turn out like men and drive 'em off? Shouldn't I be a nice sort of Christian, if I crept into a corner of my own chimney and looked on while a parcel of whiskered savages bore off Dolly – or you – ?' p. 339)

At the climax of the story, his religious values and his civic values combine to make him utterly resistant to the evils of the riots.

Looked at from a puritanical or evangelical angle – which is that used by his wife – Gabriel has some faults as a Christian. At the beginning of the novel, he does not manage to stick to his promise to his wife not to call at that den of iniquity, the Maypole Inn. Having at first shown 'resolution' (p. 28) in not calling there, he finds himself going there nevertheless to get a light, and though he is resolved 'to take nothing but a light' (p. 28), once he gets there 'Gabriel felt his firmness oozing rapidly away' (p. 29). When he later utters the phrase 'what the devil', Mrs Varden looks as if she is expecting 'visible judgment' as 'the consequence of this profanity' (p. 339). But if he does not always manage to live up to the letter of the law, he certainly understands its spirit. On issues relating to the core of Christianity he shows a clear, unwavering and brave attachment.

The society Dickens presents in the novel is a stagnant and slowly decaying one. The book opens at the Maypole Inn, whose name refers to traditional English customs, and which was reputedly built in the days of Henry VIII, though it is 'perhaps older' (p. 5). Although it has its quaint features, it is mouldering and in decay. Its stables are 'gloomy, ruinous and empty' (p. 6); its ceilings are 'blackened' (p. 7); its bricks 'had grown yellow and discoloured like an old man's skin'; its timbers 'had decayed like teeth'; its walls are 'time-worn' (p. 7). The cooing of the birds fits in with the sleepy character of the building and its little world: it 'suited it exactly, and seemed to lull it to rest' (p. 7).

The customers nevertheless find a comfort there, and the presiding spirit of the place, John Willet, fiercely opposes all change. He thus exemplifies a more general spirit of lingering in the past. Tappertit's Apprentice Association opposes 'the innovating spirit of the times' and its members 'united therefore to resist all change, except such changes as would restore those good old English customs'. They look fondly backwards to the privileges apprentices had 'in times gone by' even though these included habits in which they had 'broken people's heads by scores' and 'even achieved some glorious murders' (p. 76). As this indicates, there is little to admire in the society of which its members seem to speak so fondly. The past society

Dickens portrays is not one to feel much nostalgia about. It is a world in which crime is rife, with 'street robberies, often accompanied by cruel wounds, and not infrequently by loss of life' (p. 138), of 'lurking footpads' (p. 138), of highwaymen (p. 140). The justice system in response is brutal: hanging is commonplace, and society's barbarism is perhaps most reflected in its indiscriminate use of capital punishment. John Willet speaks approvingly of how Hugh's mother was hanged for passing forged banknotes: 'it's a blessing to think how many people are hung in batches for that, and such like offences, as showing how wide awake our government is' (p. 100). Later on we are to hear of the (real life) case of Mary Jones who:

> 'was worked off for taking a piece of cloth off the counter of a shop in Lud-gate Hill, and putting it down again when the shopman see her; and who had never done any harm before, and only tried to do that, in consequence of her husband having been pressed three weeks previous, and she being left to beg, with two young children'. (pp. 331–2)

Dennis, who relates this tale, regards such as 'the glory of England' and regards any potential change as 'going down hill' (p. 332). At the end of the novel, we witness the public hangings – a practice Dickens was famously to campaign against – of Hugh, Dennis and (almost) Barnaby. In these scenes, the author repeatedly refers to 'the bells in church towers' (p. 638), 'the spires of city churches and the great cathedral dome', the 'chime of St. Sepulchre's clock' (p. 641), the way 'the church towers, the church roof, the church yard … swarmed with life'. The churches stand in silent rebuke to the unholy deeds perpetrated by the state here,[9] as St. Sepulchre's, whose church clock was illuminated by fires set by the mob which 'shone and gleamed' (p. 534), earlier did to those perpetrated by the rioters.

Behind the barbarity of this society are bad laws and illiteracy, which Dennis the hangman sees as a positive good, the arts of reading and writing being, according to him, 'the greatest possible curse a civilised community could know' (p. 317) and detrimental to society. As things are, though, this is an ignorant society, steeped in superstition. At the beginning of the novel, Solomon relates how, on the fateful night of the death of Reuben Haredale, 'I recollected one story there was in the village, how that on a certain night in the year … all the dead people came out of the ground and sat at the heads of their own graves till morning' (p. 19). It is not surprising, therefore, that many images of decay, of an old, outworn world are to be found in the novel.

Exemplifying this old order are two figures. One is the gentleman who within seconds of meeting Barnaby and his mother is threatening them with 'the cage, the stocks and the whipping post' (p. 388) and shows a total lack of compassion for Barnaby's idiocy, which he judges merely to be 'an excuse not to work' (p. 389) and an imposture to evoke sympathy when begging: 'Most likely he's hired, at so much a day' (p. 391).

Society, however, doesn't deplore this man but rather celebrates him as the best of British, 'a genuine John Bull': 'all agreed ... that it was a pity there were not more like him, and that because there were not, the country was going to rack and ruin' (p. 390). Though 'warmly attached to the church', his behaviour as regards 'the living in his gift' shows as little genuine attachment to Christianity as do his moral attitudes, for he always appoints a clergyman who is 'a three-bottle man and a first-rate fox hunter' (p. 390).

Lack of attachment to core Christian values is also evident in the other representative of the status quo, Sir John Chester. Chester pays lip service to Christianity but no more. His commendation of Gabriel 'You are quite a Christian' (p. 627), for taking on delivering a message from Dennis that Chester does not wish to hear, is ironic; and he takes the cynical view that even men who enter the church are simply 'fortune hunters' (p. 135). Whatever does not suit him personally he classes as irreligious, as when his son refuses meekly to fall in with his father's plans for him, as we shall see below.

Even before Gordon has risen to prominence, Chester exemplifies the religious factionalism and lack of brotherhood of the age: his objections to Edward marrying Emma Haredale are partly denominational:

> In a religious point of view alone, how could you ever think of uniting yourself to a catholic, unless she was amazingly rich? You who ought to be so very Protestant, coming of such a Protestant family as you do. Let us be moral, Ned, or we are nothing. (p. 136)

It would, he asserts, be 'impossible' to set aside this objection (p. 136).

However, this is not a society on the point of collapse; even the worst riots in its history ('the largest, deadliest and most protracted ... in British history' as Linda Colley has described them)[10] do not cause it to crumble. Like the Maypole Inn, this society is 'hale and hearty', with 'a good many years of life in him yet' (p. 7), despite all its decay. There are some positive aspects of it – the cosiness of the Maypole, for example, and perhaps more significant, the civilised values of the officer commanding the soldiers engaged in controlling the riots,

> desirous to avoid rousing the people by the display of military force in the streets and ... humanely anxious to give as little opportunity as possible for any attempt at rescue; knowing that it must lead to bloodshed and loss of life, and that if the civil authorities by whom he was accompanied, empowered him to order his men to fire, many innocent persons would probably fall ... He therefore led the party briskly on, avoiding with a merciful prudence the more public and crowded thoroughfares (p. 480)

Dickens lauds this as a 'wise proceeding' (p. 480), and it demonstrates that out of the rather barbaric society of the 1770s and 1780s, there was the potential for a more civilised society to emerge.[11]

What Dickens is critical of is people living in a still barbaric age who look back longingly to the restoration of even older and more barbaric societies – at the core of which in the novel is the religious intolerance of the Protestant Association, still fighting the outrages of the reign of 'Bloody Mary' over two hundred years before.

The active participants in the Gordon Riots, though supposedly acting in a Christian cause exemplify both personally and as a mob the opposite of Christian values. Instead of love, they show hate. Instead of believing in brotherhood, their vision divides society into two groups, with one identified as the enemy. Far from loving their enemies, they do not even love their friends, but betray them – and do so out of a selfishness that is the opposite of Christian selflessness. Instead of treating people as ends, they treat them as means, exploiting them. Instead of believing in forgiveness, they believe in revenge. Instead of mercy and forbearance, they believe in cruelty. Instead of following the Prince of Peace, they believe in conflict and violence. Some pay lip service to Christianity, but in very shallow fashion; some are, in truth, even less Christian than that.

These attitudes start at the very top. Gordon's secretary, Gashford, is ready, in the light of some slight evidence of consideration in his boss to describe (and flatter) him as 'Christian from head to foot' (p. 298), but even at this early stage Gordon has already been revealed as an instrument propagating the opposite of Christian values: his unchristian avowal, not against an institution but against individual fellow human beings, 'Perish the Pope and all his base adherents' has already encouraged an attitude of hatred and vengeance – 'Down with the Papists – Vengeance on their heads' – from people willing to 'wade in blood' (p. 296). Gordon's allegiance to Christianity itself is far from firm: he tells Gashford that he has dreamt of their both being Jews and by the end of the novel he has in fact converted to Judaism. Ironically, a reflection of his muddled notions, it is only then that he embraces the Christian principles of love and universal brotherhood: when he dies, he is missed by his fellow prisoners because 'though his means were not large his charity was great, and in bestowing alms among them he considered the necessities of all alike, and knew no distinction of sect or creed' (p. 683). His attitudes at the time of the Riots, though, are revealed in a key exchange with Haredale who, having heard him speak, accuses him of a lack of brotherly love to 'speak of a large body of his fellow-subjects in such injurious language ... For shame, my lord, for shame' (p. 361). Gordon is quite overt in not acknowledging Haredale as a brother: 'we have nothing in common'. Haredale attempts to insist that they do, in their common creation by God – 'We have much in common – many things – all that the Almighty gave us', and urges Christian love, 'common charity' on him (p. 361). Gordon, though, is too caught up in factionalism to give any weight to what Haredale says: 'I can hold no communion with the worshippers of idols' (p. 361).

His secretary Gashford is a man of ostentatious religion. He approaches Gordon's room 'humming a psalm tune' (p. 299), and when talking of the Protestant Association's funds will refer to 'manna in the wilderness' and 'the widow's mite' (p. 301). Less innocent and sincere than Mrs Varden, though, his show of religion is not self-delusory but simple calculation. His strong protestations of Christianity are completely shallow: Gordon having mentioned his dream of the two of them being Jews, Gashford's subsequent private musings are that:

> provided I lost nothing by it, I don't see why that religion shouldn't suit me as well as any other. There are rich mercenary Jews; shaving is very troublesome; - yes, it would suit me well enough. For the present, though, we must be Christian to the core. (p. 307)

Gashford was, indeed, originally a Roman Catholic, and fled the church at whose altars 'his vicious life was publicly denounced', according to Haredale. By the time Haredale gives his account of Gashford's past, we have seen for ourselves that a man Haredale knew as 'a servile, false, and truckling knave ... who has crawled and crept through life ... this sycophant' has not repented and changed his ways (p. 362). According to Haredale, Gashford is a stranger to moral values who 'never knew what honor, truth or courage meant' and has behaved with 'cruelty' (p. 362). Our experience of him is as worldly and unchristian. To the extent that, however wrongheadedly, Gordon is sincere in his beliefs and is, for instance, 'no less frugal in his repasts than in his puritan attire', Gashford is, by contrast, 'more devoted to the good things of this world' (p. 307). Shortly after Haredale has denounced him he is 'breathing curses and threats of vengeance' (p. 366). Lacking Christian forgiveness, it is only too true what Dennis reports as having heard, that Gashford 'never forgot and never forgave' (p. 370). Urging Hugh and Dennis on to burning down Haredale's home, Gashford tells them to show 'no mercy' (p. 442). When Gordon is ultimately arrested, it is 'His fawning secretary' who has 'played the traitor' (p. 614); Gashford at all times serves his own self-interest and has no loyalty to his friends, much less love for his enemies. Gordon is just a means to an end, Gashford being able to exploit their relationship. For a while after his boss's arrest, for instance, he 'subsisted ... upon his traffic in his master's secrets' (p. 683). He then makes a profession out of his congenital dishonesty and lack of sincerity and loyalty, working as one of 'the honourable corps of spies and eavesdroppers'. A great survivor, dead only ten or twelve years when the story is written, Gashford has ended his life as he had lived it, sinfully, by committing suicide by taking poison. Neither in life nor in death does he conform to Christian values and principles.

Chester is an *eminence grise* behind the Gordon Riots, who helps, as he puts it himself, 'foment his disturbances in secret' (p. 336) while in public expressing 'disapprobation'. He can truthfully declare of the Protestant Association,

'I don't belong to the body' (p. 360); but as Haredale shrewdly retorts, 'Men of your capacity plot in secrecy and safety, and leave exposed posts to the duller wits' (p. 360). As this hypocrisy and exploitativeness begin to indicate, Chester thoroughly conforms to the norm among Lord George's party. His exploitative attitude extends even to his own son, whom he treats as a means rather than an end, wanting him to marry into wealth to secure his father's future. He is frank about the selfishness of this: 'I have always looked forward to his marrying well, for a genteel provision for myself in the autumn of life' (p. 107). He is dogmatic that his son's happiness must be sacrificed to his father's needs: 'As to the life I lead, I must lead it, Ned. I must have these little refinements about me. I have always been used to them, and I cannot exist without them' (pp. 135–6). Chester is strongly denominational, though mammon is ultimately even more important: of his son's plan to marry Emma Haredale, he remarks, 'how could you ever think of uniting yourself to a catholic, unless she was amazingly rich?' (p. 136). In pursuit of his ends, he is quite prepared to resort to evil means, involving what Haredale calls 'treachery and – and lying' (p. 108); Chester baulks at the terms – 'Not lying. Only a little management, a little diplomacy, a little – intriguing' (p. 108) – but not at the deeds.

Dickens describes him at one point as 'him of the world most worldly' (p. 207) and Chester seems incapable of seeing beyond worldly conditions: to him, marriage is no more than 'a civil contract' and 'people marry to better their worldly condition and improve appearances' (p. 268). The shallowness of Chester's moral and religious character is thus exposed. He can talk the language of religion, as we have seen, urging Mrs Varden, 'Let us be sincere and Protestant, strictly moral, strictly just (though always with a leaning towards mercy), strictly honest, and strictly true' but his words are 'contrived' to have the effect he wishes (p. 227); the things he says to her are 'sentiments which have nothing in them' (p. 228). If he promises to show the Christian virtues of 'mercy and forbearance' (p. 238) to Hugh, it is with selfish motives. He employs religious language in order to take the moral high ground when his son resists marrying to suit his father: 'You are so very irreligious, so exceedingly undutiful, so horribly profane' (p. 271) he tells him. Even imparting a blessing to a beggar is an egotistical act when Chester does it, given because it is 'more becoming to the face' than cursing him (p. 224).

Universal love is a concept that means nothing to Chester. At some level he does recognise the brotherhood of man, but not as a moral concept, and more as something to recoil from. He is horrified when Varden visits him directly after coming away from Newgate, because the common humanity of the prisoners and Chester himself means he might catch something from them:

> How could you be so very impudent as to come from Newgate ... where there are jail-fevers, and ragged people, and bare-footed men and women, and a thousand horrors! Peak, bring the camphor, quick! (p. 624)

Otherwise, Chester shows a lack of a sense of brotherhood in his denominationalism. However, his motivation is even worse, for there is a strong element of personal hate in his support for the riots. He has 'a personal objection' (p. 336) to Savile who introduced the Catholic Relief Bill. More deep-seated, though, is his personal hatred of Haredale. At school, Chester says, Haredale was 'My scapegoat and my drudge' (p. 249). Though Haredale was once 'my friend of later days' (p. 249), at the beginning of the novel the two men are 'enemies' (p. 105). At the end of the story, Haredale declares that he suspects Chester of being responsible for 'the foul attacks and whispered calumnies' (p. 678) that attempted to implicate Haredale in his brother's murder, and Haredale correctly concludes that the burning down of the Warren was an act of personal hatred propagated by Chester. The latter may deny the accusation that it was 'your act' (p. 678), but Haredale senses that Chester set on those who actually did the deed – 'the man I speak of, and ... your wretched son' (p. 678). We have earlier, for instance, seen Sir John urging Hugh on to entertain the prospect of 'an opportunity of revenging yourself on your proud friend Haredale' (p. 336) and relishing the idea that the rioters might 'inflict some little chastisement on Haredale'; this 'would be extremely agreeable to my feelings, and would amuse me beyond measure' (p. 337). It is noteworthy that Chester later shows no loyalty at all to those he exploits and manipulates; he refers to Hugh as 'my friend the centaur' (p. 622). Among his other motives, it seems, is an egotistical wish for self-assertion: having as a young man stolen Haredale's girlfriend, 'I triumph in the present and the past' (p. 249).

Dennis the hangman has only been to church twice in his life, including for his christening, so it is unsurprising that his awareness of, and adherence to, Christian values is little in evidence. Violence comes to be explicitly entertained when he enters the novel: 'Are we to be under orders to pull down one of them Popish chapels – or what?' (p. 310). Somehow conceiving of his job as 'Protestant work', he is strongly denominational, though he is, ironically, given to addressing others as 'brother' ('Is this axe your'n, brother?' (to Hugh) (p. 577); 'Do you want me to be throttled, brother?' (to his jailer) (p. 616)). Even this sense of brotherhood is shallow: he eventually betrays Hugh to try to save his own skin; once again, others are treated as means, not ends. Hatred overtly drives Dennis: when questioned, he confirms that he 'truly hate[s] the Papists' (p. 311). He believes in revenge: 'Let's have revenges and injuries', he urges at one point (p. 433). Only at the end, when his own life is under threat, does he discover the value of Christian principles, urging the authorities to 'have mercy on a wretched man', and to delay his execution ' for charity's sake' (p. 644).

Hugh has little to do with religion. We hear early on that when Barnaby says his prayers, Hugh does not. Having at the end of his life been spoken to by a clergyman about 'faith and strong belief', the first prayer of his life is essentially one of hatred: 'I, who never raised this hand in prayer till now, call down the wrath of God' (p. 646). A Caliban-like figure, whom John Willet speculates may not have 'any soul at all' (p. 111), Hugh is repeatedly referred to as little more than an animal, 'savage' (p. 178) and 'more brute than man' (p. 646). The riots essentially give him the opportunity fully to express this wild and savage personality; and it is this, not even denominationalism, that drives him. His lack of understanding of the cause is reflected in his rendition of 'No Popery' as 'No Property' (p. 316), a slogan reflecting only too well his anarchic, anti-social tendencies. He neither understands nor cares what he is allying himself with: as he joins Gordon's party, we are told that 'he was not at all particular, and would have leagued himself that night with anything, or anybody, for any purpose whatsoever' (p. 325). His unfocussed destructive tendencies cause him to declare that 'I'll fight the whole Parliament House single-handed, or set a lighted torch to the King's Throne itself!' (p. 325).

The riots allow him full expression of his personality. Dennis praises him for having 'so much enthusiasm' and for the way 'You hurt yourself a hundred times more than you need, because you will be foremost in everything, and will do more than the rest' (p. 430). As the riots come to a climax, so Hugh is at his wildest, and 'in every part of the riot, he was seen' (p. 560). In so far as his behaviour is more than simply a running riot of irrational tendencies within himself, his motives are, unsurprisingly, unchristian. He loves a sense of power: he revels in his intimidation of Dolly, when, having frightened her into never identifying him as the man who accosted her on her way back from the Warren, he asks if she would recognise her assailant again 'with a malicious grin' (p. 182). He asserts his attachment to revenge as part of his process of frightening her into silence: 'Bring trouble on me, and I'll bring trouble and something more on them in return' (p. 178). And it is a personal 'grudge' (p. 433) against Haredale that attaches him to Gordon's followers: 'I'd do anything to have some revenge on him – anything. And when you told me that he and all the Catholics would suffer from those who joined together under that handbill, I said I'd make one of 'em' (pp. 334–5). Significantly, he would not care, he says, 'if their master was the devil himself' (p. 335).

He has no love for his fellow men: 'I'd sooner kill a man than a dog any day. I've never been sorry for a man's death in all my life, and I have for a dog's' (p. 178). Disgracefully, and all the more so because Barnaby has been his only friend, Hugh is implicated in the exploitation of the simple-minded Rudge during the riots, knowing perfectly well what he is doing: 'the lad's a natural, and can be got to do anything, if you take him the right way' (p. 406). A cynical exploitativeness replaces Christian care for the weak and vulnerable. Even he eventually feels guilt about this, declaring that, 'if I had ten lives to lose', he would sacrifice them all to save Barnaby, whose life 'will be lost through me' (p. 646). This is the closest he comes to redemption.

The one figure in Gordon's entourage who does not share these attitudes shows the opposite to them, reveals true Christian virtues and thus acts as a foil to Gashford and the others. John Grueby is unhappy with what is going on from the beginning. He is caring about, rather than exploitative of, a man he is aware is 'half off his head' and is aware that his followers are 'ragamuffins' (p. 298), thieves who are 'very fond of spoons, I find, and silver' (p. 299). Afraid that 'more harm might be to come' (p. 299), he is totally unsympathetic to the denominationalist appeals to what happened when the Catholic 'Bloody Mary' ruled: 'I wish the blessed old creetur had never been born' (p. 298). He is the first to liken Gordon's followers to 'so many devils' (p. 299).

When the riots develop, Grueby is put on his mettle and proves his moral worth. When Haredale is at bay, facing a dangerous mob, it is Grueby who shows Christian love and compassion, as well as bravery: he advises him not to stand in defiance of the crowd but to get away, and guides him into a boat to escape. Later, when Haredale and the vintner are trapped in the latter's premises, it is Grueby who, again acting against the factionalism of Gordon's side, helps them escape. Grueby abandons Gordon's party long before the Riots are over; though unlike the others who abandon or betray Gordon personally, Grueby remains loyal to his boss: 'bluff John Grueby ... never left him until he died' (p. 683).

Grueby aside, with such people prominent in the Association, it can hardly be other, despite its avowed Protestantism, than a manifestation of the opposite of Christianity. Many of the rioters are not really religious at all, and 'had never heard a hymn or psalm in all their lives' (p. 402). People who are 'honest and sincere' soon leave Gordon's party once and for all, 'never ... to return, or to hold any communication with their late companions' (p. 415). Dickens conveys the moral evil of those who remain through recurrent comparisons of them to devils. Even in Barnaby's limited perception, London comes eventually to seem 'peopled by a legion of devils' (p. 567), and in certain passages, such references are highly concentrated. During the burning down of the Warren, for instance, the rioters are described as 'an army of devils' (p. 460); they 'plied their demon labours fiercely' (p. 460). When the fire rages, 'as though moving in that element they became fiends, and changed their earthly nature for the qualities that give delight in hell' (p. 460). The evil and criminality of what they do, the death and destruction they cause, give the lie to their supposed religious affiliations.

Dickens shows us that, without Christian values, these people have no moral values at all. Perhaps the most disturbing chapter in the whole of Dickens is Chapter 61 of *Barnaby Rudge*, with its account of Catholic families attempting to flee the rioters, and discovering themselves to be pariahs, drivers of mails and stagecoaches refusing to carry them because of their religion and people 'afraid to recognise catholic acquaintance in the street' (p. 506). Catholics discover they can find little refuge or protection in the law. A priest 'feared he might not find a magistrate who would have the hardihood to commit a prisoner to jail, on his complaint' (p. 506). Attempts to get the Lord Mayor to act to protect Catholics yield little. Instead, he blames them for their fearful predicament: 'Why couldn't you be a protestant, and then you wouldn't have got yourself into such a mess?' (p. 508). To the modern reader, there are chilling echoes here of the predicament of the Jews in Nazi Germany: a minority, outcast merely because of an identity linked to their religion, unable to take refuge in and find protection in the law. In the novel, as the forces of law and order are temporarily overwhelmed and the rioters thus not restrained by fear of the law, what is to restrain them? Only their moral values might rein them in; and that is no restraint, for they have none.

The rioters here behave as if they are outside morality. However, Dickens raises the whole issue of who, if anybody or anything, is outside morality; and this is done partly through the animal prominently featured in the novel, Grip the raven. Grip's utterances are uncomprehending mimicry, so that he is unaware of what he is saying when he constantly proclaims 'I'm a devil'. Even if he knew what he was saying, though, we would not class Grip as evil; animals exist outside the moral sphere. In turn, this raises the matter of whether any other figure in the novel is exempt from moral standards. Barnaby, mentally defective, would seem to be; but even someone as animalistic as Hugh is portrayed as morally responsible (the courts' ultimate judgement on these two reflects the difference in their moral status, with Hugh hanged and Barnaby eventually spared). And if a creature like Hugh is morally responsible then so, certainly, are the mob who act alongside him. Grip remains morally innocent even when he learns to say 'No Popery'; the humans who chant the same are never morally innocent. (Grip also unwittingly alludes to moral qualities his society needs. His cries of 'Polly put the kettle on' and constant imitation of corks being popped hint at conviviality, human friendliness and sociability, a togetherness quite at odds with the divisiveness of a factionalism-rent society; his 'Never say die' implies the need for endurance, another Christian virtue (c.f. 1 Corinthians 13:7) needed in the novel by Haredale.) Compared with the moral enormity of what the rioters have done, when, later, the leaders all betray each other, it seems by comparison a minor moral lapse.

The rioters, then, are not just wrong, but evil. The outcome of their attitudes is death and destruction. The violence and death the riots involve achieve nothing positive, but are merely destructive. Indeed, supposedly in aid of upholding the status quo, they instead threaten the order and civilisation that there are. They do not aid progress; indeed, they are an attempt to hold back progress to a more enlightened, brotherly society.

Influenced by the likes of Edmund Wilson, Steven Marcus decides that part of Dickens is a radical in his attitude to the riots despite himself:

> everyone knows now that unconsciously he identified himself with the rioters who burned into Newgate he was at the same time deliberately

> suggesting a likeness between the rabble of the Gordon riots, and the members of the Chartist agitation in the late 1830s.[12]

Similarly, John Gardiner declares that, 'Dickens the middle-class conservative speaks out in the portrayal of mob violence in *Barnaby Rudge*', but finds his attitude not 'clear cut':

> An instinctive feel for the anarchic and the violent complicates his attitude, so that outer manner and inner compulsion pull in different directions ... the stance of horrified disapproval is impeccably middle-class Victorian. But the disapproval – or more exactly the horror – is anything but sober in itself; rather, it has a visceral abandon and grim joy.[13]

To Thomas J. Rice, Dickens's class-interest makes his attitude more clear cut: in a novel in which he warns that 'political extremism of the left or right insures social instability', the author 'illustrates the most explosive of all political situations: an *alliance* between the two political extremes, radical and reactionary, the direst threat imaginable to Dickens and his middle-class audience'.[14]

Seeing things similarly less ambiguously, John Bowen decides that *Barnaby Rudge*, 'Dickens's most explicitly political novel of his early period also appears to be his most reactionary one'.[15] Referring to the description of Gabriel Varden at the end of the novel, he comments that, 'At such moments, the novel seems at its most conservative, ending the book with a deeply deterministic conclusion which starkly poses law against madness, chaos against order, and sees no middle way between them'.[16] Myron Magnet similarly argues that the 'entirely consistent vision' presented in the novel 'is that if you do not have civilisation with its concomitant personal oppression and unhappiness, then you must have universal anarchy and brutality, the war of all against all'.[17]

As I have been attempting to show, however, Dickens's stance in the novel is not a political one, either conservative or consciously or unconsciously radical. Rather, his perspective on these historical events is religious: the riots represent a breakdown of brotherhood, stirred up by people who, in their anti-Catholicism, do not recognise the brotherhood of all men. Only by the replacement of such attitudes by Christian love for one's fellow man and a sense of brotherhood can a better, happier society be achieved.

10
A Tale of Two Cities and the Persistence of Evil

FAG: So! Sir Anthony trims my master; he is afraid to reply to his father – then vents his spleen on poor Fag! When one is vexed by one person, to revenge one's self on another, who happens to come in the way – is the vilest injustice! Ah! it shows the worst temper – the basest –

Enter ERRAND BOY

BOY: Mr Fag! Mr Fag! your Master calls you.

FAG: Well, you little, dirty puppy, you need not bawl so! – The meanest disposition! the –

BOY: Quick, quick, Mr Fag.

FAG: Quick, quick, you impudent jackanapes –! Am I to be so commanded by you too? You little, impertinent, insolent kitchen-bred –

Exit, kicking and beating him

(R.B. Sheridan The Rivals Act 2 Scene 1, pp. 463–74)[1]

A Tale of Two Cities has attracted both religious and political interpretations At its centre, of course, is the French Revolution, a supremely important political event, and many critics have attempted to define in political terms Dickens's reaction to it. Just as commentators have often seen his hostility to trade unions in *Hard Times* as a matter of his middle class status making him *parti pris* as regards any threat to the stability of society in an age of Chartism and European revolution, so he has been assumed to be opposed to the insurrection from below that constituted the French Revolution on the same basis: thus, for instance, John Gross finds the 'true ring of outraged rate-paying respectability'[2] in the author's description of the Camargnole, and J.M. Rignall talks of the grindstone scene in the novel as a 'bourgeois nightmare of anarchy unleashed by the rebellion of the oppressed'.[3] This hints at a tension, though, between the writer's class interests and the sympathy for the poor, the underdog, and the mistreated we would expect in Dickens. In turn, this leads to the interpretation of the novel offered by

Cates Baldridge. Having observed that Dickens's deep dissatisfaction with the social relations fostered by his own acquisitive and aggressively individualist society leads him at times to explore with sensitivity and even enthusiasm the liberating possibilities offered by an ideology centred elsewhere than upon the autonomous self, he suggests that what emerges in the novel is 'a subversive subtext to the narrator's middle-class horror at the collectivist Revolutionary ideology promulgated behind the barricades of Paris'.[4] To avoid seeing the text as subversive involves seeing the author as having no real solution to the horrors he depicts, as Rignall observes:

> Since he sees revolutionaries as just another link in the chain of violence and oppression, and presents the efforts of individuals, like Darnay's journey to Paris, as powerless to influence the course of historical events, he can conceive no possibility, to use Benjamin's phrase, of blasting open the continuum of history by social and political action. Unlike Benjamin, Dickens can advance no alternative vision of time and history.[5]

We end up, with this approach, with an author trapped within, and biased by, his own class interests into a hostile portrayal of the revolution: a man whose whole position involves a contradiction, critical of his society yet nevertheless supporting its underpinning acquisitive values, a man whose class interests are in conflict with his professed concern for social justice. While apparently willing the end, he does not will the means, leading him to the position, as Gordon Spence remarks, in which he 'appears to have been out of sympathy with the French people, except when they were oppressed victims; he was not stirred, but his imagination was stimulated by his loathing when they committed atrocities'.[6] Furthermore, he has no solution, no 'alternative vision' to the society he portrays so critically, leaving little more than a counsel of despair. As Rignall, discussing Carton's prophecy, writes:

> Only by turning away from the course of human history can Dickens find a refuge for hope, and to express hope in such terms is tantamount to a confession of despair.[7]

In the face of this sort of confused mess, no wonder *A Tale of Two Cities* has not been highly regarded in some circles.

If a narrowly political approach to the novel, then, produces an unsatisfying interpretation of it, other critics have laid emphasis on the religious element in the novel. As Dennis Walder remarks, 'The pious manner of Sidney Carton's final moments has led to *A Tale of Two Cities* being called one of Dickens's most patently Christian novels':[8] Kenneth Sroka emphasises, for instance, points of comparison between the novel and St John's Gospel and suggests it 'may very well be another Victorian "gospel"'.[9] Here I also very much want to emphasise that Dickens's religious views are the key to his analysis of this political event. As I argued in Chapter 8, for Dickens the religious and the political are not separate: he makes sense of political events by analysing them in religious terms. In the process, he establishes why the Revolution happens, why it fails and, implicitly, what the solution to the horrors both pre- and post-Revolution that he depicts might be. There is no counsel of despair: misguided and evil values can be replaced by ones that will create a just and happy society.

In portraying the two cities of the title, Dickens by no means draws a glib contrast. London is in no way idealised. In many ways it is barbaric. It is a world of 'Daring burglaries by armed men, and highway robberies' (p. 6).[10] Capital punishment is common even for petty crimes – 'Death is Nature's remedy for all things, and why not Legislation's?' (p. 56) – and society has only just moved on from the display of criminals' 'heads exposed on Temple Bar' (p. 56). Even an ordinary man such as Jerry Cruncher sees the quartering that follows conviction for treason as 'Barbarous' (p. 62) (though Jerry has an ulterior motive for not wanting bodies to be mutilated). The threat of such punishments hanging over the accused in court cases leads to grisly, degrading tastes in humanity being pandered to: the interest Charles Darnay arouses in his court appearance 'was not a sort that elevated humanity' (p. 65) and is 'Ogreish' (p. 65). The public punishment of offenders, such as 'the whipping-post, another dear old institution' has a similar appeal to low and degraded appetites; Dickens ironically describes it as 'very humanising and softening to behold in action' (p. 63). The precarious hold of law and order and civilised values in this society engenders suspicion and distrust, as is impressed on the reader in Chapter 2 of Book 1: as they walk up the hill, the travellers on the coach are typically 'very shy of being confidential on a short notice, for anybody on the road might be a robber or in league with robbers' (p. 9) and 'the guard suspected the passengers, the passengers suspected one another and the guard, they all suspected everybody else, and the coachman was sure of nothing but the horses' (p. 9). When Jerry approaches on horseback, he too is treated with suspicion. This is not a climate in which camaraderie, or brotherhood, can be established: suspicion is so rampant, people so edgy that, if someone had suggested walking on ahead 'he would have put himself in a fair way of getting shot instantly as a highwayman' (p. 10). Darnay's trial reflects the lack of a sense of brotherhood in another sense: though a fellow 'immortal creature', he is objectified in court, merely a 'form' (p. 65) from which people, in staring at him, can derive a gruesome form of gratification. The twisting of values is reflected in court in the way the act of treachery of Darnay's servant is described as 'a holy determination' (pp. 68–9) to rifle through his belongings.

Later, the supposed funeral of Cly reflects Britain as an uncivilised place. The occasion has no dignity, 'with beer-drinking, pipe-smoking, song-roaring, and infinite caricaturing of woe' (p. 162), the crowd is 'a monster much dreaded' (p. 162) and the occasion degenerates into criminality with 'window-breaking, and ... the plundering of public-houses' and tearing up of railings (p. 164).

There is little interest, though, in changing this state of affairs: it is a country stuck in the past, which takes a perverse pride in not reforming: Tellson's Bank, we are told, is very much like the nation 'which did very often disinherit its sons for suggesting improvements in laws and customs that had long been highly objectionable, but were only the more respectable' (p. 55). For all its horrors, though, London is still a place where, in private, idylls can be created, as the Manettes do, in 'quiet lodgings ... in a quiet street corner' (p. 95), which seems to Mr Lorry 'the sunny part of his life' (p. 96).

Life in Paris, under an oppressive tyranny, is much worse. There is the same brutal regime of punishments, with punishments if anything even more cruel and extreme for offences even more trivial: thus a youth is sentenced 'to have his hands cut off, his tongue torn out with pincers, and his body burned alive, because he had not kneeled down in the rain to do honour to a dirty procession of monks which passed within his view at a distance of some fifty or sixty yards' (p. 6). This first glimpse of the French way of life, significantly involving monks and a punishment carried out 'Under the guidance of her Christian pastors' (p. 6) indicates the utter rottenness of Christianity in France, and augurs that what we will see, as we do, is a society in which Christian values are absent and betrayed. The apparent religious connections of everything we encounter in France, beginning with Saint Antoine and the unholy suffering that is later to originate from it, are revealed as utterly hollow. Later we are to hear of corrupt 'brazen ecclesiastics, of the worst world worldly, with sensual eyes, loose tongues, and looser lives', who like the military and civil officers of this society are 'totally unfit for their ... callings' (p. 110), obtained by patronage rather than vocation, dedication or any other form of merit.

Religion otherwise takes two forms in this society. There are modish groups – for fashion rules religion as it does everything else in aristocratic France – with eccentric forms of religion, such as the Convulsionists and the believers in 'the Centre of truth', whose practices supposedly 'did a world of good' though it 'never became manifest' (p. 111). Otherwise there is a blasphemous making of Monseigneur into God. His inner room is 'the Holiest of Holiests to the crowd of worshippers in the suite of rooms without' (p. 108). When he emerges 'As to bowing down in body and spirit, nothing in that way was left for Heaven – which may have been one among other reasons why the worshippers of Monseigneur never troubled it' (p. 112). His features are said to be 'beatified and beatifying' (p. 237).

Centrally, there is no sense of the brotherhood of man in French society. Instead, there is a fatal division of society into classes who show solidarity within themselves but not with each other. The ruling classes have convinced themselves that the world has been designed for their exclusive benefit: 'Creation' was 'designed expressly for Monseigneur' (p. 236); and a member of the aristocracy who dissents from this outlook is cast as a blasphemer: Stryver, in the company of French émigrés is ready to brand Darnay as 'infected by the most pestilent and blasphemous code of devilry that ever was known' (p. 248). With such an outlook, it is hardly surprising that the ruling class shows no sense of brotherhood with the poor. People barely acknowledge their own immediate families, let alone the wider human family of which they are a part. In the fashionable circles frequented by Monseigneur, Dickens comments, it would be hard to find 'one solitary wife' among those ironically described as 'the angels of that sphere' who 'owned to being a Mother ... Indeed, except for the mere act of bringing a troublesome creature into this world – which does not go far towards the realisation of the name of mother – there was no such thing known to the fashion' (p. 111). The children are farmed out to peasant women, and the author describes the grotesque situation of 'charming grandmammas of sixty' who 'dressed and supped as at twenty' (p. 111).

Their lack of recognition of their common humanity with the ordinary people is marked in a number of ways. They habitually think and speak about the peasants as animals. The Marquis, for instance, calls the peasants 'dogs' (p. 117); he looks contemptuously at Madame Defarge and 'all the other rats' (p. 117). When talking to the mender of roads, he calls him 'pig' (p. 120) and is aware of the other people listening to the conversation as 'vermin' (p. 120). Dr. Manette, taken by the Evremonde brothers to tend the dying brother of the seduced woman detects no sense of 'kindred humanity' (p. 336) in how the man is spoken about; equally his sister seems to be no more than a thing, to be used for gratification: Evremonde asked her husband 'to lend her to him' (p. 337). The Marquis similarly regards the child his carriage has killed as nothing more than 'some common thing' and views it as a commodity: he 'had paid for it, and could afford to pay for it' (p. 115). He is more concerned about the 'injury you have done to my horses' than about a fellow human being (p. 115). Quite contrary to the spirit of Christianity and brotherhood, he treats his fellow human beings as means rather than ends; leaving Monseigneur's hotel angry, having not been accorded treatment in his view due to him, it helps soothe his ruffled feelings to reassert his position by enjoying seeing the peasants scatter in panic as his coach plunges desperately ahead: it is 'rather agreeable to him to see the common people dispersed before his horses, and often barely escaping from being run down' (p. 113). In this he is typical of his breed, for the driving of his class often 'maimed the mere vulgar in a barbarous manner', but 'few cared' (p. 114) and the 'carriages were often known to drive on' (p. 114). As we see all this, Dickens's descriptions subtly underline the shared experiences and universality of the human predicament and thus the brotherhood this society refuses to acknowledge. Echoing, as Richard Maxwell points out, the Biblical text (Matthew 5:45) 'He maketh the sun to rise on the evil and the good, and sendeth the rain on the just and the unjust',[11] Dickens comments, in the wake of the killing of the child by his carriage, how 'The sweet scents of the summer night rose all around' the Marquis but also 'rose, as the rain falls, impartially, on the dusty, ragged, and toil-worn group at the fountain not far away' (p. 122). Later, he emphasises how both 'Chateau and hut ... lay under the night sky' (p. 183).

Only one member of the French aristocracy is depicted as showing any sense of brotherhood (or sisterhood) with the ordinary people. Evremonde's wife, according to Doctor Manette's account, came to try to give support to the woman her brother-in-law had seduced: 'Her hope had been, she said in great distress, to show her, in secret, a woman's sympathy'. This act of solidarity had a religious motive, in a recognition that the conduct of the aristocrats goes against the precepts of Christianity: 'Her hope had been to avert the wrath of Heaven from a House that had long been hateful to the suffering many' (p. 343). Significantly, when Charles Darnay becomes a second aristocrat to reject the outlook and values of his class, it is this woman's, his mother's, maiden name he adopts and adapts.

The consequences of the lack of brotherhood in this society are fourfold. From the beginning, Dickens stresses the three forms of affliction that he is habitually concerned about when a sense of brotherhood is lacking. The first glimpse we get of the French peasantry, when they frantically pursue the spilled wine from the broken cask in Book 1 Chapter 5, reflects their immediate suffering. So desperate are they that all the wine gets taken up, even though 'so much mud got taken up along with it' (p. 31); and the author then dwells on how prevalent 'Hunger' (p. 32) and 'Want' (p. 33) are, along with 'cold, dirt, sickness, ignorance' (p. 32) among them. Details of the peasants stress their 'starved fingers and toes' (p. 31), 'cadaverous faces'(p. 31), 'naked feet' (p. 32), the 'vestige of a garment' that constitutes their clothing (p. 32). Recurrent references to animals underline how dehumanised these people have become. The aftermath of their pouncing on the wine suggests 'there might have been a scavenger in the street' (p. 31). Some of those involved have acquired 'a tigerish smear about the mouth' (p. 32). In the conversation that follows in Defarge's shop, they are referred to as 'miserable beasts' and 'poor cattle' (p. 36). People have a 'hunted air', which suggests 'there was yet some wild-beast thought of the possibility of turning at bay' (p. 33). The latter references hint at the effect on their spiritual well-being. As the novel progresses the corruption of their moral characters into all-consuming bitterness and vengefulness is to emerge strongly; but for the time being, oppression makes this remain relatively hidden: Madame Defarge for the moment is merely 'watchful' (p. 35) and engaged in the knitting that secretly preserves her hatred. The 'great power' (p. 31) of the deprivations they suffer to create real hate, revealed for the moment only in their 'eyes of fire' and their musing about 'inflicting' 'the gallows-rope' on others (p. 33), but eventually to be so destructive, stands in ironic contrast to the 'saintly' (p. 32) character the name of the district where they live would suggest they might have.

Evident at this early stage too is a further consequence of the lack of any sense of identification with ordinary people by the powerful. The peasantry are merely there to be exploited, to fund the lives of the rich. Society is run in the interests of one class only, not for the general good. The law is a mere instrument of oppression, not applied universally but merely to bolster the position of the ruling class: the people confronting Evremonde after his carriage has killed the child are well aware 'of what such a man could do to them, within the law and beyond it' (p. 117). The source of the people's poverty is the ruthless taxation, imposed on them by the powerful sections of society in their own interests:

> Expressive signs of what made them poor, were not wanting: the tax for the state, the tax for the church, the tax for the lord, tax local and tax general, were to be paid here and to be paid there. (p. 118)

Even on a personal level, the aristocracy identify so little with the peasants as human beings that Evremonde does not enter sympathetically into the feelings of the woman whose child has just died. Ignoring her pleas, he callously has his carriage drive on. Such attitudes foster a breakdown in society: they produce factionalism, a sense of 'them and us', a strong class identity that is the equivalent of that shown by the aristocrats and which is reflected in the identification with each other that is seen in the peasants calling each other 'Jacques', and the associated political connotations of a Jacquerie. As we will see, they in turn will in due course identify the aristocracy as merely the enemy and not their fellow human beings.

A shared predicament naturally produces a sense of identification with each other: there is a 'special companionship' between all those engaged in the same activity, and for the same reasons, of desperately seizing on the spilled wine that leads to 'frolicsome embraces, drinking of healths, shaking of hands, and even joining of hands and dancing' (p. 31), the latter a foreshadowing, of course, of the later, less innocent Carmagnole. They are equally all oppressed by the same group of people. From this naturally arises a solidarity with each other and an enmity towards a defined group of other human beings.

Dickens's interest in cause and effect which leads him in *Hard Times*, for instance, to present the events of his story in terms of 'sowing' and 'reaping' is picked up in this novel. The behaviour of the aristocracy produces the effects of physical suffering, dehumanisation, corruption of the spirit and class antagonism in the peasantry, and these in turn become the causes of the Revolution. In the famous passage in which he draws conclusions about the Revolution, he sees events as having the same inevitability that we would normally expect as that of cause and effect: once again drawing on the idea of sowing and reaping he comments: 'Sow the same seed of rapacious licence and oppression ever again, and it will surely yield the same fruit according to its kind' (p. 385). Just as he draws attention to the unbrotherly exploitation of others – 'the rapacious licence' – and the lack of Christian loving kindness in their 'oppression' as the seeds of the trouble, his description of the process set in motion emphasises the dehumanisation and spiritual corruption involved: 'Crush humanity out of shape ... and it will twist itself into ... tortured forms' (p. 385).

If this is one aspect of his presentation of the French Revolution, though, it is not the only one. The theoretical speech Carton might have made at the foot of the scaffold talks of 'the new oppressors who have risen on the destruction of the old' (p. 389) and Dickens devotes considerable attention to the idea that the new society produced by the Revolution is actually no better, just as evil, and in many respects similar to the old society that has been overthrown. The motto of the French Revolution – 'Liberty, Equality, Fraternity, or Death' – is quoted several times in the novel, but the society that emerges is one in which fraternity and brotherly love are as lacking as ever.

In the old regime, power is exercised arbitrarily and ruthlessly: Dr. Manette was imprisoned without trial merely for writing a letter to a Minister revealing details of his experiences at the Evremonde chateau; Darnay only escapes being incarcerated 'indefinitely' (p. 127) because his uncle is no longer in favour enough to obtain a *letter de cachet.* In a world in which, as Evremonde relates, 'Our not remote ancestors held the right of life and death over the surrounding vulgar', a young man could be 'poinarded on the spot' for insolence, and the deterioration of such power he regards as 'real inconvenience' (p. 127). Injustice is the inevitable accompaniment of this. The peasants are aware of what Evremonde could do to them 'within the law and beyond it' (p. 117). The ordinary people are able legally to be simply exploited: as the young man dying at the hands of Evremonde tells Dr. Manette

> We were so robbed by that man ... taxed by him without mercy, obliged to work for him without pay, obliged to grind our corn at his mill, obliged to feed scores of his tame birds on our wretched crops, and forbidden for our lives to keep a single tame bird of our own, pillaged and plundered ... we were robbed, and hunted, and were made so poor (p. 337)

Under the old regime, the narrator comments at one point, referring to courts of law, 'all laws, forms and ceremonies' were 'monstrously abused' (p. 328). As this power is unjustly exercised, the innocent suffer: Darnay comments on the way his family conducted itself 'injuring every human creature who came between us and our pleasure' (p. 129), and the Marquis is free to have his carriage driven in a way that 'endangered and maimed the mere vulgar in a barbarous manner' (p. 114). The net result is a society in which fear is prevalent. As Darnay remarks, people look on him as a member of his aristocratic family with 'the dark deference of fear and slavery' (p. 128), and when Evremonde's coach recklessly kills a child the reaction of the peasants reflects this fear: there is 'no visible menacing or anger' in their looks (p. 114); they stand 'silent' (p. 114), and the one who does speak does so in 'extreme submission' (p. 115). Their 'condition' is 'cowed' (p. 117). All in all, people live under tyranny, their choices being between 'Life on the lowest terms that could sustain it' and 'captivity and Death' (p. 119). When rebellion comes, it is against 'the tyrants of the earth' (p. 283) and 'the blood of tyranny and domination by the iron hand was down' (p. 229).

This evil and undesirable society is, however, replaced by one that has exactly the same characteristics. Power changes hands with the Revolution, but it is exercised equally ruthlessly and arbitrarily. The loungers at the Defarges' shop now have 'a manifest sense of power' and their 'raggedest nightcap awry on the wretchedest head' now signifies 'do you know how easy it has grown for me,- the wearer of this, to destroy life in you?' (p. 231). Injustice is built into the regime with 'a law of the Suspected, which struck away all security for liberty or life, and delivered over any good and innocent person to any bad and guilty one; prisons gorged with people who had committed no offence, and could obtain no hearing' (p. 283).

The abuse of the law continues: Charles Darnay's trial in Revolutionary Paris takes the form of an 'unjust Tribunal' with 'little or no order of procedure, ensuring to any accused person any reasonable hearing' (p. 327); the attitudes of the Revolutionaries to the 'laws, forms and ceremonies' previously abused has been 'to scatter them all to the winds' (p. 328). The suffering of the innocent described here is reinforced by the depiction of a climate in which the arbitrary wielding of power – 'the people were so passionately revengeful and fitful' – means that 'the innocent were so constantly put to death on vague suspicion and black malice' (p. 298). The seamstress who goes with Carton to the guillotine has been accused of 'Plots' but is 'innocent of any ... Who would think of plotting with a poor little weak creature like me?' (p. 368). By the end of the novel, fear is so prevalent that even the revolutionaries are afraid of their comrades. The wood-sawyer is 'so very demonstrative' in assuring Madame Defarge that he is 'the most ardent of Republicans', for instance, that, the author comments, 'he might have been suspected ... of having his small individual fears for his own personal safety, every hour in the day' (p. 374). 'Year One of Liberty' (p. 283) may be proclaimed, but one tyranny is in reality replaced by another.

Underlying attitudes within the two regimes are also the same. The milieu of the ruling class under the old regime is one of superficiality and worldliness. The superficiality is partly a matter of people with impressive but undeserved and empty titles and positions to which they are not entitled at all: 'military officers destitute of military knowledge; naval officers with no idea of a ship; civil officers without a notion of affairs; brazen ecclesiastics, of the worst world worldly' (p. 110). It goes, though, much beyond such reflections of patronage and vanity. Babies are 'unfashionable' and so aristocratic mothers fail in their duty to their children: barely any even 'owned to being a Mother' (p. 111). All attention is to appearance:

> Such frizzling and powdering and sticking up of hair, such delicate complexions artificially preserved and mended, such gallant swords to look at, and such delicate honour to the sense of smell ... The exquisite gentlemen of the finest breeding wore little pendent trinkets that chinked as they languidly moved; these gold fetters rang like precious little bells; and what with that ringing, and with the rustle of silk and brocade and fine linen, there was a flutter in the air that found Saint Antoine and his devouring hunger far away. (p. 112)

As the end of this sentence implies, this attention to appearance diverts their attention from more important matters that need seeing to; and as the author has just ironically observed, they would be able to vindicate themselves on 'the Day of Judgment' only if it was 'a dress day' (p. 112). In their superficiality, the aristocratic are trapped in worldliness. Religion, then, means little to them. The triumph, and precedence, of worldliness over religion in them is reflected in how Monseigneur unceremoniously 'had taken his sister from a convent' to enrich the family by marrying her off to 'a very rich Farmer-General' (p. 109). As we have seen, religion largely takes the form among them of fashionable cults, and Monseigneur is surrounded by 'Unbelieving Philosophers' (p. 110) and 'Unbelieving Chemists' (p. 111). More than this, a false religion amenable to their worldliness has taken over. The Bible has been misappropriated and perverted to suit. Monseigneur's text to live by is 'The earth and the fullness thereof are mine, saith Monseigneur' (p. 109). If the text makes Monseigneur into God, he is surrounded by people subscribing to this idea, 'worshippers of Monseigneur' who, as he passes 'bow down in body and spirit' (p. 112). As we have seen, Stryver, proponent of émigré aristocrats once the Revolution has occurred, refers to Darnay's dissent from supporting the aristocratic order as 'blasphemous' (p. 248).

Divorced from Christianity and its moral values, though, the regime has a deplorable moral code. Monseigneur's very court is full of deception and treachery, for 'a goodly half' of its frequenters are 'Spies' (p. 111). Even more seriously, there is a callousness about them which means that mercy is rare in the society they dominate. The brother fatally injured in trying to protect his sister from the Evremondes tells Dr. Manette how local people were 'taxed by him without mercy' (p. 337) and Dr. Manette himself bitterly records how they have kept from him, during his imprisonment, any news of his wife, concluding that they are so alienated from God that 'they have no part in His mercies' (p. 344). The last request of Darnay's mother 'implored me to have mercy and to redress' (p. 129); but his uncle informs him that if he is seeking his help in such endeavour 'you will for ever seek ...

in vain' (p. 129). The imprisonment of Dr. Manette was an act of pure revenge, and vengefulness remains in the heart of the aristocrat toppled from power who, in exile in London, is 'boastful of what he would do to avenge himself on the rascal-people before long' (p. 246).

If Christian values like mercy and forgiveness are alien to them, so is any sense of brotherhood. They view society in terms of factions, conceived in class distinctions taken to the nth degree. Monseigneur having married his sister to 'a very rich Farmer-General, poor in family' (p. 109), nevertheless, 'superior mankind of the blood of Monseigneur, ... his own wife included, looked down upon him with the loftiest contempt' (pp. 109–10). He is conscious of the standing of those to whom he acts as a patron that they are 'nearly or remotely of the order of Monseigneur' (p. 110). Such keen awareness of class distinctions is accompanied by little sense of universality and a common humanity with everyone else. 'Creation', after all, was 'designed expressly for Monseigneur' (p. 236). As we have seen, Manette has no sense of 'pity, sorrow, or kindred humanity' (p. 336) in the way Evremonde speaks about the dying peasant, and those of a lower class are conceived of as animals. For Monseigneur, 'the pleasures of the chase' might equally be 'found in hunting the people' as 'found in hunting the beasts' (p. 236); and the Marquis looks on the peasants 'as if they had been mere rats come out of their holes' (p. 115).

These phenomena – the worldliness, the false religion, the immorality, lack of mercy, vengefulness, the lack of brotherhood – are all replicated in the new society that emerges during the Revolution. And this is a vital point: the post-Revolution French are the inheritors of an evil set of values which they have not been reformed out of – there has been no 'change of heart' among them. They are the product of the old society. It dehumanised them and corrupted them spiritually, and their natures have not changed. They are less than properly civilised human beings: at the grindstone their faces are 'more horrible and cruel than the visages of the wildest savages in their most barbarous disguise' (p. 273); a discharged prisoner is killed when 'a mistaken savage had thrust a pike' at him (p. 281). The setter of the fire at the Evremonde chateau has 'an almost barbarian aspect' (p. 237). Spectators at Foulon's hanging are 'like birds of prey' (p. 234). Under the new regime they are still essentially animals, 'wild beasts' (p. 243), showing 'beastly excitement' (p. 272) at the grindstone. The sleeping customers in the Defarges' shop are 'like slumbering bears or dogs' (p. 305). The jury at Darnay's trial are 'as a jury of dogs empanelled to try the deer' (p. 328). Spiritually they are not regenerated; in fact, their spiritual condition deteriorates as they pursue a false religion and evil moral values. There is no particular dedication to good: the attack on the Bastille is carried out 'in the name of all the Angels or the Devils – which you prefer' (p. 224). Later it seems, they are in league with the Devil, for when the revolutionaries burn the Evremonde chateau, its destruction is aided by 'a red-hot wind, driving straight from the infernal regions' (p. 241). The fires which are so much a part of the Revolution are a constant reminder of Hell. Monseigneir's class are like the man 'who raised the Devil with infinite pains', using 'many ... potent spells for compelling the Evil One' (p. 243). At the grindstone are men 'devilishly' bearing stolen goods (p. 272). Even the mild and restrained Mr. Lorry refers to those in power as 'these devils' (p. 273). The guillotine, which moves to the centre of society, being portable and able to be assembled and disassembled is 'like a toy-puzzle for a young Devil' (p. 284). Any attachment they may have had to Christianity fades: the guillotine 'superseded the Cross. Models of it were worn on breasts from which the Cross was discarded, and it was bowed down to and believed in where the Cross was denied' (p. 284). The churches become places 'where no prayers were said', 'popular revulsion... from years of priestly impostors, plunderers and profligates' leading people to abandon true religion, in the process travelling 'that length of self-destruction' (p. 326). The new and false religion of the guillotine replaces Christianity.

This false and perverted religion is one for which Madame Defarge is 'a Missionary' (p. 193) and in which she has the status of 'an Angel', like Monseigneur (p. 353). (In reality, as she strikes Miss Pross, she resembles 'the wife of Lucifer' (p. 380).) Having worked for aristocrats is proclaimed a 'sin' (p. 268), to be atoned for by declaring oneself 'ready and willing to cut his throat on the altar of the dawning Republic' (p. 268). After the Revolution, the people look for 'sacrifices and self-immolation on the people's altar', of whom Charles Darnay is to be one, his father-in-law being expected to feel 'a sacred glow' about it (p. 345). In the moral chaos of this revolutionary religion, the guillotine becomes 'popularly canonised' and the wood sawyer names his saw 'Little Sainte Guillotine' after it (p. 288). The executioners are 'the ministers of Sainte Guillotine' who are 'robed and ready', as if in clerical vestments, to perform the ceremony of execution (p. 387).

Having been imbued with the values of the society in which they grew up, and having abandoned Christianity to devote themselves to a perversion of religion, they create an evil society in which they themselves degenerate spiritually as they become more and more consumed in the opposite of Christian values. If Christianity preaches mercy, the captured Foulon throughout his mistreatment is 'always entreating and beseeching for mercy', but the only form in which it is available, is when at the third attempt to hang him, 'the rope was merciful and held him' (p. 234). Charles Darnay's return to France to attempt to 'assert the claims of mercy and humanity' (p. 252) when the life of Gabelle, as an old employee of the family, is endangered, is futile and has near-fatal consequences for him, and it takes as powerful a witness at his trial as Dr. Manette to prompt the jury into a far-from-habitual display of 'generosity and mercy' (p. 295).

Instead of mercy and Christian forgiveness, this society is driven by revenge, of which Mme. Defarge's friend, The Vengeance, is but one reflection. Before the Revolution comes, Mme. Defarge is already devoted to 'Vengeance and retribution' (p. 185); the women who help her as the Bastille is stormed are 'all armed alike in hunger and revenge' (p. 224). The Bastille's governor must not escape or 'the people's blood' will 'be unavenged' (p. 228). The Vengeance in pursuit of Foulon is likened to the deities of revenge, being 'like all the forty Furies at once' (p. 232). By the time Darnay is, briefly, acquitted at his trial, the whole climate of Paris is dominated by vengeance – 'the people ... so passionately revengeful and fitful' that Lucie dare not relax from her anxiety: rightly, as it turns out, 'a vague but heavy fear' abides in her (p. 298). Soon, Mme Defrarge's wish for revenge for the wrongs done to her family by Darnay's family drives her beyond even her husband's attempts to restrain her: 'Tell the Wind and the Fire to stop; not me!' (p. 354).

Though one of the watchwords of the Revolution is 'Fraternity', it has a highly partisan usage. It denotes not humanity in general, only the members of the revolutionary class. The 'sisterhood' Mme Defarge feels is with The Vengeance and the other Saint Antoine revolutionary women (p. 231). That it is not a concept she applies to all is evident in the scene in Book 3 Chapter 3 in which Lucie goes to plead for her arrested husband. The scene picks up a number of the major ideas we have seen are Dickens's concern. Lucie makes a desperate plea that Madame Defarge will 'be merciful' (p. 278), but it is a forlorn request. She tries to persuade Madame Defarge not to act vindictively towards Charles, appealing to their common humanity: 'O sister-woman, think of me. As a wife and mother!' (p. 278). Madame Defarge, however, does not acknowledge her as a sister human being and looks at her 'coldly as ever' (p. 278). 'Our sister-women' in her eyes are the ones they have seen 'suffer' during 'All our lives' (p. 279). They were not 'greatly considered', and she is now inclined to revenge by treating this woman in the way they once were. At Charles's second trial there is 'not a touch of human sympathy' as he is convicted (p. 345). In the factionalism that is rampant, Charles disowning his family and trying to do good count for nothing: he is condemned simply for belonging to the wrong faction: 'one of a family of tyrants, one of a race proscribed' (p. 328).

Lack of brotherly attitudes is revealed in how the aristocrats in their turn are viewed as less than human. Monseigneur has become 'A mere beast of the chase flying from hunters' (p. 268). The jury at Darnay's second trial are like 'a jury of dogs empanelled to try the deer' (p. 358). To Madame Defarge, Darnay and his family are simply 'her prey' with 'no right to live' (p. 376).

The spiritual degeneracy of the Revolutionaries is also reflected in how even virtues become perverted. Throughout Dickens's works, characters are commended for being earnest. In *Bleak House*, for instance, Allan Woodcourt's 'deep earnestness' (p. 738)[12] in love as in everything else, and in *Little Dorrit*, Amy's characteristically 'earnest face' (p. 404)[13] as she declares her devotion to Clennam, enhance their standing with the reader. In this very novel, Carton is at his best when he emerges from his lassitude and carelessness and displays the 'earnestness' (p. 215) that Darnay notes in him.

Jerry redeems himself by being, as Miss Pross remarks 'thoroughly in earnest' (p. 378) in helping when the Darnays are trying to escape. Lack of earnestness blights the characters and lives of Richard Carstone in *Bleak House* and Tip Dorrit in *Little Dorrit.*

However, Dickens is well aware that earnestness can become twisted and deployed to harmful effect. There is, for instance, the contrast between the virtuous earnestness of Arthur Clennam, and the more mordant form of it seen in his mother: Little Dorrit notes of Clennam that in his 'earnestness there was something that reminded her of his mother, with the great difference that she was earnest in asperity and he in gentleness' (p. 182). When we first meet Monsieur Defarge, it is a quality ascribed to him: 'implacable-looking ... a man of strong resolution and a set purpose ... nothing would turn the man' (p. 35); and indeed, we later discover that his first name is 'Ernest'. At this early stage he is 'good-humoured-looking on the whole' (p. 35), but there is already something slightly intimidating about his earnestness, for he is 'a man not desirable to be met, rushing down a narrow pass with a gulf on either side' precisely because 'nothing would turn the man' (p. 35). As the novel progresses this earnestness becomes a ruthless implacability intent on doing evil.

Dickens thus presents a world of rampant evil, ever spreading and deepening. Its origins lay in a world that ignored Christian values, and the society that is its product is no more Christian, no more moral or humane than its predecessor. The revolutionaries take the same position as Fag in the passage from *The Rivals*, which heads this chapter: while deploring the evil done to them, they themselves do evil as part of a chain reaction; their own suffering in no way makes them forbear in inflicting suffering on others, but rather prompts them to inflict such suffering. Evil has bred evil and as the chain reaction continues it threatens to spread out, engulf and destroy the characters we care about. Dickens does not at all present a glib picture of how a happy ending can emerge from this evil society. Sydney Carton, in his putative speech as he goes to the guillotine says 'I see the evil of this time and of the previous time of which this is the natural birth, gradually making expiation for itself and wearing out' (p. 389), and Dickens does give some indication of how this will happen.

The two societies that he portrays are places of such cruelty and suffering because they ignore God's commands about how people should live. Nevertheless, their existence raises questions about how God could allow the capacity for such evil to exist, and there is something of an implied theodicy in his study of evil in the novel. Despite, ironically, being named after a saint, Therese Defarge is the ultimate exemplar of evil in the novel, and the author uses her to expose something vital about evil: that despite being apparently strong and powerful, it has a weakness which means that it is ultimately self-destructive. It is a similar observation to the one Shakespeare makes about evil in *King Lear*: the more successful evil becomes the greedier it becomes for further success, the more rampant, the more ambitious and reckless, until it finally spirals out of control and into its own destruction. The weakness in the very nature of evil means that in the long term it does not prevail.

Madame Defarge's evil, long suppressed within her, has the opportunity to break out and be expressed rampantly once the Revolution occurs. All the bitterness and hatred that has been preserved in her knitting can now be openly expressed, and there is no-one to restrain her. Her appetite for revenge, arising not only from the general injustice and suffering she has observed around her all her life, but also from the fates of her sister and brother at the hands of the Evremondes, puts steel into her relentless and vicious pursuit of all those she identifies as enemies and has no intention of forgiving:

> imbued from her childhood with a brooding sense of wrong, and an inveterate hatred of a class, opportunity had developed her into a tigress. She was absolutely without pity. If she had ever had the virtue in her, it had quite gone out of her. (p. 375)

The very 'opportunity' the Revolution offers, however, is 'disfiguring' and in making her into a 'tigress' makes her a creature not only vicious but as irrational as animals are (p. 375). By the end of the novel it is clear that the more her lust for revenge is satisfied, the more it will be, not sated, but whetted further. The heir to the Evremondes who so mistreated members of her family has been sentenced to death, but she is not content with this. Fixed on 'pursuing this family to annihilation' (p. 373) she is determined that Lucie too will die, and doesn't demur when Jacques Three suggests also guillotining Lucie's daughter. Extraordinarily, she also wants the death of Dr. Manette, a prime victim of the regime she is supposedly avenging. The merest pretext – that Lucie and Dr. Manette were seen signalling to prisoners in La Force prison – is enough in this society in which evil is allowed to run rampant; but the comment of Jacques Three – 'We really have not heads enough' (p. 374) reveals the truth behind these executions. Revenge and state security are becoming second to an insatiable blood lust.

As her malevolence spirals out of control, she sets off armed with dagger and gun to seize her victims. By this stage she is beyond anyone's control. She knows that even her husband will baulk at sending Dr. Manette to the guillotine, so she simply by-passes him, deciding to 'act for myself' (p. 373). She considers the matter: 'Can I spare his Doctor to my husband?' – but by now her appetite for blood is such that she decides 'No; I cannot spare him!' (p. 374). When she reaches the Darnays' apartment, another weakness of evil is exposed. Centred on its gratification of self, it lacks any appreciation of the power of love for others, leading to a fatal misinterpretation of Miss Pross's behaviour. The latter is intent on fighting Mme Defarge if necessary, even though she 'had never struck a blow in her life' (p. 381), so as to keep her there and thus give Lucie the best chance of escape in the meantime. Miss Pross's courage, however, 'was of that emotional nature that it brought the irrepressible tears into her eyes. This was a courage Madame Defarge so little comprehended as to mistake for weakness' (p. 381).

The complacency enables Miss Pross to take her by surprise in attacking her. In the ensuing struggle Mme Defarge is shot and killed by her own gun, a symbol of wild self-destructiveness. In the end her hatred, vengefulness and malevolence have run away with her and taken her to an end which was inevitable sooner or later: not until stopped by death would her malevolence rest.

If there will thus be an eventual 'wearing out' of evil, the characters in the novel are confronted with the problem of how to deal with it in the meantime. They try to oppose it with goodness. When Gabelle, an employee of the Evremonde estate, is in danger of losing his life, Charles is stirred by loyalty and a sense of obligation towards 'an old servant and a good one, whose only crime was fidelity to himself and his family' (p. 250). Feeling that the compassion he showed in the past in instructing Gabelle to 'spare the people' must stand him in good stead in protecting 'his own safety' (p. 251) he returns to France. Naively, he has a 'glorious vision of doing good' once there and of having 'influence to guide this raging Revolution that was running so fearfully wild' (p. 252). Once there, of course, his hopes 'to do something to stay bloodshed and assert the claims of mercy and humanity' (p. 252) count for nothing, and he finds himself imprisoned and on trial for his life. Goodness cannot fight against this evil so simply and painlessly.

When the other characters follow him to Paris, they discover that goodness can only achieve anything in this climate of rampant evil at real cost. Within limits, while in Paris Dr. Manette can quietly go about doing good. He maintains the notion of true brotherhood by considering that 'as a physician' his 'business was with all degrees of mankind bond and free, rich and poor, bad and good' (p. 282). Thus, he can be seen showing the same sort of humanity that Allan Woodcourt did in *Bleak House*: 'Silent, humane, indispensable in hospital and prison, using his art equally among assassins and victims' (p. 284).

Not all the demands on him, though, are ones he can meet so readily. Dr. Manette is a tortured man who struggles against his own feelings of hate and vengefulness against the Evremondes. In the document eventually revealed in court that he wrote in prison, he writes bitterly of the 'hard heart' each of the brothers had in not letting him have news of his wife and in his 'unbearable agony' declares that 'I denounce them to Heaven and to earth' (p. 344). The revelation on their wedding day that Lucie's husband-to-be is an Evremonde is utterly traumatic, driving him back to his cobbler's last, and it seems to be his love for his daughter and concern for her happiness that makes him accept her husband. Once Darnay is in prison, Dr. Manette is uniquely placed, because of his status as a victim of the old regime, to help him: 'he knew himself to be invested through that old trial with forces to which' Dr. Manette and Mr. Lorry 'both looked for Charles's ultimate safety and deliverance' (p. 282). Dr. Manette's motivation seems still to be his love for his daughter: having obtained a job that involves visiting the relevant prison, 'He could now assure Lucie that her husband was no longer confined alone ... brought sweet messages to her, straight from his lips' (p. 282). In his 'gratitude and affection' he takes pride 'in rendering some service to her who had rendered so much to him' (p. 282). In due course, though, Dr. Manette rises to an even higher moral level. His testimony at Darnay's trial assures the latter's acquittal – as Darnay himself remarks: 'No other man in all this France could have done what he has done for me' (p. 297). Shortly after, Manette, tells his granddaughter a story 'of a great and powerful Fairy who had opened a prison-wall and let out a captive who had once done the Fairy a service' (p. 301). The implication here seems to be that Manette has rescued Darnay not for Lucie's sake but for Darnay's own: he has managed to forgive him.

The tendency of evil circumstances to provoke goodness in good people is reflected in Manette's managing to mount this hurdle but it is also seen elsewhere. Miss Pross furnishes another example. Her love for Lucie enables her, inexperienced though she is, to fight Madame Defarge 'with the vigorous tenacity of love, always so much stronger then hate' (p. 382), though there is a price to be paid in Miss Pross's deafness thereafter.

The supreme example of goodness being provoked by evil circumstances, though at a cost, is, of course, Sydney Carton and his sacrifice of his life. What he does has often been interpreted in the light of Jesus's saying that 'Greater love hath no man than this, that a man lay down his life for his friends' (John 15:13), as, for instance, when Andrew Sanders comments that 'Carton redeems his wasted life by laying down that life for his friend'.[14] I want to argue, though, that in the context of the novel, some other parts of Christ's teachings are also relevant. The novel portrays how evil breeds evil which then continues to spread in a kind of chain reaction. Some of the sayings of Jesus suggest how this chain reaction can be stopped, and evil contained by simply absorbing the evil:

> Love your enemies, do good to them which hate you. Bless them that curse you, and pray for them which despitefully use you. And unto him that smiteth thee on the one cheek offer also the other. (Luke 6:27–9)

In *The Life of Our Lord*, Dickens draws attention to these ideas in portraying Jesus acting in precisely this fashion when in the hands of Pilate's soldiers, transposing to this moment one of Christ's utterances on the Cross (c.f. Luke 23:34) to underline the point: 'They ill-used Him in many cruel ways; but Jesus bore it patiently, and only said "Father! Forgive them! They know not what they do!"' (p. 52).[15]

By refusing to do evil in the face of evil, by rejecting retaliation, evil is defused and defeated and the chain reaction broken. By dying in Darnay's place, Carton brings to a full stop the evil which in this case has led to the death sentence, stopping it from inflicting suffering on Darnay's family. Carton has no-one: as he soaks up the evil, the result will not be suffering and misery for others. A small link in the chain of suffering producing evil producing suffering producing evil will have been broken. He cannot bring the whole rampant evil of this society to an end but he can stand against the spread of evil in one tributary. He achieves it by sacrificing his life; but fighting evil with good comes at a real cost. The happy ending he thus furnishes for Charles, Lucie and their daughter cannot be brought about easily and painlessly in this evil world. The life he saves and the lives of the others affected will, he envisages, be 'peaceful ... prosperous and happy'; but in addition, goodness will thrive as their lives, not embittered, perverted or wrecked, will be 'useful' (a significant word, as we saw in Chapter 8) in service to others (p. 389); the realisation of a better society will be a few steps closer. Good produces good, just as evil produces evil.

The 'frightful moral disorder' which the novel portrays is 'born of unspeakable suffering, intolerable oppression, and heartless indifference' (p. 360). Both the old and new regimes are evil, and evil in the same ways. The political solution a revolution seems to offer is revealed as changing nothing. If the defining qualities of both regimes are that they represent the opposite of Christian values, the hope for a better society is the adoption of those values by each individual. Carton takes a step towards asserting Christian values and thus propagating the triumph of good over evil: it is up to each individual to commit themselves to good in their turn and thus create a better world.

It is not, then, the political structures of a society that determine whether it is a good one or not; as we have seen in Chapter 8, Dickens subscribes to the view that changing the structure and the personnel within it will not improve things unless the members of that society also change and reform.

11
A Note on Dickens and Sentimentality

Even in an age which has massively reappraised Dickens and in which his stature has grown enormously, the element of sentimentality in his works remains problematic. The very term carries pejorative overtones. The sentimental is widely attacked as marked by an insincere, false, calculating raising of the emotional temperature in art, knowingly and cynically done. Humphrey House refers to it as 'the imposition of feeling as an afterthought upon literalness'.[1] There is an element of self-indulgence in it for the reader, wallowing in an agreeably tearful state; it is mawkish and sickly. The feelings evoked are both 'unearned and undisciplined'.[2]

Critics who have attempted to defend Dickens have tended to do so by providing two sorts of context. Some, such as Fred Kaplan in *Sacred Tears: Sentimentality in Victorian Literature*, Mary Lenard in *Preaching Pity: Dickens, Gaskell and Sentimentalism in Victorian Culture*, and Valerie Purton in *Dickens and the Sentimental Tradition* have attempted to put sentimentality in a cultural context, deploying five main types of arguments. Firstly they have highlighted the respectable origins of sentimentality in eighteenth century moral philosophy, in the writings particularly of Shaftesbury, Hume and Adam Smith and their ideas that moral sentiments were innate and were expressed through spontaneous feeling.[3] Secondly, they place it in opposition within the culture to antipathetic forces such as 'utilitarianism, rationalism, scientific determinism ... Calvinism'[4] and 'industrialisation, science, mechanisation'.[5] Thirdly this in turn leads them to present sentimentality as having noble purposes. Mary Lenard argues, for instance, that 'Sentimentalist novels tried to effect change by influencing the hearts and the feelings of their readers, exploiting the 'feminine' cultural value of feeling for political purposes'.[6] Commenting on *Oliver Twist*, she notes that:

> The weepy, sentimentalist understanding of death, as embodied by Little Dick and other scenes in *Oliver Twist*, is a crucial part of the sentimental value system that Dickens proposes in opposition to a 'masculine',

> self-serving Utilitarianism which attempts to crush sympathy and sentiment in the name of 'philosophical self-interest.[7]

Purton too emphasises how Dickens strikes a blow 'against Benthamism and mechanism'.[8] More generally, as Kaplan remarks, there is the 'potential for moral reformation through an appeal to the moral sentiments'.[9]

Fourthly, these writers suggest that it is a change in our attitudes, which might be seen as a maladjustment, which makes us respond so critically to sentimentality. Commenting on how Dickens saw the suppression of innate moral sentiments as at the root of much of the corruption of Victorian society,[10] Kaplan suggests that the modern standard by which sentimental writing is judged is derived from the triumph of an anti-idealistic philosophical tradition, which involves the devaluation of human nature.[11] Lenard traces a number of factors lying behind the change of attitudes, including, in the nineteenth century, the association of sentimentality with women in an age in which there was 'suspicion of feminine qualities' in 'the high culture, the literary culture'[12] and the effect of the Aesthetic Movement in divorcing literature from having a purpose, such as sentimental writing always had.[13] Purton sees the hostility towards sentimental works as a manifestation of modernist elitism, which has resulted in a fear of emotional expression and a preference for irony, accompanying a distrust of expressing 'tender' emotions generally.[14]

This leads such critics, lastly, to suggest a re-adjustment of our attitudes and a consequent rehabilitation of sentimentality. Purton thus argues that the word should be seen simply as a critical concept, rather than a term of condemnation.[15] She contends that 'Dickens works hard to achieve effects of simplicity, intensity and excess, and to do so, crafts a complex rhetoric which merits careful analysis'.[16] Refusing to see literary sentimentality as simply a 'defect of style', she proposes that it 'should be neutrally examined as simply a mode, a literary convention, with its own rules, register and vocabulary'.[17] Modes such as sentimentalism and melodrama have 'a cultural, if not an aesthetic, value' equal to other modes of writing.[18]

A second, more straightforward context within which critics have urged that sentimental scenes in Dickens should be placed is the social historical one. Paul Davis, for instance, remarks on how

> the modern assessment of sentimentality often fails to take into account the 19th century context in which Dickens was writing. The facts of infant mortality, child labor, limited educational opportunity and poverty were more extreme than we often imagine. The suffering of children was fact, not just the imaginings of exaggerated feeling.[19]

Philip Collins argues that sentimental scenes, in the works of Victorian writers, particularly those manifesting a 'preoccupation with death-beds', need to be seen against a background both of contemporary 'philanthropic and parliamentary concern with infant mortality' and of 'the rise and decline of Evangelicalism'.[20]

Awareness of such contexts undoubtedly puts the sentimental scenes in Dickens in a different perspective, and helps explain the reactions of contemporaries. Such contextualisation is a corrective to the idea that Dickens condones wallowing self-indulgently in pathos for its own sake, something reinforced by an episode in *Bleak House* in which Mr Skimpole stands condemned for precisely such indulgent enjoyment leading to no moral action. In Chapter 31 of the novel, immediately after showing much callous indifference to the plight of Jo, he is stimulated 'apropos of our young friend' to sing a sentimental song about a peasant boy:

> Thrown on the wide world, doom'd to wander and roam
> Bereft of his parents, bereft of a home.

Despite the similarity of the predicaments of Jo and the boy in the song, Skimpole is stirred to no further action beyond revelling in its pathos: 'It was a song that always made him cry, he told us' (p. 497).[21] Knowledge of the cultural context also explains and highlights the very different response Victorian readers had, evident in the Saturday Review article, 'The Death of Mr Dickens', of 11 June 1870, in which the writer comments that:

> possibly his sentimentalism, while it wearied some of his more fastidious readers, may have helped to produce a good moral effect on the wider world which he attracted and enlightened[22]

or in Francis Jeffrey's letter of 31 January 1847 to Dickens, after he had read the death of Paul in *Dombey and Son*:

> I have so cried and sobbed over it last night, and again this morning; and felt my heart purified by these tears, and blessed and loved you for making me shed them.[23]

As we have seen, the suggestion from these critics is that Dickens wrote in a different cultural climate from the one in which we now live and that the disjunction between Victorian cultural attitudes and our own is the cause of our distaste for what was at the time a perfectly acceptable cultural mode. Kaplan describes hostility to sentimentalism as having a 'slowly gathering force', and that the term only 'came to denote ... the misuse of sentiment' at a period 'late in the nineteenth century'.[24]

It is, however, striking, that being contemporaries of Dickens did not stop a number of critics being distinctly critical of this element in his works. After his death, the tide turned against this aspect of his work remarkably quickly. At the end of his life, critics were already questioning the supposed moral effects of sentimentality. Describing Dickens's sentimentality as 'mawkish and unreal', R.H. Hutton, in a *Spectator* article of 17 April 1869, 'Mr Dickens's Moral Service to Literature' wrote that:

> Mr Dickens has brought people to think that there is a sort of piety in being gushing and maudlin, – and this is anything but a useful contribution to the morality of the age.[25]

In January of the same year, in his piece 'Charles Dickens' in the *Contemporary Review* George Stott perhaps exemplifying Lenard's argument, considered that it was only 'weak people, women and children' that Dickens made 'cry copiously'.[26]

Once he was dead, this view became even more pronounced. An unsigned article in the *Dublin Review* of April 1871 suggested that when Dickens first became famous, his sentimentality 'had many hearty admirers among his young readers', but that now, 'We suspect there are very few young people of the present day so "exceedingly young" ... as to be attracted by Mr Dickens's pathos'.[27] Equally, reviewing the second volume of Forster's biography of Dickens in *Atlantic Monthly*, and referring to Lord Jeffrey's tears over the deaths of Little Nell and Paul Dombey, William Dean Howells asked 'Does any peer of the realm now shed tears for their fate?', and went on to consider that sentimentality may have only been 'all a fashion only'.[28]

Social attitudes may simply have been moving on, and the contexts outlined by the critics discussed at the beginning of this chapter being to some extent lost. More troubling, though, is that even as Dickens was writing, not everyone seems to have regarded sentimentality in his works in the light of contexts of which they could readily have been more aware than the twenty-first century reader. As Lenard points out, hostile attitudes to sentimentality go back quite a long way. She cites Hazlitt's attack on Methodism, dating from 1815, in which he described it as 'an easy and essentially insincere approach to religion':

> How comfortably this doctrine must sit on those who are loth to give up old habits of vice ... the maudlin sentimentalist, the religious prostitute, the disinterested poet laureate, the humane war contractor.[29]

Kaplan himself quotes the criticisms of Dickens made in 1847 by Henry Hallam. Concerning the death of Paul Dombey, Hallam remarks, 'I am so hardened as to be unable to look on it in any light but pure business'. Kaplan comments here on the implication that 'Dickens had manipulated the dramatic situation, eliciting from his readers feelings that he himself did not have in order to appeal to a debased popular taste for the purpose of selling more books'.[30]

The evidence is that even when Dickens's career was at its height, sentimentality had already acquired pejorative overtones among substantial numbers of people. In the *Saturday Review* in 1857, Fitzjames Stephen wrote disparagingly of Dickens's novels, referring to their 'melodramatic and sentimental stock-in-trade'.[31] Jane Carlyle wrote approvingly of George Eliot's *Scenes of Clerical Life* being 'full of tenderness and pathos without sentimentality, of sense without dogmatism'.[32] In an article about 'The False Morality of Lady Novelists', which appeared in *The National Review* in 1859, W.R. Greg was highly critical of 'the fantastic and flatulent morality' of 'sentimental' female novelists.[33] In 1862, R.H. Hutton remarked about *The Old Curiosity Shop* and *Dombey and Son* that Dickens 'spoons and stirs the subject of grief and death'.[34]

Hallam's remark about the element of 'pure business' in the depiction of the death of Paul Dombey implies a cynicism and calculation that is part of the modern charge against Dickens's sentimentality, and others at the time also considered that the emotion might not be spontaneous and natural. 'Mr Dickens sets himself to work to make us cry just as openly and deliberately as to make us laugh', asserted Stott in the 1869 article *Contemporary Review* cited above;[35] in our own time, Barbara Hardy similarly describes Dickens as 'pursuing an inquiry into the affective life, while manipulating the responses of his readers, sometimes most blatantly'.[36] On the other hand, Mowbray Morris argued in his article 'Charles Dickens' which appeared in the *Fortnightly Review* on 1 December 1882 that 'All that we know of Dickens forbids us to doubt that he wrote such things in perfect sincerity, and not merely with a view to effect'.[37] This, however, leads us to an alternative problem about the sentimental element in Dickens's work. Walter Bagehot's assertion in an article 'Charles Dickens' in *The National Review* in 1858 that Dickens 'dwells on dismal scenes with a kind of fawning fondness'[38] only too easily gives way to Aldous Huxley's famous criticism in his 1930 book, *Vulgarity in Literature*.[39] In discussing the 'vulgar sentimentality'[40] of the presentation of Little Nell, Huxley acquits Dickens of cynical calculation: his 'really monstrous vulgarity ... is not the emotional vulgarity of one who simulates feelings which he does not have'.[41] Instead, the reverse is true:

> Dickens felt most poignantly for and with his Little Nell; that he wept over her sufferings, piously revered her goodness and exulted in her joys. He had an overflowing heart; but the trouble was that it overflowed with such curious and even rather repellent secretions.[42]

When he becomes emotional in his works 'His one and only desire ... is just to overflow, nothing else'.[43]

Dickens stands, then, accused of either mercenary calculation or, its opposite, of a lack of discipline and of self-indulgence. As Hardy comments on *The Old Curiosity Shop*,

> it seems impossible to decide whether the gross repetitions and solemn appeals in these episodes ... are the accumulated and over-charged results of self-indulgence, or arrangements made in the hope of wringing readers' hearts.[44]

Despite the valuable work done by scholars, then, the sentimental element in Dickens remains somewhat problematic; and it would seem that it is not just a matter of a cultural shift and change of fashion that determines the unease with which sentimentality in Dickens is regarded, for a similar unease was detectable even in his own age, when the contexts of his work were less remote. If he was aware of hostility to sentimentality in his own age, it may have been that he was simply defiant against the forces discussed above that were determining attitudes. However, it may also be that sentimentality has a less insistent and more complicated existence in his works than is often recognised. In what follows, I am going to argue that it is less pervasive in Dickens's works than often assumed.

A complication in attempting to discuss sentimentality in Dickens is that there seems to be a subjective element in deciding where it occurs. In a review of *Sketches by Boz*, *Pickwick Papers*, *Oliver Twist*, and *Nicholas Nickleby* in the *Edinburgh Review* in October 1838, Thomas Henry Lister confidently asserted that:

> His humanity ... is quite untainted with sentimentality. There is no mawkish wailing for ideal distresses – no morbid exaggeration of the evils incident to our lot – no disposition to excite unavailing discontent, or to turn our attention from remediable grievances to those which do not admit a remedy. Though he appeals much to our feelings, we can detect no instance in which he has employed the verbiage of spurious philanthropy.[45]

Similarly, while we have already seen Victorian commentators both rejoicing in and deploring the sentimentality of the death of Paul Dombey, the modern critic Barbara Hardy takes a different view of that and of the death of Jo in *Bleak House*:

> In the deaths of Paul and Jo he stays on the right side of the dangerous verge between sentiment and sentimentality.[46]

This in turn prompts me to ask initially, how often we find sentimentality in Dickens because we are predisposed to find it. His reputation for sentimentality goes before him, and it is at least worth asking whether when we read a scene such as the death of Jo in *Bleak House*, we respond to it as a tear-jerking scene because, once we have recognised that this is to be the death-scene of a child, we are conditioned to read it as sentimental since that is what we expect of Dickens in these circumstances. While it is undoubtedly a highly charged scene, there is actually nothing in the text to prevent us finding anger, rather than mawkishness, to be the dominant emotion in the scene. The scene does, after all, reveal a British child dying ignorant of even the most famous and basic Christian prayer, and of the concepts it contains, something that should be more an occasion for shock and dismay than an indulgent tearfulness. Usually it is read as a maudlin scene followed by an outburst of sudden anger in the last paragraph. It is, however, at least possible to read the whole scene as permeated with anger, which then rises to a crescendo in the final paragraph.

It is interesting, secondly, to note what emerges from the following passage from *A Christmas Carol*, in which the Ghost of Christmas Yet To Come is showing Scrooge a scene that may occur in the Cratchit household, after the death of Tiny Tim. Mrs Cratchit is speaking:

> 'I wouldn't want to show weak eyes to your father when he comes home, for the world. It must be near his time.'
>
> 'Past it rather,' Peter answered, shutting up his book. 'But I think he's walked a little slower than he used, these last few evenings, mother.'
>
> They were very quiet again. At last she said, and in a steady, cheerful voice, that only faultered once:
>
> 'I have known him walk with – I have known him walk with Tiny Tim upon his shoulder, very fast indeed.'
>
> 'And so have I,' cried Peter. 'Often.'
>
> 'And so have I!' exclaimed another. So had all.
>
> 'But he was very light to carry,' she resumed, intent upon her work, 'and his father loved him so, that it was no trouble – no trouble. And there is your father at the door!' She hurried out to meet him; and little Bob in his comforter – he had need of it, poor fellow – came in. His tea was ready for him on the hob, and they all tried who should help him to it most. Then the two young Cratchits got upon his knees and laid, each child a little cheek, against his face, as if they said, 'Don't mind it, father. Don't be grieved!' Bob was very cheerful with them, and spoke pleasantly to all the family. He looked at the work upon the table, and praised the industry and speed of Mrs. Cratchit and the girls. They would be done long before Sunday, he said.
>
> 'Sunday! You went today then, Robert?' 'Yes, my dear,' returned Bob. 'I wish you could have gone. It would have done you good to see how green a place it is. But you'll see it often. I promised him that I would walk there on a Sunday. My little, little child!' cried Bob. 'My little child!'

> He broke down all at once. He couldn't help it. If he could have helped it, he and his child would have been further apart perhaps than they were. He left the room, and went upstairs into the room above, which was lighted cheerfully, and hung with Christmas. There was a chair set close beside the child, and there were signs of some one having been there, lately. Poor Bob sat down in it, and when he had thought a little and composed himself, he kissed the little face. He was reconciled to what had happened, and went down again quite happy. (pp. 105–6)[47]

It is interesting to look here at where the emotion is located. If the scene is sentimental, a certain number of touches in the narration serve to raise the emotional temperature, including the references to 'little Bob' and 'Poor Bob', who is a 'poor fellow', and to the Cratchit child's 'little cheek' and Tiny Tim's 'little face'. However, it is not just the narrator who is being sentimental: the emotion of the scene is also carried in the speeches of the characters, as when Mrs Cratchit relates how it was 'no trouble – no trouble' to Bob to carry his crippled son or Bob refers to Tim as 'My little, little child! ... My little child!'. This is far from uncommon in Dickens: often in sentimental scenes, there is a distinction to be drawn between whether it is the characters, or Dickens or his narrator, who are being sentimental. This does not always involve speech. In *A Tale of Two Cities*, for instance, it is when the narrative is seeing things through the eyes of Lucie Darnay that it is described that her second, dying, child's 'golden hair, like her own, lay in a halo on a pillow round the worn face of a little boy' (p. 219);[48] the sentimental terms of the description convey her tender, loving nature.

Identifying sentimentality as a trait of personality of certain Dickens characters separate from his or his narrators' attitudes may seem to make a distinction without point. In the case of both the Cratchits and Lucie Darnay, we are plainly intended to identify with and empathise with the characters and their feelings. However, it is important to be alert to the idea that sentimentality in his characters is not necessarily something Dickens goes along with or endorses. Sometimes at least he stands at a critical distance from it. On occasion, he does this very overtly. In *Our Mutual Friend*, for instance, Mrs Veneering becomes sentimental at a celebration of her husband's election to Parliament, a victory which has involved a substantial sum of money changing hands:

> A touching little incident is related by Mrs. Veneering, in the course of the evening.
>
> Mrs. Veneering is habitually disposed to be tearful, and has an extra disposition that way after her late excitement. Previous to withdrawing from the dinner-table with Lady Tippins, she says, in a pathetic and physically weak manner:

> 'You will all think it foolish of me, I know, but I must mention it. As I sat by Baby's crib, on the night before the election, Baby was very uneasy in her sleep.'
>
> The Analytical chemist, who is gloomily looking on, has diabolical impulses to suggest 'Wind' and throw up his situation; but represses them.
>
> 'After an interval almost convulsive, Baby curled her little hands in one another and smiled.'
>
> Mrs. Veneering stopping here, Mr. Podsnap deems it incumbent on him to say: 'I wonder why!'
>
> 'Could it be, I asked myself,' says Mrs. Veneering, looking about her for her pocket-handkerchief, 'that the Fairies were telling Baby that her papa would shortly be an M.P.?'
>
> So overcome by the sentiment is Mrs. Veneering, that they all get up to make a clear stage for Veneering, who goes round the table to the rescue, and bears her out backward, with her feet impressively scraping the carpet: after remarking that her work has been too much for her strength. Whether the fairies made any mention of the five thousand pounds, and it disagreed with Baby, is not speculated on. (p. 253)[49]

On other occasions, though, things are less clear-cut, it is not as obvious that Dickens is distancing himself from the sentimentality of his characters, and it is easy to assume he is endorsing it. An example occurs in the framing story of *Mugby Junction*, which was published as the Christmas number of *All the Year Round* in 1866. In the story, the narrator, Jackson, meets a young woman, Phoebe, who was dropped as a young child and is now confined to a single room, quite unable to walk. He becomes good friends with Phoebe and her father, and at one point, watching her as she 'caressed' a musical instrument he has bought her, he is 'saddened' as he thinks that 'so might she, if her youth had flourished in its natural course, have taken to her breast that day the slumbering music of her own child's voice' (p. 498).[50] It is easy to take for granted that Dickens sympathises with this piece of sentimental fancy and wants us to feel what Jackson feels.

However, though Jackson is a sympathetic character, and though these thoughts testify to his compassionate nature, in the context of the story it is plain that we are in fact meant to look critically on this thinking. Jackson is a man who has suffered a great deal in life; everything has gone wrong for him, in both his public and his private life. We follow him in the story as he discovers how to come to terms with all this and to find serenity; and one of the ways in which he manages this is to abandon the idea that we are entitled to think that life should conform to a norm. The way to avoid the embittering experience of disappointed expectations is to accept that life is unpredictable and uncertain. Jackson's thoughts here spring out of an attitude that what would be normal for a woman would be to have children, and that Phoebe has been cheated out of something she was entitled to, just as he feels himself cheated out of things he felt he was entitled to. Phoebe herself never shows any signs of such an attitude; she is pragmatic and accepting of what has happened to her, and is thus at peace. Jackson is to learn this mind-set from her. Thus, his thoughts at this point represent an outlook that he needs to develop out of, not one Dickens would endorse.[51] This case underlines the need to distinguish carefully between the sentimentality of his characters and the author's own attitudes. In complex cases like this one, the character may be sympathetic, but misguided; and it is the character who is being sentimental, not Dickens.

Centrally, the issue of sentimentality is relevant to the theme of this book in a way that may be broached by examining the death of Stephen Blackpool in *Hard Times*. As Stephen is described lying fatally injured at the bottom of Old Hell mine shaft, and delivering his final thoughts to those attending him, a great deal is made of the star he has been able to see while in the shaft, which he thought 'were the star as guided to Our Saviour's home. I awmust think it be the very star' (p. 265).[52] As they begin to take him away from the mineshaft, he is 'overjoyed to find that they were about to take him in the direction whither the star seemed to him to lead' (p. 265). When he dies as they carry him, the narrator comments that 'The star had shown him where to find the God of the poor; and through humility, and sorrow, and forgiveness, he had gone to his Redeemer's rest' (p. 265).

Scenes in Dickens regarded as sentimental tend to be replete with religious references in this way, and such allusions are usually seen as designed to raise the emotional temperature. Religion, after all, is something with many powerful emotive connotations, and religious references in such passages can easily be interpreted as what Hardy calls 'pathetic stimuli'.[53] Thus, she describes how the death of Smike in *Nicholas Nickleby* 'is prepared and intensified by the accumulation of several sources of pathetic appeal, nostalgia, religion, nature, and hopeless love'.[54] Humphrey House finds the use of religious references in sentimental scenes part of the emotional self-indulgence we have been considering earlier and something that makes them unpalatable and even offensive to the modern reader:

> Nearly all his most embarrassing pathos is expressed in religious or semi-religious imagery and terms. The three famous deaths – those of Little Nell, Paul Dombey, and Jo – where modern readers find the uncontrolled squandering of sentiment hard not merely to appreciate, but even to understand, obviously affected Dickens very deeply, as they affected numbers of his readers ... the strongest contemporary protests against their pathos came from the religious press ... The exaggerated consolation that Jo is supposed to extract from the Lord's Prayer (which anyway he could not have understood even so far) not merely degrades the use of it into a kind of private superstition, but also has the mood of somebody

> in a state of utter emotional collapse enjoying his own prostration and mouthing formulae from another scheme of values as if they expressed his own. Apart from the use of religious terms, it is the pleasurable self-indulgence of these scenes that is so distasteful and, incidentally, so unchristian.[55]

I want to argue, though, that such allusions are included by Dickens for thematic reasons, as part of his religious critique of society; they are part of the intellectual, rather than the emotional, structure of his novels.

We have already seen that the teaching of the Lord's Prayer to the dying Jo in *Bleak House* is not some arbitrary attempt at tear-jerking; instead, it is there to underline at a climactic moment that the whole of humanity is one family, with God as its Father, at a point when Jo is dying as a result of the members of society not regarding him as a brother, entitled to all the loving care a member of the family should be given. The use of religious references as an indictment of society is far from being unique to this scene. In the extract from *A Christmas Carol* given above, the reference to Christmas could be seen as introduced to raise the emotional temperature, an allusion to a time of family togetherness at a moment when the Cratchits are experiencing family separation; but the reference can equally be seen as an indictment of the contrary values of the surrounding society, its callous, compassionless, mercenary attitudes, embodied in Scrooge, which cause the Cratchits to lead the sort of straitened lives in which Tiny Tim cannot thrive.

The religious references in the scene of Stephen Blackpool's death serve a similar purpose. The birth of Jesus, announced by the angel in Luke 2:10 as 'tidings of great joy, which shall be to all people', and heralded by the star Stephen refers to, ushered in a new covenant between God and mankind, bringing universal salvation, as underlined in Stephen's reference to Jesus as 'Our Saviour', and the narrator's allusion to Stephen's 'Redeemer', and emphasis that God is 'the God of the Poor' (p. 265). As Stephen has contemplated the star he associates with all this, the universality of God's love for mankind has made him think of the need for a similarly universal love and unity among people:

> 'lookin' up yonder, – wi' it shinin' on me – I ha' seen more clear, and ha' made it my dyin' prayer that aw the world may on'y coom together more, an get a better unnerstan'in o' one another'. (p. 264)

Stephen has come to be in his awful situation because of the absence of such a Christian outlook in society. As his society abandoned any idea of unity and brotherhood among men, splitting into factions of masters and workers, Stephen's refusal to join in led to his being victimised by both sides, losing his job and thus leaving Coketown. There was hence a need for him to return to clear his name from suspicions of robbery, his rush across the countryside leading to his falling down an abandoned mineshaft. The shaft was not fenced off, its owners never having shown any concern for their fellow human beings, as Stephen underlines:

> 'I ha' fell into th' pit, my dear, as have cost wi'in the knowledge o' fok now livin, hundreds and hundreds o' men's lives – fathers, sons, brothers, dear to thousands and thousands, an keepin 'em fro' want and hunger. I ha' fell into a pit that ha' been wi' the Fire-damp crueller than battle. I ha' read on't in the public petition, as onny one may read, fro' the men that works in pits, in which they ha' pray'n an pray'n the lawmakers not to let their work be murder to 'em, but to spare 'em for th'wives and children that they loves as well as gentlefolk loves theirs. When it were in work, it killed wi'out need; when 'tis let alone, it kills wi'out need. See how we die an no need, one way an another – in a muddle – every day!' (p. 263)

The shaft exemplifies the whole society, as is reflected in the reference Stephen goes on to make to Rachael's sister who died 'awlung o' sickly air as had'n no need to be, an awlung o' working people's miserable homes' (p. 263). The masters care not at all for the pollution they cause and its effects, neither for the social conditions their workers are forced to live in. The religious motif in this scene, though, makes the wickedness of this inescapable. The star's signification of the universality of God's love, and the identification of God as the God of 'the Poor' leaves as unjustifiable 'gentlefoks' effectively disowning their less fortunate fellow human beings and showing no responsibility to them. In the reference to lawmakers being begged to introduce regulation of working practices 'for Christ's sake', the phrase is not an oath to emphasise the campaigners' strength of feeling; it constitutes an (unsuccessful) attempt to recall the lawmakers to Christian values. It is this fundamental, immoral, irreligious wrong-headedness in society that is the 'muddle' Stephen is always referring to and that ultimately caused him to 'coom here' (p. 264) to his death.

The death of Betty Higden in Our Mutual Friend equally makes use of religious references for thematic purposes. To appreciate this fully requires examining the novel in some detail. The title *Our Mutual Friend* hints at a rich interlocking network of close relationships. It is a largely ironic title, though, for what we generally see in the novel are superficial relationships. Mr Twemlow cannot distinguish whether he is the Veneerings' newest friend or oldest friend because in reality there is no distinction between the two. The Lammles get married without in the slightest loving each other. When Charley Hexam leaves home to pursue his studies, his father 'disowns him for ever and ever' (p. 81). Rogue Riderhood used to be Gaffer Hexam's 'pardner' (p. 71) but now 'revenges himself' on him (p. 74). When the title phrase is used in the novel (p. 115), by Mr Boffin, it is actually being used facetiously, applied to Rokesmith when talking to the Wilfers. At the time, Rokesmith has only recently taken up lodgings with the Wilfers and Mr Boffin, as he says himself, has 'only seen him once' (p. 115).

Largely, relationships in the novel are frail and superficial because relationships with people are in competition with relationships with money and the latter generally win. The Lammles married simply because each supposed the other a person 'of property' (p. 127). Fascination Fledgeby's parents married simply because his mother was in debt to his father, a money-lender: 'The lady, a widow, being unable to pay the money-lender, married him' (p. 266). Mrs Lammle's apparent friendship with Georgiana Podsnap is not genuine, instead deploying 'every reassuring wile' (p. 142) and spurred on by a motive her husband identifies: 'there is money to be made out of this' (p. 146). Though Bella Wilfer has been 'fluttered' by the discovery that the apparently penniless Rokesmith 'seemed to like her' (p. 305), she does not initially consider him a marital prospect because 'I must have money ... and so I have resolved that I must marry it' (p. 317). Only the good characters value relationships above money. Unlike her brother, Lizzie Hexam puts devotion to her father before self-advancement and worldly gain: 'There am I, continuing with father and holding to father, because father loves me and I love father. I can't so much as read a book, because, if I had learned, father would have thought I was deserting him' (p. 38). Equally, such was the loyalty of the Boffins to John Harmon that they risked their livelihoods in his cause when his father disowned him. As Mr Boffin relates:

> on behalf of the poor dear boy, me and Mrs Boffin have stood out against the old man times out of number, till he has called us every name he could lay his tongue to. I have seen him, after Mrs Boffin has given him her mind respecting the claims of nat'ral affections, catch off Mrs Boffin's bonnet ... and send it spinning across the yard ... me and Mrs Boffin have ever stood, as we were in Christian honor bound, the children's friend ... me and Mrs Boffin up and faced the old man when we momently expected to be turned out for our pains. (p. 95)

It is in this context that the social theme of the book, which has Betty Higden at its centre, is presented. Betty's dilemma is that her poverty is constantly threatening to drive her to the workhouse, but what the workhouse exemplifies makes her resist with every bone in her body. For it is run in line with the values of society, exemplifying on a social level what relationships in the novel exemplify on a personal level: there is no love towards the needy; instead, any compassion is overridden by a desire to save money and look after them with as little cost to the taxpayer as possible. Betty belongs to the deserving poor. She is independent rather than a parasite on society: 'I never did take anything from any one ... I love to earn it better' (p. 203) is her response to an offer of money from Mrs Boffin. It makes no difference. The system established by the New Poor Law may have been designed to stop anyone intent on abusing it, but in the process it causes suffering to 'the best of the poor' (p. 200), with Betty hoping that 'at the last' she may have the strength, as Sloppy says,

> 'to get up from her bed and run and hide herself, and swown to death in a hole, sooner than fall into the hands of those Cruel Jacks we read of, that dodge and drive, and worry and weary, and scorn and shame, the decent poor'. (p. 200)

In Betty's eyes, the system is one which persecutes people, operating to make them 'get driven from post to pillar and pillar to post' (p. 199) and shows a complete lack of compassion: 'they are put off, put off, put off, – how they are grudged, grudged, grudged the shelter, or the doctor, or the drop of physic, or the bit of bread' (p. 199). When Johnny falls ill, Betty is reluctant to let him pass into the hands of officialdom by taking him to hospital:

> To conceal herself in sickness, like a lower animal; to creep out of sight and coil herself away and die; had become this woman's instinct. To catch up in her arms the sick child who was dear to her, and to hide it as if it were a criminal, and keep off all ministration but such as her own ignorant tenderness and patience could supply, had become this woman's idea of maternal love, fidelity, duty. The shameful accounts we read, every week in the Christian year, my lords and gentlemen and honorable boards, the infamous records of small official inhumanity, do not pass by the people as they pass by us. And hence these irrational, blind and obstinate prejudices, so astonishing to our magnificence, and having no more reason in them – God save the Queen and Con-found their politics – no, than smoke has in coming from fire! (p. 321)

The patronising class attitudes here, seeing the poor as lesser creatures, full of 'irrational, blind and obstinate prejudices' that have no 'reason in them', attest to the lack of identification with, and thus feeling for, people not recognised as brothers and sisters. The values are opposed to the ones that should obtain in 'the Christian year', just as on a personal level the Boffins found themselves opposing society's values as embodied in the form of Harmon Senior in 'Christian honor'. The result is the dehumanisation that reduces Betty to the status of a 'lower animal' who will 'coil herself away and die'; similar language, such as the reference to how she 'had crept into a copse, like a hunted animal' (p. 500), recurs in the account of her wanderings.

Regardless of how she is treated, though, it is Betty who is the more civilised human being, for not subscribing to the false values of society. She looks on people not from a class point of view but in terms of their moral stature, and so she tells Mrs Boffin, 'you were born a lady, and a true one, or there never was a lady born' (p. 203). Equally, her relationships with others are anything but superficial. Her deep affection for Johnny is expressed in the 'maternal care' (p. 195) she displays towards him and in her declaration that, 'I love him, I love him, I love him!' Loving him is also a channel for expressing the abiding love she still bears for others: 'I love my husband long dead and gone, in him; I love my children dead and gone in him' (p. 203).

In turn, she inspires deep love in others: 'Mrs Higden goes before all. None can ever be better friends to me than Mrs Higden's been', declares Sloppy (p. 332). Where relationships go deep, suffering also goes deep, so that Betty's 'fine strong old face broke up into weakness and tears' in thinking about the now-dead children she has looked after; in his intense sympathy for her Sloppy at this point 'bellowed' (p. 201). This is perhaps just in the nature of things; but in the unpropitious circumstances of the world of the novel, deep relationships become problematic in another way. In such a world, for Betty, love involves sacrifice: it would be in Sloppy's best interests to 'give me up'; since he won't, and since Betty's terror of the workhouse has created a mindset in which she cannot take help from anyone, not even the Boffins, she feels she has to 'give him up' by running away and becoming a vagrant seller of goods (p. 376).

In what follows, the unholy nature of this society is to be reflected in the way the course of action Betty is driven to provokes evil impulses in both herself and others; evil is again creating evil. During her wanderings Betty becomes tempted to suicide. A hostile and callous society means that she is already worn down by suffering: as she remarks, 'If I was young, it would all have to be gone through again, and the end would be a weary way off' (p. 375). During her wanderings, the river she comes across then seems to represent an escape from her suffering, an alternative form of relief, 'the Relieving Officer appointed by eternal ordinance to do my work', more compassionate than the alternative the State provides: 'My breast is softer than the pauper-nurse's; death in my arms is peacefuller than among the pauper-wards' (p. 497). The system corrupts people into the kind of despair that tempts them to suicide. It also provides opportunities for others to do evil, so that Rogue Riderhood is able, in a chain reaction of evil upon evil, to play on Betty's fear, and blackmail money out of her in order 'to let you go instead of handing you over safe to the Parish' (p. 502).

Once Betty has run away, the novel is heading towards a death scene that will allude to 'the Cross' (p. 505) and 'Heaven' (p. 506); but these will not be brought in spuriously as stimuli to pathos but as part of Dickens's exploration of his theme. After Betty has run away, religious references in the part of the narrative concerning her intensify. On the one hand, Betty's journey is repeatedly described as a 'pilgrimage' (p. 496, 504), perhaps signifying that her act of love for Sloppy in its selflessness takes on the status of an act of religious devotion, but also that she is straightforwardly on a religious quest, seeking a comforting refuge in a loving God that society emphatically will not offer. Much of the other religious imagery and allusion, however, is bitterly ironic; it reflects the callously perverted and unloving attitudes of a purportedly Christian society which betrays the values it pretends to. The 'Catechism' of 'my lords and gentlemen and honourable boards' expresses no holy set of beliefs. It, along with 'the Gospel according to Podsnappery', has caused society to come to

> the pass that with an enormous treasure at disposal to relieve the poor, the best of the poor detest our mercies, hide their heads from us, and shame us by starving to death in the midst of us. (p. 496)

The 'Returns of the Board of Trade', so important to a society obsessed with monetary wealth, provide no 'text for a sermon' (p. 496). Betty experiences 'horror' at the prospect of 'falling into the hands of Charity'; the 'Good Samaritan' has become 'a pursuing Fury' (p. 498). The 'Registrar General' appears as the 'Recording Angel' who tabulates unmoved the statistics of how many 'had within the last week died of want and of exposure to the weather' (p. 498). In her flight, Betty 'took refuge from the Samaritan in his latest accredited form; under a farmer's rick'; and Dickens points out to 'my fellow-Christians' that if 'the Samaritan had in the lonely night "passed by on the other side," she would have most devoutly thanked High Heaven for her escape from him' (p. 502). Her fear of being 'captured' by the system is manifest in her trying to 'escape from the Samaritan' (p. 504).

In contradistinction to the attitudes of society, though, and indicting it, is the attitude of God. All along, 'all the Light that shone on Betty Higden lay beyond Death' (p. 496). She is in 'the valley of the shadow of death' (p. 504) in two senses, but needs fear no evil, as Psalm 23 says, because of God's ever-present love. When she reaches the end of her journey, where she rests 'brought into her mind the foot of the Cross, and she committed herself to Him who died upon it' (p. 505). The idea is immediately repeated when Betty contemplates being 'found dead at the foot of the Cross' (p. 505). In contrast to the complete lack of love a supposedly Christian society has shown to Betty, the Cross signifies the enormous love God has for mankind, as Christ's own words reflect: 'God so loved the world, that he gave his only begotten Son, that whosoever believeth in him should not perish, but have everlasting life' (John 3:16). Christ's suffering death, taking the burden of all the sins of the world for the sake of saving mankind is a loving sacrifice, reference to which acts as an indictment of the unwillingness of society to sacrifice small amounts of money in order to look properly after the poor. The refuge Betty finally finds as a result of Christ's sacrifice, when Lizzie Hexam lifts her 'as high as Heaven' (p. 506) stands in contrast to the unwelcoming refuge available to the poor on Earth. This is a society in whose social policy the imitation of Christ does not even begin.

Two postscripts to Betty's death occur in the following chapter, in which the words of her funeral service are a reminder that she was 'our sister'

(p. 507), part of the human family created by God and thus deserving of better treatment, and in which the conversation soon turns to the Jewish managing partner of the mill where Lizzie works. This non-Christian and his wife 'most willingly and cheerfully do their duty to all of us who are employed here ... Indeed they do much more than their duty to us, for they are wonderfully mindful of us in many ways' (pp. 508–9). The contrast between the kindness and sense of duty here and the lack of such qualities in the Christians who run the system of poor relief further indicts the merciless mercenariness and lack of love in the conduct of mainstream society.

In 1890, Hall Caine deplored the propagation of the ideas

> that it is a poor thing to give way to strong feeling, that strong feeling is the mark of an untaught nature, and that education should help us control our emotions and conceal them.[56]

In her study, Valerie Purton argues that, in Dickens, sentimentalism 'works effectfully to evade or to numb intellectual analysis in order to produce the characteristic rush of tears which marks its successful climax'.[57] She talks repeatedly of how Dickens's rhetoric works 'to disable intellect',[58] asserts that the 'deliberate discouragement of mental activity'[59] is going on, that Dickens intends to 'disarm' such activity,[60] that he wants to 'disable thinking'.[61] At the heart of my argument here is the opposite point of view. I have argued that we should not be over-hasty in assuming a scene in Dickens is intended to be sentimental; that the sentimentality in his writings is not always his and nor does he always approve of it even when his disapproval is not blatantly obvious. Centrally, to the extent that the apparent sentimentality of a scene depends on religious references, my view is that, in the later novels at least, such references are part of the intellectual and thematic structure rather than the emotional structure. Sentimentality in Dickens may be less pervasive than we often assume.

Conclusion

Authors write, initially, for their own age; and in Dickens's case, in many of his novels he was fired by concern over contemporary social abuses and injustices. There was thus an urgent, immediate relevance to his works of social criticism at the time he wrote them. What lingering value, however, do such works have? There was a need at the time to expose what was going on in the Yorkshire schools described in *Nicholas Nickleby*, but those institutions are now long gone; what can be the point of reading about them today?

We might argue for the continuing relevance of Dickens's novels of social criticism by seeing the specific social abuses as contemporary manifestations of abiding aspects of human nature. The Yorkshire schools may no longer exist, but the callous exploitativeness that lay behind them is still all around. Equally, some of the social problems Dickens depicts have not been resolved. The problem of the relief of poverty, for instance, still abides. Over the centuries, the various measures taken in response to it – whether the Speenhamland System, the 1834 Poor Law or the modern Welfare State – have often faced the problem that they have either been humane but open to abuse, or have not been open to abuse but have been harsh. No-one has yet fully squared the circle to come up with a system that is both humane and not open to abuse. Oliver Twist asking for more is a reminder of the consequences of designing a system not open to abuse but in the process inhumane: children go hungry.

I would suggest, however, that beyond their immediate, contemporary relevance, it is the religious element in them that gives Dickens's novels of social criticism their universality and abiding relevance. As we have seen, using the circumstances of his own society, Dickens portrays the need for basing human society on Christian values. As he depicts things, the further society moves away from the teachings of Christ, the more catastrophic that society and the more suffering and unhappiness it involves. God has provided a handbook for how to make the world He created work properly; to ignore that set of rules is to create a hellish society. Dickens's novels are, to this extent, a sort of commentary on the New Testament and its teachings.[1]

Whatever his theological status, Jesus has been one of the most important and influential figures in history, and is likely to remain so. Dickens's novels, then, which present Christian values as the solution to all the problems of human society, have an abiding relevance far transcending the particular social abuses and injustices of his own age. Placing Christ's teaching at the centre of their analysis of society, they continue to present a challenging argument as to how to eliminate the suffering and injustice found in 'the prison of this lower world'.

Notes

1 Dickens's Engagement with Religion

1. *All the Year Round* 22 May 1869. Quotations are from the text as in Michael Slater and John Drew (eds), *The Dent Uniform Edition of Dickens' Journalism Volume IV: 'The Uncommercial Traveller' and Other Papers 1859–70* (London: J.M. Dent, 2000), pp. 389–90. As Drew explains in a headnote (p. 28), the *Uncommercial Traveller* pieces were originally published untitled; titles are from the later reprints in volume form.
2. Norris Pope, *Dickens and Charity* (London and Basingstoke: Macmillan, 1978), p. 13.
3. Unsigned review in the *Leader*, 27 June 1857, reprinted in Philip Collins (ed.), *Dickens: The Critical Heritage* (London: Routledge and Kegan Paul, 1971), p. 363.
4. Quoted in Dennis Walder, *Dickens and Religion* (London: George Allen and Unwin, 1981), p. 1.
5. Hugh Cunningham, 'Dickens as a Reformer' in David Paroissien (ed.) *A Companion to Charles Dickens* (Chichester: Wiley-Blackwell, 2011), p. 159.
6. To the Rev. David Macrae 1861, in Graham Storey (ed.), *The Pilgrim Edition of the Letters of Charles Dickens Volume Nine: 1859–1861* (Oxford: Clarendon Press, 1997), pp. 556–7.
7. Quoted in Walder, *Dickens and Religion*, p. 5.
8. Quoted in Walder, *Dickens and Religion*, p. 2.
9. Philip Collins, *Dickens and Education* (London: Macmillan, 1963), pp. 54–5.
10. Collins, *Dickens and Education*, p. 56.
11. Collins, *Dickens and Education*, p. 18.
12. Collins, *Dickens and Education*, p. 59.
13. Carolyn W. de la L. Oulton, *Literature and Religion in Mid-Victorian England* (Basingstoke: Palgrave Macmillan, 2003), p. 2.
14. Oulton, *Literature and Religion*, p. 23.
15. Gary Colledge, *Dickens, Christianity and 'The Life of Our Lord': Humble Veneration, Profound Conviction* (London: Continuum, 2009), p. 137.
16. Colledge, *Dickens, Christianity and 'the Life of Our Lord'*, p. vii.
17. 'Capital Punishment (Three Letters to the *Daily News*, March 9, 13 and 16, 1846)', Letter III in Charles Dickens, *Miscellaneous papers I* (Geneva: Edito-Service S.A./ Heron, 1971), p. 50.
18. John Forster, *The Life of Charles Dickens* Volume 1, edited by A.J. Hoppe, Everyman edition (further revised edn, London: Dent, 1969), pp. 337–8. Arnold argued for religious union 'on the ground that the divisions of Christians do not go so deep as is generally supposed' and proposed 'comprehending all sects in one national Church' (Francis Warre Cornish, *The English Church in the Nineteenth Century* Part 1 (London: Macmillan and Co., 1910), p. 189). This went against the grain of those who 'could not conceive of religion separated from dogma' (*English Church in the Nineteenth Century*, p. 190). Dennis Walder considers that Dickens is not referring to the whole book, more to Forster's review, in which passages quoted 'are manifestly those which would also have appealed Dickens, above all for their stress on "meaning by Religion what the Gospel teaches us to mean

by it", namely, "a system directing and influencing our conduct, principles, and feelings, and professing to do this with sovereign authority, and most efficacious influence" ... Dr Arnold's attitude, as mediated by Forster, is that the true function of Christianity lies in improving the moral and social life of the community as a whole, rather than in differences over doctrine, or modes of worship' (*Dickens and Religion*, pp. 11–2).Gary Colledge questions whether Dickens should particularly be linked to the Broad Church movement (*Dickens, Christianity and 'the Life of Our Lord'*, pp. 139–41).

19. B.G. Worrall, *The Making of the Modern Church: Christianity in England Since 1800* (third edn, London: S.P.C.K., 2004), pp. 99–100.
20. In the discussion that follows, I draw widely on Gerald Parsons's account of the Victorian Church of England in his 'Reform, Revival and Realignment: The Experience of Victorian Anglicanism' in Gerald Parsons (ed.) *Religion in Victorian Britain Volume I: Traditions* (Manchester: Manchester University Press, 1988), pp. 14–66. I follow Parsons's division of developments into administrative and pastoral; doctrinal and theological; liturgical and ceremonial; and national and constitutional.
21. Quotations from *The Mystery of Edwin Drood* are from the Penguin edition, edited by David Paroissien (London, 2002).
22. Paroissien's 'Notes' to the Penguin edition of *Edwin Drood*, p. 325.
23. Brian Heeney, 'The Theory of Pastoral Ministry in the Mid-Victorian Church of England', *Historical Magazine of the Protestant Episcopal Church*, Vol. 43, p. 217 (1974).
24. Heeney, 'Theory of Pastoral Ministry', pp. 216–7.
25. Heeney, 'Theory of Pastoral Ministry', p. 217.
26. Heeney, 'Theory of Pastoral Ministry', p. 218.
27. Heeney, 'Theory of Pastoral Ministry', p. 218.
28. Heeney, 'Theory of Pastoral Ministry', p. 219. C.f. Rosemary O'Day's account of the late eighteenth and early nineteenth century diocese of Exeter, in which services on weekdays and Holy days became neglected, in which, with the exception of the larger parishes in urban areas, one service (including a sermon) on a Sunday came to be the norm, in which Holy Communion was only occasionally celebrated and in which it was often only during Lent that catechising took place (Rosemary O'Day, 'The Clerical Renaissance in Victorian England and Wales' in Gerald Parsons, *Religion in Victorian Britain Volume I*, pp. 199–200).
29. Heeney, 'Theory of Pastoral Ministry', pp. 225–6.
30. Heeney, 'Theory of Pastoral Ministry', p. 225.
31. Heeney, 'Theory of Pastoral Ministry', p. 225.
32. Heeney, 'Theory of Pastoral Ministry', p. 227.
33. Heeney, 'Theory of Pastoral Ministry', p. 227.
34. Heeney, 'Theory of Pastoral Ministry', p. 228.
35. Heeney, 'Theory of Pastoral Ministry', p. 228.
36. Heeney, 'Theory of Pastoral Ministry', p. 229.
37. Anon. *Hints to a Clergyman's Wife; or Female Parochial Duties Practically Illustrated* (London: Samuel Holdsworth, 1832, Second edn: 1838), extracted in James R. Moore (ed.), *Religion in Victorian Britain Volume III: Sources* (Manchester: Manchester University Press, 1988), p. 247.
38. Moore, *Religion in Victorian Britain Volume III*, p. 246.
39. Moore, *Religion in Victorian Britain Volume III*, p. 246.
40. Moore, *Religion in Victorian Britain Volume III*, p. 247.

41. Quotations from *Sunday Under Three Heads* are from Michael Slater (ed.), *The Dent Uniform Edition of Dickens' Journalism Volume I: 'Sketches by Boz' and Other Early Papers 1833–39* (London: J.M. Dent, 1994).
42. Quotations from *Oliver Twist* are from the Penguin edition, edited by Philip Horne (London, 2002).
43. Quotations from *Our Mutual Friend* are from the Penguin edition, edited by Adrian Poole (London, 1997).
44. Adrian Poole, 'Notes' to Penguin edition of *Our Mutual Friend*, p. 823.
45. Michael Cotsell, 'Notes' to Oxford World's Classics edition of *Our Mutual Friend*, edited by Michael Cotsell (Oxford: Oxford University Press, 1989), p. 842.
46. Cotsell, 'Notes', p. 842. The reference was topical: the demand for clergymen to subscribe to the Thirty Nine Articles was relaxed in 1865 (Worrall, *Making of the Modern Church*, p. 99).
47. Moore, *Religion in Victorian Britain Volume III*, p. 247.
48. *All the Year Round* 26 January 1860. Quotations are from the text in Slater and Drew, *Dickens' Journalism IV*, pp. 26–40.
49. Headnote in Slater and Drew, *Dickens' Journalism IV*, p. 27.
50. Depicted as a Muscular Christian (c.f. Paroissien, 'Notes' to *Edwin Drood*, p. 325), Mr Crisparkle in *Edwin Drood*, a Minor Canon, is another example of a model clergyman in Dickens's later works. Despite a little 'harmless vanity' (p. 193) in his make-up, he is otherwise 'modest', with no 'self-assertion', and 'staunchly true to his duty', one 'really great in spirit' (p. 191). He is a man of great integrity, troubled about not being 'open', and, 'among the truest of men', he suffers scruples of conscience as he 'dreaded to add' to suspicions hovering around Neville following Edwin's disappearance by revealing all he knows (p. 180). He has no 'False pretence' (p. 255) in his nature and is 'a just man' (p. 255). He is a peacemaker, a champion of forgiveness and reconciliation, urging Neville to 'pledge me the honor of a Christian gentleman' to make his peace with Drood (p. 107). As he stands by Neville who is under grave suspicion, he attributes his staunch fidelity to his duty as a clergyman: 'I may regard my profession from a point of view which teaches me that its first duty is towards those who are in necessity and tribulation, who are desolate and oppressed' (p. 190). He believes in 'the justice that should belong to Christians' (p. 192). His practical support for Neville is, however, constrained by his serious dedication to his job: his 'Cathedral duties' make visits to see Neville 'difficult to accomplish' (p. 195).
51. Worrall, *Making of the Modern Church*, p. 9.
52. David Englander, 'The Word and the World: Evangelicalism in the Victorian City' in Gerald Parsons (ed.) *Religion in Victorian Britain Volume II: Controversies* (Manchester: Manchester University Press, 1988), pp. 22–3.
53. Parsons, *Religion in Victorian Britain Volume 1*, p. 32.
54. Parsons, *Religion in Victorian Britain Volume 1*, p. 41.
55. 'A Sleep to Startle Us' *Household Words* 13 March 1852. Quotations are from the text as in Michael Slater (ed.), *The Dent Uniform Edition of Dickens' Journalism III: 'Gone Astray' and Other Papers from "Household Words" 1851–9* (London: J.M. Dent, 1998) (pp. 49–57), p. 57.
56. 'Report of the Commissioners Appointed to Inquire into the Condition of the Persons Variously Engaged in the University of Oxford' *The Examiner* 3 June 1843. Quotations are from the text as in Michael Slater (ed.), *The Dent Uniform Edition of Dickens' Journalism II: 'The Amusements of the People' and Other Papers: Reports, Essays and Reviews 1834–51* (London: J.M. Dent, 1996) (pp. 59–63), p. 62.

57. Graham Storey (ed.), *Pilgrim Edition of the Letters of Charles Dickens Volume Ten: 1862–1864* (Oxford: Clarendon Press, 1998), p. 444.
58. 'Review: *The Poetry of Science, or Studies of the Physical Phenomena of Nature* by Robert Hunt' *The Examiner* 9 December 1848. Quotations are from the text as in Slater, *Dickens' Journalism II* (pp. 129–34), p. 131.
59. Michael Slater, *The Genius of Dickens: The Ideas and Inspiration of Britain's Greatest Novelist* ([1999] London: Duckworth Overlook, 2011), p. 169.
60. Colledge, *Dickens, Christianity and 'The Life of Our* Lord', p. 50.
61. Letter to W.W.F. De Ferjat, 28 May 1863 in Storey, *Pilgrim Letters Volume Ten*, p. 253.
62. 'The Sunday Screw', *Household Words*, 22 June 1850. Quotations from the text as in Slater, *Dickens' Journalism Volume II*, p. 251.
63. To Frank Stone 13 December 1858 in Graham Storey and Kathleen Tillotson (eds), *Pilgrim Edition of the Letters of Charles Dickens Volume Eight: 1856–1858* (Oxford: Clarendon Press, 1995), pp. 718–9.
64. Colledge, *Dickens, Christianity and 'The Life of Our Lord'*, p. 50.
65. Letter to W.W.F. De Cerjat, 28 May 1863, *Pilgrim Letters Volume Ten*, pp. 252–3.
66. Parsons, *Religion in Victorian Britain Volume I*, p. 47.
67. Ian Bradley, *Abide with Me: The World of Victorian Hymns* ([1997] London: Faber and Faber, 2010), p. 1.
68. Bradley, *Abide with Me*, p. 1.
69. Bradley, *Abide with Me*, p. 16.
70. Bradley, *Abide with Me*, p. 30.
71. Bradley, *Abide with Me*, p. 30.
72. Bradley, *Abide with Me*, p. 31.
73. Bradley, *Abide with Me*, p. 3.
74. Bradley, *Abide with Me*, p. 37.
75. Parsons, *Religion in Victorian Britain Volume I*, pp. 49–50.
76. Quotations from *Sketches by Boz* are from the text as in Slater, *Dickens' Journalism Volume I*.
77. 'City of London Churches', *All the Year Round*, 5 May 1860. Quotations are from Slater and Drew, *Dickens' Journalism Volume IV*, p. 110.
78. 'Report of the Commissioners Appointed to Inquire into the Condition of the Persons Variously Engaged in the University of Oxford', Slater, *Dickens' Journalism II*, p. 62.
79. Slater, *Dickens' Journalism II*, p. 59.
80. To Macvey Napier, 16 September 1843, in Madeline House, Graham Storey and Kathleen Tillotson (eds), *Pilgrim Edition of the Letters of Charles Dickens Volume Three: 1842–1843* (Oxford: Clarendon Press, 1974), p. 565.
81. 'A December Vision', *Household Words*, 14 December 1850. Quotations are from the text in Slater, *Dickens' Journalism II* (pp. 305–9), p. 307.
82. K.J. Fielding, *The Speeches of Charles Dickens* (Oxford: Clarendon Press, 1960), p. 329, footnote 3.
83. Fielding, *Speeches*, p. 329, footnote 2.
84. Quotations from Dickens's speeches are from Fielding, *Speeches*.
85. *All the Year Round*, 25 February 1860. Quotations are from the text as in Slater and Drew, *Dickens' Journalism IV*, pp. 52–62.
86. H. Mann, *Census of Great Britain, 1851: Religious Worship, England and Wales. Report and tables presented to both Houses of Parliament by command of Her Majesty* (London: H.M.S.O., 1853), extracted in Moore, *Religion in Victorian Britain Volume III*, p. 315.

87. *Liverpool Courier*, 3 March 1860, p. 6.
88. *Liverpool Courier*, 14 March 1860, p. 5.
89. *Liverpool Courier*, 21 March 1860, p. 5.
90. Quotation from the text as in Slater, *Dickens' Journalism II* (pp. 290–6), p. 293.
91. 'A Sleep to Startle Us', *Household Words*, 13 March 1852. Slater, *Dickens' Journalism III*, p. 51.
92. 'Review: *The Drunkard's Children. A Sequel to the Bottle.* In Eight Plates, by George Cruikshank', *The Examiner*, 8 July 1848. Quotation here from the text as in Slater, *Dickens' Journalism II*, p. 105.
93. Quotation taken from the text as in Slater, *Dickens' Journalism II*, p. 226.
94. Janet L. Larson, *Dickens and the Broken Scripture* (Athens: The University of Georgia Press, 1985), pp. 8–9.
95. Larson, *Broken Scripture*, p. 6.
96. Larson, *Broken Scripture*, p. 9.
97. Larson, *Broken Scripture*, p. 13.
98. Larson, *Broken Scripture*, p. 314.
99. Vincent Newey, *The Scriptures of Charles Dickens: Novels of Ideology, Novels of the Self* (Aldershot: Ashgate, 2004), p. 3.
100. Newey, *Scriptures of Charles Dickens*, p. 18.
101. Newey, *Scriptures of Charles Dickens*, p. 19.
102. Newey, *Scriptures of Charles Dickens*, p. 20.
103. Newey, *Scriptures of Charles Dickens*, p. 74.
104. Newey, *Scriptures of Charles Dickens*, p. 179.
105. Newey, *Scriptures of Charles Dickens*, p. 1.
106. Barry V. Qualls, *The Secular Pilgrims of Victorian Fiction: The Novel as Book of Life* (Cambridge: Cambridge University Press, 1982), p. 96.
107. Qualls, *Secular Pilgrims of Victorian Fiction*, p. 89.
108. Qualls, *Secular Pilgrims of Victorian Fiction*, p. 110.
109. Qualls, *Secular Pilgrims of Victorian Fiction*, p. 108.
110. Larson, *Broken Scripture*, p. 6.
111. Qualls, *Secular Pilgrims of Victorian Fiction*, p. 96.
112. Qualls, *Secular Pilgrims of Victorian Fiction*, p. 98.
113. Forster, *Life of Charles Dickens Volume 1*, pp. 282–3.
114. John Forster, *The Life of Charles Dickens* Volume 2. Edited by A.J. Hoppe, Everyman edition (further revised edn: London: J.M. Dent, 1969), p. 379.
115. Forster, *Life of Charles Dickens Volume 2*, p. 380.
116. Forster, *Life of Charles Dickens Volume 2*, p. 380.
117. Printed as an Appendix in Forster's *Life of Charles Dickens Volume 2*, pp. 419–23.
118. Forster, *Life of Charles Dickens Volume 2*, p. 422.
119. Andrew Sanders further demonstrates the consistency of Dickens's religious attitudes in comparing a letter the author wrote the day before his death with one he wrote in 1843, concerning the need not to be showy in declaring one's religious allegiances (Andrew Sanders, *Charles Dickens: Resurrectionist* (New York: St. Martin's Press, 1982), p. xi).
120. 'Crime and Education' (Letter to the *Daily News*, 4 February 1846) in Dickens, *Miscellaneous Papers I*, p. 28.
121. To Frank Stone, 13 December 1858. *Pilgrim Letters Volume Eight*, p. 718.
122. *Pilgrim Letters Volume Eight*, p. 244.
123. 'A Nightly Scene in London', *Household Words*, 26 January 1856. Text quoted as in Slater, *Dickens' Journalism III* (pp. 346–51), p. 349.

2 Dickens and Early Victorian Christian Social Attitudes

1. Rev. Thomas Gisborne, *Friendly Observations Addressed to the Manufacturing Population of Great Britain* (Third edn, 1827), quoted in Norris Pope, *Dickens and Charity* (London and Basingstoke: Macmillan, 1978), pp. 5–6.
2. Gerald Parsons, 'Social Control to Social Gospel: Victorian Christian Social Attitudes' in Gerald Parsons (ed.) *Religion in Victorian Britain Volume II: Controversies* (Manchester: Manchester University Press, 1988), p. 43.
3. Quoted in Robert S. Dell, 'Social and Economic Theories and Pastoral Concerns of a Victorian Archbishop', *Journal of Ecclesiastical History,* Vol. 16, p. 206 (1965).
4. Dell, 'Social and Economic Theories', p. 207.
5. Dell, 'Social and Economic Theories', p. 207.
6. Dell, 'Social and Economic Theories', p. 207.
7. Dell, 'Social and Economic Theories', p. 200.
8. Dell, 'Social and Economic Theories', p. 200.
9. Owen Chadwick, *The Victorian Church* Part 1 (London: Adam and Charles Black, 1966), p. 95.
10. Chadwick, *The Victorian Church*, p. 96.
11. Gertrude Himmelfarb, *The Idea of Poverty: England in the Industrial Age* (London and Boston: Faber and Faber, 1984, 1985), p. 174.
12. Quoted in Peter Murray, *Poverty and Welfare 1830–1914* (London: Hodder and Stoughton, 1999), p. 20.
13. Quoted in Murray, *Poverty and Welfare*, p. 20.
14. Quoted in Pope, *Dickens and Charity*, p. 6.
15. Chadwick, *The Victorian Church*, p. 96.
16. G. Kitson-Clark, *Churchmen and the Condition of England 1832–1885: A Study in the Development of Social Ideas and Practice from the Old Regime to the Modern State* (London: Methuen and Co. Ltd., 1973), p. 159.
17. Quotations from *American Notes* are from the Penguin edition, edited by Patricia Ingham (revised edn, London, 2004).
18. Letter to Cornelius Felton, 2 March 1843, quoted in Gary Colledge, *Dickens, Christianity and 'The Life of Our Lord': Humble Veneration, Profound Conviction* (London: Continuum, 2009), p. 85.
19. Quotations from 'A Manchester Strike' in *Illustrations of Political Economy* Volume III are from the first edition (London: Charles Fox, 1834), pp. 102–3.
20. 'Lord Ashley's Bill', *The Inquirer*, No. 5, 6 August 1842.
21. 'The Charter or the Corn-Law Repeal', *The Inquirer*, No. 8, 27 August 1842.
22. Quoted in Cecil Driver, *Tory Radical: The Life of Richard Oastler* ([1946] New York: Octagon Books, 1970), p. 108.
23. Quoted in Driver, *Tory Radical*, p. 190.
24. Driver, *Tory Radical*, p. 342.
25. Raymond V. Holt, *The Unitarian Contribution to Social Progress in England* (London: George Allen and Unwin, 1938), p. 165.
26. Holt, *Unitarian Contribution to Social Progress*, p. 166.
27. Holt, *Unitarian Contribution to Social Progress*, p. 165.
28. Holt, *Unitarian Contribution to Social Progress*, pp. 197–204.
29. Holt, *Unitarian Contribution to Social Progress*, p. 205.
30. Holt, *Unitarian Contribution to Social Progress*, p. 165.
31. W.R. Greg, *Essays on Political and Social Science* (London: Longman, Brown and Green, 1853), p. 284, 290. J.T. Ward describes Greg as an 'anti-religious writer' (J.T. Ward,

The Factory System 1830–1855 (London: Macmillan and Co., 1962), p. 39), and Mary B. Rose records how while attending Edinburgh University, he joined the Plinian Society 'which challenged orthodox religious beliefs' and how the publication of his *Creed of Christendom* in 1851 confirmed 'his reputation as religious sceptic'. (Mary B. Rose, 'Greg, William Rathbone (1809–1881)', *Oxford Dictionary of National Biography* (Oxford: Oxford University Press, 2004). Online edn, May 2008. [http://oxforddnb.com/view/article/11446, accessed 4 September 2014]). Nevertheless, he was brought up in a strongly Unitarian environment. His mother came from 'a prominent Unitarian family' and her 'interest in religion and education ... had a lasting impact on her younger sons, especially Samuel and William' (Mary B. Rose 'Greg, Samuel (1758–1834)', *Oxford Dictionary of National Biography* (Oxford: Oxford University Press, 2004). Online edn, May 2012. [http://www.oxforddnb.com/view/article/59911, accessed 4 September 2014]). In addition, he was educated at a Unitarian school in Bristol (Mary B. Rose, 'Greg, William Rathbone (1809–1881)', *Oxford Dictionary of National Biography.* Online edn). On the basis of his upbringing and education, then, we may thus assume a Unitarian element in his outlook.

32. Quotations from *Mary Barton* are from the Everyman edition, edited by Alan Shelston (London: J.M. Dent, 1996).
33. W.R. Greg Review of *Mary Barton, Edinburgh Review*, Vol. 89 (1849).
34. Quotations from *Michael Armstrong* are from the Nonsuch edition (Stroud, 2007).
35. Driver, *Tory Radical*, p. 105.
36. Driver, *Tory Radical*, p. 452.
37. J.C. Gill, *The Ten Hours Parson: Christian Social Action in the Eighteen-Thirties* (London: S.P.C.K., 1959), p. 180f.f.
38. Nicolas Edsall, *The Anti-Poor Law Movement 1834–44* (Manchester: Manchester University Press, 1971), p. 22.
39. G.D.H. Cole, *Chartist Portraits* ([1941] London: Cassell, 1989), p. 70.
40. Edsall, *Anti-Poor Law Movement*, p. 41–2.
41. Edsall, *Anti-Poor Law Movement*, p. 63.
42. Figures such as Oastler and Stephens are now little remembered, but in the 1830s and 1840s, they were national figures, their speeches and deeds reported, as we shall see, in such publications as *The Times* and the *Annual Register*. A number of these campaigners, including Ashley, Sadler, Oastler, Bull and Tonna, were Evangelicals (Pope, *Dickens and Charity*, p. 7; Mary Lenard, *Preaching Pity: Gaskell, Dickens and Sentimentalism in Victorian Culture* (New York: Peter Lang, 1999) 55), a group known for their social involvement. Others among them were emphatically not part of this branch of the Church. The High Church Trollope, for instance, attacked Evangelicalism in her 1837 novel *The Vicar of Wrexhill*. The clergyman of the title is villainous, and Evangelicalism is depicted as splitting families up. Those converted to it have been 'perverted' (*The Vicar of Wrexhill* (Stroud: Alan Sutton Publishing, 1996), p. 86), and characters to whom we are sympathetic refer to the 'grievously schismatic road into our national church which these self-chosen apostles have made' (*Vicar of Wrexhill*, p. 127) and sum it up as 'the most mischievous sect that ever attacked the established church' (*Vicar of Wrexhill*, p. 131). Its doctrines are variously described as 'gloomy and unchristianlike' (*Vicar of Wrexhill*, p. 131), 'sinful' and 'impious' (*Vicar of Wrexhill*, p. 193). Dickens's relationship with Evangelicalism was complex. From the beginning of his career, he portrays it in a hostile light. Evangelicalism, of course, straddled the Church of England and Methodism, and in *Sunday Under Three Heads* he describes a preacher immediately identifiable as Evangelical from his being 'clad in rusty black' and uttering 'an extempore prayer' preaching in a chapel that is 'a stronghold of

intolerant zeal and ignorant enthusiasm' (*Sunday Under Three Heads*. Quotation from the text as in Michael Slater (ed.), *The Dent Uniform Edition of Dickens' Journalism Volume I: 'Sketches by Boz' and Other Early Papers 1833–39* (London: J.M. Dent, 1994), p. 480); and the portrait of Stiggins in *Pickwick Papers* is similarly unsympathetic. Nevertheless, as we shall see, there was some common ground between Dickens and Evangelicals. As Carolyn Oulton points out, he shared the Evangelical endorsement of the work ethic (Carolyn W. de la L. Oulton, *Literature and Religion in Mid-Victorian Britain* (Basingstoke: Palgrave Macmillan, 2003), p. 31); and centrally, he shared their social concern. He showed an early interest, for instance, in the Ragged School movement in which such Evangelicals as Ashley were so important (cf. 'Crime and Education Letter to the *Daily News* 4 February 1846' in Charles Dickens, *Miscellaneous Papers I* (Geneva: Heron/Edito-Service, 1971), pp. 25–9).

43. A religious viewpoint was common among the supporters of the Factory Movement apart from the ones discussed here. Support among the clergy was widespread (c.f. e.g. Ward, *Factory System*, pp. 47, 141, 196, 315, 423) and political campaigners often adopted a religious critique of the factory system. Thus, William Busfeild Ferrand declared that the factory system was 'unscriptural and at variance with the Divine Word of God, for that blessed Book tells us that man shall earn his bread by the sweat of his brow; but unregulated machinery prevents him from doing that' (J.T. Ward, *Factory System*, p. 274). (Even opponents of the Movement recognised a religious imperative behind it, however keen they were for it to be disregarded: Sydney Smith told Countess Grey that, 'it does seem to be absurd to hinder a woman of 30 from working as long as she pleases; but mankind are getting mad with humanity and Samaritanism' (Ward, *Factory System*, p. 289)). Others, though, such as John Fielden, who eventually guided the 1847 Bill through Parliament, regardless of their religious outlook, took another view. His *The Curse of the Factory System* of 1836 presents a rather different set of arguments and perspectives from the ones discussed here.
44. Driver, *Tory Radical*, p. 40.
45. Driver, *Tory Radical*, p. 42.
46. Gill, *Ten Hours Parson*, p. 186.
47. Michael S. Edwards, *Purge This Realm: A Life of Joseph Rayner Stephens* (London: Epworth Press, 1994), p. 31.
48. Edwards, *Purge This Realm*, pp. 31, 32.
49. Driver, *Tory Radical*, p. 403.
50. Mary Lenard, *Preaching Pity: Dickens, Gaskell and Sentimentalism in Victorian Culture* (New York: Peter Lang, 1999), p. 55.
51. J. Douglas Holladay, '19th Century Evangelical Activism: From Private Charity to State Intervention, 1830–50', *Historical Magazine of the Protestant Episcopal Church*, Vol. 50, p. 55 (1982). The Society's aim was to influence both government and press as regards religious and moral matters.
52. *The Political Preacher*, 6 January 1839, pp. 13–14 quoted in Eileen Groth Lyon, 'Stephens, Joseph Rayner (1805–1879)', *Oxford Dictionary of National Biography* (Oxford: Oxford University Press, 2004). Online edn, January 2008. [http//www.oxford.com/view/article/26389, accessed 29 May 2008].
53. Richard Turnbull, *Shaftesbury: The Great Reformer* (Oxford: Lion, 2010), p. 88.
54. Quoted in Driver, *Tory Radical*, p. 295.
55. Edwards, *Purge This Realm*, p. 43.
56. Ward, *Factory System*, p. 124. Historians such as G.D.H. Cole have similarly argued that the Whig government viewed the implementation of the New Poor Law as

'an essential part of their policy of giving *laissez-faire* capitalism every chance' (Cole, *Chartist Portraits*, p. 65). The opposite point of view is forcefully expressed by Norman McCord: 'It would be very difficult indeed to establish the argument that the 1834 Poor Law Amendment Act was dictated by a desire to serve the needs of an industrial society. On the contrary, one of the major criticisms levelled against the Act has been its irrelevance to the then social needs of the growing industrial sector, and the Act was certainly passed by a legislature which was very far from being under the control of capitalist industrialists' (Norman McCord, 'The Poor Law and Philanthropy' in Derek Fraser (ed.) *The New Poor Law in the Nineteenth Century* (London and Basingstoke: Macmillan, 1976), p. 89).

57. *The Times*, 17 March 1832.
58. Quoted in J.T. Ward, 'Two Pioneers in Industrial Reform', *Bradford Textile Society Journal* 1963–4, p. 35.
59. Quotations from *Helen Fleetwood* are from the fourth American edition (New York: Baker and Scribner, 1848).
60. *The Times*, 12 March 1844.
61. *The Times*, 8 January 1839.
62. *Annual Register for 1839*, p. 67.
63. A reference to the way the sexes were separated in the workhouse.
64. *The Times*, 8 January 1839.
65. J. Wesley Bready, *Lord Shaftesbury and Social-Industrial Progress* (London: George Allen and Unwin, 1926), p. 269.
66. It was claimed in a court case of November 1843, for instance, that a seamstress 'had only three halfpence for making a shirt' (*Northern Star*, 25 November 1843). Henry Moses, the slopseller in the real-life case which inspired 'The Song of the Shirt' (see Alvin Whitley, 'Thomas Hood and The Times', *Times Literary Supplement*, 17 May 1957, p. 509), defended himself in a letter to *The Times* on the grounds that such low wages were the result of the competition at the core of a free market: 'surrounded by a competitive market, I am compelled to sell as cheaply as my neighbours' (*The Times*, 31 October 1843).
67. Quotations from Hood's poems are from Walter Jerrold (ed.), *The Complete Poetical Works of Thomas Hood* (London: Henry Frowde, 1906).
68. *The Times*, 14 October 1840.
69. Quotations from 'The Cry of the Children' are from the poem as it appears in John Robert Glorney Bolton and Julia Bolton Holloway (eds), *Aurora Leigh and Other Poems* (London: Penguin, 1995).
70. Quoted in David Englander, *Poverty and Poor Law Reform in 19th Century Britain 1834–1914: From Chadwick to Booth* (Harlow: Longman, 1998), p. 38.
71. Bready, *Lord Shaftesbury*, p. 126.
72. *Leeds Mercury*, 30 October 1830.
73. Quoted in Bready, *Lord Shaftesbury*, pp. 268–9.
74. *The Times*, 14 October 1840.
75. Quoted in Gill, *Ten Hours Parson*, p. 37.
76. *The Times*, 29 February 1844.
77. Quoted in J.L. Hammond and Barbara Hammond, *Lord Shaftesbury* (fourth edn, London: Frank Cass, 1969), p. 73.
78. It is, of course, the particular selection of perspectives and preoccupations that is distinctive of this group; individually, some at least may be drawn on by others. The parallel between slavery and factory labour, for instance, was widely drawn, and for a variety of purposes, as Catherine Gallagher demonstrates in 'Workers and Slaves: The Rhetoric of Freedom in the Debate over Industrialism', the first

chapter of her *The Industrial Reformation of English Fiction 1832–1867* (Chicago and London: The University of Chicago Press, 1985), pp. 3–35.

79. Via the poet Edward Fitzgerald, Ashley offered to have Dickens shown what the cotton factories were like during a tour the latter made of the Midlands and North Wales during October and November of 1838 (Lenard, *Preaching Pity*, p. 97). In a letter of 29 December 1838, Dickens writes to Fitzgerald that on a visit to Manchester he has seen both 'the *worst* cotton mill' and 'the best' and that 'There was no great difference between them' (Madeline House and Graham Storey (eds), *The Pilgrim Edition of the Letters of Charles Dickens Volume One: 1820–1839* (Oxford: Clarendon Press, 1965), p. 483). With another visit impending, he says, 'I should be most happy to avail myself of any introduction from Lord Ashley which, in the course of an hour or so, would enable me to make any fresh observations' (House and Storey, *Pilgrim Letters Volume One*, pp. 483–4). He declares that what he has seen 'has disgusted and astonished me beyond all measure. I mean to strike the heaviest blow in my power for these unfortunate creatures' (House and Storey, *Pilgrim Letters Volume One*, p. 484), and so asks Fitzgerald 'Will you make known to Lord Ashley (confidentially) my intentions on this subject, and my earnest desire to avail myself, either now or at some future time, or both, of his kind assistance? Pray thank him warmly, from me, for tending it' (House and Storey, *Pilgrim Letters Volume One*, p. 484). (Dickens was not, of course, to write a novel about the industrial world until *Hard Times* in 1854. Lenard considers that with both Trollope and Tonna writing about the industrial world, 'any contribution by Dickens would probably have seemed superfluous' (Lenard, *Preaching Pity*, p. 99). Similarly, Priti Joshi (in 'An Old Dog Enters the Fray; or, Reading *Hard Times* as an Industrial Novel', *Dickens Studies Annual*, Vol. 44, pp. 221–41 (2013)) argues that Dickens was 'Put out by the news' (p. 224) that Trollope was working on *Michael Armstrong*, and cites the assertion of Pamela Neville-Singleton that Dickens regarded her as 'a serious rival' at the time (p. 225); 'upset' at 'The seeming convergence between his and Trollope's novel' he 'seemed to wash his hands of industrial fiction altogether' (p. 225)). The evidence of the Pilgrim edition of Dickens's letters is that, of the political and religious campaigners discussed here (as opposed to the writers – Dickens corresponded with both Fanny Trollope and Thomas Hood), Dickens was in touch only with Ashley. The two men had quite a bit of contact over the years, without apparently becoming close friends. In addition to the common ground discussed in this chapter, in 1843 both became interested in ragged schools (Pope, *Dickens and Charity*, p. 154), both supported home missions (Dennis Walder, *Dickens and Religion* (London: George Allen and Unwin, 1981), p. 142), both opposed teetotalism (Pope, *Dickens and Charity*, pp. 117, 121) and both saw emigration as a way of solving the problems of poverty (Pope, *Dickens and Charity*, pp. 185–7). Dickens commented warmly on Ashley's work on several occasions. In the 1838 letter to Fitzgerald, he writes that 'With that nobleman's most benevolent and excellent exertions, and with the evidence which he was the means of bringing forward, I am well acquainted' (House and Storey, *Pilgrim Letters Volume One*, p. 484). At a dinner in 1843 in aid of the Sanatorium, Dickens and Ashley paid each other compliments, the former describing the latter as the man who 'had sacrificed party spirit and politics that he might advance the cause and interests of the neglected and forlorn, – who had boldly stood forward among seven hundred legislators, and maintained that women should not be compelled to do the work of harnessed brutes ... To Lord Ashley the most oppressed and neglected classes would have to return thanks for ages to come' (Speech of 29 June 1843 in K.J. Fielding (ed.), *The Speeches of Charles Dickens* (Oxford: Clarendon

Press, 1960), p. 43). In 'The Sunday Screw' (*Household Words*, 22 June 1850), he wrote of Ashley as one 'who has done much good, and whom we mention with every sentiment of sincere respect' (text as in Michael Slater (ed.), *The Dent Uniform Edition of Dickens' Journalism Volume II: 'The Amusements of the People' and Other Papers: Reports, Essays and Reviews 1834–51* (London: J.M. Dent, 1996), p. 251) and referred to his 'indisputably humane and benevolent impulses' (p. 254). In a speech delivered at a banquet of the Metropolitan Sanitary Association in 1851, Dickens proposed the toast to Ashley as a man 'whose Earnestness in all good works no man can doubt, and who has always the courage to face the worst and commonest of cants; that is to say, the cant about the cant of philanthropy and benevolence.' (Speech of 10 May 1851 in Fielding, *Speeches*, p. 132). He described Ashley's 1851 Common Lodging-Houses Act, designed to tackle the problem of immorality and the corruption of youth in common lodging-houses by licensing such establishments in London and opening them to police inspection as 'the best law ... ever passed by an English parliament' (Pope, *Dickens and Charity*, p. 168). Nevertheless, the relationship was not close. Ashley's strong Evangelicalism, for one thing, was a barrier between them. 'The Sunday Screw' is concerned, for instance, with Ashley's attempt to put a stop to all Sunday collections and deliveries of letters, something Dickens expresses emphatic opposition to: 'it is the beginning of a Sabbatarian Crusade, outrageous to the spirit of Christianity ... and the true religious feeling, of the community' (Slater, *Dickens' Journalism II*, p. 250). (Ashley, and Sadler, had served on a select committee investigating Lord's Day Observance as early as 1832 (Pope, *Dickens and Charity*, p. 49), and according to an account by Shaftesbury himself, he was introduced to George Stringer Bull by Sir Andrew Agnew, whose attempts to get Sabbatarian legislation passed during the 1830s prompted Dickens to write *Sunday Under Three Heads* (R.W. Cooke-Taylor, *The Factory System and the Factory Acts* (London: Methuen & Co., 1894), p. 43)). Writing to Forster on 17 December 1871, in praise of the latter's biography of the author, Shaftesbury expressed the view that God had given Dickens 'as it were, a general retainer for all suffering & oppression; and tho I cannot hold it to be a fact a propos writers on human woes, that "he best can paint them, who can feel them most", I fully believe that it was so with him. He felt what he wrote, and he wrote what he felt; and, as a result, he obtained, &, I am sure, to his heart's joy, a mighty alleviation of tyranny and sorrow.' Shaftesbury went on to add, perhaps a trifle unfairly, 'And yet, strange to say, he never gave me a helping hand – at least, I never heard of it' (Quoted in Graham Storey (ed.), *The Pilgrim Edition of the Letters of Charles Dickens Volume Twelve: 1868–1870* (Oxford: Clarendon Press, 2002), p. 521). In his journal on 20 December 1871, Shaftesbury speculated that Dickens had been sent 'to rouse attention to many evils and many woes; and though not putting it on Christian principle (which would have rendered it unacceptable), he may have been, in God's singular and unfathomable goodness as much a servant of the Most High as the pagan Naaman "by whom the Lord had given deliverance to Syria"!' (Extracted in Philip Collins (ed.), *Dickens: The Critical Heritage* (London: Routledge and Kegan Paul, 1971), p. 568).

80. 'The Paradise at Tooting', *The Examiner*, 20 January 1849. Text quoted here as it appears in Slater, *Dickens' Journalism II*, p. 155.
81. Quotations from *Oliver Twist* are from the Penguin edition, edited by Philip Horne (London, 2002).
82. For example, Philip Horne in the Penguin edition, p. 491; and Stephen Gill in the Oxford World's Classics edition, edited by Kathleen Tillotson, with an Introduction and Notes by Stephen Gill (Oxford: Oxford University Press, 1999, p. 464).

83. Quotations from *Hard Times* are from the Penguin edition, edited by Kate Flint (revised edn, London, 2003).
84. *Morning Chronicle*, 25 July 1842. Text as in Madeline House and Graham Storey (eds), *The Pilgrim Edition of the Letters of Charles Dickens Volume Two: 1840–1841* (Oxford: Clarendon Press, 1969), pp. 279–80, 285.
85. Quotations from *The Chimes* are from the text as it appears in *Christmas Books*, Oxford Illustrated Dickens edition (London: Oxford University Press, 1954).
86. Quotations from *The Old Curiosity Shop* are from the Penguin edition, edited by Norman Page (London, 2000).
87. Speech to Conversazione of the Polytechnic Institution: Birmingham, 28 February 1844 in Fielding, *Speeches*, p. 61.
88. Quotations from *The Haunted Man* are from the text as it appears in the Oxford Illustrated Dickens edition of *Christmas Books* (London: Oxford University Press, 1954).
89. Quotations from *The Pickwick Papers* are from the Penguin edition, edited by Mark Wormald (London, 1999).
90. Quotations from 'Full Report of the Second Meeting of the Mudfog Association For the Advancement of Everything' are from Slater, *Dickens' Journalism I*, pp. 530–51.
91. Text of 'The Hymn of the Wiltshire Labourers' as in F.G. Kitton (ed.), *Charles Dickens: Poems* ([1903] Richmond: Alma Classics Ltd., 2013), pp. 86–7.
92. *Household Words*, 11 February 1854. Quotations from the text here are from Michael Slater (ed.), *The Dent Uniform Edition of Dickens' Journalism III: 'Gone Astray' and Other Papers from 'Household Words' 1851–9* (London: J.M. Dent, 1998), pp. 196–210.
93. Quotations from *Little Dorrit* are from the Penguin edition, edited by Stephen Wall and Helen Small (revised edn, London, 2003).
94. Driver, *Tory Radical*, p. 434.
95. Driver, *Tory Radical*, p. 433.
96. Quotations from *Jessie Phillips: A Tale of the Present Day* are from the Nonsuch edition (Stroud, 2006).
97. Gill, *Ten Hours Parson*, p. 20.
98. A reference to a controversial speech in which Oastler had threatened to teach factory workers how to sabotage machines by using knitting needles to damage the spindles. See Driver, *Tory Radical*, p. 327.
99. Edwards, *Purge This Realm*, p. 41.
100. Edwards, *Purge This Realm*, p. 85. Victorian clergymen continued to feel the need to justify their involvement in such social issues as sanitary reform, housing and industrial relations, and often argued their case, to a little dissent from some colleagues. c.f. Brian Heeney, 'The Theory of Pastoral Ministry in the Mid-Victorian Church Of England', *Historical Magazine of the Protestant Episcopal Church*, Vol. 43, p. 219f.f (1974).

3 *Oliver Twist* and Fagin's Jewishness

1. David Vital, *A People Apart: The Jews in Europe 1789–1939* (Oxford: Oxford University Press, 1999), pp. 186–7.
2. Harry Stone, 'Dickens and the Jews', *Victorian Studies*, Vol. 2, p. 228 (1959).
3. Deborah Heller, 'The Outcast as Villain and Victim: Jews in Dickens's *Oliver Twist* and *Our Mutual Friend*' in Derek Cohen and Deborah Heller (eds) *Jewish Presences in English Literature* (Montreal: McGill-Queen's University Press, 1990), p. 39.

4. Quoted in Stone, 'Dickens and the Jews', p. 223.
5. Graham Storey (ed.), *The Pilgrim Edition of the Letters of Charles Dickens Volume Ten: 1862–1864* (Oxford: Clarendon Press, 1998), p. 270.
6. David Englander, 'Anglicised not Anglican: The Jews and Judaism in Victorian Britain' in Gerald Parsons (ed.) *Religion in Victorian Britain Volume I: Traditions* (Manchester: Manchester University Press, 1988), p. 239; Cecil Roth, *A History of the Jews in Britain* (Oxford: Clarendon Press, 1941), p. 246.
7. Vital, *People Apart*, p. 41.
8. Cited in Roth, *History of the Jews*, p. 247.
9. Cited in Roth, *History of the Jews*, p. 247.
10. Roth, *History of the Jews*, pp. 249–51.
11. *The Times*, 14 April 1834.
12. Roth, *History of the Jews*, p. 252.
13. Roth, *History of the Jews*, pp. 252–3; *The Times*, 18 November 1835.
14. *The Times*, 30 January 1835.
15. Vital, *People Apart*, p. 186.
16. Roth, *History of the Jews*, p. 243.
17. *The Times*, 6 January 1830.
18. Henry Mayhew, *Mayhew's London, Being Selections from 'London Labour and the London Poor'* (London: Spring Books, 1957), pp. 275–6.
19. Anne Aresty Naman, *The Jew in the Victorian Novel: Some Relationships between Prejudice and Art* (New York: AMS Press, Inc., 1980), p. 54.
20. V.D. Lipman, 'The Age of Emancipation, 1815–1880' in V.D. Lipman (ed.) *Three Centuries of Anglo-Jewish History: A Volume of Essays* (Cambridge: Heffer and Sons, Ltd., 1961), pp. 78–9.
21. Mayhew, *Mayhew's London*, p. 276.
22. Anne and Roger Cowen, *Victorian Jews through British Eyes* (Oxford: Oxford University Press, 1986), pp. 16–7.
23. Cowen, *Victorian Jews*, p. 18.
24. Cowen, *Victorian Jews*, p. 24.
25. Cowen, *Victorian Jews*, p. 123.
26. Stone, 'Dickens and the Jews', p. 233.
27. Heller, 'The Outcast as Villain and Victim', p. 41.
28. Heller, 'The Outcast as Villain and Victim', p. 49.
29. Efraim Sicher, 'Imagining "the Jew": Dickens Romantic Heritage' in Sheila A. Spector (ed.) *British Romanticism and the Jews: History, Culture, Literature* (New York and Basingstoke: Palgrave Macmillan, 2002), p. 140.
30. Sicher, 'Imagining "the Jew"', p. 139.
31. Sicher, 'Imagining "the Jew"', p. 140.
32. Storey, *Pilgrim Letters Volume Ten*, p. 269.
33. Quotations from *Oliver Twist* are from the Penguin edition, edited by Philip Horne (London, 2002).
34. Henry Mayhew, *The Morning Chronicle Survey of Labour and the Poor: The Metropolitan Districts* 6 Vols (Firle: Caliban Books, 1980–82), Volume II, p. 135.
35. Mayhew, *Mayhew's London*, p. 286.
36. Mayhew, *Mayhew's London*, p. 285.
37. Mayhew, *Morning Chronicle Survey*, p. 35.
38. Cates Baldridge, 'The Instability of Inheritance in *Oliver Twist*', *Studies in the Novel*, Vol. 25, pp. 184–95 (1993).
39. Quoted in Storey, *Pilgrim Letters Volume Ten*, p. 269.
40. Storey, *Pilgrim Letters Volume Ten*, p. 269.

41. Dickens uses a very similar device in *Our Mutual Friend*. Betty Higden dies in circumstances that are an indictment of the callous arrangements made by a Christian society for the care of the poor: she dies homeless rather than enter the workhouse. Immediately after her death in Book the Third Chapter 8, and her funeral at the beginning of Chapter 9, Lizzie Hexam describes the humanity of her Jewish employer, who, in allowing Betty's body to be placed in his store-room, in the end provided her with a compassionate refuge of a sort not available to her during her life from Christian society, and whose help was important in carrying out Betty's final request that her body should not end up in the hands of the Parish, for, as Lizzie remarks, 'I should not have had the power, without our managing partner'. Of him and his wife, she goes on to remark, 'there cannot be kinder people in the world' (*Our Mutual Friend*, edited by Adrian Poole (London: Penguin, 1997), p. 508).

4 Christian Social Vision in the Novels of the 1850s: *Bleak House, Hard Times* and *Little Dorrit*

1. Richard Turnbull, *Shaftesbury: The Great Reformer* (Oxford: Lion, 2010), p. 89.
2. J.T. Ward, *The Factory Movement 1830–1855* (London: Macmillan, 1962), p. 346; Cecil Driver, *Tory Radical: The Life of Richard Oastler* ([1946] New York: Octagon Books, 1970), p. 472.
3. Ward, *Factory Movement*, p. 347.
4. Ward, *Factory Movement*, p. 371; Driver, *Tory Radical*, p. 492.
5. Ward, *Factory Movement*, p. 372.
6. Ward, *Factory Movement*, p. 356.
7. Ward, *Factory Movement*, p. 358.
8. Ward, *Factory Movement*, pp. 382–3.
9. Ward, *Factory Movement*, p. 385.
10. Ward, *Factory Movement*, p. 388.
11. Ward, *Factory Movement*, p. 389.
12. Driver, *Tory Radical*, p. 518.
13. Ward, *Factory Movement*, p. 390.
14. Ward, *Factory Movement*, p. 400.
15. Norman Longmate, *The Workhouse* ([1974] London: Pimlico, 2003), p. 133.
16. Adrian Poole (ed.), *Our Mutual Friend* (London: Penguin, 1997), p. 799.
17. Quoted in Longmate, *Workhouse*, p. 274.
18. Longmate, *Workhouse*, pp. 279, 280.
19. Longmate, *Workhouse*, p. 284.
20. Trevor May, *The Victorian Clergyman* (Princes Risborough: Shire, 2006), p. 8.
21. Gerald Parsons, 'Social Control to Social Gospel: Victorian Christian Social Attitudes' in Gerald Parsons (ed.) *Religion in Victorian Britain Volume II: Controversies* (Manchester: Manchester University Press, 1988), pp. 45–6.
22. Norris Pope, *Dickens and Charity* (London and Basingstoke: Macmillan, 1978), p. 8.
23. B.G. Worrall, *The making of the modern Church: Christianity in England since 1800* (third edn, London: S.P.C.K., 2004), p. 43.
24. Parsons in Parsons, 'Social Control to Social Gospel', p. 47.
25. Parsons, 'Social Control to Social Gospel', p. 47.
26. Parsons, 'Social Control to Social Gospel', p. 48.
27. Parsons, 'Social Control to Social Gospel', p. 49.
28. Speech to Metropolitan Sanitary Association, 6 February 1850 in K.J. Fielding (ed.), *The Speeches of Charles Dickens* (Oxford, Clarendon Press, 1960), p. 106.

29. Speech to dinner for Royal Hospital for Incurables, 5 June 1856 in Fielding, *Speeches*, p. 223.
30. *All The Year Round*, 20 June 1863. Quotations are taken from the text as in Michael Slater and John Drew (eds), *The Dent Uniform Edition of Dickens' Journalism Volume IV: 'The Uncommercial Traveller' and Other Papers 1859–70* (London: J.M. Dent, 2000), pp. 237–47.
31. 'On Duty with Inspector Field', *Household Words*, 14 June 1851. Quotations are from the text as in Michael Slater (ed.), *The Dent Uniform Edition of Dickens' Journalism Volume II: 'The Amusements of the People' and Other Papers: Reports, Essays and Reviews 1834–51* (London: J.M. Dent, 1996), pp. 3612. We may compare, in the visual arts, G.F. Watts's painting 'Under A Dry Arch' (c. 1849–50), which depicts a homeless woman sheltering under a bridge; St. Paul's Cathedral is visible in the background.
32. Quotations from *Bleak House* are from the Penguin edition, edited by Nicola Bradbury (revised edn, London, 2003).
33. Quotations from *Hard Times* are from the Penguin edition, edited by Kate Flint (revised edn, London, 2003).
34. Quotations from *Little Dorrit* are from the Penguin edition, edited by Stephen Wall and Helen Small (revised edn, London, 2003).
35. Kathleen Tillotson, *Novels of the Eighteen Forties* (Corrected edn, London: Oxford University Press, 1961), p. 157.
36. Tillotson, *Novels of Eighteen Forties*, p. 154.
37. Michael Goldberg, *Carlyle and Dickens* (Athens: University of Georgia Press, 1972), pp. 10, 12.
38. Goldberg, *Carlyle and Dickens*, p. 78.
39. Goldberg, *Carlyle and Dickens*, p. 79.
40. Quotations from *Oliver Twist* are from the Penguin edition, edited by Philip Horne (London 2002).
41. Ward, *Factory Movement*, p. 145.
42. Ward, *Factory Movement*, p. 170.
43. Ward, *Factory Movement*, p. 250.
44. Ward, *Factory Movement*, p. 301.

5 *Bleak House*: Law, Religion and Civilisation

1. To the Rev. David Macrae, 1861, in Graham Storey (ed.), *The Pilgrim Edition of the Letters of Charles Dickens Volume Nine: 1859–1861* (Oxford: Clarendon Press, 1997), p. 556.
2. 'Capital Punishment (Three Letters to *Daily News*, March 9, 13, and 16, 1846)', Letter III in Charles Dickens, *Miscellaneous Papers I* (Geneva: Edito-Service S.A./ Heron, 1971), p. 49.
3. Quotations from *Bleak House* are from the Penguin edition, edited by Nicola Bradbury (revised edn, London, 2003).
4. Victorian understanding of dinosaurs was still evolving, so Dickens's implications in this image may not have been precisely those the modern reader may take from it. In 'Notice on the Megalosaurus or Great Fossil Lizard of Stonefield; Observations on the Beginning of *Bleak House*' (*Dickensian*, Vol. 78, pp. 97–104 (1982)), Philip James Wilson discusses how fossils were at this time interpreted as 'relics of the Biblical Flood' (p. 98), although by the 1850s 'the idea of the Flood being the agent for extinction was being questioned' (p. 102). Dickens's

subscribing to this idea makes sense of the reference to 'the waters' being 'newly retired from the face of the earth' (*Bleak House*, p. 13). If the image suggested to him something less remote than an age of dinosaurs some sixty five million years ago, such as we now imagine, it nevertheless conjures up a world in a very primitive state. In the Biblical account, with the Flood God in effect goes back to the Creation; in his promise to Noah after the Flood, God promises that he will never again send such a flood 'to destroy the earth' (Genesis 9:11).

5. The other narrative, that of Esther, equally begins with an account of her upbringing by Miss Barbary, whose name, reminiscent of 'barbarian', also suggests we are not in a civilised world.
6. See, for instance, Humphrey House's discussion of the matter in *The Dickens World* (second edn, Oxford: Oxford University Press, 1942), pp. 30–33.
7. D.A. Miller, 'Discipline in Different Voices: Bureaucracy, Police, Family and *Bleak House*', *Representations*, No. 1, 1983. Reprinted in Harold Bloom (ed.), *Modern Critical Views: Charles Dickens* (New York/New Haven/Philadelphia: Chelsea House Publishers, 1987), p. 205.
8. Miller argues that Mrs Snagsby's suspicions satisfy her need to see herself as wronged and thus to consolidate the basis of her domestic tyranny ('Discipline in Different Voices', p. 206).
9. Kevin McLaughlin, 'Losing One's Place: Displacement and Domesticity in Dickens's *Bleak House*'. Originally published in *Modern Language Notes*, Vol. 108 (1993). Quotation used here is from the text as reprinted in Jeremy Tambling (ed.), *Bleak House*, New Casebook series (Basingstoke: Macmillan Press Ltd., 1998), p. 230.
10. B.G. Worrall, *The Making of the Modern Church: Christianity in England since 1800* (Third edn, London: S.P.C.K., 2004), p. 47.

6 'Oh my Friends and Brothers': Industrialism and Trade Unionism in *Hard Times*

1. Quotations from *Bleak House* are from the Penguin edition, edited by Nicola Bradbury (revised edn, London, 2003).
2. Nicola Bradbury, 'Appendix 1: Chancery' in the Penguin edition of *Bleak House*, p. 990.
3. Quotations from the text of 'The Fine Old English Gentleman' are from F.G. Kitton (ed.), *Charles Dickens: Poems* ([1903] Richmond: Alma Classics, 2013), p. 57.
4. Kitton, *Charles Dickens*, p. 57.
5. Kitton, *Charles Dickens*, p. 58.
6. These ideas are explored in detail by J. Hillis Miller in his study of *Bleak House* in Chapter 6 of his *Charles Dickens: The World of his Novels* (Cambridge: Harvard University Press, 1959), pp. 160–224, esp. p. 190f.f.
7. Quotations from *Hard Times* are from the Penguin edition, edited by Kate Flint (revised edn, London, 2003).
8. This was a topical issue. In a circular of January 1854, inspectors had asserted the need to fence shafts; however, the circular was modified after a deputation of masters persuaded Palmerston in March 1854 that it was not necessary to fence shafts over seven feet from the floor. (J.T. Ward, *The Factory Movement 1830–1855* (London: Macmillan, 1962), p. 400). As Ward goes on to state, 'Many masters continued to ignore safety precautions and the toll of mangled operatives continued, especially among maintenance workers'.
9. F.R. Leavis, *The Great Tradition* (London: Chatto and Windus, 1948), p. 246.

10. For an account of his visit to Preston, see my 'Dickens the Journalist: The Preston Strike and "On Strike"', *Dickensian*, Vol. 88, 129–38 (1993).
11. The origins of the Preston Strike lay as far back as 1847, when, during a commercial crisis, wages within the cotton industry had been cut by ten per cent. The factory workers at least understood that the ten per cent would be restored when prosperity returned. By 1853, trade had apparently improved once more, and workers began to campaign for the restitution of the ten per cent. It was eventually conceded in such towns as Stockport and Blackburn, but in Preston the Masters' Association determined to resist. Following strikes at some Preston mills, the Masters' Association announced a general lock-out to begin on 15 October 1853. By this time, both the spinners and the weavers were organised into unions, George Cowell and Mortimer Grimshaw being prominent in the leadership of the weavers. The Strike was to last over six months, the operatives being financially supported by contributions from workers in other towns. Despite various efforts to bring the conflict to an end, it was only in May 1854 that the strikers abandoned their claim and returned to work. For a full account of the Preston Strike, see H.J. Dutton and J.E. King, *'Ten Per Cent and No Surrender': The Preston Strike 1853–1854* (Cambridge: Cambridge University Press, 1981).
12. *Preston Chronicle*, 4 February 1854; *Manchester Guardian*, 1 February 1854. Both these visits to the union meetings were relatively brief. The *Preston Chronicle* reports that he attended the Sunday meeting 'for a short time' and that he stayed at the Monday meeting 'for about ten minutes'.
13. 'On Strike', p. 208. References to and quotations from the article, originally published in *Household Words* on 11 February 1854, are to the text as in Michael Slater (ed.), *The Dent Uniform Edition of Dickens' Journalism Volume III: 'Gone Astray' and Other Papers from 'Household Words' 1851–9* (London: J.M. Dent, 1998).
14. This matter has been discussed by, for instance, Geoffrey Carnall in his 'Dickens, Mrs Gaskell and the Preston Strike', *Victorian Studies*, Vol. 8, pp. 31–48 (1964), and by Anne Smith in her '*Hard Times* and *The Times* Newspaper', *Dickensian*, Vol. 69, pp. 153–62 (1973).
15. *Household Words*, 11 February 1854.
16. Dutton and King, *'Ten Per Cent and No Surrender'*, p. 46.
17. Dutton and King, *'Ten Per Cent and No Surrender'*, p. 31.
18. H.I. Dutton and J.E. King, '"A fallacy, a delusion, and a snare": Arbitration and Conciliation in the Preston Strike, 1853–4', *Transactions of the Historic Society of Lancashire and Cheshire*, Vol. 131, p. 70 (1983).
19. Dutton and King, *'Ten Per Cent and No Surrender'*, p. 42. See also Dutton and King, '"A fallacy, a delusion, and a snare"', p. 70.
20. Dutton and King, 'A fallacy, a delusion, and a snare', p. 71.
21. In addressing the Society of Arts' Conference on Strikes and Lockouts: c.f. *Supplement to the Journal of the Society of Arts*, Vol. 2, p. 204 (1854).
22. Henry Ashworth, *The Preston Strike, an Enquiry into its Causes and Consequences* (Manchester: Simms, 1854), p. 27. In this, Ashworth later acknowledges that the leaders of the strike 'exerted, upon the whole, a useful influence in repressing violence, and restraining the operatives within the limits of moral force' (p. 29).
23. The reports of the Sunday meeting in the *Preston Chronicle* (4 February 1954), *Preston Guardian* (4 February 1854), *Preston Pilot* (4 February 1854), *The Times* (31 January 1854), *Manchester Guardian* (1 February 1854) and *Reynold's Newspaper* (5 February 1854) make no mention of Cowell, though it should be noted that some of these reports are very brief.

24. The conference is reported in *Supplement to the Journal of the Society of Arts*, Vol. 2, pp. 189–207 (1854).
25. Dutton and King, *'Ten Per Cent and No Surrender'*, p. 111.
26. *Preston Chronicle*, 4 February 1854.
27. *Preston Chronicle*, 4 February 1854.
28. *Manchester Guardian*, 1 February 1854.
29. Dutton and King, *'Ten Per Cent and No Surrender'*, p. 46.
30. *Eliza Cook's Journal*, p. 227, 19 August 1854; quoted in Dutton and King, *'Ten Per Cent and No Surrender'*, p. 47.
31. Ashworth, *The Preston Strike*, pp. 28–9. On the personalities and behaviour of Cowell and Grimshaw, see also Carnall, 'Dickens', esp. pp. 34ff, 40f.
32. Dutton and King, *'Ten Per Cent and No Surrender'*, p. 46.
33. Humphrey House, *The Dickens World* (second edn, Oxford: Oxford University Press, 1942), p. 209.
34. *Preston Chronicle*, 28 January 1854.
35. Ashworth, *The Preston Strike*, pp. 26–7.
36. Patrick Brantlinger, 'The Case Against Trade Unions in Early Victorian Fiction', *Victorian Studies*, Vol. 13, p. 48 (1969).
37. Dutton and King, *'Ten Per Cent and No Surrender'*, p. 27.
38. Ashworth, *The Preston Strike*, pp. 5–6.
39. *Illustrated London News*, 12 November 1853.
40. Preston itself formed a good example of the factionalism Dickens attacks in *Hard Times*, and not only because the workers had become organised into unions. The Preston employers had long had an association: 'As early as the 1820s the Masters' Association in Preston was regarded as one of the strongest in Lancashire' (Dutton and King, *'Ten Per Cent and No Surrender'*, p. 21). Its history went back continuously, however, 'no further than the great strike of 1836' (Dutton and King, *'Ten Per Cent and No Surrender'*, p. 20). Nevertheless, as such, it was one of the oldest Masters' Associations. In 1853, the Masters' Association was revived before the Preston spinners' union began its agitation; the Preston weavers only formed a combination a couple of months later: c.f. Dutton and King, *'Ten Per Cent and No Surrender'*, pp. 28–31.
41. c.f. the vacillation between the two sets of terms among speakers at the Society of Arts' Conference on Strikes and Lockouts in the account given in *Supplement to the Journal of the Society of Arts*, Vol. 2, pp. 189–207 (1854).
42. *Preston Pilot; and County Advertiser*, 4 February 1854.
43. *Preston Chronicle*, 28 January 1854.
44. *Preston Guardian*, 28 January 1854.
45. *Preston Pilot*, 28 January 1854.
46. Carnall, 'Dickens', p. 41–2.
47. *Preston Guardian*, 28 January 1854. These sentiments were also reported in the other local newspapers, the *Preston Chronicle* and the *Preston Pilot*, of the same date.
48. *Preston Guardian*, 4 February 1854.
49. *Preston Guardian*, 4 February 1854.
50. *Household Words*, 11 January 1851.
51. Quotations from 'Railway Strikes' are from the text as printed in Michael Slater (ed.), *The Dent Uniform Edition of Dickens' Journalism Volume II: 'The Amusements of the People' and Other Papers: Reports, Essays and Reviews 1834–51* (London: J.M. Dent, 1996), pp. 316–22.
52. In the novel, the formation of a union by the workers is directly following the example of the employers who are, as Bitzer points out, 'united' (p. 115).
53. *'Railway Strikes'*, p. 317.

54. In exploring the reasons for Stephen's refusal to join the union, some critics, including Kate Flint and Nicholas Coles, have drawn attention to a passage excised from the published novel in which Stephen relates the industrial accident that happened to Rachael's younger sister and comments bitterly on employers' resistance to boxing off dangerous machinery. As Flint relates, 'Rachael tells Stephen to let such things be, since too much anger will only lead to hurt, and submissively – over-submissively, perhaps – he agrees.' This then becomes, 'the basis of the promise which is alluded to later in the text' (Kate Flint Introduction to Penguin edition of *Hard Times*, pp. xiv–xv). Even if we take this deleted passage into account, Stephen's reason for not joining the union remains the same, for Rachael is guiding him away from the anger and bitterness that leads to the 'them and us' mentality that leads in turn to factionalism and is so inimical to a sense of brotherhood. We may compare Coles's regretful comment that the passage's inclusion 'would ... have given his refusal of the union the thematic meaning of a rejection of un-Christian angry retaliation to the masters' callousness' (Nicholas Coles, 'The Politics of *Hard Times*: Dickens the Novelist versus Dickens the Reformer', *Dickens Studies Annual*, Vol. 15, p. 178 (1986)); as I have been arguing, my opinion is that this element is still present in the novel as published.

7 *Little Dorrit*: Serving Mammon

1. Quotations from *Little Dorrit* are from the Penguin edition, edited by Stephen Wall and Helen Small (revised edn, London, 2003).
2. Quotations from *Bleak House* are from the Penguin edition, edited by Nicola Bradbury (revised edn, London, 2003).
3. Quotations from *American Notes* are from the Penguin edition, edited by Patricia Ingham (revised edn, London, 2004).
4. As Patricia Ingham notes, Louise H. Johnson in her article 'The Source of the Chapter on Slavery in Dickens' *American Notes*' (*American Literature*, Vol. 14, 427–30 (1943)) identified the catalogue of examples of brutality as being directly taken from an 1839 publication of the American Anti-Slavery Society, Theodore D. Weld's *American Slavery As It Is* (Patricia Ingham Introduction to Penguin edition of *American Notes*, p. xvi).
5. Quotations are from the text as in David Lodge *Deaf Sentence* ([2008] London: Penguin, 2009).
6. Albeit that man's activity in the contemporary world is said to be making some of these things worse.
7. See Penguin edition, pp. 864–71.
8. Catherine Waters, *Dickens and the Politics of the Family* (Cambridge: Cambridge University Press, 1997), p. 116.
9. Waters, *Dickens and the Politics*, p. 115. Waters further argues that a changing social order was leading to other instances of the shrugging off of personal responsibility. Mr Casby's conduct in business, for instance 'exemplifies the early nineteenth-century shift to a less paternalistic form of social organisation', in which landlords were no longer deeply rooted where they lived, and thus didn't have strong bonds with their tenants: 'Mr Casby is simply a landlord concerned only about money, and who lacks the sense of duty towards his tenants upon which the viability of a paternalism based on property depended' (Waters, *Dickens and the Politics*, p. 103).
10. See Heather Small's note in the Penguin edition of the novel, p. 965.
11. Small points out the reference to Acts 5:15 in her Notes to the Penguin edition, p. 974.

12. Small, in her Notes to Penguin edition, p. 970.
13. Quotations from *Our Mutual Friend* are from the Penguin edition, edited by Adrian Poole.

8 Dickens and Politics: Temporary and Permanent Revolution

1. Speech to Administrative Reform Association, 27 June 1855, in K.J. Fielding (ed.) *The Speeches of Charles Dickens* (Oxford: Clarendon Press, 1960), p. 200.
2. Michael Slater, *The Genius of Dickens: The Ideas and Inspiration of Britain's Greatest Novelist* ([1999] London: Duckworth Overlook, 2011), p. 86.
3. *Nicholas Nickleby*, edited by Mark Ford (London: Penguin, 1999), p. 5.
4. Mark Ford, Notes to the Penguin edition, p. 798.
5. 'The Agricultural Interest', *Morning Chronicle*, 9 March 1844. Quotation from the text as in Michael Slater (ed.), *The Dent Uniform Edition of Dickens' Journalism Volume II: 'The Amusements of the People' and Other Papers: Reports, Essays and Reviews 1834–51* (London: J.M. Dent, 1996), p. 65.
6. Slater, *Journalism Volume II*, p. 66.
7. Quotations from 'The Fine Old English Gentleman' and the other poems discussed here are from the texts as printed in F.G. Kitton (ed.), *Charles Dickens: Poems* ([1903] Richmond: Alma Classics Ltd, 2013), pp. 58–9.
8. Kitton, *Charles Dickens*, p. 61. Forster explains the reference here: 'A celebrated address had been delivered at Tamworth, in which the orator, though in those days big with nothing much larger or graver than a sliding scale, had made a mystery of it as an infallible specific for public affairs, which he refused to prescribe till regularly called in; and this was good-humouredly laughed at in a quack-doctor's proclamation.' (John Forster, *The Life of Charles Dickens* Volume 1, edited by A.J. Hoppe, Everyman edn (further revised edn, London: J.M. Dent, 1969), p. 163).
9. Kitton, *Charles Dickens*, p. 83.
10. Kitton, *Charles Dickens*, p. 86.
11. Kitton, *Charles Dickens*, p. 87.
12. Forster, *Life of Charles Dickens*, p. 164.
13. Speech to the Birmingham and Midland Institute: Annual Inaugural Meeting: Birmingham, 27 September 1869, in Fielding, *Speeches*, p. 407.
14. Speech to the Administrative Reform Association, 27 June 1855, in Fielding, *Speeches*, p. 202.
15. Quotations from *Hard Times* are from the Penguin edition, edited by Kate Flint (revised edn, London, 2003).
16. 'Judicial Special Pleading', *The Examiner*, 23 December 1848. Quotations are from the text as in Slater, *Journalism Volume II*, p. 139.
17. 'To Working Men', *Household Words*, 7 October 1854. Quotation is from the text as in Michael Slater (ed.), *The Dent Uniform Edition of Dickens' Journalism Volume III: 'Gone Astray' and Other Papers from 'Household Words' 1851–9* (London: J.M. Dent, 1998) (pp. 225–9), p. 226. 'The Tooting Farm' (*The Examiner*, 27 January 1849) also presents a highly critical picture of Chartist leaders: they 'found the mass of their audience among the discontented poor', 'The foremost of them had not the plea of want to urge for themselves', 'their misrepresentations were addressed to the toiling multitudes, on whom social irregularities impossible to be avoided, and complicated commercial circumstances difficult to be explained to them, pressed heavily' (Charles Dickens, *Miscellaneous Papers I* (Geneva: Heron Books/Edito-Service S.A., 1971), p. 159). The narrator of 'A Poor Man's Tale of a Patent' (*Household Words*, 19 October 1850) gives a slightly more sympathetic view of

Chartism. Though personally the narrator 'never was' a Chartist, 'I don't mean to say but what I see a good many public points to complain of'; however, 'I don't think that's the way to set them right.' He knows 'many good men and workmen who are Chartists', but he carefully emphasises 'Note. Not Physical force'. Quotations are from the text as in Slater, *Journalism Volume II*, p. 285.
18. 'Old Lamps for New Ones', *Household Words*, 15 June 1850. Quotation is from the text as in Slater, *Journalism Volume II*, p. 244.
19. Philip Collins, *Dickens: The Critical Heritage* (London: Routledge and Kegan Paul, 1971), p. 300.
20. T.A. Jackson, *Charles Dickens: The Progress of a Radical* ([1937] New York: International Publishers, 1987), p. 7.
21. Jackson, *Charles Dickens*, p. 88.
22. Jackson, *Charles Dickens*, p. 102.
23. Vincent Newey, *The Scriptures of Charles Dickens: Novels of Ideology, Novels of the Self* (Aldershot: Ashgate, 2004), pp. 5–6.
24. Newey, *Scriptures of Charles Dickens*, p. 41.
25. Newey, *Scriptures of Charles Dickens*, p. 42.
26. Newey, *Scriptures of Charles Dickens*, p. 43.
27. Newey, *Scriptures of Charles Dickens*, p. 43.
28. Newey, *Scriptures of Charles Dickens*, p. 41.
29. Newey, *Scriptures of Charles Dickens*, p. 47.
30. Humphrey House, *The Dickens World* (second edn, Oxford: Oxford University Press, 1942), p. 50.
31. Sonia Orwell and Ian Angus (eds), *The Collected Essays, Journalism and Letters of George Orwell Volume I: An Age Like This 1920–1940* ([1968] Harmondsworth: Penguin, 1970), p. 457.
32. Orwell and Angus, *Collected Essays*, p. 460.
33. Orwell and Angus, *Collected Essays*, p. 468.
34. F.R. Leavis and Q.D. Leavis, *Dickens the Novelist* (London: Chatto and Windus, 1970), p. 140.
35. Nicholas Coles, 'The Politics of *Hard Times*: Dickens the Novelist versus Dickens the Reformer', *Dickens Studies Annual*, Vol. 15, p. 149 (1986).
36. Coles, 'The Politics of *Hard Times*,' p. 151.
37. Coles, 'The Politics of *Hard Times*,' p. 172.
38. Coles, 'The Politics of *Hard Times*,' p. 173.
39. John Relly Beard, *The Religion of Jesus Christ Defended from the Assaults of Owenism* (London: Simpkin, Marshall and Company; and Smallfield and Son, 1839), pp. 40–1.
40. Beard, *Religion of Jesus Christ*, p. 41.
41. Beard, *Religion of Jesus Christ*, pp. 41–2.
42. Beard, *Religion of Jesus Christ*, p. 43.
43. Beard, *Religion of Jesus Christ*, p. 43.
44. Quotations from *Aurora Leigh* are from the poem as printed in John Robert Glorney Bolton and Julia Bolton Holloway (eds), *Aurora Leigh and Other Poems* (London: Penguin, 1995).
45. Speech to Birmingham and Midland Institute: Annual Inaugural Meeting: Birmingham, 27 September 1869, in Fielding, *Speeches*, p. 398.
46. Orwell himself seems to understand that this is Dickens's position. He writes that 'two viewpoints are always tenable' when confronting the ills of society: 'The one, how can you improve human nature until you have changed the system? The other, what is the use of changing the system before you have improved human

nature?'(Orwell and Angus, *Collected Essays*, p. 469). However, this is a point that has tended to get lost in many later discussions of Dickens and the 'change of heart'.

47. J.T. Ward, *The Factory Movement 1830–1855* (London: Macmillan & Co, 1962), p. 426.
48. Quotations from *Our Mutual Friend* are from the Penguin edition, edited by Adrian Poole (London, 1997).
49. Quotations from *Hard Times* are from the Penguin edition, edited by Kate Flint (revised edn, London, 2003).
50. The concept of usefulness provides another link between Dickens and the Evangelicals, to whom it was also important, as Juliet Baker notes: '"Usefulness" was the watch-word of the Evangelicals' (*The Brontes* (second edn, London: Abacus, 2010), p. 33). Thus, the young Patrick Bronte was noted to be a man with a 'desire for usefulness in the ministry' (Barker, *Brontes*, p. 33), and in due course he paid tribute to a fellow clergyman who had 'lived *an useful life*' (Barker, *Brontes*, p. 83).
51. Speech to the Charitable Society for the Deaf and Dumb, 23 May 1843, in Fielding, *Speeches*, p. 42.
52. Speech to the First Annual Soiree of the Athenaeum: Manchester, 5 October 1843, in Fielding, *Speeches*, p. 45.
53. Fielding, *Speeches*, p. 51.
54. Speech to the First Annual Soiree of the Athenaeum: Glasgow, 28 December 1847, in Fielding, *Speeches*, p. 90.
55. Speech to the Newsvendors' Benevolent Institution, 27 January 1852, in Fielding, *Speeches*, p. 137.
56. Quotations are from Charles Dickens, *The Life of Our Lord* (Southampton: Ashford Press Publishing, 1987).
57. Quotations from *A Tale of Two Cities* are from the Penguin edition, edited by Richard Maxwell (revised edn, London, 2003).
58. Quotations from *Little Dorrit* are from the Penguin edition, edited by Stephen Wall and Helen Small (revised edn, London, 2003).
59. Speech to the Administrative Reform Association, 27 June 1855, in Fielding, *Speeches*, p. 202.
60. Quotations from *A Child's History of England* are from the text as in *Master Humphrey's Clock and A Child's History of England*, Oxford Illustrated Dickens edition (Oxford: Oxford University Press, 1958).
61. Quotations from *Pictures from Italy* are from the Penguin edition, edited by Kate Flint (London, 1998).
62. Carolyn W. de la L. Oulton, *Literature and Religion in Mid-Victorian England* (Basingstoke: Palgrave Macmillan, 2003), p. 10. Dickens was far from alone in perceiving theocratic intentions on the part the Roman Catholic church. In December 1847, the *Quarterly Review* saw some actions by the Pope as reflecting an 'intention of proving that he has power and authority, both temporal and spiritual, here in England itself' (Francis Warre Cornish, *The English Church in the Nineteenth Century Part 1* (London: Macmillan and Co., 1910), pp. 340–1). At the time of the Papal Aggression, in response to an address from the episcopate, Queen Victoria declared that, 'you may rely on my determination to uphold alike the rights of my Crown and the independence of my people against all aggressions and encroachments of a foreign power' (Cornish, *English Church*, p. 346); and in the Speech from the Throne in Parliament in February 1851, referred to various addresses presented to her by numerous of her subjects, and how 'I have assured them of my resolution to maintain the rights of my Crown and the independence of the nation' (Cornish, *English Church*, pp. 348–9).

63. John Bowen Introduction to the Penguin edition of *Barnaby Rudge*, edited by John Bowen (London, 2003), p. xv. Bowen goes on to detail some ways in which the novel is untypical of historical novels, a matter he also discusses in his *Other Dickens: Pickwick to Chuzzlewit* (Oxford: Oxford University Press, 2000, p. 163 f.f). In an extended footnote (*Other Dickens*, p. 163), he details how a number of critics have seen the relationship between *Barnaby Rudge* and Scott's novels. He later describes Dickens's novel as one 'which settles accounts with, moves beyond or, alternatively, lamely imitates the historical fiction of Walter Scott' (*Other Dickens*, p. 165).
64. Andrew Sanders, *The Victorian Historical Novel 1840–1880* (London and Basingstoke: Macmillan Press Ltd., 1978), p. 89.

9 *Barnaby Rudge* and the Struggle for Brotherhood

1. Quotations from *Barnaby Rudge* are from the Penguin edition, edited by John Bowen (London, 2003).
2. Quotations from *Pictures from Italy* are from the Penguin edition, edited by Kate Flint (London, 1998).
3. K.J. Fielding (ed.), *The Speeches of Charles Dickens* (Oxford: Clarendon Press, 1960), p. 225. When parts of what became *Pictures from Italy* were printed in the *Daily News*, Dickens on one occasion added a footnote stating that in recording aspects of the Italian people's religious practices he had 'no intention ... to disparage their religious belief. When any offshoot of it, strikes me as being ridiculous or offensive, I simply write down my own impression of that particular exhibition or practice, and desire to go no further' (26 February 1846). Quoted in Kate Flint, Notes to Penguin edition of *Pictures from Italy*, p. 193.
4. C.f. Carolyn Oulton's remark that in the period after the Catholic Emancipation Act of 1829, there remained widespread prejudice about 'two perceived evils' represented by Roman Catholicism, 'the restriction of individual freedom and the dangerous influence of the Catholic priesthood' (Carolyn W. de la L. Oulton, *Literature and Religion in Mid-Victorian Britain* (Basingstoke: Palgrave Macmillan, 2003), p. 8).
5. 'A Crisis in the Affairs of Mr John Bull, As Related by Mrs Bull to the Children', *Household Words*, 23 November 1850. Quotations are taken from the text as in Michael Slater (ed.), *The Dent Uniform Edition of Dickens' Journalism Volume II: 'The Amusements of the People' and Other Papers: Reports, Essays and Reviews 1834–51* (London: J.M. Dent, 1996), pp. 297–305.
6. Quotations from *A Child's History of England* are from *Master Humphrey's Clock and a Child's History of England*, Oxford Illustrated Dickens edn (Oxford: Oxford University Press, 1958).
7. In his chapter on the novel in Steven Marcus, *Dickens: From Pickwick to Dombey* (London: Chatto and Windus, 1965).
8. Quotations are from Charles Dickens, *The Life of our Lord* (Southampton: Ashford Press Publishing, 1987).
9. Though it is Dickens's opposition to the public nature of hangings that is well-known, in the 1840s, as Philip Collins observes in his *Dickens and Crime* (London: Macmillan and Co. 1962), he opposed capital punishment more generally. He was 'sympathetic to the cause' of its abolition at least as early as May 1840 (*Dickens*, p. 223), and argued in his letters to the *Daily News* in 1846 for 'the total abolition of the Punishment of Death, as a general principle, for the advantage of society, for the prevention of crime, and without the least reference to, or, tenderness for

any individual malefactor whatever' (*Dickens*, p. 226). Collins notes that Dickens began to compromise on the issue in 1849 (*Dickens*, p. 244), and that 'within a few years, he ... had abandoned his opposition to hanging' (*Dickens*, p. 245).

10. Cited in John Bowen, *Other Dickens: Pickwick to Chuzzlewit* (Oxford: Oxford University Press, 2000), p. 159.
11. Though Dickens was hardly complacent about his own society, some relevant progress had been made by the time *Barnaby Rudge* was written: the first public grants to aid education had been made in 1833; hanging had become restricted to being the punishment for murder since 1838; and religious toleration had taken important steps forward with the repeal of the Test and Corporation Acts in 1828 and the passing of the Catholic Relief Act in 1829.
12. Marcus, *Dickens*, p. 172.
13. John Gardiner, 'Dickens and the Uses of History' in David Paroissien (ed.) *A Companion to Charles Dickens* (Chichester: Wiley-Blackwell, 2011), p. 247.
14. Thomas J. Rice, 'The Politics of *Barnaby Rudge*' in Robert Giddings (ed.) *The Changing World of Charles Dickens* (London and Totowa: Vision and Barnes and Noble, 1983), p. 53.
15. Bowen, *Other Dickens*, p. 178.
16. Bowen, *Other Dickens*, p. 179.
17. Myron Magnet, *Dickens and the Social Order* (Philadelphia: University of Pennsylvania Press, 1985), p. 102.

10 *A Tale of Two Cities* and the *Persistence of Evil*

1. Quotations from *The Rivals* are from the New Mermaids edition, edited by Elizabeth Duthie (London: A&C Black, 1989).
2. John Gross, '*A Tale of Two Cities*' in John Gross and Gabriel Pearson (eds) *Dickens and the Twentieth Century* (London: Routledge and Kegan Paul, 1962), p. 192.
3. J.M. Rignall, 'Dickens and the Catastrophic Continuum of History in *A Tale of Two Cities*' *English Literary History*, Vol. 51, p. 579 (1984).
4. Cates Baldridge, 'Alternatives to Bourgeois Individualism in *A Tale of Two Cities*', *Studies in English Literature*, Vol. 30, p. 634 (1990).
5. Rignall, 'Dickens and the Catastrophic Continuum of History', p. 586.
6 Gordon Spence, 'Dickens as a Historical Novelist', *Dickensian*, Vol. 72, p. 27 (1976).
7. Rignall, 'Dickens and the Catastrophic Continuum of History', p. 586.
8. Dennis Walder, *Dickens and Religion* (London: George Allen and Unwin, 1981), p. 198.
9. Kenneth M. Sroka, 'A Tale of Two Gospels: Dickens and John', *Dickens Studies Annual*, Vol. 27, p. 145 (1998).
10. Quotations from *A Tale of Two Cities* are from the Penguin edition, edition by Richard Maxwell (revised edn, London, 2003).
11. Maxwell Notes to Penguin edition, p. 462.
12. Quotations from *Bleak House* are from the Penguin edition, edited by Nicola Bradbury (revised edn, London, 2003).
13. Quotations from *Little Dorrit* are from the Penguin edition, edition by Stephen Wall and Helen Small (revised edn, London, 2003).
14. Andrew Sanders, *The Victorian Historical Novel 1840–1880* (London and Basingstoke: Macmillan Press Ltd., 1978), p. 93.
15. Quotation is from Charles Dickens, *The Life of Our Lord* (Southampton: Ashford Publishing, 1987).

11 A Note on Dickens and Sentimentality

1. Humphrey House, *All in Due Time* (London: Rupert Hart-Davis, 1955), p. 93.
2. Fred Kaplan, *Sacred Tears: Sentimentality in Victorian Literature* (Princeton: Princeton University Press, 1987), p. 18.
3. Kaplan, *Sacred Tears,* pp. 3–4, 18–20, 25–7; Mary Lenard, *Preaching Pity: Dickens, Gaskell and Sentimentalism in Victorian Culture* (New York: Peter Lang, 1999), p. 11–3; Valerie Purton, *Dickens and the Sentimental Tradition: Fielding, Richardson, Goldsmith, Sheridan, Lamb* (London: Anthem Press, 2012), pp. xvi, xx.
4. Kaplan, *Sacred Tears,* p. 4.
5. Purton, *Dickens and the Sentimental Tradition,* p. 5.
6. Lenard, *Preaching Pity,* p. 46.
7. Lenard, *Preaching Pity,* p. 88.
8. Purton, *Dickens and the Sentimental Tradition,* p. xviii.
9. Kaplan, *Sacred Tears,* p. 39.
10. Kaplan, *Sacred Tears,* p. 40–1.
11. Kaplan, *Sacred Tears,* p. 40.
12. Lenard, *Preaching Pity,* p. 23.
13. Lenard, *Preaching Pity,* pp. 26–7.
14. Purton, *Dickens and the Sentimental Tradition,* pp. xiii–xiv.
15. Purton, *Dickens and the Sentimental Tradition,* p. xiv.
16. Purton, *Dickens and the Sentimental Tradition,* p. xv.
17. Purton, *Dickens and the Sentimental Tradition,* p. xvi.
18. Purton, *Dickens and the Sentimental Tradition,* p. 156.
19. Paul Davis, *The Penguin Dickens Companion* ([1998] London: Penguin, 1999), p. 441.
20. Philip Collins, *From Manly Tear to Stiff Upper Lip: The Victorians and Pathos* (Wellington: Victoria University Press, 1974), p. 18.
21. Quotations from *Bleak House* are from the Penguin edition, edition by Nicola Bradbury (revised edn, London, 2003).
22. Philip Collins (ed.), *Dickens: The Critical Heritage* (London: Routledge and Kegan Paul, 1971), p. 511.
23. Collins, *Critical Heritage,* p. 217.
24. Kaplan, *Sacred Tears,* p. 12.
25. Collins, *Critical Heritage,* p. 490.
26. Collins, *Critical Heritage,* p. 498.
27. Collins, *Critical Heritage,* p. 551.
28. Collins, *Critical Heritage,* p. 581.
29. Lenard, *Preaching Pity,* p. 15.
30. Kaplan, *Sacred Tears,* p. 47.
31. Lenard, *Preaching Pity,* p. 23.
32. Lenard, *Preaching Pity,* pp. 23–4.
33. Lenard, *Preaching Pity,* pp. 24–9
34. Kaplan, *Sacred Tears,* pp. 47–8.
35. Collins, *Critical Heritage,* p. 498.
36. Barbara Hardy, *Forms of Feeling in Victorian Fiction* (London: Methuen & Co., 1985), p. 63.
37. Collins, *Critical Heritage,* p. 603.
38. Collins, *Critical Heritage,* p. 397.
39. Extracted in George H. Ford and Lauriat Lane Jr., *The Dickens Critics* (Westport: Greenwood Press, Publishers, 1972), pp. 154–9.
40. Ford and Lane, *Dickens Critics,* p. 155.

41. Ford and Lane, *Dickens Critics*, p. 153.
42. Ford and Lane, *Dickens Critics*, p. 153.
43. Ford and Lane, *Dickens Critics*, p. 154.
44. Hardy, *Forms of Feeling*, p. 68.
45. Collins, *Critical Heritage*, p. 73.
46. Hardy, *Forms of Feeling*, p. 68.
47. Quotations from *A Christmas Carol* are from Michael Slater (ed.), *A Christmas Carol and Other Christmas Writings* (London: Penguin, 2003).
48. Quotations from *A Tale of Two Cities* are from the Penguin edition, edited by Richard Maxwell (revised edn, London, 2003).
49. Quotations from *Our Mutual Friend* are from the Penguin edition, edition by Adrian Poole (London, 1997).
50. Quotations from *Mugby Junction* are from *Christmas Stories*, Oxford Illustrated Dickens edn (Oxford: Oxford University Press, 1956).
51. I discuss these matters in more detail in my forthcoming *Dickens Quarterly* article, 'Railways and the Troubled Protagonist of the "Mugby Junction" Framing Story'.
52. Quotations from *Hard Times* are from the Penguin edition of the novel, edited by Kate Flint (revised edn, London, 2003).
53. Hardy, *Forms of Feeling*, p. 63.
54. Hardy, *Forms of Feeling*, p. 65.
55. Humphrey House, *The Dickens World* (Second edn, Oxford: Oxford University Press, 1942), p. 132.
56. Hall Caine, 'The New Watchwords in Fiction', *Contemporary Review*, April 1890, quoted in Collins, *From Manly Tear*, p. 20.
57. Purton, *Dickens and the Sentimental Tradition*, p. xv.
58. Purton, *Dickens and the Sentimental Tradition*, p. xviii.
59. Purton, *Dickens and the Sentimental Tradition*, p. 18.
60. Purton, *Dickens and the Sentimental Tradition*, p. 41.
61. Purton, *Dickens and the Sentimental Tradition*, p. 156.

Conclusion

1. Compare Dickens's own comment on his Christmas books: 'In every one of those books there is an express text preached on, and the text is always taken from the lips of Christ.' Letter to the Rev. David Macrae, 1861, in Graham Storey (ed.), *The Pilgrim Edition of the Letters of Charles Dickens Volume Nine: 1859–61* (Oxford: Clarendon Press, 1997), pp. 556–7.

Bibliography

Primary sources

Literary

Dickens

American Notes ed. Ingham, Patricia (Revised edn London: Penguin, 2004)
Barnaby Rudge ed. Bowen, John (London: Penguin, 2003)
Bleak House ed. Bradbury, Nicola (Revised edn London: Penguin, 2003)
A Christmas Carol and Other Christmas Writings ed. Slater, Michael (London: Penguin, 2003)
Christmas Books Oxford Illustrated Dickens edn (London: O.U.P., 1954)
Christmas Stories Oxford Illustrated Dickens edn (Oxford: O.U.P., 1956)
Hard Times ed. Flint, Kate (Revised edn, London: Penguin, 2003)
The Life of Our Lord (Southampton: Ashford Press Publishing, 1987)
Little Dorrit ed. Wall, Stephen and Small, Helen (Revised edn London: Penguin, 2003)
Master Humphrey's Clock and A Child's History of England Oxford Illustrated Dickens edn. (Oxford: O.U.P., 1958)
The Mystery of Edwin Drood ed. Paroissien, David (London: Penguin, 2002)
Nicholas Nickleby ed. Ford, Mark (London: Penguin, 1999)
The Old Curiosity Shop ed. Page, Norman (London: Penguin, 2000)
Oliver Twist ed. Horne, Philip (London: Penguin, 2002)
Our Mutual Friend ed. Poole, Adrian (London: Penguin, 1997)
Pickwick Papers ed. Wormald, Mark (London: Penguin, 1999)
Pictures from Italy ed. Flint, Kate (London: Penguin, 1998)
Poems ed. with commentaries Kitton, F.G. ([1903]Richmond: Alma Classics Ltd., 2013)
A Tale of Two Cities ed. Maxwell, Richard (Revise edn. London: Penguin, 2003)

The Dent Uniform Edition of Dickens' Journalism
Volume I: '"Sketches by Boz" and Other Early Papers 1833–39' ed. Slater, Michael (London: J.M. Dent, 1994)
Volume II: '"The Amusements of the People" and Other Papers: Reports, Essays and Reviews 1834–51' ed. Slater, Michael (London: J.M. Dent, 1996)
Volume III: '"Gone Astray" and Other Papers from *Household Words*, 1851–9' ed. Slater, Michael (London: J.M. Dent, 1998)
Volume IV: '"The Uncommercial Traveller" and Other Papers 1859–70' ed. Slater, Michael and Drew, John (London: J.M. Dent, 2000)

Miscellaneous Papers Volume I (Geneva: Edito-Servo S.A./Heron, 1971)

The Pilgrim Edition of the Letters of Charles Dickens
Volume One: 1820–1839 ed. House, Madeline and Storey, Graham (Oxford: Clarendon Press, 1965)
Volume Two: 1840–1841 ed. House, Madeline and Storey, Graham (Oxford: Clarendon Press, 1969)
Volume Three: 1842–1843 ed. House, Madeline, Storey, Graham and Tillotson, Kathleen (Oxford: Clarendon Press, 1974)

Volume Eight: 1856–1858 ed. Storey, Graham and Tilloson, Kathleen (Oxford: Clarendon Press, 1995)
Volume Nine: 1859–1861 ed. Storey, Graham (Oxford: Clarendon Press, 1997)
Volume Ten: 1862–1864 ed. Storey, Graham (Oxford: Clarendon Press, 1998)
Volume Twelve: 1868–1870 ed. Storey, Graham (Oxford: Clarendon Press, 2002)

The Speeches of Charles Dickens ed. Fielding, K.J. (Oxford: Clarendon Press, 1960)

Other

Browning, Elizabeth Barrett *Aurora Leigh and Other Poems* ed. Bolton, John Robert Glorney and Holloway, Julia Bolton (London: Penguin, 1995)
Gaskell, Elizabeth *Mary Barton* ed. Shelston, Alan (London: J.M Dent, 1996)
Hood, Thomas *The Complete Poetical Works of Thomas Hood* ed. Jerrold, Walter (London: Henry Frowde, 1906)
Lodge, David *Deaf Sentence* ([2008] London: Penguin, 2009)
Martineau, Harriet *Illustrations of Political Economy* (London: Charles Fox, 1834)
Sheridan, R.B. *The Rivals* ed. Duthie Elizabeth ([1979] London: A&C Black, 1989)
Tonna, Charlotte Elizabeth *Helen Fleetwood* (New York: Baker and Scribner, 1848)
Trollope, Frances *Jessie Phillips: A Tale of the Present Day* (Stroud: Nonsuch, 2006)
——— *Michael Armstrong* (Stroud: Nonsuch, 2007)
——— *The Vicar of Wrexhill* (Stroud: Alan Sutton Publishing, 1996)

Non-fiction

Newspapers and Magazines

Edinburgh Review
Illustrated London News
The Inquirer
Leeds Mercury
Liverpool Courier
Manchester Guardian
Northern Star
Preston Chronicle
Preston Guardian
Preston Pilot and County Advertiser
Reynold's Newspaper
The Times

Books and reports

Annual Register for 1839
Anonymous *Hints to a Clergyman's Wife; or Female Parochial Duties Practically Illustrated* (Second edn London: Samuel Holdsworth, 1838). Extracted in ed. Moore, James R. *Religion in Victorian Britain Volume III: Sources.*
Anonymous *Supplement to the Journal of the Society of Arts*, 2, 1854.
Ashworth, Henry *The Preston Strike. An Enquiry into its Causes and Consequences* (Manchester: Simms, 1854)
Beard, John Relly *The Religion of Jesus Christ Defended from the Assaults of Owenism* (London: Simpkin, Marshall and Company; and Smallfield and Son, 1839)
Fielden, John *The Curse of the Factory System* ([1836] London: Frank Cass and Co. Ltd., 1969)

Forster, John *The Life of Charles Dickens* Volumes I and II ed. Hoppe, A.J. (Further revised edn. London: J.M. Dent, 1969)
Greg, W.R. *Essays on Political and Social Science* (London: Longman, Brown and Green, 1853)
Mann, H. *Census of Great Britain, 1851: Religious Worship, England and Wales. Reports and Tables Presented to Both Houses of Parliament by Command of Her Majesty* (London: H.M.S.O., 1853) Extracted in ed. Moore James R. *Religion in Victorian Britain Volume III: Sources.*
Mayhew, Henry *Mayhew's London. Being Selections from 'London Labour and the London Poor'* (London: Spring Books, 1957)
Mayhew, Henry *The Morning Chronicle Survey of Labour and the Poor: The Metropolitan Districts* Volume II (Firle: Caliban Books, 1980–82)

Secondary sources

Baldridge, Cates 'Alternatives to Bourgeois Individualism in *A Tale of Two Cities*' *Studies in English Literature* 30, 1990 633–54
Baldridge, Cates 'The Instability of Inheritance in *Oliver Twist*' *Studies in the Novel* 25, 1993 184–95
Barker, Juliet *The Brontes* (Second edn. London: Abacus, 2010)
Bowen, John Introduction to Penguin edition of *Barnaby Rudge* (London, 2003)
Bowen, John *Other Dickens: Pickwick to Chuzzlewit* (Oxford: O.U.P., 2000)
Bradbury, Nicola 'Appendix 1: Chancery' in Penguin edition of *Bleak House* (Revised edn London, 2003)
Bradley, Ian *Abide with Me: The World of Victorian Hymns* ([1997] London: Faber and Faber, 2010)
Brantlinger, Patrick 'The case Against Trade Unions in Early Victorian Fiction' *Victorian Studies* 13, 1969 37–52
Bready, J. Wesley *Lord Shaftesbury and Social-Industrial Progress* (London: George Allen and Unwin, 1926)
Butterworth, R.D. 'Dickens the Journalist: The Preston Strike and "On Strike"' *Dickensian* 88, 1993 129–38
Butterworth, Robert D. 'Railways and the Troubled Protagonist of the "Mugby Junction" Framing Story' *Dickens Quarterly* (Forthcoming)
Carnall, Geoffrey 'Dickens, Mrs Gaskell and the Preston Strike' *Victorian Studies* 8, 1964 31–48
Chadwick, Owen *The Victorian Church* Part 1 (London: Adam and Charles Black, 1966)
Cole, G.D.H. *Chartist Portraits* ([1941] London: Cassell, 1989)
Coles, Nicholas 'The Politics of *Hard Times*: Dickens the Novelist versus Dickens the Reformer' *Dickens Studies Annual* 15, 1986 145–79
Colledge, Gary *Dickens, Christianity and 'The Life of Our Lord': Humble Veneration, Profound Conviction* (London: Continuum, 2009)
Collins, Philip *Dickens and Crime* (London: Macmillan and Co., 1962)
Collins, Philip *Dickens and Education* (London: Macmillan, 1963)
Collins, Philip *Dickens: The Critical Heritage* (London: Routledge and Kegan Paul, 1971)
Collins, Philip *From Manly Tear to Stiff Upper Lip: The Victorians and Pathos* (Wellington: Victoria University Press, 1974)
Cooke-Taylor, R.W. *The Factory System and the Factory Acts* (London: Methuen & Co., 1894)
Cornish, Francis Warre *The English Church in the Nineteenth Century* Part 1 (London: Macmillan and Co., 1910)

Cotsell, Michael Notes to Oxford World's Classics edition of *Our Mutual Friend* (Oxford: O.U.P., 1989)

Cowen, Anne and Roger *Victorian Jews Through British Eyes* (Oxford: O.U.P., 1986)

Cunningham, Hugh 'Dickens as a Reformer' in ed. Paroissien, David *A Companion to Charles Dickens*

Davis, Paul *The Penguin Dickens Companion* ([1998] London: Penguin, 1999)

Dell, Robert S. 'Social and Economic Theories and Pastoral Concerns of a Victorian Archbishop' *Journal of Ecclesiastical History* 16, 1965 196–208

Driver, Cecil *Tory Radical: The Life of Richard Oastler* ([1946] NewYork: Octagon Books, 1970)

Dutton, H.I. and King, J.E. '"A fallacy, a delusion, and a snare": Arbitration and Conciliation in the Preston Strike, 1853–4' *Transactions of the Historic Society of Lancashire and Cheshire* 131, 1982 63–86

Dutton, H.I. and King, J.E. *'Ten Per Cent and No surrender': The Preston Strike 1853–1854* (Cambridge: Cambridge University Press, 1981)

Edsall, Nicholas *The Anti-Poor Law Movement 1834–44* (Manchester: Manchester University Press, 1971)

Edwards, Michael S. *Purge This Realm: A Life of Joseph Rayner Stephens* (London: Epworth Press, 1994)

Englander, David '"Anglicised Not Anglican": The Jews and Judaism in Victorian Britain' in ed. Parsons, Gerald *Religion in Victorian Britain Volume I: Traditions*

Englander, David *Poverty and Poor Law Reform in 19th Century Britain 1834–1914: From Chadwick to Booth* (Harlow: Longman, 1998)

Englander, David 'The Word and the World: Evangelicalism in the Victorian City' in ed. Parsons, *Gerald Religion in Victorian Britain Volume II: Controversies*

Fielding, K.J. Footnotes in *The Speeches of Charles Dickens* (Oxford: Clarendon Press, 1960)

Flint, Kate Introduction to the Penguin edition of *Hard Times* (Revised edn London: Penguin, 2003)

Ford, Mark Notes to the Penguin edition of *Nicholas Nickleby* (London: Penguin, 1999)

Gallagher, Catherine *The Industrial Reformation of English Fiction 1832–1867* (Chicago and London: The University of Chicago Press, 1985)

Gardiner, John 'Dickens and the Uses of History' in ed. Paroissien, David *A Companion to Charles Dickens*

Gill, J.C. *The Ten Hours Parson: Christian Social Action in the Eighteen-Thirties* (London: S.P.C.K., 1959)

Gill, Stephen Notes to Oxford World's Classics edition of *Oliver Twist*, ed Tillotson, Kathleen, (Oxford: O.U.P., 1999)

Goldberg, Michael *Carlyle and Dickens* (Athens: University of Georgia Press, 1972)

Gross, John '*A Tale of Two Cities*' in ed. Gross, John and Pearson, Gabriel *Dickens and the Twentieth Century* (London: Routledge and Kegan Paul, 1962)

Hammond, J.L. and Hammond, Barbara *Lord Shaftesbury* (Fourth edn London: Frank Cass, 1969)

Hardy, Barbara *Forms of Feeling in Victorian Fiction* (London: Methuen & Co., 1985)

Heeney, Brian 'The Theory of Pastoral Ministry in the Mid-Victorian Church of England' *Historical Magazine of the Protestant Episcopal Church* 43, 1974 215–30

Heller, Deborah 'The Outcast as Villain and Victim: Jews in Dickens's *Oliver Twist* and *Our Mutual Friend*' in ed. Cohen, Derek and Heller, Deborah *Jewish Presences in English Literature* (Montreal: McGill-Queen's University Press, 1990)

Himmelfarb, Gertrude *The Idea of Poverty: England in the Industrial Age* (London and Boston: Faber and Faber 1984, 1985)

Holloday, J. Douglas '19th Century Evangelical Activism: From Private Charity to State Intervention, 1830–50' *Historical Magazine of the Protestant Episcopal Church* 50, 1982 53–79
Holt, Raymond V. *The Unitarian Contribution to Social Progress in England* (London: George Allen and Unwin, 1938)
House, Humphrey *All in Due Time* (London: Rupert Hart-Davis, 1955)
House, Humphrey *The Dickens World* (Second edn Oxford: O.U.P., 1942)
Huxley, Aldous *Vulgarity in Literature* (1930) Extracted in ed. Ford, George H. and Lane Jnr, Lauriat *The Dickens Critics* (Westport: Greenwood Press Publishers, 1972)
Ingham, Patricia Introduction to the Penguin edition of *American Notes* (Revised edn London: Penguin, 2004)
Jackson, T.A. *Charles Dickens: The Progress of a Radical* ([1937]New York: International Publishers, 1987)
Joshi, Priti 'An Old Dog Enters the Fray; or, Reading *Hard Times* as an Industrial Novel' *Dickens Studies Annual* 44, 2013 221–41
Kaplan, Fred *Sacred Tears: Sentimentality in Victorian Literature* (Princeton: Princeton University Press, 1987)
Kitson-Clark, G. *Churchmen and the Condition of England 1832–1885: A Study in the Development of Social Ideas and Practice from the Old Regime to the Modern State* (London: Methuen and Co Ltd., 1973)
Larson, Janet L. *Dickens and the Broken Scripture* (Athens: The University of Georgia Press, 1985)
Leavis, F.R. *The Great Tradition* (London: Chatto and Windus, 1948)
Leavis, F.R. and Leavis Q.D. *Dickens the Novelist* (London: Chatto and Windus, 1970)
Lenard, Mary *Preaching Pity: Dickens, Gaskell and Sentimentalism in Victorian Culture* (New York: Peter Lang, 1999)
Lipman, V.D. 'The Age of Emancipation 1815–1880' in ed. Lipman, V.D. *Three Centuries of Anglo-Jewish History: A Volume of Essays* (Cambridge: Heffer and Sons, Ltd., 1961)
Longmate, Norman *The Workhouse* ([1974] London: Pimlico, 2003)
Lyon, Eileen Groth 'Stephens, Joseph Rayner (1805–1879)' *Oxford Dictionary of National Biography* (Oxford: O.U.P., 2004) Online edn., January 2008. http://www.oxfod.com/view/article/26389, accessed 29 May 2008
Magnet, Myron *Dickens and the Social Order* (Philadelphia: University of Pennsylvania Press, 1985)
Marcus, Steven *Dickens: From Pickwick to Dombey* (London: Chatto and Windus, 1965)
Maxwell, Richard Notes to Penguin edition of *A Tale of Two Cities* (Revised edn London: Penguin, 2003)
May, Trevor *The Victorian Clergyman* (Princes Risborough: Shire, 2006)
McCord, Norman 'The Poor Law and Philanthropy' in ed. Fraser, Derek *The New Poor Law in the Nineteenth Century* (London and Basingstoke: Macmillan, 1976)
McLaughlin, Kevin 'Losing One's Place: Displacement and Domesticity in Dickens's *Bleak House*' Original publication in *Modern Language Notes* 108, 1993. Reprinted in ed. Tambling, Jeremy *Bleak House* New Casebook series (Basingstoke: Macmillan Press Ltd., 1998)
Miller, D.A. 'Discipline in Different Voices: Bureaucracy, Police, Family and *Bleak House*' Original publication in *Representations* 1, 1983. Reprinted in ed. Bloom, Harold *Modern Critical Views: Charles Dickens* (New York/New Haven/Philadelphia: Chelsea House Publishers, 1987)
Miller, J. Hillis *Charles Dickens: The World of His Novels* (Cambridge: Harvard University Press, 1959)

Moore, James R. *Religion in Victorian Britain Volume III: Sources* (Manchester: Manchester University Press, 1988)

Murray, Peter *Poverty and Welfare 1830–1914* (London: Hodder and Stoughton, 1999)

Naman, Anne Aresty *The Jews in the Victorian Novel: Some Relationships between Prejudice and Art* (New York: AMS Press, Inc., 1980)

Newey, Vincent *The Scriptures of Charles Dickens: Novels of Ideology, Novels of the Self* (Aldershot: Ashgate, 2004)

O'Day, Rosemary 'The Clerical Renaissance in Victorian England and Wales' in ed. Parsons, Gerald *Religion in Victorian Britain Volume I: Traditions*

Orwell, George 'Charles Dickens' in ed. Orwell, Sonia and Angus, Ian *The Collected Essays, Journalism and Letters of George Orwell Volume 1: An Age Like This 1920–1940* (Harmondsworth: Penguin, 1970)

Oulton, Carolyn W.de la L. *Literature and Religion in Mid-Victorian England* (Basingstoke: Palgrave Macmillan, 2003)

Paroissien, David ed. *A Companion to Charles Dickens* (Chichester: Wiley-Blackwell, 2011)

Paroissien, David Notes to the Penguin edition of *The Mystery of Edwin Drood* (London: Penguin, 2002)

Parsons, Gerald 'Reform, Revival and Realignment: The Experience of Victorian Anglicanism' in ed. Parsons, Gerald *Religion in Victorian Britain Volume I: Traditions*

Parsons, Gerald ed. *Religion in Victorian Britain Volume I: Traditions* and *Volume II: Controversies* (Manchester: Manchester University Press, 1988)

Parsons, Gerald 'Social Control to Social Gospel: Victorian Christian Social Attitudes' in ed. Parsons, Gerald *Religion in Victorian Britain Volume II*

Poole, Adrian Notes to Penguin edition of *Our Mutual Friend* (London: Penguin.1997)

Pope, Norris *Dickens and Charity* (London and Basingstoke: Macmillan, 1978)

Purton, Valerie *Dickens and the Sentimental Tradition: Fielding, Richardson, Goldsmith, Sheridan, Lamb* (London: Anthem Press, 2012)

Qualls, Barry V. *The Secular Pilgrims of Victorian Fiction: The Novel as Book of Life* (Cambridge: Cambridge University Press, 1982)

Rice, Thomas J. 'The Politics of *Barnaby Rudge*' in ed. Gittings, Robert *The Changing World of Charles Dickens* (London and Totowa: Vision and Barnes and Noble, 1983)

Rignall, J.M. 'Dickens and the Catastrophic Continuum of History in *A Tale of Two Cities*' *ELH* 51, 1984 575–87

Rose, Mary B. 'Greg, Samuel (1758–1834)' *Oxford Dictionary of National Biography* (Oxford: O.U.P., 2004). Online edn., May 2012. http://www.oxforddnb.com/view/article/59911, accessed 4 September 2014

Rose, Mary B. 'Greg, William Rathbone (1809–1881)' *Oxford Dictionary of National Biography* (Oxford: O.U.P., 2004). Online edn., May 2006. http://www.oxforddnb.com/view/article/11446, accessed 4 September 2014

Roth, Cecil *A History of the Jews in Britain* (Oxford: Clarendon Press, 1941)

Sanders, Andrew *Charles Dickens: Resurrectionist* (New York: St. Martin's Press, 1982)

Sanders, Andrew *The Victorian Historical Novelist 1840–1880* (London and Basingstoke: Macmillan Press Ltd., 1978)

Sicher, Efraim '"Imagining the jew": Dickens' Romantic Heritage' in ed. Spector, Sheila A. *British Romanticism and the Jews: History, Culture, Literature* (New York and Basingstoke: Palgrave Macmillan, 2002)

Slater, Michael *The Genius of Dickens: The Ideas and Inspiration of Britain's Greatest Novelist* ([1999] London: Duckworth Overlook, 2011)

Small, Heather Notes to Penguin edition of *Little Dorrit* (Revised edn London: Penguin, 2003)

Smith, Anne '*Hard Times* and *The Times Newspaper*' *The Dickensian* 69, 1973 153–62
Spence, Gordon 'Dickens as a Historical Novelist' *The Dickensian* 72, 1976 21–9
Sroka, Kenneth M. 'A Tale of Two Gospels: Dickens and John' *Dickens Studies Annual* 27, 1998 145–61
Stone, Harry 'Dickens and the Jews' *Victorian Studies* 2, 1959 223–53
Tillotson, Kathleen *Novels of the Eighteen Forties* (Corrected edn., London: O.U.P., 1961)
Turnbull, Richard *Shaftesbury: The Great Reformer* (Oxford: Lion, 2010)
Vital, David *A People Apart: The Jews in Europe 1789–1939* (Oxford: O.U.P., 1999)
Walder, Dennis *Dickens and Religion* (London: George Allen and Unwin, 1981)
Ward, J.T. *The Factory System 1830–1855* (London: Macmillan and Co., 1962)
Ward, J.T. 'Two Pioneers in Industrial Reform' *Bradford Textile Society Journal* 1963–4 33–51
Waters, Catherine *Dickens and the Politics of the Family* (Cambridge: Cambridge University Press, 1997)
Whitley, Alvin 'Thomas Hood and *The Times*' *Times Literary Supplement* 17 May 1957 509
Wilson, Philip James 'Notice on the Megalosaurus or great fossil lizard of Stonefield: observations on the beginning of *Bleak House*' *The Dickensian* 78, 1982 97–104
Worrall, B.G. *The Makings of the Modern Church: Christianity in England since 1800* (Third edn. London: S.P.C.K., 2004)

Index

Printed and bound by CPI Group (UK) Ltd, Croydon, CR0 4YY